The Chalice of the DAWN

DAVID CARTER

Book Two of the Falconia Trilogy

Published in Australia by Sid Harta Books & Print Pty Ltd,
ABN: 34632585293
23 Stirling Crescent, Glen Waverley, Victoria 3150 Australia
Telephone: +61 3 9560 9920, Facsimile: +61 3 9545 1742
E-mail: author@sidharta.com.au

First published in Australia 2023
This edition published 2023
Copyright © David Carter 2023
Cover design, typesetting: WorkingType (www.workingtype.com.au)

The right of David Carter to be identified as the
Author of the Work has been asserted in accordance with the
Copyright, Designs and Patents Act 1988.

This book is a work of fiction. Any similarities to that of
people living or dead are purely coincidental.

Carter, David
The Chalice of the Dawn
ISBN: 978-1-922958-36-5
pp462

ABOUT THE AUTHOR

David Carter is a retired tax accountant. These days he spends his time buying and selling antiques and collectables and one day he may actually make a profit. He also enjoys playing chess and reading. His favourite author is Bernard Cornwell, but he also enjoys many more historical and other writers.

He lives near the picturesque Port Noarlunga and Christies Beach in Adelaide, South Australia, and is fortunate to live near one of the best wine regions in the world.

Other titles by David Carter

This book is dedicated to the memory of Judith Millar.

I wish she could have heard the ending.

I acknowledge the help I received for this book and thank Alison, Charlotte, Stuart and Judith. I also thank Marie Pietersz, Luke Harris, my editor Jenn Zabinskas and Sid Harta Publishers.

Map of Strasia

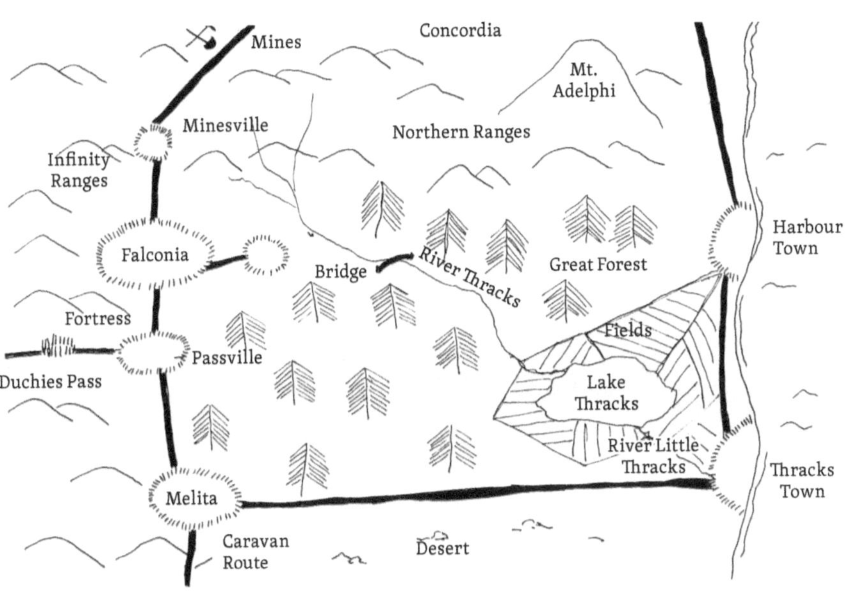

CHAPTER ONE

/| t's probably a mirage seen by a drunken shepherd.' Captain Andrew Richardson, who at six foot three inches, was taller than the person he was riding next to; the captain was broad with short, dark hair and complexion, brown eyes and a small scar on his forehead and he was tired of riding around the lush green foothills on an almost perfect late spring day. They were near the town of Minesville, and he continued, 'I mean a sixty foot snake that's over four foot wide, you must admit, it is a little ridiculous.'

He was speaking to Sir Philip Concord, the King of Falconia and the head of the Falconian army, who was at least ten years younger than himself.

'I have learnt that there are many strange and wondrous

creatures in this world. I wouldn't rule out anything,' his sovereign answered. 'And there's plenty of food around for any sort of carnivore.' He gazed at the small groups of two or three sheep that dotted the countryside.

There were eight of them from the fort near Minesville. The six guardsmen were led by Captain Richardson with Sir Philip as their ultimate commander. Queen Charlotte and King Philip had decided to keep a permanent standing army because of what they perceived, quite rightly, to be constant threats to Falconia. There were two new forts, one near Minesville and the other near Passville. The plan was to have a thousand men in each fort. The reality at that time was just over two hundred in each. Sir Philip was inspecting the troops in the fort near Minesville when reports came in about a giant snake in close proximity of the Infinity Ranges foothills. Sir Philip decided to take out a patrol to investigate.

'We'll continue for another hour then we'll head back,' Sir Philip continued. 'It's starting to get late.'

Sir Philip called a halt while scanning the horizon of the foothills. He and Captain Richardson were in full armour; Sir Philip's though was the new lighter, stronger armour from Concordia, whereas Captain Richardson's was the basic older type. They both carried sword, battleaxe, throwing axe and shield, whereas the other six members of the patrol were dressed in little more than what a castle guard would wear. Front and back plates over chain mail which reached their knees and an open helm. The patrol members all carried sword and shield and a short lance. The shields were all painted sky-blue and grass-green, the colours of Falconia and showed a black falcon holding the Great Ring of Falconia, except for Sir Philip's which was white with a red fist in the centre, a Concordian shield as Sir Philip Concord was the nephew of the King of Concordia. Sir Philip planned to have all members of the Falconian army equipped and armoured as fine as anyone in the Concordian army as soon as possible.

Sir Philip was, on horseback, taller than any other member of his patrol, mainly because his horse was three hands taller than any of the others. Jenny was jet-black and a hardened battle horse with heavy iron horseshoes and her extra height helped Sir Philip check the area.

'We'll go around that hill and then head back towards the fort.' Sir Philip pointed at a low hill about a mile away.

The patrol reached the bottom of the hill and started around it. As they rode around the hill, from what looked like caves in the hill, came a loud hiss. Sir Philip and his men halted and spread out into a line and rode towards the caves slowly.

As they neared the caves, a huge snake slithered

out at speed towards them. 'I reckon that shepherd underestimated,' Captain Richardson whispered to Sir Philip.

'I think you're right,' Sir Philip answered.

The snake must have been at least seventy feet long and maybe five and a half feet wide. It had brown, green and grey jagged stripes all the way down its body to its tapered tail. What had all the men mesmerised though was the huge gaping hole that was its mouth. Two long fangs dipped down from the roof of its mouth, both over three feet long, it also had two sets of backward-curving teeth. As it approached the patrol it slowed and stopped, its yellowy-white eyes with their black vertical slit seemed to stare at each member of the troop.

Sir Philip tried to stroke his chin and struck his helmet. He raised his visor and spoke loudly to the others. 'Usually, large snakes aren't poisonous but neither do they have fangs. This thing has fangs and teeth so let's suppose it's poisonous. Be extra careful. Snake tails are usually a soft spot so that's where we'll make our serious attack. Captain, it will be your job to cut off its tail.' Sir Philip handed his battleaxe to the largest of his men, a blond youth of about six feet six inches and extremely broad. 'Jacob, you go with him and help. The rest of us will keep it occupied. Try to stab it in the eyes with your lances,' he told the others.

'Been in a few fights that one,' the soldier to Sir Philip's left observed, seeing the damage that had occurred to its fangs. They had nicks and chunks missing in them and in places the enamel was hanging off.

'Yes, everyone be careful.' Sir Philip lowered his visor. 'Advance!'

They advanced towards the snake which raised its head fifteen feet into the air and looked down at them. 'Paul and Barry try to stab its underbelly; the rest of us will approach and attack its head when it lowers it.'

Paul and Barry increased speed to a canter with their lances lowered, while the others continued their advance while watching the snake's head for movement. Captain Richardson and Jacob kept riding to get to the rear of the snake.

As Paul and Barry neared the underside of the snake, its head moved with lightning speed and Barry was being dragged off his horse by the sharp backward-facing teeth. He gave a loud scream as he was swallowed in two gulps. Sir Philip and the others with him accelerated towards the snake's head.

Paul stabbed his lance into the softer underbelly of the snake and a trickle of blood appeared. The snake gave a hissing roar and lowered its head so it could also swallow Paul. It was just about to bite down on him when

Sir Philip's throwing axe caught it in the corner of its right eye. The snake started to rear as it continued to bite down on Paul, so that instead of Paul slipping between its fangs helped by its teeth, the snake's right fang impaled him through his back and out through his stomach. Paul screamed as blood dribbled from the holes in his armour. The screams quickly stopped as Paul started to turn blue. 'Definitely poison,' Sir Philip shouted. 'Be extra careful,' and drew his sword.

Paul started to slide off the fang but then caught on a loose piece of enamel that was hanging from the fang and stuck fast. The snake reared up and shook its head, trying to remove the body without success. Sir Philip and the three survivors all rode towards the underbelly of the snake and started to stab at it with various degrees of success. Suffice that it was left with several small bleeding wounds. The snake shook its head and struck towards one of its attackers. Its aim was off, and it only knocked the rider off his horse rather than swallowing him. 'Its balance is off, attack from the left,' Sir Philip cried. The three riders moved to the left of the creature's head while the soldier who had lost his horse, scrambled away after recovering his lance.

The snake shook its head again to try to remove Paul's body, once more without success. It lowered its head watching the three riders who had stopped moving, watching for an opening to attack. The snake's forked tongue flickered in and out while it watched the men; both they and it were waiting for the other to make a wrong move.

The snake suddenly reared up and gave an excruciating, screaming roar. It had just lost about three feet off its tail. Captain Richardson and Jacob had dismounted and chopped down in unison from either side of the tail. It flicked what was left of its tail away from the men with the axes, who dived away to avoid it. It turned and advanced on its new attackers. As it did so, its head started to slip to its right as Paul continued to affect its balance. The snake slowed as it attempted to regain its balance. Jacob took the opportunity to drop his axe and pick up his lance. He ran towards the snake and when he was about fifteen feet away, he threw it with all his strength straight into the beast's left eye.

The snake shook its head, then it attempted to bite down on its attacker. Jacob leapt away and the snake missed him by inches. The snake now had damage to both its eyes and its tail as well as various wounds to its body. It started to turn back towards the caves.

Sir Philip and the two others that were still mounted rode close to the body of the beast and endeavoured to wound it some more, but the snake's tough upper skin resisted their efforts. The riders halted and watched it reach the caves. Before it entered it turned its head and gave the men a last look with its injured eyes, the lance still protruding from the left one and then slithered into the caves. Sir Philip and his men did not follow.

Captain Richardson and Jacob walked to the three riders. 'That was some battle,' Captain Richardson observed. 'I didn't think for a while there we would beat it.'

'I'd call it a draw.' Sir Philip looked down as Jacob handed him back his battleaxe. 'Even half-blinded and without its tail I'm not sure we could have beaten it, and as for you,' he added, looking at Jacob severely, 'what sort of idiot runs full pelt at a seventy foot snake?' Sir Philip shook his head. 'Well done sergeant,' he added with a smile.

Jacob took a step back with his jaw hanging. He tried to answer but it came out as a sputter, 'Thank ... thank you, sir.'

'Just make sure you continue to deserve it,' Sir Philip answered, then added more seriously, 'Now make sure all the weapons and horses are collected and we'll head back to the fort.'

Jacob saluted by placing his fist over his heart. 'Yes,

sir.' He turned and organised the search with the other soldiers.

'Never heard of anything that big in any of Falconia before,' Captain Richardson commented to Sir Philip.

'It must have come from somewhere deep in the Infinity Ranges. Anything could be living in that expanse. Some people think that dragons still survive there,' Sir Philip answered. 'What worries me, is what sort of creature could have driven that thing out of the ranges into Falconia.'

'I hate to think, but it must be really monstrous.' The captain paused, then continued, 'I don't mean to criticise your action, sir, but do you think it was a good idea to promote Private Lipson like that?'

'Sergeant Lipson now. Yes, I do. We need to encourage bravery and fast decision making if we want an army that can stand up to anyone.'

'The dwarfs shouldn't be that hard to beat,' Captain Richardson answered. 'The fort at the mines should hold them easily.'

'Even Sir George doesn't have any intelligence about the dwarfs.' (Sir George Potts, the Royal Falconer, oversaw Falconian intelligence.) 'There could be thousands of them hiding in the caverns and tunnels in the mountains just waiting to take the mines back.' Falconia had beaten the dwarfs over two hundred years previously and taken the mines from them. In fact, no dwarf had been seen in the mountains since then except for a few that had been soundly beaten by the now dead, Queen Katerina, just over a year before. 'And there could be other enemies.'

'Surely you don't mean the duchies?' the captain asked. 'Queen Charlotte is the Duchess of Mayflor's granddaughter.'

'And is responsible for the death of her twin sister Scarlett who I'm sure would be the Duchess's favourite, and don't forget Braidos, the God of Chaos killed Queen Katerina, the Duchess's daughter, because of Katerina's failure to destroy Charlotte. I'm sure she will be plotting something.'

'When you put it like that it explains the reasoning of having our second major barracks near Passville and strengthening the Duchies Pass Fort.'

'The fort didn't need much strengthening, it was pretty strong to begin with. I've never seen it and I must admit I've only been to Passville once,' Sir Philip smiled at the memory, 'and that was before Charlotte became Queen. I plan to go and inspect the new fort near Passville after the twins are born.'

'You must be looking forward to being a father,' Captain Richardson observed with a smile.

'I'd be happier if it weren't going to be twins, especially after all the fun we had with Charlotte's twin.' Sir Philip grimaced.

Sergeant Lipson approached the two and again saluted by placing his fist over his heart. 'We've collected all the horses and weapons, sir, we're ready to leave as soon as you give the order.'

Sir Philip looked at the sun that was slowly setting. 'We'll mount and set off immediately, it'll be after dark when we get back, but I'd rather that, than camp out here with that thing about.' He nodded towards the caves. 'Let's go.'

He mounted Jenny and the others all mounted their horses and they set off back to the fort.

CHAPTER TWO

The shrill, frightening scream rang out loudly in the still, foggy night air. The eight-man patrol stopped and listened for a clue to decide in which direction to follow. Sir George Potts quickly made a decision. 'This way.' He pointed with the hook that had become his left hand and headed off down a narrow alley in the poorer section of the town of Falconia. 'Bloody wraiths, almost impossible to see in this fog.'

Sir Philip Concord, the husband of Queen Charlotte of Falconia, followed. 'Look for the eyes, they have a slight glow,' he ordered the other men in this extraordinary patrol. All were eminent guards whose normal job was to protect the Queen. They were all wearing front and back plates and open helms and wore sky-blue and grass-green tabards, emblazoned with the Falconian symbol of a black falcon, holding the Great Ring of Falconia in its claws. Except one, who was finding it difficult to keep up. He was wearing black sheepskin trousers and a white sheepskin jacket and used a six foot staff with a bear's head carved into the top of the wood. On top of this was a nugget of blackened metal holding two crystals, a green one and a purple one. When asked what the staff could do, he always said it was just to help him walk, his limp on his right leg was quite pronounced. He also carried a large leather pouch. 'And don't forget, go for between the eyes, that's the only way to kill them,' Sir Philip continued.

It was four days after the encounter with the snake. Although Queen Charlotte was due to give birth to twins at any moment, Sir Philip had decided to join the patrol. He had more experience fighting wraiths than anyone else in Falconia.

They came to a junction of three alleys and almost tripped over a body. A poorer person of Falconia, going by his clothes, was lying at the entrance of one of the alleys. There was a hole in his chest where his heart had been torn out, which was slowly filling with blood.

Sir George took in the scene using his one good eye. 'We'll have to split up. Sir Philip, you take Josh and Guy, Sam you stay here with Colin, you other two with me.'

Sir Philip's group took the right alley where the body lay and Sir George's the left, both groups hurrying down the alleys leaving Colin and Sam behind. Colin stood in the centre of the junction while Sam leant against a wall. Sam smiled at Colin. 'May as well make ourselves con——'

Sam never finished the sentence, he just looked down at the claw protruding from his chest with his heart clasped within it. Colin watched in dread as the wraith finished floating through the wall and Sam's slowly crumpling body.

The wraith stopped and faced Colin, who had limped back to the opposite wall. It made a sound that could have been a hissing chuckle. 'Your friends are chasing fog. I will be well-rewarded for taking the queen's sorcerer's heart.'

Colin raised his hand. 'Stop! Before you kill me, who sent you?'

The wraith didn't answer but continued to float towards Colin, its one claw outstretched towards his chest. Colin, his staff held between his hands, smashed it down on where the top of the wraith's head should have been. The wraith paused and hissed. 'Do you think a stick with a bit of silver slag on the end can harm me?'

'The crystal may hold you.' Colin whispered some words and the purple crystal began to glow and a purple light flashed towards the wraith.

The wraith gave a sibilant laugh. 'I'm smoke, I have no substance. Your crystals cannot harm me. Goodbye fool.'

The wraith's claw continued its movement towards Colin's chest. It suddenly gave a great hiss and then slowly started to dissipate as a hook's tip inserted itself between its eyes. 'Colin's stick might not hurt you, but my hook can,' the gruff voice of Sir George told it. 'Are you all right Colin?'

'Yes, thank you,' Colin answered with a slightly quivering voice. 'Much better than Sam, may Craidos have mercy on him.'

'Yes,' Sir George answered, the two guards that had accompanied him stood behind him. 'You were lucky that alley was a short dead-end, so we had to come back. I keep forgetting that these things can float through walls.'

As he was speaking, Sir Philip and his two men ran back into the junction, he looked down at the dead body of Sam and asked, 'What happened?'

Colin, now calmer, informed Sir Philip, 'It was hiding inside the wall. It killed Sam and would have killed me if it hadn't been for Sir George.'

'Think nothing of it.' Sir George's smile wrinkled his scared face. 'But we'd better be getting back to the castle.' He looked at Sir Philip with a slight frown. 'You shouldn't have come. You should be with Charlotte.'

Sir Philip nodded. 'I know, but I've had more

experience fighting these things than anyone else in Falconia. This was the fourth I've encountered. Charlotte has the best midwives in the country with her and there's nothing I could really do to help. I'm sure the twins will be born safely.'

'True,' Sir George agreed. 'But now it's dead, we should get back immediately.' He looked at the guards. 'Sorry boys, you'll have to take these poor unfortunates to Craidos, the God of Order's Temple.' He nodded towards the two dead bodies. 'Don't forget the hearts.'

Sir George, Sir Philip and Colin left the others to retrieve the bodies.

They made an interesting threesome as they entered the castle. Sir George, a noble in his early sixties, tall and straight-backed with long, black hair to his shoulders and a long scar from his milk-white left eye down his left cheek to his chin. Colin, slightly shorter but stooped, with short black hair, about forty years old, hobbling with his staff. And Sir Philip, almost looking tiny beside them, with long, blond hair, also to his shoulders, blue eyes and almost twenty. Sir George and Sir Philip didn't look like normal guards even though they were wearing the same uniform, as guards all had short hair, not hair showing beneath their helmets. The guards on the gate snapped to attention as soon as the three were spotted.

'Well, have you thought of names yet?' Sir George asked as they climbed the stairs towards Queen Charlotte's quarters.

'We're waiting until we know the sexes before we decide,' Sir Philip answered. 'I just hope it's not two girls. Two girls caused so much trouble for Falconia, although I'm extremely happy one turned out to be Charlotte.'

'Well, if one of them is like Scarlett you could always ask Sharag to spirit her away,' Colin joked. Sharag was the leader of a group of strange creatures that were created through the magic of Queen Katerina, Charlotte's dead mother, they now lived at the edge of the Great Forest. When Charlotte was born with her twin Scarlett, Queen Katerina had one of the creatures take Charlotte away, hoping to never hear from her again.

'I don't think Charlotte would find that funny,' Sir Philip answered. 'I just wish we had Scarlett's body so we could have burnt it. I'm not still comfortable about the way Charlotte absorbed Scarlett after the pendant fused together.' They finally arrived at the queen's quarters. 'Would either of you like to see her?'

Colin shook his head. 'I'm just next door if you need

me or any of my crystals, facing a wraith was a bit scary, I think I'll lie down.'

Sir George, Charlotte's great uncle also shook his head. 'I'm going to check on the guard. This is not the night we want any more trouble.'

They both left as Sir Philip opened the door to the anti-chamber. As he entered, the door to the bedroom also opened and one of the midwives exited together with the noise of a crying baby.

Sir Philip looked at her, lifted his arms and asked, 'Well?'

The mid-wife looked at him and smiled, 'Triplets.'

Sir Philip collapsed back into a chair.

CHAPTER THREE

I t was now over a year since Charlotte had been crowned ruling Queen of Falconia, probably the richest kingdom or place on the continent of Strasia, just a few days before her wedding to Sir Philip, now King Philip, the king consort. She was blonde, blue-eyed, had a peaches and cream complexion and full lips, and was five feet eight inches tall. She had prayed that the twins she had been expecting would not be like her and her twin, Scarlett, who had tried so hard to kill her. Queen Charlotte felt that Scarlett had not completely gone and sensed her presence like a bitter aftertaste in her new life and this had changed her to some degree. She was concerned that one of her children may turn out like Scarlett. Colin told her they should be all right. Charlotte wasn't going to sell her soul to a demon for power like her mother Queen Katerina did, was she? But now with triplets she didn't know what to think.

Queen Charlotte thought a lot of Colin's advice. She would not have been alive without his help. He now walked with a staff and limped which sometimes disguised his true height of six feet four inches. His limp had been caused when he was severely injured in the fight the previous year with the Redcap Goblins where originally everyone thought him dead. His friend Bruno the Bear, one of the Silver creatures created by Charlotte's adoptive parents, was killed in the fight, but Colin had survived with the help of his crystals and maybe Charlotte's magical powers. He had then been nursed back to health by a pack of werewolves. Colin had many crystals, which did many various things, and Charlotte had only beaten Scarlett with their help. Colin had his staff carved with a bear's head on top and this was topped by a lump of silver and two crystals.

There had been many changes in Falconia since Charlotte had become queen. She had first to appoint a new Royal Chamberlain. Sir John Amberleigh the previous Royal Chamberlain had offered to stay but Queen Charlotte did not want someone who had served her evil mother and sister. In truth he had been given forty-eight hours to get out of Falconia as had almost all her mother and sister's senior assistants and advisors. A numerous number of minor officials and guards had also been exiled. Sir George Potts had been offered the position of Royal Chamberlain, but had refused, preferring to remain the Royal Falconer, he and Sir Philip went hunting quite often together. Colin had also been offered the position. He said he had been a hermit for over ten years and did not wish to be burdened with a position at court, although he ended up running a school for magic users there. In the end, taking the advice of Sir George, she had appointed Gillian Stevens, tall at six feet three inches, thin, mature at about forty, with short, dark brown hair. A leading member of the Falconian Merchants Association, Gillian, Queen Charlotte had been told, had some experience at court. He was also promoted to Sir Gillian Stevens.

The new captain of the guard was Jack Clough. He was another tall, six feet five inches, broad man with brown hair. He was the ex-sergeant of Thomastown and had also been instrumental in helping Charlotte become queen.

The ex-captain of the guard had been the first of many people to be exiled, also many of the palace guards. Most of the senior officers in the Falconian army and some of the troops were exiled. Very few ordinary citizens went. The head of the Merchant Association was one who was exiled, as was the Mines Manager. Both were replaced by people suggested by the new Royal Chamberlain, as were most of the new advisors. Sir Philip became head of the army with his main officers suggested by Sir George.

Some of the exiles had made their way to Thrackstown, fewer to Harbourtown and even fewer to the Kingdom of Concordia on the other side of the Northern Ranges which was where Sir Philip was born. Some headed into the Great Forest to become bandits. Some braved the desert to the south of Melita using the only known caravan trail through it. Most had, however, headed west through the narrow Duchies Pass to the duchies beyond. There were seven duchies, one of which, the Duchy of Mayflor, was where Queen Katerina, Charlotte's mother, had been born. Katerina had been a daughter of the Duke and Duchess of Mayflor and had had the title of Lady Katerina of Mayflor. Most of the exiles went to the Duchy of Mayflor, although some distributed themselves amongst the other six duchies.

The vast majority of people in Falconia were extremely happy that Charlotte was the new queen. They had lived under tyranny for sixteen years and they loved their new freedoms. All in all, Falconia was a much happier and better ruled place than just over a year ago.

It was the morning, three days after the encounter with the wraith and the birth of the triplets. Queen Charlotte and Sir Philip were sitting on their thrones on the dais of the throne room. They had had new ones made as neither wanted to use the ones used by Queen Katerina and Princess Scarlett. Both thrones were the same size and were made of wood covered with gold leaf and padded with red velvet. Queen Charlotte wore the jewellery she always wore, the Great Ring of Falconia, the wolf ring, the eagle brooch, the double dolphin-headed bracelet and a necklace with the medallion that had beaten her sister. It showed a star and the moon and had a jagged line running through the centre of it. When Charlotte had joined the two halves together it had emitted a burst of light that had destroyed Scarlett with rays of rainbow light, entering Charlotte from Scarlett. Queen Charlotte was never without all of these items.

The throne room itself was vast. It was thirty feet high and the ceiling was painted with murals of various vistas of Falconia. The mountains to the north and west, the forest to the east and the rolling hills to the south. The walls were painted white and there were paintings of previous rulers and country scenes. Paintings of Queen Katerina and Princess Scarlett had been removed even though she and Queen Charlotte looked exactly alike.

There was just the one each of Queen Charlotte and King Philip wearing their regal robes and crowns. Doors on one side of the room opened out onto a large balcony that overlooked the castle courtyard. At one end of the room was a three foot dais, the back, and sides of which were covered in ruby-red curtains edged in gold and on this the thrones were placed. Around the room, at the entrances and the edges of the dais, members of the Queen's guard had been stationed.

In front of the thrones below the dais three cots had been placed. Two were alike, both solid brown wood and sturdy with rockers at the base. One had blue bedding the other pink. The third had been acquired somewhat quickly as there had been no expectation that it would have been needed. This was painted white and had thinner wood than the other two. It likewise had rockers at the base and had pink bedding.

The triplets were all amazingly asleep considering the large number of people in the room who were slowly queuing past them, giving them little waves and going 'coo, coo'. Two large midwives guarded the triplets from their admirers, not getting in the way but keeping a sharp eye on the babies and the crowd. Sir Gillian Stevens, the Royal Chamberlain controlled the crowd, making sure they remained in single file as they queued past. Two of the babies looked exactly alike and without checking, it was impossible to tell which was the boy and which the girl, both having blonde hair and blue eyes like their parents. The third in the white cot was smaller than the others and she had red hair and green eyes. Sir Gillian Stevens has expressed surprise that one of the babies didn't have the blonde hair that all the members of the Mayflor family had. Sir Philip explained to him that his father and his uncle King Regis of Concordia had married two sisters, both of whom had vivid red hair and it should be noted that the Crown Prince of Concordia's son had vivid red hair. Sir Philip laughingly noted that he and his cousin were fortunate that the red hair had skipped a generation.

People kept asking Sir Philip and Queen Charlotte what the babies' names were going to be, and all were informed that no decision had been yet made.

While this was happening Captain Jack Clough entered the throne room and went straight up to Sir Gillian and whispered something into his ear. Sir Gillian immediately turned and bowed to Sir Philip and Queen Charlotte. 'Please excuse me, Your Majesties, an important matter has come up that requires my most urgent attention.'

Queen Charlotte answered, 'Certainly, Sir Gillian, I hope that whatever the matter is, it can be solved quite easily.'

Sir Gillian nodded, 'So do I. Thank you, Your Majesties.' He turned and went to leave the room with the captain of the guard, just pausing long enough to order one of the guards to take over keeping the crowd organised.

An hour later the crowd filing past the babies started to reach the end. Sir Philip and Charlotte had kept giving each other glances that seemed to say, *'Hang on, not much longer.'*

Sir Gillian, Captain Clough along with Colin still carrying his bag, entered the throne room followed by a dozen fully armoured guards. Everyone stopped moving and all eyes were on Sir Gillian as he signalled the guards to halt and approached the thrones.

Queen Charlotte and Sir Philip had both stood. Sir Philip looked down at Sir Gillian and asked, 'What's the meaning of this? What is happening?'

Queen Charlotte asked simultaneously, 'Colin what's happening?'

'May I suggest that this parade be halted at once.' Sir Gillian looked around at the shocked faces. 'Temporarily of course, but something extremely important has come up.'

Queen Charlotte looked at Colin who nodded. Sir Philip announced, 'Quickly everybody, we will continue this tomorrow and we may have come up with names by then.' Everybody except the guards, the midwives, Sir Gillian, and Colin started to file out of the throne room.

Sir Gillian approached the dais and signalled for Queen Charlotte and Sir Philip to bend down so he could whisper to them. 'May I also suggest that the babies be sent to a guarded place of safety.'

Both Queen Charlotte and Sir Philip looked shocked. Sir Philip ordered the guards that had been originally in the throne room and the midwives to carry the cots to the royal nursery and not to leave them unless they were personally ordered to do so by either himself or Queen Charlotte. Sir Gilliam supervised this personally.

The other dozen guards then spread out in front of the dais, all were carrying halberds and were holding them in the ready position across their chests. While they were doing this Sir George entered the throne room and strode towards the dais. He looked at Colin and nodded towards Queen Charlotte and Sir Philip, 'Do they know?'

Colin shook his head. 'We're waiting for Sir Gilliam to return.'

The Royal Chamberlain re-entered the throne room followed by six fully armoured guards. Queen Charlotte gave Sir Gillian a questioning look as the six guards also took places around the dais looking out. The guards were all carrying halberds across their chests in a ready for action position. Queen Charlotte still standing glowered at Sir Gilliam. 'I demand to know what is happening,' she ordered.

Colin answered, first glancing towards Charlotte's hands to make sure she was wearing the Great Ring of Falconia, and the wolf ring, even though he knew she always wore them. 'You have visitors.'

'Who would warrant all this?' Queen Charlotte asked waving at the guards.

'Your cousin is here, and he's bought Sir John Amberleigh, someone called Sir Roger Livermore, and a score of men at arms with him.'

'What!' exclaimed Queen Charlotte.

The Royal Chamberlain replied, 'The men-at-arms are being held in the courtyard surrounded by fifty guards with crossbows. As your family is known to use magical weapons, we are taking all the precautions we can.'

'Sir John Amberleigh is to be thrown into the dungeons at once,' Sir George ordered. 'He has been exiled from Falconia and ordered never to return on pain of death.'

The Royal Chamberlain headed towards the door. 'No, wait,' Queen Charlotte ordered. 'We will first find out what brings them here and then decide their fate.'

Sir George turned to Queen Charlotte. 'Your Majesty, if we allow Sir John Amberleigh to return unpunished, we will have most of the exiles returning also expecting nothing to happen to them.'

Queen Charlotte raised her hand. 'I am Queen, I will handle this matter. Show them in.' Sir George's face creased in a frown, and he crossed his arms as the Royal Chamberlain left the throne room.

Two minutes later he was back, followed by three men who in turn were flanked by five guards with drawn short swords on either side. None of the three men had observable weapons. The leading man, the queen's cousin, the Marquis Sir Peter Mayflor was six feet tall, had long shoulder length blond wavy hair, blue eyes, broad shoulders, and was probably the most handsome man that anyone in the throne room or indeed the whole of Falconia had ever seen. He wore a rich red satin shirt and black satin trousers and long, black riding boots. He was possibly just a little older than Sir Philip, who hated him on sight. Just behind him to his right was another tall man. This one was older, dark and had short-cropped hair, was extremely thin and dressed in total black. The man just behind the Marquis Sir Peter Mayflor on his left was a small, dark-haired, mousey, beady-eyed man. This was Sir John Amberleigh.

The procession stopped about six feet short of the dais. The Marquis Sir Peter Mayflor took one extra step forward and bowed, copied by his two companions. All the guards stayed still. He then flung his arms open and walked towards Queen Charlotte. 'Dear cousin Charlotte you look — ' He never got to finish saying what Charlotte looked like as two halberds came down crossing in front of him and just missing his nose.

Sir Philip had stood up. 'That's Your Majesty to you and you do not approach the queen without permission.'

Sir Peter stepped back and gave a slight bow. 'My apologies, Your Majesty. Please forgive the fact I was excited to meet my cousin for the first time.'

Sir Philip continued, 'Really? Queen Charlotte has been on the throne of Falconia for over a year and this is the first time any of her family from Mayflor has visited. Not just that, Sir Gillian please read out which towns and countries attended Queen Charlotte and my wedding.'

Sir Gillian answered, 'Fortunately, I can recite them from memory. All the towns and mines from Falconia obviously. Your brother, who was the envoy from your uncle, the King of Concordia. Burghers from Harbourtown and Thrackstown. Envoys from the Duchies of Blange, Deccells, Fliume, Plaige, Riverworth and Yocum. And representatives of Melita and the desert peoples of the south, Your Majesty.'

'Thank you, Sir Gillian, but you did not mention Mayflor.'

'Mayflor did not send a representative, Your Majesty,' Sir Gillian replied, bowing.

While this exchange was going on Sir Peter stood looking bored and tapping his foot. When Sir Gillian had finished, he bowed to Queen Charlotte with a great flourish. 'Mayflor apologises for missing your wedding, Your Majesty. If you remember, circumstances at the time made us think that your family at Mayflor might not be extremely welcome. The Duchess's daughter and granddaughter had just died under ... hmm, interesting circumstances.'

'I am their granddaughter also, but does not that matter?'

'It was thought to be more ... hmm, safer for future relations to wait a while before attempts to resume contacts were made.'

Sir Philip at this point decided to join the conversation once again. 'What makes you think that we want a relationship with a place that worships Braidos.'

Sir Peter looked at Sir Philip in surprise. 'Did you not know? Braidos's temple in Mayflor has been torched and totally destroyed. The Duchess was angry at the way Braidos killed her daughter. The god is no longer welcome in Mayflor.'

Queen Charlotte, Sir Philip, Sir George and Colin, all

gave each other astonished looks.

Queen Charlotte asked, 'And what did Braidos think of this?'

Sir Peter smiled, 'The Duchess is strong enough to even worry a god. As I said Braidos is now no longer welcome in Mayflor, as far as I know he now has no temples anywhere. I assume you destroyed the one here.'

Queen Charlotte answered, 'It was one of the first things we did. And why is John Amberleigh with you. He was exiled upon pain of death.'

'I am sorry; we thought that his presence would be useful.' He turned and walked to the guard closest to John Amberleigh and snatched the guard's sword out of his hand, turned and plunged it into John Amberleigh's stomach, gave it a twist and pulled it out. He then returned the sword dripping in blood to the astonished guard. John Amberleigh gave a gasping sound and collapsed to the ground with his hands clutching the bleeding wound. Everyone else in the room had gone still, surprised by Sir Peter's actions.

Queen Charlotte turned to Colin. 'Help him.' Colin limped immediately to the dying man, grabbing a green crystal from his bag. Queen Charlotte looked angrily at Sir Peter and shouted, 'What was the meaning of that?'

Sir Peter and Sir Roger Livermore, the man wearing

black, were quickly surrounded by guards holding swords or halberds at their throats or torsos. Sir Peter threw his arms wide. 'I was obeying your royal command, cousin.'

Queen Charlotte, still glaring at Sir Peter, spoke to Sir George Potts. 'Escort them to one of the fortified guest rooms and leave a strong guard on the door. They are not to leave for any reason.'

Sir George took charge and all the guards in the room, except two that remained at the entrance to the throne room, escorted the two Mayflorians to a fortified guest room. They were built so they could be extremely hard to enter, or in this case, leave. A fortified guest room had its own bathroom but no windows and only one door. Colin had gone to the wounded man and was bending over him pressing his green crystal against the wound. The green crystal was about three inches long and was diamond-shaped. It was an immensely powerful crystal; it had already saved the lives of Sir Philip and Colin just over a year ago. Queen Charlotte had also grabbed a bag that she kept behind the throne and was already mixing herbs and extracts together in a bowl to make a poultice with the water kept in a flask in the bag. Queen Charlotte, before she had become Queen, had owned the apothecary at Harbourtown and was an accomplished healer, both with herbs and her magic. It was now run by her friend Pat who had bought her up after her adoptive parents had been murdered. Queen Charlotte called to one of the guards at the door, while mixing the poultice. 'Get a stretcher and take him to the infirmary immediately.' He ran to get a stretcher.

Queen Charlotte pressed her hastily made poultice to the wound and Colin placed his crystal on top, where it was bandaged to the wound. The guard returned with two pages and a stretcher, and they carried John Amberleigh out. Queen Charlotte and Colin followed together with the two guards. Sir George re-entered the throne room and found Sir Philip alone. Sir Philip said to Sir George, 'Well, that was very strange. Who would have thought that Sir Peter would have stabbed John Amberleigh after bringing him here all the way from Mayflor?'

'Yes, it was very strange,' Sir George replied frowning.

'Well, he was lucky to have probably the two best healers in Falconia, if not Strasia, in the same room with him.'

Sir George rubbing his chin nodded, 'Yes, wasn't he?'

CHAPTER FOUR

ust over an hour later, Charlotte and Colin entered the Queen's consulting room. This was a small room about fifteen feet square with two doors, one opened into a corridor which led to the throne room and the other to the royal chambers. A table for eight people with eight chairs was in the centre. All the walls were covered in closed dark walnut-brown cupboards. It was lit by a globe of light hovering near the ceiling in the centre of the room. There was a large carafe of water on the table and eight glasses. Sir Philip and Sir George were already sitting at the table. Charlotte dropped into her chair at the head of the table and wiped her forehead with her handkerchief, Colin took a side seat. Sir Philip asked, 'Well did he survive?'

Colin answered, 'Yes, a nasty, painful wound but not fatal if attended to at once.'

'That's what Sir George and I thought. In fact, we first thought that it could have been planned so that Sir John got wounded in order to make us think we could trust him and any information he may have.'

Sir George took up the narrative. 'However, even though Sir John was a superb administrator, he was, and we assume is, somewhat of a coward and it is thought by myself and others that used to know him, that there is no way he would agree to being stabbed in the stomach even if he knew he would not die. What is more important however, is why the fort at Duchies Pass didn't send a pigeon informing us of the Mayflorians coming. I have sent for an explanation of this.'

'Hmm, so what should we do with Sir Peter and Sir Roger?' Charlotte asked.

'Sir George and I will go and see them now and find out exactly what they want here. I have had their men-at-arms disarmed, and they are now camped in the stables under guard,' Sir Philip answered.

'Good, I feel tired. I will await you in our rooms.' She smiled at Sir Philip. 'Will you escort me please, Colin?'

Colin bowed. 'Certainly, Your Majesty.'

Charlotte tut-tutted. 'Colin, please. You know it's

Charlotte to you when we are with friends.'

'Yes, Charlotte.' Colin smiled and moved to help her stand. There was suddenly a heavy knocking on the door which led to the throne room. Both Sir Philip and Sir George stood with their hands immediately dropping to their swords. Colin looked at them. 'Feeling a bit edgy, can't blame you but surely we would have heard if someone had overpowered the guards.'

Sir Philip answered, 'You should know more than anyone what magic can do.'

Colin frowned. 'True.' Then went and opened the door. Sir Gillian, accompanied by two guards, looked extremely agitated.

Queen Charlotte, still sitting, ordered, 'Sir Gillian, please enter.'

Sir Gillian entered and bowed. 'Your Majesties, Sir George, Colin. I have urgent news.'

Queen Charlotte started to rise from her seat. 'What has Sir Peter done now?'

Sir Gillian answered, 'Nothing as far as I know. We have a message from the mines. They've spotted dwarfs.'

'What!' everyone exclaimed at once.

Sir Philip added, 'Exactly where and how many?'

'To the south-east of the mines. In the foothills.'

'That's near the forest and there have been reports of

increased goblin activity. Could they be connected?' Sir Philip asked.

Sir George replied, 'If they are getting together that would be extremely bad news for Falconia, especially with this entirely new incident with Mayflor.'

Queen Charlotte spoke to Sir Gillian. 'Arrange a meeting of all my advisors for two o'clock this afternoon. That is about two hours away. In the meantime,' she looked at her husband, 'you and Sir George see what you can find out from Sir Peter and Sir Roger. Oh, Sir Gillian, send a message to Sharag asking him if he can contact Helmut and to ask Helmut if he can find out what is happening in the forest with the goblins.' Sharag was one of several creatures created by Charlotte's mother. He had a combination of a lion's head, a bull's body, and an elephant's legs and feet. Helmut was a werewolf who, together with his pack, had saved Charlotte and Sir Philip's lives on more than one occasion. Queen Charlotte had issued a proclamation banning the hunting of werewolves and had granted Sharag and the four other creatures, which were also created by the dead Queen Katerina, land on the edge of the forest. The water creatures Queen Charlotte's mother had created still lived in the moat. She turned to Colin. 'How are your contact crystals going?'

Colin replied, 'Slowly, I hope we will have four or five intact within two weeks.'

Sir George asked, 'How many did you start with again over six months ago?'

Colin replied, 'You know very well it was over two hundred. If it weren't for the old Queen's laboratory I could never have started.'

'I just hope they are worth it, if and when we ever get any,' Sir George observed. 'Let us go and see these Mayflorians.' He left with Sir Philip.

There were four guards and a sergeant outside the door where Sir Peter and Sir Roger were held. When Sir Philip and Sir George arrived, the sergeant saluted, and the guards came to attention. The sergeant spoke, 'There has been no noise from inside, sir. They were both searched, and all their possessions confiscated.'

Sir Philip answered, 'Thank you, you and one of your men will accompany us inside. Now open the door.'

The sergeant opened the door while saying, 'Levin with me. The rest of you stay alert.'

The room was large and beautifully decorated with murals of the Falconian countryside on the walls and ceiling. There was a large fireplace on one wall. There was a purple-draped four-poster bed in one corner of the room next to a walnut dressing table. The rest of the room had four large, blue armchairs and a walnut table and four dining chairs. Sir Peter Mayflor and Sir Roger Livermore were lounging in two of the armchairs when Sir Philip, Sir George and the guards entered the room. They did not get up.

'You do realise that imprisoning us like this is against diplomatic protocol?' Sir Peter told them as they came in.

Sir George answered looking around him, 'Doesn't look much like a prison to me.'

'You mean we're free to go?'

'You and your men may leave Falconia immediately, as long as you never come back,' Sir Philip answered.

'Hmmm, that would leave my mission unfinished.'

Sir Philip asked, 'What mission would that be?'

'To improve relations between Mayflor and Falconia.'

'Not doing a particularly good job are you.'

'I was just trying to help.'

'By murdering a man in the throne room in front of the Queen?'

'You told me he was under sentence of death.'

'Enough of this. Is there anything you want to say before you and your men are escorted out of Falconia?'

'I've messed up badly. I am here to improve relations between my cousin Queen Charlotte and our grandmother. She wishes to meet Charlotte and her great-grandchildren before she dies. Please forgive me my error in the throne room. Justice in Mayflor is quick and absolute. I thought I was doing the right thing.'

'I don't like you, but I will not stand in the way of Queen Charlotte and her family. I will tell her what you have said, and you may wait for her reply.' Sir Philip turned towards the door, followed by Sir George and the guards. 'Do not attempt to leave this room. I will have food and wine brought for you.'

The four left with no more words. Sir Peter looked at Sir Roger, gave him a wink and smiled.

Colin had gone to the old Queen's laboratory, now his, where he was welcomed by his two assistants, Jackie and Liam. Jackie was a little older than Charlotte and looked much like her. She was slightly taller at five feet nine inches but also had long blonde hair and blue eyes. She had known Charlotte all her life and they had thought themselves related; Jackie having been the niece of Charlotte's adoptive mother Julie Silver, who had bought up Charlotte as her own without telling her she was not her real mother. Jackie and her parents and siblings lived in a village to the south of Harbourtown. Jackie used to live there until she became one of Colin's assistants in Castle Falconia. The other assistant was Liam. He was fourteen and shorter than Jackie by over six inches. He had long brown hair and was stocky and strong. His eyes were green, and he had a dark complexion. Both showed signs of magical powers. Jackie's family had an extensive line of magic users including Julie Silver who, with the help of Colin, had created the Silver jewellery that turned into animals. Liam was discovered in Town Falconia by Charlotte. He was begging in the streets and Charlotte felt stronger than usual magical vibes coming from him. Liam did not know his parents or lineage. Jackie and Liam were very fond of each other.

Colin asked as he walked in, 'How are the communication crystals going?'

Liam answered with a wry smile, 'Slowly and we lost another one. That only leaves four left.'

Colin shook his head. 'We must try another approach next time. Let's see how your lessons are going. Liam explain *The Magic* to me.'

'*The Magic* is everywhere and in everything. It is stronger in some than in others. It is what gives the gods their powers and the gods can magnify its powers in individuals. It has extremely strict rules and is not all powerful. There are ways to overcome it.' Liam paused.

'That is good. Remember both of you, knowledge can be more important. I have no *Magic* as such, but I can control and use crystals, which is just as good.'

Jackie piped in, 'I have some good news.'

Colin looked at her, 'Oh yes, what?'

'I think I have found a confusion spell among the old Queen's books.'

Colin laughed. 'I don't think we need that, you two are confusing enough just as you are.'

Both Jackie and Liam rolled their eyes.

CHAPTER FIVE

t was two o'clock and Queen Charlotte and her advisors were all sitting around the large and long table in a room that could seat twenty. This was Queen Charlotte's consulting room for meetings between herself and her advisors. The room was panelled in oak over thick stone and had a glass ceiling. A person, to enter the room, had to go through two pairs of doors with a small anti-room between them. It had been built so that none of the conversations in there could be overheard. All Queen Charlotte's advisors were there. There were sixteen of them, ranging from Sir Philip to Sir Giles Ramsbottom, a short bald mousey man, the Master of the Castle, who oversaw almost all the servants in Castle Falconia. The captain of the castle guard was also an advisor.

'Well, what news do we have?' Queen Charlotte asked the gathering.

Sir Giles immediately spoke up. 'We are having some problems in the kitchens. Some of the cooks——'

'Silence!' Sir Philip shouted. 'We are not here to discuss trivia. We have weighty matters to decide upon.' Sir Giles went quiet immediately, while suddenly finding his shoes remarkably interesting.

Sir Philip continued, 'John Amberleigh, I feel that he has lost the right to call himself a knight, is going to live. We have not yet been able to question him. It is hoped that we may do so in the morning. Sir Peter Mayflor claims that he was just trying to improve relations with us when he tried to murder John Amberleigh and states that he does not wish to leave Falconia yet as he is charged by his grandmother to improve relations between her and her surviving granddaughter and great-grandchildren. We have to decide whether we will enter talks with Mayflor and if so, whether to do so through Sir Peter.'

Queen Charlotte nodded towards Sir Philip. 'Thank you, how is security with their men?'

'There has been no——' his words were suddenly interrupted by a loud urgent knocking on the inner of the great doors. Jack Clough rose from his seat and opened the door.

A castle guard stood breathless from running. 'The mines are under attack from dwarfs. The outer areas have fallen, and the main mines are under siege from the outside and from the depths.'

Sir Philip immediately took charge and ordered Captain Clough, 'Sound the general alarm and get all spare troops that are not guarding the Mayflorians and needed for castle security ready to ride within the hour. And send a pigeon to Captain Richardson telling him to get to the mines as soon as possible.'

Captain Clough saluted by placing his right fist on his chest and replied, 'Yes, sir,' and turned and left the room leaving the doors open. Sir Philip then turned to Sir George Potts. 'Do we have any information about the dwarfs?'

Sir George rubbed his chin. 'Well, last year a delegation of dwarfs turned up at the mines after 237 years of not being seen after the battle of Minesville where they were savagely beaten. They demanded the return of the mines to them. Queen Katerina and Princess Scarlett went to meet them and killed all of them except one, who escaped. The mines were fortified after this incident which is probably why they have not fallen yet. Colonel Blayton oversees mine security. He's one of the few senior officers that were kept after Queen Charlotte was crowned. He is very capable. The mines used to have wraiths patrolling the surrounding areas and depths, but since Queen Charlotte took over, they have all disappeared.'

'Good riddance too,' Sir Philip added. 'I've had enough of those things, and now we have the creatures bothering us again.'

A loud ringing carried through the castle as the alarm sounded and there were the sounds of shouting and running in the corridors as troops rushed to their emergency posts. Queen Charlotte rose. 'We must plan for our defence of the mines. It will take us two days to get there, will the mines be able to hold out that long?'

'Dear cousin, we can be there a lot sooner than that.'

Everyone turned to the doorway where Sir Peter Mayflor leant against the doorjamb.

'How did you get here?' Sir Philip snarled.

'Does it matter? What does matter is that I can get you and your men to the mines in a few hours, not days.'

'You are not going to get anyone anywhere,' Sir Philip replied. He moved to the doorway and shouted, 'Guards, guards!' He turned back to Sir Peter. 'I will have you thrown into the cells.'

Queen Charlotte sighed. 'Stop, Philip. Let us hear what he has to say.'

Sir Peter smirked at Sir Philip. 'Thank you, cousin, I mean, Your Majesty,' he added as Sir Philip growled at him. 'There is a secret passage in the castle that leads to a portal that will get us to the mines in a flash of the eye. We can be there in three hours and attack the dwarfs from the rear. I also volunteer my men to help.'

'I don't like it; we can't trust him,' Sir Philip growled.

Queen Charlotte looked at Sir George. 'What's your opinion?'

'We'll have Captain Richardson's force and guards from Minesville there in a day. If we can reinforce before then it would be to our advantage. If we take Sir Peter's men, we can also take the fifty men guarding them and an extra one hundred and fifty from the castle. I will immediately send messages to all the towns and villages to send men to Minesville, but it will take several days to get those men organised and we cannot be sure of the number until they get there. If Sir Peter can be trusted, we should use him.'

'That's a big if,' Sir Philip added.

Sir Peter spread his hands in a gesture of frustration. 'They're your mines, do you want to rescue them or not?'

Queen Charlotte banged her fist on the table. 'No more bickering. We must save the mines. We go. Sir George consult with Sir Peter and have the men ready as soon as possible. This meeting is ended, all of you leave, Sir Philip, Colin, please stay.'

Everyone rose from the table and left the room except Queen Charlotte, Sir Philip and Colin. Sir George and Sir Peter proceeded to the stables and barracks to organise the soldiers, the others went back to their general duties.

Once they had all left, Charlotte closed and sealed the doors with a click of her fingers. 'Philip, I know Sir Peter cannot be trusted but I think we will need his help to rescue the mines from the dwarfs. Just keep an eye on him until we can send him back to Mayflor.'

Sir Philip nodded and took his wife's hand. 'Yes, you are right, the mines must come first.'

Charlotte then looked at Colin. 'Colin, please keep an eye on the triplets while we are at the mines. I will leave Sir George in charge of the castle.'

'You can't go!' Sir Philip cried, startled. 'It's only three days since you had the triplets.'

'Who else has the power to hopefully force a truce with the dwarfs. I'm a lot more powerful than I was a year ago. Colin has helped make me stronger in *The Magic*, that could be the deciding factor. Besides, I have powerful bodyguards in Jason and Great Wing.'

Sir Philip nodded. 'That is true, but please be careful, I won't leave your side.'

Charlotte looked at Sir Philip quizzically. 'But will you not be leading the troops? Or would you rather Sir Peter did?' she added with a wicked smile.

'I will lead,' Sir Philip answered and gave Charlotte a kiss. 'I'd better go and get ready.' He rose and left the room, closing the doors behind him.

'Colin, please make sure the triplets come to no harm.'

'I will do all in my power, but as all the Mayflorians are going with you, they should be safe,' Colin replied.

'Yes, that's true, but I'm still worried about their real reason for being here, and now with this trouble with the dwarfs, the babies picked a great time to arrive.'

'I'll arrange roast stork for dinner tomorrow so that you can get revenge.' Colin smiled.

Charlotte laughed and gave Colin a quick kiss on the cheek and took his hand. 'I have a lot to thank you for, especially for being such a good and loyal friend.'

'It's what your parents were to me.' Colin gave a sad smile. 'Stephen and Julie would be extremely proud of you.'

'That's what we'll call the two blonde babies,' Charlotte exclaimed still holding Colin's hand. 'Thank you for the inspiration. Now I must go and prepare for whatever else may occur this day.' She rose from the table, smiled at Colin and left the room, leaving Colin deep in thought.

CHAPTER SIX

ess than an hour later, over two hundred and twenty men were paraded in the castle courtyard. The men and their commanders had all eaten a small meal as they were planning to travel as light as possible, just carrying weapons and armour. Sir Philip was addressing them, informing the troops of what was expected of them. He kept it short so they would have plenty of daylight left on the bright, late spring day. Queen Charlotte, Sir George Potts, Captain Clough, Sir Peter, and Sir Roger were in a separate group, listening.

Jackie, Colin's assistant joined the group and approached Queen Charlotte in order to speak to her. From a distance, except for the clothes, it was hard to tell the difference between them. Queen Charlotte was dressed in green doublet and tights, feeling that it would be more appropriate than a dress for a battle. Sir Peter, in black armour as was Sir Roger, came up to Queen Charlotte. 'You look absolutely stunning, cousin. If you ever want to get rid of Sir Philip, please give me a call. You do know that Scarlett and I were to be married. You would make a great substitute.'

'I'm not a substitute for anyone or anything,' Queen Charlotte retorted angrily. 'Are you sure you're not here to worsen relations between Falconia and Mayflor? Because you're doing well.'

Sir Peter bowed. 'My apologies, Your Majesty, I did not mean to offend. I'm sure after we beat the dwarfs, things will improve between us.'

Queen Charlotte turned her back on him and spoke quietly to Jackie, who was also wearing doublet and tights, but hers were brown. 'Why are you here Jackie? Do you have a message from Colin? Are the triplets alright?'

Jackie spoke quietly back. 'Everything is alright, but I do have a message from Colin. He wants both of us to watch Sir Peter closely so that we will be able to use whatever method he uses to get us to the mines ourselves without him.'

'You're not coming, it's too dangerous,' Queen Charlotte told Jackie.

'I'll stick close to you, but Colin wants both of us to watch so nothing gets missed,' Jackie replied.

Queen Charlotte grimaced. 'Well, where magic is concerned Colin is in charge, but be incredibly careful. I do not want you hurt.'

'I'll be behind you, Your Majesty,' Jackie answered.

Sir Philip finished his speech to the troops and joined the command group. 'Well, we're ready to go. Lead the way.' The last comment was to Sir Peter.

Sir Roger started to walk away from the group. 'I'll join our men in the centre of the force.' It had been decided that the twenty Mayflorians would be sandwiched between a hundred Falconians on either side. Every fifth man, whether Falconian or Mayflorian, had been given a torch soaked in pitch and a tinder box.

Sir Peter bowed to Queen Charlotte. 'Your Majesty, please lead the way to the royal reading room.'

Queen Charlotte and Sir Philip gave each other a quizzical look. 'This way,' Queen Charlotte answered and led the way into the castle followed by Sir Peter and then the rest of the command group and then the soldiers two by two. The fifty crossbowmen were the last to enter.

When they got to the reading room door, there was a long queue of troops snaking its way back to the castle courtyard. Queen Charlotte opened the door and stood back to allow Sir Peter to enter first. The reading room was used by Queen Charlotte and before her, her predecessors, to study documents before signing. It was not a large room and had narrow, slotted, square, wooden panels on three of the walls, and the fourth contained large glass windows to let in as much light as possible for reading. There was a table and just the one extremely comfortable chair in there.

Sir Peter turned to Queen Charlotte and suggested, 'I think that just you, Sir Philip and I should enter the room until it is prepared for the rest of the men.'

Queen Charlotte, Sir Philip and Sir Peter entered the room and shut the door. Sir Peter then knocked twice on one of the wooden panels at the back of the room and part of the wall silently slid aside. It revealed a stairway leading down into what seemed to be an awfully dark, gaping hole. Sir Philip uttered to Sir Peter, 'Interesting what you know about this castle that none of the rest of us do.'

Sir Peter answered, 'Yes, isn't it; but this is not the time to discuss it. Would you like to get the men ready?'

Sir Philip went to the door and left the room. He addressed the command group. 'Jackie, you go and join the queen inside.' Jackie left. 'Sir George, please go to the end of the column to make sure everyone gets here, and Captain Clough make sure everyone who has a torch lights it before they enter the passage inside. Do it inside the room and try to make sure none of the men set it on fire. Thank you.' Sir George left for the rear of the column while Sir Philip and Captain Clough entered the reading room followed by the first men in the column.

Meanwhile, the three in the room provided their own light. Queen Charlotte had created a ball of light that floated in front of her, while Sir Peter and Jackie both held their left hand palm up from which a flame burned without harming them.

As Sir Philip entered the room he took in the scene. 'Well, it looks like you three should lead, we'll follow.'

Sir Peter stated, 'Normally, I would offer to go first, but you, dear cousin, have the best light, so after you.'

Sir Philip drew his sword. 'That sounds fair enough, but I'll be right behind you with my sword at your back. So be careful. And it's "Your Majesty" to you.'

'I understand completely, Sir, I mean King Philip. Just please don't slip and fall on the stairs,' Sir Peter quipped.

The long passage at the bottom of the many stairs terminated in a cave on the side of a hill behind the castle and the town. Outside the cave was a small clearing surrounded by dense wood. It was still only mid-afternoon, and the sun shone brightly in the clearing. The light ball in front of Queen Charlotte disappeared as did the flames on the hands of Sir Peter and Jackie. Sir Peter walked to near the edge of the clearing, followed closely by Queen Charlotte and Jackie and waved his hands twice in front of his face and a shimmering haze about ten feet in diameter appeared in front of them, causing some mutterings among the soldiers that had already entered the clearing.

Sir Philip addressed the first sergeant that had appeared from the cave. 'Sir Peter and I will be the first through whatever that thing is, followed by Queen Charlotte and Jackie. After that I'm relying on you to keep the men moving. Have them leave half of the torches here and bring the rest.'

The sergeant saluted and answered, 'Yes, sir.'

Sir Philip went up to Sir Peter, still with his drawn sword in his hand he gestured towards the haze, 'Shall we?'

Sir Peter smiled, nodded and walked towards the haze with Sir Philip at his side. They entered, closely followed by Queen Charlotte and Jackie. The troops then started to follow with some trepidation.

They exited through a matching haze in a small valley in the mountains, all feeling exhausted. Sir Peter declared to Sir Philip, 'Have the men rest for a little while, they will need it.'

Sir Philip ordered the men who followed through the haze to rest until a sergeant came through and he delegated the responsibility to him while he went and sat with Queen Charlotte, Jackie, Captain Clough and Sir Peter. 'Which way now?' he asked Sir Peter.

'I don't know,' Sir Peter answered. 'I've never been here before. I just know the mines are close. I suggest you send out scouts.'

They were in a valley between mountains and there were only two ways to go, east and west. Sir Philip sent five men who had rested, in each direction, with orders not to go more than two miles before returning. Fifteen minutes later, while men were still entering the valley through the haze, a soldier returned from the west. He approached Sir Philip and saluted with his fist over his heart. 'I didn't see it, sir, and the others went forward to investigate, but it sounds like fighting in that direction.' He pointed back to the west.

Sir Philip nodded and said, 'Thank you.' He then looked at Captain Clough. 'You will lead with twenty men, followed by the crossbowmen. We,' he indicated himself, Queen Charlotte, Jackie and Sir Peter, 'will be next with a hundred Falconians, then Sir Roger with the Mayflorians and then the rest of the Falconians.' He looked around. 'Where is Sir Roger?'

No one knew. Sir Philip turned on Sir Peter, 'What trickery is this?'

Sir Peter spread his hands at his head height. 'I know nothing of this. He should be with our men.'

'I'll want a full explanation when we get back. Let's get started. All the men are through now.' The sergeant that had been organising the men on the other side of the haze had passed through several minutes before and the haze had disappeared.

Queen Charlotte spoke, 'Sir Peter, you'll have to teach me how to use that haze.' Sir Peter bowed but said nothing. She continued, 'One change, I'll be with the crossbowmen.'

'That's far too dangerous,' Sir Philip retorted.

'I'm probably the most powerful person here. I should be near the front,' Queen Charlotte answered.

Sir Philip realising the truth of the statement replied, 'All right, but I'll be right with you.'

'So will I,' Sir Peter exclaimed. 'Magic users will be especially useful.'

'That includes me then,' Jackie added.

Sir Philip gave up. 'Captain Clough, move out.'

The column started moving towards the mines.

There was a loud knock on the door of the nursery. Colin looked at the triplets as he opened the door. The two guards that were standing guard outside had a page between them. The page bowed to Colin, 'Sir, you are urgently required at the infirmary immediately. They think that Sir John Amberleigh is about to die.'

Colin's face formed a frown. 'That shouldn't happen. I'll come immediately.' He spoke to the two guards outside the door and the two inside, as well as the two nursemaids. 'Do not open the door to anyone except myself, Sir George or the King and Queen.' He turned to the page. 'Go and find Sir George immediately and have him come here at once.' The page rushed off down the corridor with Colin limping behind him with his staff and pouch of crystals. In the shadows Sir Roger watched with an unpleasant grin on his face.

CHAPTER SEVEN

After the column had walked almost three-quarters of a mile, they started to hear the sounds of battle from the mines. Sir Philip ordered them to increase their pace to get there quicker. Queen Charlotte, against all advice, joined Captain Clough at the front of the column. She ordered Sir Philip and Sir Peter to stay with the crossbowmen and have them ready to fire a volley as soon as ordered. The column spread out as they entered the valley at the base of the three mountains. The sight they saw was alarming. In the year since Charlotte became queen the men at the mining camp had built a strong, ten foot tall palisade around it, constructed of both stone and wood. Hundreds of dwarfs were climbing over and on top of each other to get to the top of the palisade where bitter fighting was causing casualties on both sides, but mainly the dwarfs'. There was a group of dwarfs at the entrance of the northern gap of the valley who seemed to be directing the battle plan of the dwarfs. Queen Charlotte pointed her fingers at a rocky outcrop near this group and a bolt of lightning emitted from them, causing an explosion that startled them and brought their attention to the troops spreading out behind her. Charlotte magnified her voice. 'Stop this attack at once or the next explosion will be in the centre of your group and my crossbowmen will open fire on your men at the wall immediately.'

The dwarfs at the wall stopped their attack and waited at the base of it for orders. A large (in girth) dwarf in full armour and an open helm turned towards them. He was about three foot six inches tall and, like all the dwarfs, had long brown hair and beard. His voice boomed in the valley. 'Why should I heed the daughter of the witch who killed my brother? Borin Steelhammer and others came here in peace to talk. You and your mother killed them, save one you left as a witness.' He pointed at a companion armoured like him to his left. 'Balor Hardfall watched you kill them all and revenge will be ours. Even now while you watch us, a thousand dwarfs are pouring out of the mine entrances inside your fort. Even if I die soon, all of you will be dead also.'

'Sorry, but I don't think that's going to happen.' A giant of a man, six feet ten inches, fully armoured but without his helmet, on top of the wall shouted, 'As soon as you attacked, we blocked all of the entrances with some of Sir Philip's there,' he gestured towards Sir Philip, 'stronger Concordian steel gates and dropped huge boulders on top of that. It will take some time even for your best miners to get through that.' He waved his meaty hand with a flourish. 'Even so, I'm extremely glad to see you, Your Majesties.' His smile made his extremely scarred face even uglier.

Charlotte and Sir Philip waved back smiling. 'Could you get the mine manager up there with you, Colonel Blayton?' Queen Charlotte shouted back. 'I think we'll need him for negotiations.'

Before Colonel Blayton could move, Sir Peter moved forward. 'You're not going to negotiate with those scum.' He pointed his hand at the group of dwarfs and lightning emitted from his fingers but before it could hit the dwarfs a ray of green light flashed out from the Great Ring of Falconia on the right ring finger of Queen Charlotte's hand, which intercepted the lightning with an explosion that, although not killing or hurting anyone, knocked a number of the crossbowmen off their feet.

Sir Peter turned on Queen Charlotte with such a scowl that made even his immensely handsome face ugly. 'You stupid interfering floozy.' He started to aim his hand at Queen Charlotte but stopped as he found himself flat on his back with a giant, black wolf's front paws on his chest and a large mouthful of teeth drooling over his face.

Queen Charlotte smiled. 'Hi Jason, if he moves, bite his head off.'

Jason gave a small growl and moved his jaws closer to Sir Peter's head. Sir Peter remained totally immobile.

Queen Charlotte turned her attention again to the dwarf leader. 'I killed no one. My mother and my twin sister, both of whom now are dead, did that. I am Queen Charlotte and I have only been in Falconia for just over a year. The incident that you refer to took place before I got here.'

The dwarf leader answered, 'Why should we believe you?'

'I could have let Sir Peter there,' she nodded towards the prostrate Sir Peter, 'kill all of you if that's what I wanted. You said that you sent people here in peace to talk, so talk to me.'

The dwarf leader twirled the end of his long beard for several heartbeats. 'My name is Malgon Steelhammer. I am leader of the Northern Ranges Tribes of Dwarfs. I am here to demand the return of the mines that were stolen from us over two hundred years ago.' He took a step forward. 'Will you return them?'

Queen Charlotte looked at the palisade where Colonel Blayton had returned with the mine manager, a shorter man, only six feet three, bald with a ruddy complexion. 'Sir Robert, which are our two northernmost mines?'

'Marshall and Nexus, Your Majesty. Two of our richest diamond mines.'

'Thank you.' She turned back to the dwarf. 'As a sign of our good faith, they are yours.'

Malgon Steelhammer looked astonished. 'Just like that?'

Queen Charlotte smiled. 'Just like that. There is a condition.'

The dwarf grimaced. 'I should have known.'

Queen Charlotte continued, 'They are not bad. First the fighting must stop, we have more reinforcements already on the way and more fighting will only cause a massive loss of life on both sides. Secondly, you agree to talks between us on the future of the mines. You have to understand that the mines are the wealth of Falconia and we cannot and will not just give them away; but we do wish peace with you and the dwarfs, so a compromise must be found. Do you agree?'

Malgon Steelhammer bowed. 'I wish that your mother and sister had had your wisdom. I agree.' He waved at the dwarfs under the palisade and pointed back up the northernmost valley. The dwarfs started to move. 'We must go and tend our wounded. We will send a delegation here in two days to commence talks. Thank you, Your Majesty.'

Queen Charlotte nodded her head to the dwarf. 'Thank you, Malgon Steelhammer.'

Sir Philip walked up to Queen Charlotte and gave her a kiss on the cheek. 'You were magnificent; but I must wonder what happened to the young girl I saved from the manticore and used to carry bags of sneezing powder to put off suitors.' (A manticore is a creature with a human face and head, the body of a lion and a scorpion's tail.)

Queen Charlotte gave a sad smile. 'She's still in there somewhere. It's been a strange year and I've had to be stronger than I was.' She looked around at Sir Peter. 'One more problem. Would you like Jason to bite your head off or just eat you slowly?'

Sir Peter gave Queen Charlotte a beseeching look. 'No, please,' he muttered in a quivering voice.

'You didn't answer me before when I asked if you would show me how to use the haze.'

'I meant to say, *yes*, of course. Honestly, Your Majesty, nothing would give me greater pleasure.' Sir Peter was sweating.

'Jason, let him up. Someone tie his hands to make sure we see no more lightning.'

Jason stepped off Sir Peter's chest and he got to his feet and started to wipe the wolf's saliva off his face, but before he could do much, his arms were seized, and his hands tied behind him. Queen Charlotte looked at him. 'Unfortunately, we have no lockable steel gloves with us to stop most of your magic and I know you can untie those ropes just like that.' She clicked her fingers. 'But Jason will be behind you all the way back to the haze.'

Colonel Blayton had left the palisade and walked up to join them. He bowed to Queen Charlotte. 'Any orders, Your Majesty?'

Queen Charlotte gave him a beaming smile. 'You did well in defending the mines, your covering of the mine openings inside the palisade was brilliant. It won the fight. I am so glad you stayed on as the commander here.'

Colonel Blayton beamed happily as he bowed again. 'Thank you, Your Majesty.'

'As for orders,' she paused a moment in thought, 'continue holding the mines here as best you can. I will leave you a hundred extra men and twenty crossbowmen. I hope that will be enough.' She looked at the exiting dwarfs. 'I believe that Malgon Steelhammer will keep his word but it's best to play safe.'

'Yes, Your Majesty and I will reinforce the barriers at the mine openings.'

'Good idea and send a pigeon to Minesville ordering Captain Richardson to divert his men to Castle Falconia.'

Colonel Blayton bowed yet again. 'Yes, Your Majesty, I will do so immediately.' He turned and returned to the palisade.

Queen Charlotte called out, 'Captain Clough, to me.'

The captain came running up and saluted with his fist over his heart. 'Yes, Your Majesty.'

'You are to disarm all the Mayflorians immediately and have all their hands tied behind them. If we can't trust their commander, we certainly can't trust them. Then have one hundred of the men and twenty of the crossbowmen reinforce Colonel Blayton and they can take the Mayflorian's weapons with them. And then get ready to leave with the Mayflorians as prisoners. All the other crossbowmen are to target Sir Peter.' She made sure that Sir Peter heard her last order.

Captain Clough set about obeying her orders while she, Sir Peter and Jackie waited. 'Jackie, when Sir Peter shows us how to work the haze, I want you to watch and learn.'

Jackie answered, 'Yes, Your Majesty.'

It was almost dark by the time they set out back to where the haze was. They were glad they had plenty of torches.

Sir Roger looked at the two sleeping guards and the two sleeping nursemaids and smiled. The guards outside were also asleep and the door had been no problem for him. He then looked at the three cots and then down at his hand which held two, what looked like, small black seeds. *None of us expected triplets,* he thought to himself, *I'll use the big ones.* He went to the brown cots ignoring the white one. He picked up the baby with the blue bedding and turned him on his stomach. He felt for the top of the boy's spine and slowly pushed one of the seed-like items into the baby's head at the top of his spine. It left a tiny red mark. He turned him back onto his back. He then repeated the same procedure with the blonde sister. He then went to leave, just before he got to the door it swung open and Colin was standing there. Colin exclaimed while threatening Sir Roger with his staff, 'What are you doing here? Why are the guards sleeping?'

Sir Roger answered by waving his right hand across his body and Colin went flying into the wall, dropping his staff and collapsing to the ground. 'You're not even a real magic user, you're nothing without your crystals. I'm not even going to use magic to kill you.' He drew his sword and advanced on Colin. 'No one was supposed to die, but you came back too soon.'

He pulled his arm back for the killing thrust and

hesitated as he looked down at six inches of steel protruding from his sternum which then twisted. Blood started to pour from the wound as Sir Roger slowly crumpled to the ground.

'That's twice this week, you're really going to have to be more careful.'

'Thank you once again,' Colin mumbled to Sir George as he used his staff to help pull himself back onto his feet. 'I think it must be because of my attempts to stay out of danger.' He frowned. 'But why was he here and why did he put everyone to sleep.'

Sir George looked at the cots in alarm. 'The triplets! What has he done to the triplets?' He went to the door and shouted in a parade ground voice, 'Guards! Guards! Call out all the castle guards, this is an extreme emergency! Everyone to their posts!' His words could be heard echoing as the guards within hearing repeated them while rushing to their posts.

Colin and Sir George went to check on the triplets as the noise from the rest of the castle increased. Four guards appeared at the door to the nursery. Sir George ordered, 'Check on the guards and the nursemaids,' as he and Colin checked the triplets for injuries.

'Well, they all seem healthy enough, there's a tiny pimple I haven't seen before at the top of the boy's spine but nothing else I've not seen before,' Colin observed. 'When the nursemaids recover, we'll get them to check also.'

Sir George, holding the redheaded daughter, observed, 'Well, there's no pimple on this one, although I think there was one on her,' he nodded towards the other girl, 'but him and her they're as alike as twins. What happens to one happens to the other. This one is the odd one out.'

'Maybe I interrupted him before he could do what he intended. I hope so.'

'I'm going to enjoy asking Sir Peter and his men about this when they get back. The torture chamber hasn't been used since Charlotte became queen.' Sir George smiled as he rubbed his hands.

CHAPTER EIGHT

When Queen Charlotte and the rest of her entourage from the mines arrived back at Castle Falconia, it was fully dark. They were surprised at the alarm and having all the castle guards at their posts. Queen Charlotte and Sir Philip immediately thought of the triplets and ordered Captain Clough to put all the Mayflorians in the dungeons while they rushed to the nursery. When they got there, they found a full squad of a dozen men standing guard. The sleeping guards and the nursemaids had been taken to the infirmary. Queen Charlotte and Sir Philip entered the nursery. Colin and Sir George were still in there, together with a nurse from the infirmary to help with the triplets. The body of Sir Roger lay against a wall where it had been placed.

Charlotte and Sir Philip went immediately to the triplets' cots while Charlotte asked in alarm, 'What happened? Are the babies safe?'

Sir George answered, 'We think so, at least we can't find anything wrong with them. Colin came back to find the guards and the nursemaids asleep and Sir Roger in the room.'

Charlotte looked at Colin accusingly. 'Came back? From where?'

Colin looked directly at Charlotte. 'I was called to the infirmary. John Amberleigh is dead. Obviously, his death was timed to draw me away. I sent for Sir George to take my place while I was away. John Amberleigh was dead when I got to the infirmary, so I came straight back and found the outside guards asleep. I came in and found Sir Roger just inside the door. Sir Roger attacked me and was just about to kill me when Sir George arrived and saved my life again. We've checked the babies, the blonde ones both have a flea bite at the base of their heads near the spine. We couldn't find anything on the redheaded girl.'

Charlotte had been listening intently as Colin spoke. 'I'm sorry Colin, I should have known it would have had to be an emergency to lure you away.' She picked up the male blond baby and looked at and felt the flea bite and then did the same thing for the female. 'I can sense nothing extra strange about them, they both seem to have no magic, but the marks look remarkably alike. No one is to enter this room. Colin, please stay and watch them, and do not leave for any reason. Also, please search Sir Roger's body for any clue about what he was doing.' Colin nodded assent. 'The guards will stay outside. Sir George please have Sir Peter brought to us in the throne room under heavy guard. You'll find him in the dungeons.'

Sir George's eyebrows rose an inch. 'Good place for him.' Sir Philip nodded in agreement.

'Sir Philip and I will await you there.' Sir George, Charlotte and Sir Philip left leaving Colin and the nurse watching the babies.

Sir Peter was brought into the throne room by ten guards with halberds all pointing at him. They walked slowly as the guards leading were walking backwards so that they could watch Sir Peter. Captain Clough guided them all so that they didn't trip over each other. Ten more guards stood between the group and the thrones in front of the platform.

Both Queen Charlotte and Sir Philip had stood when the group entered the throne room. Sir Peter bowed when he and his guards halted. 'Once again, I apologise, Your Majesty, for a stupid fit of anger in the heat of the moment in front of an enemy. Many have done the same thing. It is not new. Please forgive me, Your Majesties. I did give you and your friend the secret of the haze.'

Queen Charlotte signalled Sir Philip to sit while she answered, 'Threatening my life is an offence punishable by death. I am prepared to overlook this as we are related and you did tell us about the haze, which saved our men at the mines. What I cannot and won't forgive, is the threat to the lives of my children!' Her voice started to get louder. 'What was your and Sir Roger's intentions towards them?'

Sir Peter paled. 'I know nothing of this.'

'Sir Roger put the guards and midwives to sleep and then entered the triplets' nursery. What he did in there we do not know, except he attempted to kill Colin before Sir George killed him.' Queen Charlotte stared down at Sir Peter. 'Are you trying to tell me that you didn't know that Sir Roger had slipped away from your forces to threaten the children?'

Sir Peter tore open his red satin shirt exposing his bare chest. 'I knew nothing of Sir Roger's actions. My sole mission was to improve relations between you and Mayflor. If you think me guilty, please kill me now. I will not resist. I do not know how our grandmother will take it though.'

'Hmmm, our grandmother.' Queen Charlotte paused. 'I find it hard to believe that Sir Roger would have been acting without orders from someone and my loving grandmother is the most likely culprit. Whether or not you knew of whatever they were planning is uncertain. Because of this and the fact that you have made it possible to get men to and from the mines extremely quickly, I am not going to have you executed. In the morning you and your men will be escorted from Falconia never to return. You will spend the night in the cells. Take him away.'

'Wait,' Sir Peter called out. 'Please let me succeed in part of my mission. Allow an embassy from Mayflor, so that relations between our two countries will eventually improve.'

Queen Charlotte put up her hand. 'Wait.' She stood thinking for almost two minutes. 'I will allow an embassy; it will not be here but in Passville and no relative of ours will be allowed to be the ambassador. Mayflor can communicate with us from there by Falconian messenger. In fact, no Mayflorian from today will be allowed in Castle Falconia or the town. Everything will go through Passville.' She turned to Sir Philip. 'Sir Philip will you please organise the escort for the prisoners and inform the Mayor of Passville of our decision.'

Sir Philip bowed and answered, 'Certainly, Your Majesty.'

Queen Charlotte looked into Sir Peter's eyes. 'There, you have succeeded in your mission. The condition is there is no trouble from you, or your men, when you are escorted out of Falconia tomorrow.'

Sir Peter bowed. 'I promise on our grandmother's life, we will cause no trouble, cousin. I mean, Your Majesty.' He smiled at a scowling Sir Philip.

'I'm not sure our grandmother would like to hear you swear that.' Queen Charlotte smiled. 'Take him away and leave Sir Philip and me alone.' Everyone exited the throne room.

Charlotte knelt next to Sir Philip and took his hand. 'Do you think the triplets will be alright?'

Sir Philip looked into Charlotte's deep blue eyes. 'Well, you, Colin and the nursemaids have checked them out from head to toe and the only thing found was those two flea bites and you have checked for magical interference and have found nothing. All we can hope is that Colin interrupted Sir Roger before he was able to do whatever he planned. We will have the triplets watched around the clock to make sure they're safe.'

Charlotte looked at Sir Philip and nodded. 'Yes, thank you Philip, but I'll still worry for a while.'

Sir Philip stood and smiled at her. 'As will I,' he continued after helping Charlotte to her feet. 'I will command the escort tomorrow. I will order the force at the pass fort to be ready for anything and to improve their already extremely robust fortifications, then go to Passville to prepare them for the Mayflorian embassy.'

Charlotte nodded. 'I have thought of names for the twin triplets, I would like to call them Stephen and Julie, after my adoptive parents.'

Sir Philip answered, 'I totally agree, great names. I have a suggestion for the third, Rose, not just because of her hair, but because the rose pendant you gave me saved my life on more than one occasion.'

Charlotte clapped her hands. 'Brilliant, that's all settled then, I will call Sir Gillian and have it announced at once.'

Sir Philip took Charlotte's hands and gave her a big kiss. 'It was the happiest day of my life when I saved you from that manticore. I love you.'

Charlotte replied, 'It was for me also. I love you too.'

They kissed again and then went about their royal duties.

CHAPTER NINE

ate the next day Duchies Pass came in sight to the military column. Captain Richardson had arrived with his two hundred men during the night. 'We left immediately we received your pigeon.' And they now garrisoned Castle Falconia.

Sir Philip told him, 'You will take over garrisoning the castle while the current garrison borrow your horses. They leave for the fort at Duchies Pass in the morning. I will have your horses returned to you as soon as possible.'

The normal garrison along with the crossbowmen now escorted Sir Peter and his Mayflorians, watching them closely. Sir Peter rode at the head of the column along with Sir Philip and Captain Clough. Jackie had talked to Sir Peter throughout the long ride, trying to find out more information about *the haze* and whether there was another one near the pass which had been used by the Mayflorians to get past the fort and at the battle of the Duchies Pass almost nineteen years before. Unfortunately, she learnt nothing new.

When they had reached the turnoff to the pass on the Passville road they met up with a hundred men from the fort near Passville, who had been sent the order to join them by pigeon. Sir Peter had looked at the extra men and had ridden up to Sir Philip and asked if was sure he had enough men to watch the twenty-one Mayflorians. Sir Philip had ignored him.

The column entered the pass and immediately saw the massive fort that guarded the Falconian end. It was built into the mountain itself. There were walls only on two sides and were twenty feet thick and sixty feet high. The closed gate was made of thick oak and was thirty feet above the pass floor. The only access was via a ramp which looked just wide enough for two wagons to pass abreast. The bottom thirty feet of the wall only protected the tightly packed rubble that the inside of the fortress was built on.

It was almost dark when Sir Philip signalled the fort to open its gates then ordered the Mayflorians to camp in the pass surrounded by all the Falconians, except Sir Philip, Jackie and two guards who rode up to the fort. Sir

Peter asked if he could come too and was not too politely refused.

As the four rode through the gate Sir Philip noted the two deep, parallel, thick groves which were cut into the stone floor about a foot from the sides of the gate and which continued up the street behind the gate until they passed under two huge wooden gates into an equally huge building. As they dismounted, they were greeted by the fort commander, Sir James Oliver, who had the rank of a colonel.

Sir James was a tall, thirtyish, thin man with jet-black hair, wearing a scarlet silk shirt with matching tights and armed with a rapier and dagger. He bowed. 'Welcome to the fort at the end of Duchies Pass, Your Majesty. We received a message by pigeon telling us to expect you. These men will look after your horses.'

Sir Philip smiled. 'Please call me Sir Philip and if you will show me where the stables are, I will look after Jenny.' He gave Jenny's ears a rub. 'When we are away from Castle Falconia, I am the only one to look after her.' Jenny gave a short snort and gave Sir Philip a nuzzle.

Sir James bowed again. 'As you command, Your ... I mean Sir Philip. There is food prepared and these men will escort you to the stables and then to my personal dining hall.'

Sir Philip nodded his thanks and followed Sir James's men to the stables.

Sir Philip was shown to Sir James's private dining room. It was a moderately sized room cut out of the mountain with just one wall made of a light wood with the room's only door, that was left open. It had a dark hardwood table with ten matching chairs. The floor had an exotic woollen carpet that looked like it came from the desert lands, south of Melita. It was lit by dozens of candles. The cutlery and plates were made of silver and each place had a golden goblet. There was a choice of lamb or beef and several silver platters of various vegetables and fruit. The centrepiece was a platter of crab, lobster and prawns. There were golden jugs of wine, water and cordials. In all, it looked like a feast fit for a king, which it was.

Sir Philip looked at the room and the food. 'Nice, we don't often eat this well at Castle Falconia and rarely have seafood.' He looked at Sir James. 'Are you sure this is a frontline fort?'

Sir James shrugged. 'I was fortunate enough to have been born rich. We trade with the Duchies, two of which have access to the sea, hence the seafood, but let me introduce you to the others.' He indicated the other four people at the table who had stood when Sir Philip entered. 'Jackie, who you obviously know.' Jackie, halfway down the table, smiled and nodded. 'The lady at the bottom of the table,' he indicated to a gorgeously dressed, tall blonde woman who had slightly overdone her makeup, so she seemed to have very dark eyes and purple lips with bright red cheeks, she also wore a magnificent diamond cluster necklace with matching earrings, 'is my wife, the Lady Margaret of Yocum.' The Lady Margaret rose and curtsied. 'These two men are Captain Wilson, my second in command and Timothy Jenkins, who takes care of all the non-military affairs of the fort.' Captain Wilson who was in Falconian uniform stood and saluted by placing his right fist over his heart. He was about forty, six feet two inches tall, had short, cropped brown hair and a scar over his left eye. Timothy Jenkins stood and bowed. He was only about twenty-five, short and had long wavy black hair. They both sat to Sir Philip's left, Sir Philip having been given the head of the table, and Sir James sat to his right.

Sir James clapped his hands and two maids came in pushing a trolley holding an embossed silver soup tureen with matching bowls and spoons and started ladling some fish soup to all of the diners with Sir Philip first.

'Excellent, this fish soup is superb, I'm sure you'll really enjoy it, Your... I mean Sir Philip.'

Sir Philip took a sip. 'Very true, this is an excellent soup. You seem to have an abundance of seafood here. It's a luxury we don't often get at Castle Falconia.'

Sir James smiled at his wife. 'Yocum is one of the two duchies that have a coastline on the Western Sea. My wife's brother, the Duke of Yocum, is very generous with his supplies of seafood. In fact, trade with all the duchies is excellent.'

'I hope it stays that way, but I fear it could change.'

Sir James looked perplexed. 'Change, Sir Philip?'

'The Queen and I want you to build a wall with a walkway on top so it can be defended from both sides, leaving a space on both sides, which can be attacked by missiles from the fort and with the fort gate on the Falconian side. It will have a strong gate only wide enough for one laden wagon at a time each way and can be blocked extremely quickly.'

Sir James now looked ashen. 'Your Majesty, I assure you we watch the pass with all vigour. We cannot understand how the Mayflorians got through the pass to get to Castle Falconia, but I feel we are not to blame. Is this wall really necessary?'

'We do not blame you. We think we know how they got

into Falconia and I assure you, you are not to blame. An incident occurred at the castle that because of certain recent events at Castle Falconia makes us think we should make ourselves secure against a possible attack from the duchies, not necessarily by an army.'

'We have plenty of stone, it will be a wall you can be proud of, Your Majesty.'

'I'm sure it will be. I will leave most of the troops outside here with you, to help with the construction.'

The rest of the meal was eaten in comparative silence with just a little small talk and with the two maids bringing in extra food and making sure that everyone's plate or goblet was never empty.

Sir Philip patted his stomach. 'That was one of the best meals I have ever eaten. Thank you very much, Sir James.' Jackie nodded her agreement.

'You are very welcome, Sir Philip; it was my very immense pleasure.'

'I have heard a little about the way the fort gate is defended and as we entered, I saw grooves in the paving of the entrance, which entered a building further down the street. How does this work?' Sir Philip asked.

'Yes, the giant blocks of stone.' Sir James looked thoughtful. 'They were last used in earnest almost twenty years ago when we were attacked by the duchies, led by the Duchess of Mayflor, and they saved the fort. We test them once a year.'

'Only once?'

'Yes, a massive amount of grease is needed and every time they are used, repairs have to be made to the grooves. The blocks are on a trolley, which itself has been made extremely strong and magically enhanced, the wheels fit into the grooves and the trolley is moved by several ropes and a series of pulleys powered by ten enormous and extremely strong cart horses. When the trolley gets to the gate the grooves deepen so the trolley rests on the ground with the stone blocks supporting the gate. When we need to open the gates again the horses pull it back.'

'I would have liked to see it work.'

'We have only just finished the repair work and need to get more grease, Sir Philip, to use it now would use up the rest of our supply.'

'I will make sure you get extra grease when I visit Passville tomorrow. I must arrange for them to accept an embassy from Mayflor. Maybe next time.'

'It would be my pleasure to show you.'

'Could you please show us to our rooms.' Sir Philip indicated himself and Jackie.

'Certainly. I will have the maids do so. Goodnight.'

Sir Philip and Jackie were shown to their rooms.

Chapter Ten

The next morning, Sir Philip, Jackie and the two guards rode down to where the Mayflorians and the Falconian troops were camped. Captain Clough reported to Sir Philip at once. 'They were quiet as mice, sir. Not a peep out of any one of them.'

'Hmm. I thought Sir Peter would have been complaining about his lack of comforts,' Sir Philip mused.

'If you don't mind me saying so, sir, I think that Sir Peter is a lot tougher than he looks,' Captain Clough volunteered.

'Unfortunately, I think you're right. I just hope he goes back to Mayflor and never comes back.' Sir Philip grimaced. 'Anyway, come with me and we'll see them off.'

They found the Mayflorians getting ready to leave the camp, still being watched by the Falconian troops. Sir

Philip and Captain Clough approached Sir Peter. 'I hope you had an uncomfortable night,' Sir Philip exclaimed.

'Extremely. Thank you.' Sir Peter gave Sir Philip a nasty look. 'One day I hope to return some of your hospitality.'

'I can assure you that I'm never going to visit the duchies, so fortunately, that's very unlikely. However, we will keep a nice cold, damp cell for you in case you ever come back and don't forget your ambassador will not be a member of your or the Duchess's family.'

'Fortunately, unlike Falconia, Mayflor has an abundance of talented people, one of whom will be chosen to come and slum it over here,' Sir Peter retorted.

Sir Philip and Captain Clough let the Mayflorians finish their preparations in silence. When they had finished, they mounted up. Sir Peter looked down at Sir Philip. 'Don't forget, you still owe us weapons. I will expect them sent to us. Give my love to my cousin.' Without waiting for a reply, the Mayflorians rode out of the camp, down the pass towards the duchies.

'Good riddance.' Sir Philip scowled. 'If I never see that man again it will be too soon. Captain Clough, pick twenty good men to accompany us to Passville. We will ride out immediately. The rest will join the garrison here, including the crossbowmen. I think they'll find they are going to be kept terribly busy.'

Captain Clough saluted and went to obey the order.

Later that day they rode through the north gate of Passville set in the wooden wall that surrounded the town. The gate was left open during the day, protected by two armoured guards carrying halberds that immediately came to attention as the column passed through. The gate would be closed at dusk. Everyone who lived near the Great Forest barricaded themselves in at night. The first building they rode past was the especially functional-looking gate guard post. Shortly after, they saw an inn. It was larger than most, having three storeys, and was painted in the very distinctive black and white that most inns were decorated. There was a swinging inn sign over the front door showing a sleeping man on a wagon, underneath were the words "The Merchants Rest".

'Have the sergeant take the men to the barracks and have him warn the mayor I will be there to see him later to organise the Mayflorian embassy,' Sir Philip ordered, then smiled. 'You and I are going visiting.'

They tied Jenny and Captain Clough's horse to the rail outside. 'Jenny doesn't need this but it's town regulations.' They also left their helmets on their saddle pommels.

They entered the double front doors into the taproom of the inn. It was a large square room with a long bar on one side which ran for most of its length. A pair of doors completed the wall. On the opposite wall was a large fireplace with a big pile of logs on either side. There was a small fire burning even though it was early afternoon on a pleasant late spring day. There were two large bay windows on the same wall as the door. Oil lamps were burning from the ceiling. The many tables were mainly unoccupied at this early hour. Behind the bar was a short, balding, middle-aged, extremely well-muscled man with a broken nose and bushy eyebrows. There were also two pretty serving girls in green dresses and white aprons.

The man behind the bar looked up and his face burst into a broad smile. He almost ran from behind the bar with his arms wide in a welcoming manner. 'Phil, Phil, it's been a long time. How are yer?'

The man suddenly stopped as he found a sword at his throat. 'You address King Philip as Your Majesty, peasant.' Captain Clough had drawn his sword and now threatened the innkeeper.

'Wait, put away your sword.' Sir Philip pulled the captain's arm down. 'Claude is the only person in the kingdom allowed to call me Phil. Sorry about that,' he added to Claude while shaking his hand.

Claude had a look of amazement on his face. 'You're the King? I thought you were Philip Concade from Concordia.'

'Well, I am from Concordia, but my real name is Sir Philip Concord, the nephew of King Regis of Concordia and now King of Falconia; but in this place I'm Phil and it's good to see you.'

'It's good to see you too, Your Majesty.' Claude bowed.

'I wasn't joking Claude, I'm Phil to you.' He turned and indicated Captain Clough. 'And this is Jack.' The captain didn't look happy. 'Could you get us two mugs of ale and some of your delicious bread and cheese? We'll take my table by the back door.'

Claude beamed. 'Certainly, Phil. Will you need a room or stabling?'

'No, we'll be staying with the mayor. We have important business with him.' Phil and Jack took their table near the back door.

A few minutes later one of the serving girls, an attractive about seventeen-year-old, brought them two mugs of ale and some bread and cheese. She spoke to Sir Philip after curtsying. 'Are you really the King, sir?'

Sir Philip looked at her and answered, 'Yes.' He then added to Captain Clough, 'Just over a year ago Claude and I rescued this young girl from receiving a thrashing from three obnoxious merchants.' He then turned back to the girl. 'I hope you've had no trouble since then.'

'No, Claude is extremely protective. He's even hired a guard for the evenings since the incident.' She paused. 'Does this mean I've been kissed by the King?'

Sir Philip smiled, 'No, I wasn't King then.' He rose and gave her a kiss on the cheek. 'Now you have.'

The girl giggled and raised her hand to the spot she had been kissed. She curtsied again. 'Thank you, Your Majesty. I'll never wash that spot again.' She backed away curtsying all the way back to the kitchen.

Phil and Jack finished their repast while chatting to Claude, then left for their business with the mayor.

CHAPTER ELEVEN

t was the thirteenth birthday of the triplets. Many things had changed in Falconia since they were born. Everyone was thirteen years older to start with. Queen Charlotte had grown into a great beauty and Sir Philip had grown a beard. Their fairness in dealing with everyone was legendary, although it must be admitted there was a little bias against Mayflor, whose ambassador still resided in Passville. The wall across the pass still enabled trade between the duchies and the rest of the continent of Strasia, although the merchants of Melita, Thrackstown and Harbourtown, together with those of the duchies, were not too happy.

The truce between the dwarfs and Falconia held well, although there were those on both sides who were not happy. All of the mines more than a mile north of the main mine camp had been given back to the dwarfs with all others kept by Falconia. This meant that Falconia wasn't as rich as it once was but was still immensely wealthy. There was now trade between the dwarfs and Falconia so that the dwarfs now enjoyed Falconian lamb, Concordian beef and produce from The Field.

The Field was between the ports of Harbourtown and Thrackstown and several miles inland. It was a huge area of arable land which was the main food crop source of all the major towns and kingdoms on the continent of Strasia. In its centre was the large lake called Lake Thracks. Canals from the lake had been built to help irrigate The Field.

Most of the remainder of the continent south of the Northern Ranges and north of the Southern Desert was the Great Forest. It was flanked by the Eastern Sea except for The Field and an area between ten and a hundred miles wide between it and the Infinity Ranges north of the Southern Desert. The only break in the Infinity Ranges was the Duchies Pass which led to the Seven Duchies.

At Castle Falconia Sir George had retired as the Royal Falconer. His head of security, Fabian Hastings had taken over. Sir George, being the Queen's great-uncle, hadn't had to vacate his living quarters but now shared them with Fabian. Fabian, now a man in his late thirties, five foot ten inches, dark hair greying at the temples, wiry but surprisingly strong, had been trained by Sir George for over twenty years, was exceptionally competent and in the words of Sir George, "a worthy successor".

Colin, with Charlotte, Jackie and Liam's help, all of whom were still learning themselves, had increased the number of his new magic students to twenty-seven including the triplets, Charlotte and Rose being the best students. Colin had finally managed to get some of his communication crystals working. He hadn't many and their top range was not quite a hundred miles. They also needed a magic user to work. Only seven were in constant use. There was one at the mines, one at Minesville, one at Thomastown, one at Passville, one at the Duchies Pass Fort, one each at the two new forts which now had almost full complements, with the northern one called Fort Charlotte and the southern one called Fort Philip, and several at Castle Falconia. The magic users at each of these places were rotated every two months. However dependable, these crystals sometimes failed to work, although this was becoming rarer, all posts that used the crystals still kept a plentiful supply of pigeons as back up.

The triplets had discovered they could feel each other's emotions. They couldn't mind-read each other but could tell what each of the others were feeling. Stephen and Julie could tell each other's feelings stronger than Rose was able to.

Jenny had long retired as a warhorse and had been put out to pasture, though Sir Philip still rode her at least once a month and occasionally stabled her. A herd of horses just over a decade previously had been driven the long distance around the Great Forest from Concordia to Falconia and Jenny had taken one as a mate. She now had five children, one for each of the main royal family. The triplets had not yet received one. Sir Philip had trained the horses, four mares and one stallion, keeping the eldest one, a mare for himself. He called her Cherry after her reddish-brown colour. Cherry was as tall as Jenny and had the same temperament.

Falconia, even with the loss of a sizeable number of its most profitable mines, was still a vibrant, prosperous kingdom that many looked towards as a major influence on the continent.

The castle that morning was at its busiest with everyone preparing for the big party that evening. Sir Gillian Stevens, still the Royal Chamberlain and Sir David

Reading, the grandson of Paul Reading, Mayor of Thomastown, who had been one of Charlotte's major allies in her fight against her twin sister seemed to be just about everywhere, making sure that the preparations were going to be perfect for the party celebrating the triplets becoming teenagers. Sir David, in his mid-twenties, tall at six foot six inches, brown-haired and very slender was the new master of the castle, having taken over from Sir Giles Ramsbottom who had been murdered over two years previously.

The kitchens were busy, and the throne room was busy being decorated and tables and chairs brought in for the party that afternoon.

The triplets, each of whom had their own separate rooms, met in a corner of the kitchen for breakfast. The head cook had given each of them some bread and cheese and a glass of milk, wished them all a happy birthday and asked them all to stay out of the way while the party preparations continued. Stephen was just under five feet tall, short blonde hair, blue-eyed, powerfully built and with what seemed usually to be a permanent smile but had lost it this morning. He complained of having a slight headache. Julie who looked almost exactly like Stephen but with softer, more attractive features, slightly shorter and much less well-built and with much longer hair had the same complaint. Rose at four foot eight inches was the shortest of the three. She had the longest hair though, reaching halfway down her back. She had green eyes and a darker complexion than the others, who were quite pale-skinned, and told the others that she was feeling marvellous and was really looking forward to the party later that day.

Just as they were finishing their breakfast, Sir David entered the kitchen and informed them that their father wanted to see them in the castle courtyard. He led them to the courtyard to find their father with three grooms. Each groom held one of Jenny's children.

'Good morning and happy birthday teenagers. The first of your presents.' Sir Philip gave his children a bow and half-turned, using his arm to present the horses. All three children gave a squeal of delight. 'You can decide between you which one each of you want.'

Stephen shouted while running straight to the stallion, 'I'll take the stallion.'

Julie pouted. 'That's not fair!'

Sir Philip lifted her up. 'The best horse I've ever known and one of the best horses in Concordia, if not the best, was a mare.'

Julie looked down. 'Jenny?'

Sir Philip smiled. 'Yes, Jenny.'

Stephen who had been listening and was having problems with the stallion yelled, 'Hey, I want to change. This one is rejecting me.'

Sir Philip put Julie down. 'Too late, you chose first. Now it's the girls' turn.'

Rose indicated that Julie could have the first choice and she picked the larger of the mares leaving Rose with the smaller.

Rose and her horse seemed completely happy while Julie's did the same as Stephen's and seemed to be skittish and not liking their new riders.

Sir Philip looked nervous. 'Well, horses sometimes take a while to get used to people. Sir David, please take the children to see their mother. She's in the lab with Colin. Oh, and tell Captain Clough that I want to see him.'

Sir David led the children back into the castle while Sir Philip and the grooms checked the horses. None of them could find anything wrong.

Captain Clough entered the courtyard. 'You wanted me, Sir Philip?'

'Yes, two of these horses did appear to be skittish, which seems to have stopped now, and in all of their training this hasn't happened before. However, the last time Jenny was skittish a wraith was nearby. It's probably nothing but have all the castle guards put on a discrete alert to be on the lookout for anything strange happening in the castle and if so, to bring it to my attention immediately.'

'Yes, Sir Philip, I will do so immediately.'

'Oh, and do not mention this to the Queen or anyone else. As I said, it's probably nothing.'

Captain Clough left to carry out his orders.

The royal family had lunch in their private dining room. This was a bright, well-lit, small, square room with large windows and a glass roof and plain cream walls. It had a table with five chairs around it. They had been served a light lunch of ham and cheese sandwiches, with water to drink as it was expected they would have more than enough to eat at the party that evening. Even so, Stephen and Julie ate little and complained about worsening headaches. All three of them complained that Colin had informed them that now they were teenagers, they would have to take turns watching the communication crystals at the castle, although it still would be a few more years before they were considered for the outlying ones.

Charlotte had sent to the castle apothecary for a powder that she herself had made to cure headaches. This had been brought back by Colin but had made no difference and Charlotte and Sir Philip were starting to become worried about them.

When Colin had brought them the powder from the apothecary, he also brought three packets which he gave to Charlotte. Charlotte thanked Colin and he went back to stand by the door.

Charlotte handed each of the triplets one of the packages which they opened immediately. Each contained a silver necklace on which was a delicate silver rose. Charlotte smiled. 'These are a present from myself and Colin. My parents gave me one when I was a baby, and it saved your father's life.'

Sir Philip nodded. 'Yes, it saved me from a rather nasty poison.'

Charlotte continued, 'Your adoptive grandparents were incredibly talented, as you know they created Jason, Great Wing, Speedy and Slinky. I'm not trying to say that Colin and I were able to match their talent, but we brought Grandpa Stephen's best apprentice from Harbourtown, who now is the major silversmith there, to help make these. If they are just a fraction as powerful as the original, they should be useful to you all.'

As the triplets started to thank Charlotte and himself, Colin thought back to the creation of the three roses. The research and reading of Grandma Julie's journals to try to work out how Stephen and Julie had done it. Finding out if the new master silversmith had any ideas or information that had been taught to him from his master that could help. The creation of the new royal rose garden to hide the three rose bushes that the pendants were linked to, so it would be difficult to destroy the pendants by destroying the pendant's roses. When the original rose pendant had saved Sir Philip, it had destroyed itself, at the same time the climbing rose on the front wall of Charlotte's apothecary in Harbourtown had shrivelled and died. Also, when Bruno had been killed, the silver bear pendant had been destroyed and turned into a misshapen lump of silver. This lump of silver now adorned the top of Colin's staff.

After the triplets had thanked their mother and Colin for the pendants, Colin informed them just before he left, 'Tell no one what these are. They'll be able to help you best if they're kept a secret.'

All three children agreed. A short while later Stephen and Julie complained that the pendant didn't seem to be helping with their headaches. Charlotte suggested to them that Stephen and Julie should go to the castle infirmary for treatment but both the children, fearing that they would miss the party later that day, declined to go. There was a sudden knocking on the dining room door.

Charlotte clicked her fingers and the door opened and Sir Gillian Stevens entered. 'Prince Rudolf of Concordia is here, Your Majesties.'

The three children all shouted at once, 'Rudi!' and scrambled from the table towards the door.

Queen Charlotte shouted, 'Stop!' The triplets stopped. 'You must not forget that you are a prince and princesses of Falconia. You will go and greet Prince Rudolf with politeness and decorum.'

The triplets all nodded and replied, 'Yes, Mother, certainly.'

They all quickly walked to the door and out into the corridor where the next thing to be heard was the sound of three excited children running as fast as they could.

Sir Philip smiled at Queen Charlotte. 'Well, at least they made it to the corridor.' He turned to Sir Gillian. 'Go and prepare rooms for Prince Rudolf and I assume his companions?'

Sir Gillian answered, 'Sir Rudolf is with five companions and six wyverns that are busy scaring everything human and animal in the castle courtyard.'

'Hmmm ...' Sir Philip frowned in thought. 'Have a field prepared outside the town for the wyverns and tents for whoever gets the job of watching them.' Sir Philip raised his hand for Queen Charlotte to take. 'Shall we go and greet my cousin, second in line to the throne of Concordia?'

'Yes, it's been a while since we've seen him.' Queen Charlotte smiled. 'He's the only person I know of whose hair is as red as Rose's.'

'Well, that's what happens when two brothers marry two redheaded sisters. And now we should go and rescue him from the triplets.' Sir Philip laughed.

As Queen Charlotte and Sir Philip entered the castle courtyard, the first thing they saw were six wyverns. The wyverns were assorted colours ranging from bright red to off-white, each one with its own distinct colour. They all stood about ten feet tall at the tip of their almost triangular heads and eighteen feet long from their heads to the tips of their long tails. They had two strong, thick rear legs that looked incredibly powerful which they walked around on, and two much shorter legs in approximately the top of their chests just below their long necks. Halfway down their backs were the wings. They seemed to be almost gossamer-thin so that the wyvern's bones and veins could be seen in them. They had a wingspan of almost thirty-five feet which couldn't be seen at this time as the wings were tucked in close to their bodies. All the wyverns wore specially made saddles just where their necks touched their bodies and had large, strange-looking, box-like saddlebags attached to their front legs. All six were wandering around the courtyard which made sure everything else there stayed well out of their way.

In one corner of the courtyard a tall, redheaded, green-eyed youth of about eighteen, wearing a full set of armour minus the helmet and with a white tabard with the red fist of Concordia on it, was surrounded by five other men clad the same way, all had a crossbow on their backs. But of more interest to the King and Queen were the three smaller figures busily trying to dress in the armour, which was Prince Rudolf's present to them, that lay at their feet.

As Queen Charlotte and Sir Philip approached the group, Sir Philip called out, 'Rudi, you made it after all.'

Prince Rudolf gave a laugh. 'As if I'd miss my three favourite cousins becoming teenagers. I think you're in for a lot of trouble in future.'

Prince Rudolf's last remark brought howls of protest from the three new teenagers who were still trying to get into the armour.

Queen Charlotte answered, 'I fear you're probably

right.' She continued, 'Children you can try on the armour later, right now we must house Prince Rudolf and his companions and clear the castle courtyard. A field is being prepared outside the town walls for your pets.'

'Dangerous pets, they are trained for war. They've proved invaluable against the northern tribes and the northern tribes are now finally agreeing to peace.' Prince Rudolf looked at one of his men. 'Joseph take the wyverns to the field we used before.' He looked at Sir Philip who nodded.

Prince Stephen asked, 'But won't they just fly off in all directions with only one being ridden?'

Joseph answered, 'They're good at playing follow-the-leader as long as one of them is being ridden.'

Everyone headed into the castle except Joseph who mounted his wyvern and led the rest to the field that was being prepared for them.

CHAPTER TWELVE

t was late afternoon and the triplets' birthday guests were making their way into the throne room. Queen Charlotte and Sir Philip weren't sitting on their thrones, but at either end of a long table that had been placed parallel to the dais. In the centre were the triplets and the rest of the table was taken by their closest friends including Prince Rudolf and most of Colin's magic school. The rest of the throne room was taken up by tables lengthways to the dais and many children and their parents were seated at them. This included some from the poorer area of Town Falconia, who had been invited after they had won a spot in a free lottery. The table closest to the balcony sat a number of royal advisors and friends.

The dais just before the throne was a mass of parcels.

All were presents from the many children and their parents, the royal court and some sent from towns and villages in Falconia.

Everyone in the throne room, except the few guards who were stationed either side of the double doors and on the dais, was either talking or helping themselves to the finger food that was on the tables in front of them. This was mainly biscuits and small pastries. The only exceptions to this were Stephen and Julie who were still complaining of a headache.

Queen Charlotte stood and the Royal Chamberlain, who was sitting at the head of the table that contained the royal courtiers, struck the small gong that was in front of him. All talking stopped, as it was obvious that Queen Charlotte wished to speak. 'Thank you all for coming. The number of gifts you have brought,' she waved a hand at the pile in front of the throne, 'will keep the triplets busy for hours opening them. Before I give them my present, I think we should wish them a happy birthday with a song.'

Liam who was sitting at a table in the main hall stood and waved a hand. The melodic sound of the birthday song rang out. When the song got to the name, all three names were garbled quickly. When the song had finished all three of them had turned red.

Queen Charlotte clapped her hands and smiled. 'That

was magnificent. I thank you all and I'm sure Stephen, Julie and Rose do also.' Stephen, Julie and Rose, far from looking appreciative, were slowly sinking into their seats.

Queen Charlotte continued, 'This is a special day for Stephen, Julie and Rose, and what better way for them to remember it for ever.' She clicked her fingers and the double doors to the throne room swung open.

Standing there was an extremely small man, about five feet two inches. He was totally bald but made up for it by having eyebrows that were even bushier than Sir Philip's, and a large bushy black beard. His skin was darker than the average Falconian and he wore a black and white, vertically striped kaftan. His hands seemed too big for his arms and body and his fingers seemed even longer. 'I present to you Shorman Del Longe, the greatest living artist on the continent of Strasia!' Shorman bowed to the gathering from his position at the door. 'He is going to paint the portraits of each of my children. This is my present to them.' As if on cue, the assemblage rose and applauded the famous artist as he made his way to the head table. When he reached it, he raised his hands for silence. He spoke with a thick raspy voice. 'I thank Queen Charlotte for this opportunity to paint three persons, whom I'm sure will make great names for themselves not just in Falconia, but in the history of our continent.'

He turned and swept out his arm to include the birthday children. 'But for now, you must please excuse me as I sit down.' He looked around and saw Sir Gillian Stevens standing behind an empty chair and signalling that it was for him. 'It's a long journey from Melita and I have been here less than an hour.' He bowed again and went to sit down.

Queen Charlotte still standing clapped her hands, the sound magically amplified. 'Enough talking, I'm sure everyone is hungry, bring in the food.' A procession of food and drink laden servants suddenly appeared at the doors.

As everyone was eating the sun was setting. The magic users including Queen Charlotte had created balls of light that hovered near the ceiling. As the last rays of sunlight disappeared, both Stephen and Julie rose from their seats screaming. They both held their heads in their hands as everyone stopped to watch them as they both collapsed unconscious to the floor. Queen Charlotte stood and started to speak, but her words were never uttered as she also collapsed to the ground. Panicking parents and children started to run for the doors of the throne room as Colin and his students, along with Sir Philip, Sir George, the captain of the guard and other courtiers and guards went to surround the unconscious royalty. Colin called out, 'Don't touch anyone until I've examined them with my crystals.'

'There's no need for that,' the voice seemed to come from the lifeless Queen Charlotte, although her lips were not moving. The medallion that had beaten her sister, the medallion that showed a star and the moon and had a jagged line running through the centre of it, flared and turned into a lump of metal. 'I'm just going to take possession of either my nephew or niece. Do I wish to remain female, or shall I try being a man?'

As these words seemed to emanate from Queen Charlotte a mist started pouring from her head. The mist rose and began to take form; it looked like Charlotte had thirteen years previously. Sir Philip who had grabbed a sword from one of the guards slashed at the apparition, but the sword just went straight through it.

The apparition laughed. 'Your weapons cannot harm me, but enough, your children await.' Scarlett, Charlotte's twin, who had now completely formed, started to glide towards the motionless Stephen and Julie. Colin and the other magic users moved between Scarlett and the children, attempting to form a magical barrier between them. Scarlett laughed as she totally ignored it.

'Wait!' Shorman Del Longe stood to the side of Scarlett.

Scarlett paused. 'Have no fear, when I am Queen, I will

commission you to create a portrait of me and I will pay you well.'

'I do not work just for money, and it may not take that long.'

Scarlett frowned as Shorman Del Longe waved his hands in the air and a large canvas appeared next to him. It was large enough for a full-sized life-like portrait. He commenced to wave his hands at Scarlett, and she started to be drawn towards him.

Scarlett screamed. 'What's happening, you can't do this. Stop! My grandmother will destroy you.'

Shorman Del Longe completely ignored her as he waved his hands, moving Scarlett towards the canvas. Soon she was right next to it, and she started to sob. 'No, please no, not after all this time.'

Shorman Del Longe clicked his fingers and there Scarlett was. In the canvas.

CHAPTER THIRTEEN

All the guests had left the throne room and Rose had been sent to bed, escorted by her cousin Prince Rudolf, two of his men and Jackie, after crying to her parents that she could no longer feel her sibling's feelings. They had promised to stand guard over her all night. Extra guards, magic users, a healer and the children's nurses were now in there. Queen Charlotte had regained consciousness and had looked in amazement at the remains of her medallion. She was now looking at the *portrait* of her twin sister, Princess Scarlett. 'I thought when she dissipated fourteen years ago we'd seen the last of her.' She turned to Colin who was examining Stephen and Julie with the healer. 'Can you help them?'

The healer looked at Colin, who answered, 'I do not

know; they're still breathing but seem to be in a coma. There is a red swelling at the top of their spines in the same place that they had that pimple when they were babies, when we caught Sir Roger Livermore in their room.'

'But that would mean this was planned thirteen years ago by the Duchess of Mayflor!' Queen Charlotte exclaimed. 'Is that possible?'

'The Duchess is extremely powerful. Even Braidos, the powerful God of Chaos, fears her. It may be that she wanted an almost-adult, blood relative for Scarlett to take possession of.' Colin got up and walked over to inspect the *portrait*.

Scarlett was standing with her hands next to her head on either side. She was wearing the clothes she was wearing for her coronation, which never happened. Her dress was low-cut and jet-black. She wore a ruby choker that looked the colour of blood. There were rubies and diamonds sewn around her dress and she wore strong, black, leather ankle boots. She also had a black fur cloak with grey ermine edges. Her long, blonde tresses were tied up in a bun. She was perfectly still except for her eyes which darted around everywhere looking frightened.

Sir Philip joined them. 'I will order this monstrosity burnt immediately, that should get rid of Scarlett once and for all.'

'I wouldn't do that,' a rasping voice intoned. 'It wouldn't kill her but just release her from her prison.'

Sir Philip grimaced. 'Pity.' He looked down at Shorman Del Longe. 'That was some trick. I must thank you for saving my children.'

'I must admit I do use magic in a lot of my paintings. I sometimes put a subject in a canvas then sketch around them in order to make the likeness perfect.'

Colin smiled. 'That is amazing. How long will the canvas hold her?'

'Until the canvas is destroyed, or I release her, which in her case may be never.'

Queen Charlotte was examining her children. 'How long will they be like this?'

Colin answered, 'I will have all my students who aren't otherwise performing other duties scour the library for information. In the meantime, we will make arrangements for their protection. We should also have that thing,' he indicated the canvas, 'put in a secure place.'

Sir Philip looked at Shorman Del Longe. 'Will she feel her surroundings? I mean does she feel temperature or atmosphere, and can she hear us?'

Shorman Del Longe answered, 'Yes, I usually like to keep my subjects comfortable.'

Sir Philip gave a wicked grin. 'Good, I'll have her put in

the darkest, coldest and most damp dungeon in the castle.' He called two guards over. 'You heard me, do it. Oh, and have some pots and saucepans set up so that they clash against each other constantly. We wouldn't want her to think she had gone deaf.'

One of the guards smiled as he saluted with his fist over his heart. 'You'll even 'ear it up 'ere, sir.'

As the guards turned to leave with the portrait, Sir Philip added, 'Make sure there are eyes on that portrait at all times, the guards may wear earplugs.' The eyes in the portrait gave Sir Philip a hateful glare as it was taken away.

Fabian Hastings, the Royal Falconer, entered the throne room, he bowed to Queen Charlotte. 'Your Majesty, I have sent for extra troops from Fort Charlotte. Two hundred will be here tomorrow. Five hundred men from Fort Philip will arrive at the Duchies Pass Fort in the morning. Extra patrols are right now being organised to patrol the roads between here and the Duchies Pass Fort in case Mayflor sends men through one of those fast-travel hole things. The castle guards were already on alert, but they have been doubled.'

Queen Charlotte nodded her thanks to the royal falconer and turned to the captain of the guard who had also entered the throne room. 'Captain Clough, why were the castle guards on alert? Did you expect trouble?'

Captain Clough looked at Sir Philip who answered for him. 'I ordered it. The horses were nervous earlier today and I thought there may be a small chance their actions could portend a magical problem. I thought better safe than sorry, but something like this was not expected in any way.'

Colin spoke to Queen Charlotte. 'Your Majesty, with your leave I will prepare the room that Sharag and his companions were kept in, for the use of the royal children. It's probably, except for the dungeons, the most secure room in the castle.'

'Good idea, Colin. Do it immediately and let me know the second it's ready.' Queen Charlotte looked at Fabian Hastings. 'Have the Mayflorian Ambassador brought here immediately under a strong, armed guard and have all our informants of any kind look for information that may help the children get back to normal.'

Fabian Hastings bowed. 'It shall be done immediately, Your Majesty.' He left the throne room.

Queen Charlotte went to Sir Philip, and they gave each other a hug. 'Will we be able to save them?'

Sir Philip gave Queen Charlotte a kiss on the forehead. 'Of course. You are a great magic user and I'm sure Colin will find how to help in the library. It's a great store of information and if we have to, I'm sure the seven duchies will not be able to stand against the combined armies of Falconia and Concordia, especially now that Concordia has wyverns.'

'Well, I'm going to the library to help look for the answer. I wouldn't be able to sleep anyway.' Charlotte gave Sir Philip a last kiss and hug and left the throne room.

Sir Philip followed her out. He wouldn't be able to sleep either. There was no point in him going to the library, he wouldn't know what to look for. He would check all of the guard posts and hope one had seen a wraith. He would look forward to stabbing one between the eyes.

Colin had taken control of looking after Stephen and Julie and two comfortable beds and other furniture had been moved into the room behind the strong, locked iron door. Behind the door, stairs went down about ten feet into a large square room. There had been old iron beds, tables and chairs in the room, all oversized, which had been there from when it had been occupied by Sharag and his companions and still leave plenty of room for them to move. These had all been removed. There was nothing behind the walls except for the base rock the castle was built on, so that even a wraith couldn't walk through them. Colin had had a staff made from a tree branch which he had set up in the centre of the room. He then took a large yellow crystal from his bag and placed it on top of the staff, it stayed there without adhesive, he then took smaller yellow crystals out of his bag and placed them around the outside of the room, all less than three yards from each other. After the Prince and Princess had been settled into their beds and with two heavily armed guards and a magic user left to guard them, he then placed both hands on the large crystal and whispered a few words. A yellow mist fountained above the staff and spread until all the small crystals were reached and then stopped, leaving an opaque, yellow, dome-shaped screen around the room.

Colin addressed the guards and the magic user. 'Everything moving through this yellow screen will be reduced to about a tenth of its normal speed, this includes magic. Cooper,' he indicated the magic user, a tall, skinny, dark-haired youth of about eighteen, 'has been given a communication crystal which will be able to communicate very slowly with the one that will be kept by another magic user behind the iron door at the top of the stairs. The iron door will be locked and on the other side will be the other magic user and two more guards. The stairs are there, where I have put that green stone. It should be the only way to enter the screen as the rest is against the walls that are backed by thick solid rock therefore should be impenetrable, but remember we are up against powerful magic so keep checking. No one will enter unless a message has been sent via the communication crystal first and your reply and counter reply has been made. Cooper has the first set of passwords. If something goes wrong with the communication crystals use a stone with parchment tied around it to throw on the stairs.' Colin paused for a few seconds. 'It used to be the screen would only be stable for a day at a time, but it has been improved since then. I will be back later with these improvements and one of the more powerful magic users, who will have to be used to maintain it. Cooper when you are relieved, you will be given training to master this magic also.' Cooper nodded. 'Well, I hope you stay bored because that will mean there are no attacks. I will come back soon.' Colin exited the screen very slowly where the green stone indicated the stairs were.

He climbed the stairs and entered the castle laboratory, locking the iron door behind him. He gave instructions to two more guards and a magic user with a communication crystal who were stationed right outside the iron door, then left to report to Queen Charlotte in the library.

CHAPTER FOURTEEN

t was early the next morning. Very few people in Castle Falconia got a full night's sleep. Queen Charlotte and some of the other magic users had spent all night in the library keeping themselves awake magically while searching for an answer. Colin, after reporting to Queen Charlotte, had consulted his large, two feet in diameter, clear crystal, which in the past had given him answers or insights into many questions. Sir Philip had patrolled the castle all night joined by Sir George and unfortunately, they hadn't seen a wraith anywhere. Sir Philip now dozed while sitting on his throne.

Fabian Hastings, the Royal Falconer, ran into the room shouting. 'Your Majesty, Your Majesty.' He looked around. 'Where is Queen Charlotte?'

Sir Philip, now fully awake, stood and answered, 'She's in the library. What's the matter?'

'The troops from Fort Charlotte have arrived and we have a message from Thomastown through the communication crystal,' Fabian panted. 'Sharag is there with a message from Helmut. They already know what happened here yesterday and they have urgent information to give us.'

Sir Philip immediately called for a guard to summon Queen Charlotte with the message to meet them in the consulting room. He also sent for Colin, Sir Gillian Stevens, Sir George Potts, Captain Jack Clough and Sir David Reading as he, like Captain Clough, was from Thomastown and may have local knowledge.

It took over half an hour before everyone was present. Sir George had spent the previous night in the castle visitor's rooms so he could be close if needed.

Colin took the longest to arrive as he was with Stephen and Julie and so had to make his way through the screen after the message had finally got to him. Prince Rudolf invited himself as he was talking to Captain Clough when the message arrived.

Queen Charlotte took charge of the meeting. 'Fabian, what is this about?'

Fabian bowed to the queen. 'Your Majesty, we have

received a message from Thomastown. Sharag is there with a message from Helmut. Queen Lumina and Aengus want a party of us to meet them at the fairy bridge. They have information that may help us save Prince Stephen and Princess Julie. Sir Philip has been there before.'

Everyone looked at Sir Philip who shook his head. 'That's an experience I'll never forget, at least I feel Aengus can be trusted.'

Fabian continued, 'Helmut will help guide the party if necessary. Queen Lumina and Aengus have let Helmut know they may have a way to find out how to help Prince Steven and Princess Julie.'

Sir Philip stood. 'I'll get a force together to head to the Great Forest immediately, especially now we have the troops from Fort Charlotte to help.'

Prince Rudolf raised his hand. Queen Charlotte looked at him. 'Do you wish to say something?'

'Yes,' Prince Rudolf answered. 'If we take my wyverns we should be there quicker.'

Sir Philip looked at his second cousin. 'There's no place near the bridge for them to land and if Queen Lumina takes a disliking to them, we will have completely wasted our time. I'll just take a couple of hundred men and no enemies in the forest will dare approach us.'

Fabian, who had been listening patiently, gave a small

cough. 'Your Majesties, there is another problem to both your plans. Helmut has instructed that our group be of no more than a dozen. That is non-negotiable.'

'What?' exclaimed several people around the table.

Sir George declared, 'That would leave them vulnerable to attack from renegade dwarfs, goblins, shadow walkers and any strange creature they may come across.'

Fabian answered, 'I think Helmut's werewolves would deter most enemies, but that is not all.' Fabian paused. 'One of the group must be, and I quote, "the red-haired one".'

Queen Charlotte slammed her fist on the table. 'Never! I will not permit it. Rose may be the last of my children to live, if the worst comes to the worst.'

'Unfortunately, we may not have a choice if we wish to save the other two children, Your Majesty,' Fabian continued, 'and Helmut is a remarkable creature who I feel could be reliably trusted to protect her.'

'Helmut has saved my life three times and yours twice. I will also be one of the twelve and I will protect Rose with my life,' Sir Philip told his wife. 'And if this is the only way to save Stephen and Julie, we must give it a try.'

'Hang on a minute, my hair is red too. They may be referring to me.' Prince Rudolf had stood up. 'I insist that I be included in the twelve.'

'Don't be ridiculous. You are the son of Concordia's Crown Prince. There would be chaos to pay if you got hurt or killed,' Sir Philip told Prince Rudolf. 'And besides, you are too young.'

Prince Rudolf objected. 'When you made yourself famous by fighting the Northern Tribes you were younger than me and Rose is younger than I am.'

'I would feel better if Rose was *not* going. And I am *not*' Sir Philip emphasised the word "not" twice, 'the son of the Crown Prince of Concordia.'

'But how do you know I'm not the red-haired one?' Prince Rudolf looked around the table as if asking for support.

Sir Philip shook his head. 'The fairies could not have known you were here and——'

Colin had given a loud cough and stood up. 'How could they know what happened here yesterday? But obviously they do. I have to agree with Prince Rudolf.' Sir Philip started to protest, and Colin raised a hand to stop him. 'Think, Sir Philip. You are probably right but, there is a chance you are wrong. It isn't worth risking the lives of your children if it is Prince Rudolf they want. They both must go.'

'Well, if you put it like *that*, I'll withdraw my objection. Who else goes?'

Prince Rudolf, grinning, stated, 'I must take my two best men. They are supposed to be my bodyguards.'

Queen Charlotte had retaken her seat while the conversation continued. She clapped her hands and the room resounded with loud thunder. Everyone except her immediately put their hands over their ears. 'Hmm, I was just wondering whether or not, as Queen, if I had a say in this?' She spoke quietly but with menace.

There were murmurings of, 'Yes, Your Majesty' and 'Of course, Your Majesty,' and finally, 'What does Your Majesty wish?'

'I do not like the idea of Rose going. If she does, she will need strong protection. I would like Jackie and Liam to go with her. I will also lend her Jason and Great Wing. I do not see how Sleeky and Speedy could help her, but I will lend her that bracelet also. I agree with Prince Rudolf that he should go, just in case he is the red-haired one they mean. I do not know a braver man than Sir Philip, who has slain more than one monster to keep me alive. That's five. Prince Rudolf may choose one of his men for his bodyguard.'

'But I should have two,' the prince interrupted.

'I do not doubt their loyalty and courage but all of you were obviously chosen for your size and weight for flying with wyverns. I want big strong Falconian warriors to protect my daughter and they will be the last six. My decision is final.'

Sir Gillian Stevens asked, 'Who will be the head of the army while they are away for what we must realise, is an unknown amount of time?'

Sir George Potts stood. 'May I suggest Colonel Blayton? He is probably our most experienced soldier, and no one could possibly doubt his bravery and tactical ability.'

Queen Charlotte nodded. 'Colonel Blayton it is.' She turned to Colin. 'Colin, could you please ask Jackie to go through the haze to get him, with a suitably strong military escort. The colonel has never been through the haze. I should like to know what he thinks of it.'

Colin stood. 'Immediately, Your Majesty. And I will also prepare some communication crystals along with some other crystals they may find useful to be taken with the group.' He left the room.

'Sir Philip, go and find six volunteers to go with you and choose a dozen good horses from the stables.' She turned to Sir David. 'Sir David, go immediately and prepare supplies for a dozen people for three weeks. I hope this crisis will be over long before then but it's best to have a little too much than not enough.' She clapped her hands again, this time without the thunder. 'This meeting is over, I will expect everything to be organised before noon. I want you in Thomastown before nightfall and, if possible, at the Great Forest.'

As everyone left the room, Sir Philip went up to Sir David. 'Make sure everyone gets a pouch with two gold pieces and five silver pieces of both Falconian and Concordian coins, with instructions to tie them to their sword belts. Queen Lumina can get a little greedy and crafty at times and make sure everyone realises that this is communal mission money. I will give everyone a bonus when we get back.'

Sir David bowed. 'It will be done, Your Majesty.'

They also left the room.

Prince Rudolf joined Sir Philip as he went down to check on the newly arrived troops from Fort Charlotte. As they entered the courtyard, the men who were standing ready next to their horses came to attention and saluted by placing their right fist over their hearts. An officer who had his back to Sir Philip and Prince Rudolf turned to see who had entered. He saw Sir Philip and his mouth erupted into a broad smile as he too saluted. Sir Philip grinned back and walked up to the officer and slapped him on his back. 'Sergeant Lipson, it's great to see you. Where is the officer in charge?'

'Captain Lipson now, sir. I got promoted last month and the officer in charge is me.'

'Well done, Captain.' Sir Philip turned to Prince Rudolf. 'I knew this man when he was just a green private. I promoted him to sergeant after he charged a hundred foot snake on foot with just a short sword.' Sir Philip turned his head and winked at the captain. 'Well, Rudi, I think we've found one of our volunteers.'

'Volunteer, sir? What for?' Captain Lipson asked with a little concern on his face.

'No need to worry, Captain, none of us are probably going to come back alive and you'll die in illustrious company.' Sir Philip told him with a smile.

'In that case, I'm definitely volunteering. Is there anything else I can do?'

'Yes, find five more volunteers, your best men.'

'Yes, sir.' Captain Lipson saluted again.

Sir Philip went to turn away, but Prince Rudolf addressed the captain first. 'Captain, did you really charge a one hundred foot snake on foot with just a short sword?'

The captain smiled. 'Of course not, sir.' He paused. 'It was one hundred and twenty foot and all I had was my bare hands.'

The prince gave the captain a startled look, the captain

and Sir Philip burst into laughter, a couple of seconds later so did the prince.

136

CHAPTER FIFTEEN

Just over an hour later, the group was ready to leave. Everyone, except the older magic users, were in full armour. Rose wore the armour that had been a gift from Prince Rudolf, and the men from Fort Charlotte had been issued with Concordian plate, which was the strongest known. Prince Rudolf when he had mounted his horse, which had been provided for him, had counted the members of the group and then ridden over to Sir Philip mounted on Cherry, Jenny's daughter. 'I think someone here can't count. I see eighteen riders, not twelve,' Prince Rudolf told Sir Philip.

Sir Philip smiled. 'There are eighteen but only twelve of us will proceed all the way to the fairy bridge. Two groups of three, which include two guardsmen and a magic user with a communications crystal, will provide a communication relay back to Thomastown and from there to here, so that we can be in contact with Castle Falconia for the longest amount of time. I hope Helmut will agree to provide extra protection for the two groups.'

'Good idea.' The prince nodded. 'We don't know what we'll meet and if there are any problems it's nice to know we can call for help.'

'It was Colin's idea. I think he just wants to come up with ways to show how good these communication crystals are. Most people still don't think of them as dependable. We'll lose communications after we reach the bridge unless they tell us to come back, and I really don't think that will happen. Jackie hasn't returned from the mines yet with Colonel Blayton so we're taking Lizzy.' Sir Philip nodded towards a tall girl with dark brown hair, about seventeen years of age with a bright, laughing smile and brown eyes. She had a large black raven on her left shoulder. 'The raven is called a familiar I believe, and Lizzy and it can communicate with each other.'

'Sounds more dependable than Colin's communication crystals.' Prince Rudolf laughed. He then rode away to speak to one of his wyvern riders who was standing in the courtyard watching.

Queen Charlotte entered the courtyard and

approached Sir Philip, who bent in his saddle to give her a kiss. 'Even after all this time we still have problems with your armour.' Queen Charlotte smiled as Sir Philip took off his helmet and tried again. 'Look after yourself and Rose, I will be extremely annoyed if anything happens to either of you. Come back soon.'

'I'll be as fast completing this mission as I possibly can. I want to see Stephen and Julie back on their feet at the soonest possible time,' Sir Philip answered.

Queen Charlotte said with a tear in her eye, 'I love you.'

Sir Philip gave her a smile. 'I love you too.' He then turned to address the riders. 'We are about to embark on a mission that will affect the future of Falconia. We do not yet know what that mission will entail but I am sure everyone amongst us will thrive to make it a success. I wish all of you the strength and luck to make it succeed.' Sir Philip pointed to the courtyard gate. 'Forward.' They rode out of the castle.

It was mid-afternoon when they arrived at Thomastown. During the ride, Prince Rudolf had had a long chat to Captain Lipson and had found out the true story of the snake. They also talked about various training methods and the qualities of their respective armies. Captain Lipson decided to ask about the quality of wyverns in battle. 'They look scary enough but are they useful in any other way?'

Prince Rudolf nodded. 'They turned the tide in our struggles with the Northern Tribes. The Tribes sued for peace after we started using them. Wyverns are a distant cousin to dragons you know.'

'Some people think that dragons are a myth,' Captain Lipson mused.

'So are seventy foot snakes.'

Captain Lipson nodded.

Prince Rudolf continued, 'Who knows what sort of monstrosities exist in the Infinity Ranges. Anyhow, wyverns can spout a fifty-to-seventy foot flame for up to five seconds.'

'Wow, that's going to put us poor soldiers out of business,' Captain Lipson observed.

'Not really, after the flame burst, a wyvern needs over two hours until it is able to do it again. That's the reason all of us wyvern riders carry crossbows, so that we can use them while our wyverns are recovering.'

'Couldn't you use weights to drop on your opponents?' the captain asked.

'Not really,' was the reply. 'We use small men in light

armour for a reason. The more weight a wyvern carries is less time they can stay in the air.'

'Hmmm ... still, the initial attack would be devastating.'

'Yes, but we still need ground forces to finish an enemy off.'

Captain Lipson asked, 'How many do you have?

'We have twelve. Half of which are now in Falconia. My grandfather hoped we wouldn't be here for long, but I think he's going to be disappointed.'

Captain Lipson gave a thoughtful nod and the column rode on.

⁂

All the riders ate while in their saddles riding, having not taken a break on their journey. When they came into sight of Thomastown most of the riders were surprised to see three tied wyverns with the ropes staked into the ground there. Sir Philip called Prince Rudolf to his side. 'I suppose you know nothing about this.'

'On the contrary, I ordered them here to give us some air cover for the first part of our mission. As you said we do not yet know what the mission will entail. So, I thought the more force we have while we can use them, the merrier. But why are they staked?'

Sir Philip nodded. 'I wonder if it's because of Sharag.' He pointed to where a creature was walking towards them from the direction of the great forest. Sharag was a combination of a lion's head, a bull's body, and an elephant's legs and feet and was eight-feet tall.

Prince Rudolf blinked. 'Yes, I imagine that even a wyvern would be afraid of that.'

Sir Philip replied, 'Yes, I wouldn't like to fight him. One of his companions died fighting at my side fourteen years ago. They are very fierce. Talking about the wyverns, when we move deep into the forest you can send them home, the foliage will be too thick for them to help us.'

While they waited for Sharag to approach they looked at the gates in Thomastown's wall. They opened and two guards with halberds and half-armour came out. One of them shouted inside and four men emerged from the town. Three were in the uniform of Concordian wyvern riders and they went to tend their animals. The fourth was the mayor, Mayor Andrews, a mid-height, slightly shorter that Sir Philip, man who had long grey curly hair. He wore the mayoral robes and a gold chain. Both Sharag and the mayor reached the column at the same time. Both Sharag and the mayor bowed at the same time. The mayor spoke first. 'Welcome to Thomastown, Your Majesty, food and wine await your party at the Town Hall.'

Sir Philip looked down at the mayor. 'Thank you, but we're not stopping.'

He dismounted and shook Sharag's hoof, which was almost as flexible as a man's hand. 'Welcome, Sharag. I wish we were meeting under better circumstances. What news do you have?'

'Helmut came to our camp with the message that was sent to you. He did not feel he would be welcome himself in Thomastown. I also was refused entry.' He gave an angry glance at the mayor.

Sir Philip raised his hand to pause Sharag and looked at the mayor. 'You may return to your town immediately and be assured we will talk of this when I return.'

The mayor gulped and then bowed. 'Certainly, Your Majesty.' He turned and almost ran back to the gate.

Sir Philip turned back to Sharag. 'Please continue.'

'There is not much else to say. Helmut and his pack are camped just outside the forest by the Northern Ranges, so they'll be easy to find. If you leave now, you should be there before nightfall. I will not be able to match the speed of your horses.' Sharag nodded towards the wyverns. 'Or your flying creatures.'

'Thank you for your help, Sharag. We leave immediately.' Sir Philip remounted and saw Prince Rudolf's bodyguard riding back from where he had obviously gone to talk to the other wyvern riders.

Sir Philip looked at Prince Rudolf who shrugged. 'Just making sure they're ready to follow.'

Sir Philip shook his head and pointed north-east towards the forest. 'At the canter, ride.'

Chapter Sixteen

While they were riding, Sir Philip called Lizzy to ride at his side. After a little small talk, which included him telling her to call him Sir Philip and not Your Majesty, he asked her, 'Can you communicate with your raven?'

'Edgar is my closest friend; we discuss and share everything together,' she answered immediately.

'Nice name for a raven. How far away can he go and still remain in contact with you?' Sir Philip asked.

'We have mind-communicated over distances of almost ten miles. I think we probably could over longer distances. Why?' She gave Sir Philip a suspicious look.

'I was wondering if I could through you, ask him if he could fly ahead and locate Helmut's camp so we can save some time by riding straight to it rather than having to search.'

'Edgar's eyes are superb. He'll find it easily.' She looked at the raven. 'Go, Edgar. Find Helmut's camp.' The raven flew off to the north-east.

'One more thing,' Sir Philip hesitated, 'this is a favour I must ask. You are the only other female in this group besides Rose. Will you look after and keep an extra eye on her for me? Please?'

Lizzy gave a small laugh. 'You are too late. Your wife, the Queen has already asked this of me, and I have agreed.'

Sir Philip smiled. 'I'm sure she offered you her gratitude to which I must add my own. Thank you. The Royal house of Falconia owes you a favour. We will not forget.'

Lizzy rode back to join Rose.

Just before they were to enter the Great Forest near where it met the Northern Ranges, Lizzy rode up again to Sir Philip, who was riding with Prince Rudolf and his bodyguard, shouting, 'Sir Philip, Sir Philip, Helmut's camp is under attack.'

'Did Edgar tell you who by and where they are?' Sir

Philip asked with concern.

'Two different tribes of small men. They look different but fight together. Helmut's camp is about five miles away. Edgar is on his way back to guide us.'

While they were talking Prince Rudolf had removed his crossbow from his back and was selecting a specific crossbow bolt from his sheaf on his belt and loaded the crossbow. 'Excuse me,' he spoke to Lizzy, 'May I trouble you for a light?'

Lizzy and Sir Philip looked at him in surprise. 'For the bolt please.' Lizzy put her hand over the bolt and the point started to burn. Prince Rudolf immediately aimed the crossbow into the sky and fired. The bolt soared into the sky leaving a smoke trail behind it. When it reached its apex, it burst into a cloud of bright stars. 'Good, isn't it? Doesn't even use magic, although it is our magic users that prepare them. Some powders they get from the northern mountains.' Prince Rudolf smiled. There was a loud flapping of wings as the three wyverns flew down to join the column. 'Please excuse me, I have to go and give some orders.' He turned to Lizzy. 'Will Edgar guide the wyverns?'

'I will ask him.' Lizzy closed her eyes and concentrated for a few seconds and smiled. 'Only if they can keep up.'

'If they don't, I'll be getting some new wyvern riders.' Prince Rudolf laughed and proceeded to talk to his men.

The prince gave his men their orders quickly and they immediately flew off in a north-easterly direction, keeping an eye out for Edgar.

Sir Philip raised his voice so the entire column could hear him. 'We will ride at a fast canter and when we see the battle, form line. Liam will ride next to me, and the other magic users will stay back with two guards.' Rose started to object, and Sir Philip glared at her. 'This is a military patrol and everyone will obey my orders.' Rose went quiet. 'Forward.' They rode after the quickly disappearing wyverns.

When they reached Helmut's camp, they found they weren't able to form a battle line due to lack of space between the trees and the rocks which were the start of the Northern Ranges, not that there was any need, the fight was just about over.

The wyverns had done an excellent job. The first had burnt the dwarfs and goblins that were just a little way from the forest, being careful not to set it on fire. The second had attacked the enemy that were just leaving the rocks and the third had burnt mainly dwarfs who were in the rocks with bows. The survivors were attempting to retreat rapidly. The ones in and near the rocks were being targeted by the wyvern riders with crossbows. The dwarfs and goblins who had been too close to the forest, so escaping the wyvern fire, were being attacked by wolves as they attempted to retreat. Fortunately for them, only four wolves left the forest so that most of the retreating dwarfs and goblins reached the rocks. Sir Philip's men charged at the retreating enemy but only caught up with a few before the panicked enemy reached the rocks. They found that because the enemy was short their sword strokes went over most of the dwarfs and goblins heads, allowing them to escape. The wolves had halted so they wouldn't get trampled by the horses who, as yet, had not caught the werewolves' scent. They may not have noticed anyway as the stench of burning flesh permeated the entire clearing.

Sir Philip's men captured two unhurt dwarfs. There were many dead and injured dwarfs and goblins on the ground. Sir Philip noted that the goblins had been redcap ones. (Goblins are about three feet tall, have large heads and eyes and extra-wide mouths with sharpened teeth. They are also yellow. There are several tribes of goblins with each tribe wearing different coloured clothing.) The Redcap Goblins were the same tribe that had tried to ambush and kill him, Charlotte and Colin amongst others fourteen years before. They had been rescued that time by Helmut and he felt proud he had been able to return the favour.

He gave the order to put the too seriously injured out of their misery and the magic users went to help the lesser injured. Helmut and the other three werewolves turned back into humans, there were three naked males and one naked female. Sir Philip went over to Helmut and told him that his daughter Rose was with them, and Helmut and his comrades found what was left of their clothes in the camp and dressed. Shortly after, ten wolves charged into the camp. Helmut told them to wait in the forest. He told Sir Philip that when they were attacked, he had sent for reinforcements but luckily for them the wyverns and the humans had got there first. Sir Philip commented that it was a pleasant change for him to rescue Helmut, but he was still two down.

Helmut, who was tall, dark, very slender and very hairy, told Sir Philip that there had been twelve werewolves in the camp when the dwarfs and goblins attacked. Fortunately for them, the dwarf archers had fired too early and most of Helmut's force made it into the forest. He had lost more as the enemy followed. He had lost a total of eight comrades in the fight and would have been completely overwhelmed if the wyverns hadn't have arrived. Helmut was extremely impressed by the wyverns and commented that he was happy that his werewolves and the humans were now friends.

Sir Philip then addressed the matter that had brought him there. 'What do you know about the attack on my children?'

'Personally, nothing. We received a message from Aengus stating that he and Queen Lumina had information that could help you and to get you to their bridge as quickly as possible. There should be twelve of you, you are too many. Not that I mind, your numbers have helped win the day.'

'Not all of us are going all the way. Colin thought we should leave a couple of communication points to stay in contact with Castle Falconia. Would you and your people help guard them?'

'My people? My *people* will be glad to. We have much to thank you for here today.'

Sir Philip continued, 'It's strange that dwarfs and goblins are fighting together, while not exactly enemies, no one would have thought them friends.' He called for Liam. 'Liam, send a message immediately to Thomastown to pass on to Castle Falconia about what has happened here and to reinforce the mines at once.'

'At once, Sir Philip. Dwarfs and goblins fighting

together could be very bad news.' Liam walked to his horse to get the required crystal.

The wyverns managed to find enough room in the clearing to land after the horses were led out of it. Edgar came back and landed on Lizzy's shoulder, and she approached Sir Philip. 'Edgar tells me that the *little people* are still running, and he thinks they may end up crossing the Northern Ranges, they are going so fast.'

Prince Rudolf approached Sir Philip. 'What are we going to do with the prisoners?'

Helmut answered, 'My werewolves will take care of them.'

Prince Rudolf looked at Sir Philip. 'Do you really want to leave them here for these creatures?'

'These *creatures* are my friends and allies. I, Charlotte and Colin would be dead several times over if it wasn't for them.'

Prince Rudolf looked at Helmut. 'I apologise if I have given any offence,' there could still be heard some reserve in his voice, 'but in Concordia we don't usually butcher prisoners.' In the last part of his speech, he was staring at Sir Philip of Concordia.

'We have no facilities for prisoners, so we will question them and release them in just their underwear and bare feet. Then they can fend for themselves.' Sir Philip looked at Helmut. 'Will that satisfy you?'

'Do I have a choice? I know the goblins would kill every one of my kind if they had the opportunity,' Helmut answered, glaring at Prince Rudolf.

'Break the fingers of their right hands so that it will be some time before any of them can fight again. Will that satisfy you, my brave lycanthrope friend?' Prince Rudolf set his face into a smile and held out his hand to Helmut.

Helmut smiled back and took his hand. 'Certainly, we will take care of our dead enemies though. And once again I ask for help with the funeral pyres for our comrades.'

Sir Philip answered, 'Of course we will, it is extremely late in the day, and this will make a good place to camp for the night and we will resume our journey in the morning. It will take us several days to get to the bridge, especially as we have to work around three sets of cliffs.'

Helmut gave Sir Philip a blank look. 'Three sets of cliffs? Er ... what three sets of cliffs?'

Sir Philip, looking puzzled, answered, 'The three sets of cliffs that the rapids move down. I almost had to navigate them when Queen Lumina didn't want to let me cross her bridge, until she saw the rose that Charlotte had given me.'

'Oh, those three sets of cliffs.' Helmut did his best not to bend over in laughter but failed. 'And Queen Lumina told you about them?' Helmut collapsed to the ground in laughter.

Sir Philip, attempting to look dignified, uttered, 'There's no three sets of cliffs, is there?'

Helmut shook his head and Prince Rudolf started to laugh as well.

'I wonder what the penalty for throttling a fairy queen is,' Sir Philip growled, crossing his arms.

'They'd probably turn you into a toad.' Helmut laughed, then turned serious. 'We must get to work, there is not much light left and we do have at least a two-day trip ahead of us, even without the cliffs.' He gave Sir Philip a *friendly* pat on the back.

The work in the camp continued.

CHAPTER SEVENTEEN

Even the occasional screams didn't stop the humans from sleeping that night. They were all tremendously tired after an exceptionally long day. They had prepared eight funeral pyres for the werewolves and the heat from these kept the camp warm all night. In the morning, Helmut sought out Sir Philip and Prince Rudolf.

'We have only broken fingers from the prisoner's right hands. We implied that we were going to do much worse, especially to the goblin prisoners and one of them didn't get his fingers broken because he talked to us. He'll probably have to change tribes.' Helmut hesitated.

Prince Rudolf broke the silence. 'Well, what did he say?'

'Balor Hardfall of the dwarfs has formed an alliance with Iggord of the Redcap Goblins.'

Sir Philip interrupted. 'Balor Hardfall was the only survivor of Queen Katrina's meeting with the dwarfs but who is this Iggord?'

'Iggord is the son of Loftynut, who I killed myself. Balor and Iggord were just finalising their alliance when one of their scouts spotted us coming out of the forest to wait for you. They thought we would make an easy target to cement their alliance. They've never seen wyverns before. Well, neither had we.'

'But did you find out why the alliance?' Sir Philip asked.

'Besides the old saying, "the enemy of my enemy is my friend", Balor has offered Iggord better dwarf-made weapons and treasure if he'll form an alliance of goblins, shadow walkers, slime tunnellers, human bandits and whatever else they can find to besiege Thomastown to draw our forces, so as to make it easier for the dwarfs to take back the rest of the mines.'

Sir Philip grimaced. 'Does Malgon Steelhammer know of this?'

'Your guess is as good as mine.'

Sir Philip nodded. 'Thank you, Helmut, for this information. I will get Liam to inform Thomastown immediately and then we'll set off for the bridge.' He glanced at Prince Rudolf. 'I must admit, I'm tempted to leave the prisoners to Helmut's tender mercy, but we will let them go. Having broken fingers will slow them down and make it harder for them to fight.'

Prince Rudolf nodded.

As the communication crystals could only send short messages, Prince Rudolf wrote a letter to Queen Charlotte describing the events of the previous day and also informing her of the information procured by Helmut. He also wrote a second letter to his father, the Crown Prince of Concordia. This letter was taken by one of the wyvern riders and he immediately set off over the Northern Ranges towards Concordia. The other letter he gave to one of his two remaining wyvern riders, and they left immediately for Castle Falconia.

The next two days seemed to go extremely slowly for the group. Even without three sets of cliffs, the terrain was hard to get through. The fortunate thing, because of the size of the group, was there were no more incidents on the journey. They left two guards and a magic user with a communications crystal at the clearing where they stopped at on the first night. Helmut left four of his werewolves with them.

They stopped mid- to late afternoon in a clearing on the second day. Sir Philip wanted to go on, but Helmut informed him that the clearing was as far as he or any of his werewolves went.

'Queen Lumina would rather not have werewolves too close to her bridge,' Helmut told Sir Philip and Prince Rudolf. 'I suggest we camp here for the night, and you can set up your second communications base. In the morning if your party rides off that way,' Helmut pointed south-east, 'I'm sure you'll find the bridge.'

'Could we make it tonight?' Sir Philip asked. 'I would really like to get Stephen and Julie recovered as soon as possible.'

'You've met Queen Lumina. Does she seem the type who would welcome strangers camping next to her precious bridge for the night?'

Sir Philip gave a rueful smile. 'No, you're right of course. We'll proceed in the morning.'

They set up camp for the night.

When the two wyvern riders got back to Castle Falconia they once again landed in the castle courtyard, frightening the guards and horses. The rider with the letter left the other with the wyverns and entered the castle, demanding to see Queen Charlotte at once.

He was led into the queen's consulting room where Queen Charlotte sat at the head of the table. Also sitting at the table were Colin, Colonel Blayton, Fabian Hastings, Sir Gillian Stevens, Captain Clough and Sir George Potts who had come down to join them even though he was now *retired*. The wyvern rider was invited to sit at the other end of the table to Queen Charlotte. He passed Prince Rudolf's letter around the table to the Queen who opened it. She read the letter then passed it around the table so everyone including the rider could read it. When everyone had read the letter, Queen Charlotte addressed the rider. 'Well, what do I call you?'

'Sergeant Alexander, Your Majesty,' the sergeant, a short, lithe, brown-haired man, answered.

'Well, Sergeant Alexander, is there anything you can add to this letter?' the queen enquired.

'We think we were observed leaving by a goblin in the forest but there was nothing we could do about it unless we wanted to set the forest on fire or went back to inform the others. The prince had told us to deliver the letter at speed, so we decided to fly on.'

'There seems to be a lot of interesting information in

the letter, not just about the incident with the dwarfs and the goblins, but some useful information about their intentions. How was this information obtained?'

Sergeant Alexander reddened. Everyone, even in Concordia, knew how Queen Charlotte felt about torture. 'We were given the information by Helmut.'

Sir George Potts banged his fist on the table. 'Excellent, well there's one person we can rely on to get the job done.'

Queen Charlotte gave her uncle a dirty look. 'Well, Sergeant Alexander, thank you for your efforts. You may now go and get something to eat, and rooms will be prepared for you and your companion.'

Sergeant Alexander stood and bowed. 'Thank you, Your Majesty.' He turned to leave the room.

Fabian Hastings stood. 'Wait.' Sergeant Alexander turned back. 'Three wyverns and their riders left Castle Falconia to meet with Sir Philip's party and only two have returned, what happened to the other one?'

Sergeant Alexander was silent for a few seconds and then said, 'Prince Rudolf sent Cameron back to Concordia.'

Fabian Hastings asked, 'Why?'

Sergeant Alexander answered more quickly. 'I believe he was carrying a letter.'

The Royal Falconer continued, 'And what was in this letter?'

'The prince does not confide his plans or correspondence with me.'

'Make a guess.'

Sergeant Alexander rubbed his chin. 'Well, with all that has happened in the last three days it would not surprise me to see assistance appear from Concordia. What that assistance will be?' The sergeant shrugged. 'That's all I can say.'

Fabian Hastings nodded to the sergeant. 'Thank you, sergeant. You have been most helpful. Do not let me hold you up any longer.'

The sergeant nodded back and then saluted the room with the Concordian salute of touching his forehead with the back of his hand. He then turned and left.

Queen Charlotte addressed the room. 'Send for Jackie and have her take …' she looked at Colonel Blayton, 'will three hundred men be enough for the protection of the mines?'

Colonel Blayton answered, 'That's all the spare men here at the moment. I will send a message to Fort Charlotte ordering two hundred more men to march to the mines and three hundred more to come here. Two hundred of these we will send to Thomastown. I will also order a hundred men from Fort Philip to patrol the road between here and the Duchies Pass Fort in case some

Mayflorians suddenly appear, and another hundred to keep an eye on the forest.'

Fabian Hastings asked, 'Will a hundred be enough?'

Colonel Blayton shook his head. 'No, but that's all we can spare if we want to keep some reserves. I will send for as many senior commanders or their representatives that I can and work out the best places for the reserves according to the threats. With all the possible threats that are surrounding us, we will be pretty thin on reserves.'

Sir George joined the conversation. 'All these possible threats happening at the same time surely can't be coincidental.'

Queen Charlotte stood. 'If we think about it, except for the attack on my children, there is not a definite attack against Falconia, only possible ones. I thank you, Colonel, for your efforts, your recommendation to be head of the army was worthwhile.' She nodded to the colonel and Sir George. 'All these defensive measures will be carried out, but what we really need to do is to attack the source of our problem and unfortunately, except for that despicable painting in the cells, we do not know what that is.' She paused for several seconds. 'Sir Gillian, write a letter for Jackie to take to the mine manager asking him to get in touch with Malgon Steelhammer asking him what he knows about this alliance of the dwarfs with the redcap goblins.'

Sir Gillian answered, 'Yes, Your Majesty.'

Queen Charlotte then asked, 'Is the Mayflorian ambassador here yet?'

Fabian Hastings answered, 'He should be here later today.'

'When he gets here, have Sir George give him a tour of the torture chamber.'

Everyone looked at Queen Charlotte in surprise except Sir George, who was smiling and rubbing his hands.

The Mayflorian ambassador who arrived at Castle Falconia was a massive man, about six foot two inches tall and almost that in girth. He had huge arms and legs but an incredibly small head. He was bald with no eyebrows, so his head looked like a ball. He wore the garb of a typical ambassador, a purple silk shirt with black linen pantaloons and thin purple cotton slippers. Sir George with two guards took him on a tour of the torture chamber implying all the while that the ambassador could be its next guest. The ambassador said very little but gave out many grunts. When the tour was over the ambassador did ask what the noise was, that was coming from the direction of the cells. All Sir George answered was they had a special prisoner.

The ambassador was then taken by Sir George into the throne room where Queen Charlotte was waiting. Also, in the throne room was Sir Fabian Hastings, Colonel Blayton and Captain Clough with half a dozen guards.

'What do you know about the events of the last three days?' Queen Charlotte asked the ambassador.

The ambassador looked puzzled. 'What events? We're a bit slow getting the latest news in Passville.'

'Do you expect me to believe you?' Queen Charlotte glared at the ambassador. 'Or would you prefer Sir George to take you back to the torture chamber?'

'Now that would be news.' The ambassador smiled. 'I would be the first official prisoner taken there since you became Queen.'

'Official prisoner?' Queen Charlotte queried while looking at Sir George, who had suddenly found one of the paintings on the wall extremely interesting. She shook her head, then looked back at the ambassador. 'You are no longer welcome in Falconia. I hope you enjoy your walk back to Mayflor. You may start at once.'

'Surely you mean after I get all my belongings and carriage from Passville,' the ambassador stated.

'Don't you listen? I said AT ONCE!' The queen shouted

the last two words.

The ambassador looked down at what he was wearing, especially his slippers. 'Please, Your Majesty, I'm not prepared for a walk. Your men grabbed me away before I could make any sort of preparation.'

Queen Charlotte looked down at the ambassador. 'Why are you still here? Captain Clough, get some guards to escort him to Duchies Pass. He's not to stop for anything, even sleep.'

The ambassador dropped to his knees. 'Please, Your Majesty, that could kill me.'

Queen Charlotte said nothing but looked down at the ambassador. Captain Clough held the guards back waiting to see what would happen. The ambassador shook his head. 'All I can say is that a rider warned me to be ready to receive someone from Castle Falconia very soon and to be ready to send a message through the pass to Mayflor and have several men prepared to do what the someone ordered at a moment's notice.'

'Who was this someone?'

'I don't know. I was told I would know them when I saw them.'

'I believe you. Captain Clough, escort this man back to Passville where he is to pack up and leave for Mayflor immediately. His associates are to be arrested and sent as prison workers to The Field.'

Two guards helped the ambassador to his feet and led him out of the throne room, as he kept saying, 'Thank you' to Queen Charlotte. Captain Clough started to follow but stopped and addressed the queen. 'Is he not to have any other punishment, Your Majesty?'

'I'm sure my grandmother will come up with a suitable punishment for his failure, greater than anything I could do.'

Sir George Potts moved towards Queen Charlotte with a look of admiration on his face, quietly clapping his wrists. 'Who needs a torture chamber when we have you, Your Majesty.' He bowed.

Queen Charlotte looked down at him. 'Thank you, Uncle. However, when this is all over, you and I are going to have a talk about "official" and "unofficial" prisoners.'

Sir George looked up at Queen Charlotte, smiled and said, 'I'm retired, Your Majesty.' He then turned and marched out of the throne room.

CHAPTER EIGHTEEN

Early the next morning, the twelve riders that were to go on left the camp in a south-easterly direction, leaving two guards and a magic user, along with Helmut and several other werewolves. Helmut had told Sir Philip he would leave four werewolves to help protect the guards and magic user from the perils of the forest. They had travelled less than two miles when the riders spotted something fluttering about in the lower canopy of the trees. Sir Philip called a halt and sat waiting for whatever it was to approach.

Shortly, the creature fluttered down and approached Sir Philip. She was incredibly beautiful even though she was only six inches tall. She had thin gossamer wings, dark brown hair, brown eyes and pointy ears. She wore a brown and purple dress to just above her knees. She stopped about two feet in front of Sir Philip's face and curtsied in mid-air. 'Your Majesty, King Philip,' (Sir Philip decided not to tell her to call him Sir Philip as he thought it would be more advantageous to remain on equal footing with Queen Lumina), 'my name is the Lady Yolande, my mistress Queen Lumina awaits you. The bridge is still over two hours away, we should start immediately.'

Sir Philip asked, 'Is Aengus there also?'

The fairy curtsied again. 'Yes, Your Majesty,' and turned to leave.

Sir Philip nodded. 'Good,' and added in a quiet whisper to Prince Rudolf, 'Well, at least that is good news. We should get honesty from him if not Queen Lumina.'

Lady Yolande turned back and smiled. 'We fairies have excellent hearing, Your Majesty, I will not mention your comment to my mother.' She continued to smile. 'This time.'

Sir Philip gave a wry smile. 'Thank you, Lady Yolande.'

Lady Yolande led them away.

It was over two hours later when they heard a faint constant noise. As they rode on, it became louder and louder until the roaring drowned every other noise in the forest. Then, suddenly, there were no more trees. In front of them was a twenty foot wide ditch which contained a wild, fast, rocky river rapid. Two hundred yards away down rapids there was the bridge. It was the strangest looking bridge the riders, except for Sir Philip, had ever seen. It looked as if a giant spider had woven it. It was very narrow, had a single arch and only a low balustrade. It was like a strange cobweb of silk.

As they got closer to the bridge, the noise from the rapids decreased. Sir Philip half-expected to be slowed down as if wading through treacle, which had happened to him the last time he had seen the bridge, but it didn't happen. As the column approached the end of the bridge, they could see a huddle of tiny creatures awaiting them. Sir Philip signalled a halt and dismounted while ordering everyone else to remain mounted.

As soon as Sir Philip dismounted, he bowed. 'I am honoured to meet you again, Your Majesty.'

Two of the tiny creatures left the group and flew up to join Lady Yolande who was hovering about three feet in front of Sir Philip's face. One, a female, was dressed in red and had blonde hair, she had incredibly pale skin, pointy ears and green eyes. The other was a male fairy in blue attire. He was older, greying and distinguished.

The female, Queen Lumina, spoke to Sir Philip. 'It is good to see you again also, Your Majesty. You have raised yourself greatly since our last meeting when you were just a knight. You have made good time to get here so quickly.'

Sir Philip smiled. 'Yes, although the three sets of cliffs did slow us a little.'

Queen Lumina blushed and the male fairy, Aengus, put his hand to his mouth to hide a smile. 'As I said, the last time we met you were just a knight, not a king,' Queen Lumina paused for a second. 'And we did let you over our bridge.'

'For which I am eternally grateful. I have ordered all my men to carry coins so we may pay for passage over your bridge.'

A flash of anger crossed Queen Lumina's face. 'We are royalty together! Your coins have no value here. You may all cross our bridge if you wish, but I feel that none of you will want to.'

'I'm sorry if I have offended you, Your Majesty,' Sir Philip said quickly, feeling puzzled. 'I am worried about my children, I just wish to save them from the evil magic that has them in thrall.'

Queen Lumina looked down. 'Evil magic, yes, evil magic.' She looked back up. 'Aengus will lead you on the next step of your journey, but it is not across our bridge; you will be heading south. Aengus will explain while you travel. We will not talk of evil in this sacred place. I will leave now, but I assure you, King Philip, I wish you and your family nothing but good and I hope all your problems disappear soon.'

Sir Philip bowed. 'Thank you, Your Majesty.'

Queen Lumina and Lady Yolande turned and flew down to the group at the end of the bridge, who all then disappeared.

'Well, King Philip, we'd better get started.' Aengus flew close to Sir Philip. 'We've a long way to go.'

'Sir Philip to you, Aengus. What is happening and how did you find out about what happened at Castle Falconia?'

Aengus frowned. 'We will talk when we are away from the bridge. Queen Lumina was serious when she said that we should not talk of evil in this place.'

Sir Philip, looking both puzzled and worried, remounted Cherry and followed the flying Aengus into the forest, with the others following in single file.

After they had travelled about a mile, Aengus flew down to Cherry and lay back in her mane. 'Very comfortable, Your Majesty. I should travel like this more often.'

Sir Philip smiled. 'You are welcome anytime and

while we're travelling call me Sir Philip.' He then turned serious. 'But to weightier matters. Where are we going and what do you know?'

'Where we're going is easy. We're off to see Braidos.'

'What!' Sir Philip had stopped without warning causing the other riders to bunch up. Prince Rudolf who had been next in line rode up to join Sir Philip.

'What's the matter? Why did we stop?'

Sir Philip turned his head to address the prince. 'We're off to see Braidos.'

'You're joking.' Prince Rudolf looked down at Aengus. 'What's this about?'

Aengus ignored Prince Rudolf and spoke directly to Sir Philip. 'I suggest we keep travelling and I will explain everything to you.'

Sir Philip resumed the journey with Prince Rudolf falling in behind. 'Well, what's going on?'

Aengus rubbed his chin. 'Four evenings ago, a bluecap goblin approached our territory with what it said was a message for Queen Charlotte from Braidos. It informed us of what had happened at Castle Falconia and that Braidos could put it right. He stipulated that your number should be twelve and that the red-haired one should be one of your number. We got in touch with Helmut immediately.'

'But why would Braidos send a bluecap goblin

messenger to you in the forest. There must be better ways to send a message.'

Aengus chuckled. 'Poor old Braidos is having a bit of a tough time at present.' Sir Philip looked puzzled. 'You and Queen Charlotte destroyed his temple and drove out his priests in Falconia and the Duchess of Mayflor did the same thing in the Seven Duchies after he destroyed her daughter, Queen Katerina. Once the Duchess got rid of him, the other duchies followed, they're not going to defy her.'

'But why is he here in the Great Forest?' Sir Philip asked. 'There must be better places for him.'

'Like where? He was only just getting established in Falconia when you got rid of him. He obviously thought he could afford to destroy Queen Katerina as Princess Scarlett would eventually turn to him. Something that Queen Charlotte messed up. His main base of operation has been for centuries, the Seven Duchies. The Duchess may have forgiven him Queen Katerina, if Scarlett had taken over in Falconia, but that didn't happen. So, he's here, in the Great Forest among the bluecap goblins with a pathetic wooden temple, trying to plan ways to make a return.'

'Does he really think that Charlotte and I will help him?'

'Do you want Stephen and Julie cured? I think a bargain will be made. Unfortunately, you have little choice.'

Sir Philip looked grim.

It was close to noon with Aengus still riding in Cherry's mane, when the group entered a clearing where a group of well-armed bluecap goblins was waiting for them. With them was a man who stood slightly in front of the goblins. He was tall, about six foot seven inches, which was almost all that could be said about him. He wore a black habit and cowl in the manner of a monk and none of his features were visible under the hood. All that could be seen of the man were his skeletal hands clasped together in front of him. Sir Philip stopped just less than halfway across the clearing so that the others could enter it also.

Sir Philip spoke with his most authoritarian voice. 'I would say good morning, Roget, but wherever you are, nothing can possibly be good.'

Roget, the high priest of Braidos the God of Chaos, bowed. 'Welcome, Your Majesty. Your group has made good time, but there is a problem.'

Sir Philip sat back in his saddle and crossed his arms. 'What? You've brought us halfway across the continent just to tell me there is a problem!' Sir Philip's last words ended in a shout which made the bluecap goblins reach for their weapons, a move that was mirrored by Sir Philip's group.

Roget spread his arms and turned to the goblins. 'Wait, put away your weapons.' He turned back to Sir Philip who had also signalled for his group to put away their weapons. 'The fault is yours. You were told to bring twelve. I count fourteen.'

'Oh, Aengus was our guide.' Aengus flew up and bowed to Sir Philip.

'Well, I'm going. I wish you all luck and remarkable success in your quest.' He flew back into the trees.

Sir Philip spoke again to Roget. 'That's it, we are now twelve.'

Roget's voice was soft. 'I still count thirteen.'

'You need to learn to count Roget. I would have thought Braidos would have a high priest who would at least know his numbers.'

'There is a semi-intelligence among you. Not human.'

Sir Philip thought for about ten seconds and then burst into laughter. 'Surely you don't mean Edgar. Edgar's just a dumb bird.'

Edgar seemed to give Sir Philip a nasty look but remained quiet as Lizzy stroked its feathers.

'Hmm, a familiar. I would never call a familiar dumb. I will leave the final decision to the Great One. I will summon him.' Roget turned back to the goblins and signalled with his hands to one of them at the back. The goblin approached Roget while carrying a large golden chalice. Roget intoned a few words so quietly no one could hear. He then drank from the chalice and returned it to the goblin.

Everyone in the clearing waited silently for over two minutes, then there was a sound like a thunderclap and the clearing darkened. A black whirlwind started to grow in the centre of the clearing. Both Sir Philip and his group and Roget and the goblins moved back. In the centre of the whirlwind, a large dark figure started to appear. The dark figure slowly continued to form from the top of the head down. It looked like a male. He was bald with scarlet-coloured, glowing skin. The eyes were jet-black, the nose little more than a slit and the lips a deep blood-red. He wore a jet-black cloak over his bare back. He looked extremely muscular. His legs were not seen, if they existed, as the whirlwind still swirled below his waist. When Braidos had finished forming, he had his back to Roget and the goblins, and faced Sir Philip.

Braidos did not bow and spoke in a loud and hollow voice. 'King Philip, you have finally arrived.' He pointed a long slim finger at Sir Philip. 'What do you offer me to help you save your children?'

Sir Philip gave Braidos a hateful glare. 'I need offer you nothing. As we speak the greatest minds on the continent are searching for a solution. I'm sure they'll find it.'

Braidos laughed. 'You've enlisted the Duchess of Mayflor?' Sir Philip looked puzzled. 'Excuse me I thought you said you had enlisted the greatest minds on the continent.' Braidos shook his head. 'Your *minds* will never find the answer, this is a new one from the Duchess.'

Sir Philip spat out his next words. 'What do you want? Your temple back? Falconia will never let that happen.'

Braidos's eyes flashed as he laughed. 'What, a temple in Falconia that you will tear down as soon as you get the chance? No, but I tire of only having a wooden temple here in the Great Forest. I would be mighty again. Give me the painting, so I can bargain with the Duchess.'

'You would trust the Duchess?'

'I have ways to ensure a bargain between myself and the Duchess will be honoured. So, is the painting worth your children?'

'How do I know I can trust you?'

Braidos answered angrily, 'No one, living or dead, can accuse me of not keeping my word.'

'Tell me, no, get my children back and you can have

Scarlett.'

'Firstly, you must get the Chalice of the Dawn.'

'Why don't you get it?' Sir Philip asked.

'Gods can do many things but holding physical items in this world is not one of them, which is why you will give the painting to Roget.' Roget bowed at the mention of his name. 'Moreover, the Chalice is on the furthest of the Eastern Isles where *The Magic* has no power. You must sail there from Harbourtown.'

'Do we have a map?'

'Roget will join you.' Sir Philip started to protest. 'This is also not negotiable, both Roget and your daughter will have to lift the Chalice at the same time for it to be able to be moved.'

This last comment caused gasps of surprise from Sir Philip's group. Sir Philip asked angrily, 'What's Rose got to do with this?'

'It has to be lifted by an agent of mine and an agent of Craidos, which will be your daughter. Do not question this, it is just what is. Roget has a map and all the details that you will need, and he will inform you of them during your journey. Your number is now thirteen, a nice lucky number. The raven will not be counted amongst you, even though it can go with you. Neither will I count the wolf, eagle and dolphins that your daughter possesses.' He looked at Roget. 'You have to be more observant Roget, you missed those.'

Roget bowed to Braidos. 'I apologise master. I did not look for items of magic.'

'Be more careful in future,' Braidos told Roget.

Sir Philip asked, 'What happens after we get the Chalice?'

'Roget will explain all. Do we have an agreement?'

'What happens after we get the Chalice?' Sir Philip repeated.

'You will need to concoct a mixture which your children will be able to drink even though they are in a coma. You have a long journey, plenty of time for Roget to explain. Do we have an agreement?'

'I cannot speak for Queen Charlotte, but if she is agreeable, I promise to give Roget the painting when, and not until, Stephen and Julie are cured.'

As soon as Sir Philip agreed, a goblin brought a white horse out of the forest for Roget.

Sir Philip spoke again. 'It will take time to get Queen Charlotte's agreement to this.'

Braidos smiled. 'I think not. Aengus who is hiding in the trees will take a message to your closest men with a crystal and a message should not take long to get to Falconia. The answer should be waiting for you when you reach Harbourtown. Now I will leave you.' There was another thunderclap as Braidos clapped his hands and he shrank back into the whirlwind, which then faded until it disappeared altogether.

Roget had mounted his horse and rode over so that he was close to Sir Philip who still couldn't make out any of Roget's features.

'Shall we start?' Roget asked.

Sir Philip answered, 'You will ride next to me. I have many questions.' The thirteen rode out of the clearing.

CHAPTER NINETEEN

The column rode in pairs except for Prince Rudolf who rode just behind Sir Philip and Roget so that he could attempt to listen to their conversation. He was only partly successful. The sky was dark with clouds threatening heavy rain and there was an annoying drizzle, which not only dampened the trail but their spirits also. They moved to the south of Queen Lumina's lands as Roget wouldn't have been welcome there. Roget showed Sir Philip his map of the Eastern Isles and explained that the island they needed to go to, to get the Chalice was not on his map, but was further east than any of the others. 'When we get to the main port of the islands, Danziger, which was named after its founder, we will find someone to guide us the rest of the way.'

'And what happens after we get the Chalice?' Sir Philip asked.

'We must put it in a lead-lined box as no one may touch it except your daughter and I together. We must take it back to your castle, mix up the potion in the Chalice and give it to your children. Then you give me the painting and give me escort to Duchies Pass.'

'You make it sound easy.'

'Unfortunately, we don't know what to expect on the islands which is why we are thirteen, a lucky number for Braidos.'

'And what's in the potion?'

'It's quite an easy one actually, call your senior magic user.'

Sir Philip called for Liam to join them, which annoyed Prince Rudolf as he was forced by this to ride further back.

Sir Philip told Liam, 'Roget is going to list the ingredients that we will need for the potion to cure Stephen and Julie. I want to know if we will have any problems getting them.'

Liam took some parchment, a quill and some ink out of his saddlebags and got ready to write. 'Ready, Sir Philip.'

Sir Philip gave a wave of his hand to Roget. 'Continue.'

'Firstly, you will need some dragon's blood.'

'No problem with that one, we have plenty in the castle laboratory both liquid and dried,' Liam said while writing. 'Next.'

'Crushed rubies.'

Sir Philip noted, 'This sounds like an expensive potion.'

Liam nodded in agreement. 'True, but it's easy enough for we magic users to crush up a few rubies.'

'The red petals of the lace leaf flower.'

Liam looked up. 'They're poisonous. The lace leaf is a type of Anthurium, a very poisonous species.'

Roget looked impressed. 'Not many would know that. However, it is mainly the stem and leaves that are poisonous, and you will only need five petals for each child.

'So, that's ten petals, correct?' Liam looked at Roget.

'Correct,' repeated Roget.

'Charlotte or one of the others will be able to collect those from the forest,' Liam noted.

Roget looked at Liam in surprise. 'You would call your queen by her first name?'

Liam who had been thinking as if he was in one of Colin's classes answered, 'No, it was just a slip of the tongue.' He looked at Sir Philip. 'No disrespect was meant, Your Majesty.'

Sir Philip, who knew how informal things were

between the magic users, answered, 'No problem.' He looked at Roget. 'Continue.'

'And last but very much not least, you'll need the berries of the red mountain ash.'

Liam looked up. 'That could be hard. It's a deep mountain tree. We may have to ask the dwarfs for some.'

'Then let us hope that Malgon Steelhammer had nothing to do with the alliance with the redcap goblins,' Sir Philip mused.

While they were talking, they entered a clearing. Sir Philip asked Roget, 'Do you know how far away the river is.'

'I was told we would reach it before nightfall,' was the answer.

Sir Philip ordered, 'We'll take a ten-minute break to stretch our legs and whatever and then we'll ride on fast to camp at the river.'

Everyone was relieved to take a break. The girls took a couple of saddle blankets to find a private spot and the men moved to the trees around the clearing. Suddenly there was a scream. Everyone turned around. One of Captain Lipson's men had what looked like a giant, white, six foot long maggot with large squinty eyes on stalks and a large round mouth surrounded by teeth, climbing up his leg, with the man's leg inside its mouth. Liam immediately sent a bolt of lightning to hit the creature at the far end of its body. The creature let out a loud sibilant scream, as the back third of its body disappeared and it slid back down the soldier's leg, unfortunately taking the soldier's foot with it, leaving just a bloody stump with the armour around it melted. Others of the creatures started to appear from new holes in the ground. Sir Philip shouted, 'They're slime tunnellers. Try to hack them to pieces. Be careful the slime's acidic.'

Fortunately for the group, Roget clapped his hands and an extremely bright light suddenly appeared in the clearing. The slime tunnellers immediately stopped and started to tunnel back underground. Roget called out, 'Everybody back on their horses. Those things hate bright light, but it won't last for long.' Captain Lipson and one of his men helped Graham, the wounded soldier back on his horse, then remounted themselves with the soldier leading Graham's horse. They left the clearing at a fast canter and did not slow down until they were over a mile away. They then paused while Rose and Lizzy did what they could for the wounded man's leg. Liam gave them a small green crystal for them to tie to the stump. 'It's not Colin's big one, but it should help,' he told the girls. They then set off again towards the river.

About an hour before dark, they came to the River

Thracks. It was about thirty feet wide at this point and only about four feet deep. Sir Philip decided, although they could ride across, they would be better off dry for the night, so he called a halt and they set up camp.

The soldiers set about building a fire, while the magic users tended the wounded man. Rose applied a poultice that had been taught to her by her mother, and then they refastened the green crystal to the stump. Sir Philip stated that he had a lot of faith in Queen Charlotte's poultices as they had helped save his life. Prince Rudolf and his bodyguard started to prepare a meal.

Sir Philip spoke to Roget. 'Thank you for your quick thinking back there. I think we could have beaten the slime tunnellers but not without more casualties. We'll leave Graham with the authorities at The Field where he can get more medical attention.'

'Slime tunnellers are nasty creatures but cannot stand bright light. But your man, we cannot leave him.'

'Why?'

'He is now one of the thirteen. The thirteen of us who started this quest must land on the Eastern Isles, there may be no substitutes. That is the way it is.'

'You're very glib with your "That is the way it is".'

'That cannot be helped. Braidos and I want you to succeed in this quest as it will help our cause also. As long as the thirteen of us land on the island of the Chalice of the Dawn we have a chance. He may be left there if you wish. But there are things I cannot tell you. I know it's hard, but you must trust us.'

'That is very hard to do,' Sir Philip answered. 'The two of you don't exactly inspire trust.'

'Unfortunately for you, you have no choice if you want your children back. Accept this and our mission should be successful.'

'As you say, I have no choice. But be warned, I will be watching you every step of the way.'

Sir Philip's attempt to keep the group dry for the night failed miserably. Shortly after his conversation with Roget, the clouds that had been threatening rain all day opened and before long the entire camp was soaked. Thanks to the magic users, their fires were not washed out, but everyone who was wearing armour had water inside of it and squished every time they moved. By the next morning everyone was wet and miserable. As the fires had been protected by the magic users, they at least had a hot breakfast. After they had eaten, the sun came out and the clouds started to dissipate. The magic users checked and put a fresh poultice and dressing on Graham's leg.

After everyone had mounted, Graham had his injured

leg tied to his stirrup strap, Sir Philip spoke to the group. 'Well, crossing the river shouldn't get us any wetter than we already are. I want us to have reached The Field by the end of today and hopefully partway past it. I want us at Harbourtown by the end of tomorrow and a boat hired and ready to go by the next day. I was going to leave Graham at one of the settlements surrounding The Field but our *friend* here,' he nodded towards Roget, 'informs me that all thirteen of us have to reach the Eastern Isles for our mission to be a success. Captain Lipson, I'm putting you in charge of making sure that Graham is able to keep up. Rose has learnt a lot about medicine from her mother so she and Lizzy will help you. Well, we may as well get started so let's go and get even wetter.'

Sir Philip led the group in single file across the river.

It was late that day when they reached The Field. They had been fortunate that the day had been fine and warm after the previous night's downpour. Everyone had dried out and even Graham had kept up a relatively cheerful demeanour. He had not slowed the group much at all with Rose and Lizzy riding next to him in turns, making sure he was riding well. There had been no more incidents during the day, something everyone in the group was thankful for.

One minute they were in the forest and the next they were on the wide road that surrounded The Field. This part of the field was predominately root crops and the short green tops of the various plants went on for miles. 'They look like carrots,' Prince Rudolf observed, riding up to Sir Philip and looking at the nearest plants.

'Hmm, never did like carrots,' Sir Philip answered. 'But we will camp here and go on in the morning.'

Prince Rudolf smiled. 'Excellent, Evan and I will start preparing a meal.' He looked at Sir Philip. 'With lots of fresh carrots.'

Sir Philip gave the prince a nasty glare and went to help prepare their camp.

CHAPTER TWENTY

n a small, black brick, windowless room, lit only by a brazier in the corner, a small woman in a black, hooded gown sat on a stool staring at a crystal ball on a stand in front of her. There was no other furniture in the room and the only entrance was through a small, curtained tunnel. Only the woman's hands could be seen, which were also small, but smooth and dark. She had long fingers which were extended by her three-inch-long, painted black fingernails. In the crystal, she could see Sir Philip's group following the men from The Field. The woman picked up a leather pouch that lay on the floor at her feet. She opened it and poured two small piles of green powder on the floor. She waved her hands over the piles and they became two formless green veils of mist.

She walked to the curtained tunnel and lifted the curtain. 'The red-haired girl is the weak link. Destroy her.'

The two veils of mist made no sound as they left the room through the tunnel.

⚜

Everybody in the group had slept in their armour or clothes. Early the next morning Sir Philip was woken by the guard that was on watch. 'Sir Philip.' The guard continued to shake him until Sir Philip began to stir. 'Sir Philip, riders, sir, about twenty of them.

Sir Philip stood and watched the riders approach from the north. The guard tapped Sir Philip on the shoulder. 'There too, sir.' The guard pointed to the south where another dozen men had appeared, riding towards them.

Sir Philip picked up his sword and shield and started banging them together. 'Alarm, alarm, everyone to horse immediately.'

The horses had all been tethered to trees with their saddles on in case of emergencies at the edge of the forest and as everyone awoke in the camp, they left all their equipment except for their weapons to mount as soon as possible. Rose and Lizzy helped Graham to mount.

The group bunched up so, if necessary, they could attack together as a powerful punch with the magic users just behind the men-at-arms. Sir Philip spoke in a loud voice. 'Remember, these men are probably just The Field's security force checking to see who we are. We do not want trouble with them, so no one is to start anything.'

They waited until the larger group of riders got close to them and stopped. The second group, still some distance away kept coming. They all wore front and back plates and had half-helmets. They all gripped short lances which made them some concern to Sir Philip's group, as the short lances gave them extra reach. They also carried sheathed swords on their hips, and bucklers. They all wore surcoats showing a sheaf of wheat on a blue background. The man at the front of the group of riders was small, slender and had brown hair and eyes. He also had a scar on his left cheek. He had a yellow feather in his helmet which Sir Philip recognised as the mark of an officer. The officer moved a little ahead of his men and looked over Sir Philip's group.

The officer smiled and shook his head. 'Hmm. Most of you wear the livery of Falconia and two of Concordia. Who are you? Why are you here and why are you stealing from The Field?'

Sir Philip nudged Cherry forward. 'I'm Sir Philip Concord, King of Falconia.' He turned and indicated Prince Rudolf. 'This is Prince Rudolf of Concordia, the son of the Crown Prince of Concordia, heir to the throne of Concordia. The others are our associates. We are on our way to Harbourtown and seem to have taken a wrong turning somewhere. I apologise for using some of The Field's carrots, but we are willing and able to pay for what we have used. And whom am I addressing?'

The officer cast a critical eye over the bedraggled group. 'You're the King of Falconia, right?' Sir Philip nodded. He then looked at Prince Rudolf. 'And you're the heir to the Concordian throne?' Prince Rudolf nodded. 'Well, I'm pleased to meet you. I'm the Grand Duchess of Mayflor.' The officer gave a small laugh which was echoed by his men. While this conversation was taking place, the other riders had arrived, so that Sir Philip's group was effectively surrounded.

Sir Philip smiled back. 'I must admit you do bear a striking resemblance to my grandmother-in-law, but I've never heard of her describing herself as the Grand Duchess of Mayflor, just the Duchess of Mayflor.' The smile was gone from the officer's face to be replaced by a scowl. 'I suggest you just charge us for the carrots and then escort us to Harbourtown where you will find numerous burghers, constables and local citizens who will vouch for me.' Sir Philip had also lost his smile and held eye contact with the officer.

'I'm Captain Jason Ride of The Field Defence Force and

I'm the authority here,' the officer answered Sir Philip. 'Now order your men to drop their weapons and we will escort you to Harbourtown.'

Both Sir Philip and Prince Rudolf bristled. Sir Philip answered first. 'You have no authority over the King of Falconia and I must take this as a declaration of war.'

Prince Rudolf added, 'At this moment over five hundred members of the Concordian army are approaching Harbourtown on the way to Falconia. Unless you change that last *request*,' Prince Rudolf emphasised the word request, 'the troops will divert themselves to The Field and take it over, you and your men will then find yourselves as new field workers. You know what that means.'

Captain Ride, visibly shaken, answered, 'Be careful, you and your men might not make it to Harbourtown.'

Sir Philip turned in his saddle. 'Liam, the top of that tree.'

Liam pointed at the top of the tree and a lightning bolt sprang from his hand setting the top on fire, as all the trees were still wet from the rainfall two nights previously the fire did not last long. Sir Philip then turned to Roget. 'Roget, more light, please.' Roget clapped his hands together and a large ball of light appeared directly above Captain Ride and his men.

'You may now address me as Your Majesty and Prince Rudolf here as Your Highness. We will of course pay you for the carrots. How much were they?'

A gleam came to the nervous captain's eye. 'Looking at the patch that has been removed, I would estimate, about five gold pieces.' He hesitated before finally adding, 'Your Majesty.'

'What! Five gold pieces. You're worse than Queen Lumina. I shall have all our accounts with The Field checked when I get back to Castle Falconia and you can be sure that I will be contacting The Farm Council over this.' Sir Philip had taken his purse from his saddlebag and counted out five gold pieces and held them out. Captain Ride ordered one of his men to ride over to Sir Philip and receive them. The man immediately gave the coins to his captain.

'I want a receipt,' demanded Sir Philip.

Captain Ride wrote a receipt on a small piece of parchment. 'Follow us,' Captain Ride ordered, then turned his men around and started off down the road. Sir Philip immediately followed.

Prince Rudolf joined Sir Philip. 'Well, that was fun. What about all our camp gear?'

'Leave it,' was the answer. 'We'll resupply in Harbourtown.' The prince nodded. 'And Rudi,' the prince looked up, 'never serve me carrots again.'

⁂

Sir Philip and his group rode on the good road between the two groups of The Field soldiers. They rode in pairs with Roget by himself in the centre of the group. Rose and Lizzy took turns to ride with Graham.

As they rode, they spotted here and there among the plants, free farmers harvesting their crops. Sir Philip and several other members of the group waved and occasionally one or two of the farmers would wave back, although most just stood and watched as they rode by.

They also saw various buildings scattered among the crops. Most were obviously barns, but there were some that no one in the group could guess at. They also passed the occasional hamlet, home of the free farmers.

Just before noon, the root crops gave way to tomatoes. Between the root crops and the tomatoes, the group saw prison workers dressed in the striped uniform of red and yellow, digging a new irrigation trench. They were guarded by several armed soldiers wearing the surcoats with a sheaf of wheat. All the nations on Stasia sent prisoners to The Field to serve their sentences, except for either really serious or relatively minor crimes, which were dealt with by the nation involved. The prison workers were usually given the hardest and most unpleasant jobs to do.

Soon the tomatoes gave way to beans, then to various peppers. Prince Rudolf asked Sir Philip, 'When do you think they'll stop for lunch. None of us had breakfast and I'm sure it's not just me who is hungry.'

Sir Philip gave a mirthless laugh, 'You should watch our escort. They've all been eating from their saddlebags while riding. I don't think we're going to stop.'

Prince Rudolf gave a groan and shook his head. 'I'm going to faint from hunger.'

Sir Philip laughed. 'No, you won't, and just think, we left all our food and cooking equipment back at our camp this morning. We probably won't eat until tomorrow.'

Prince Rudolf's eyes went wide. 'I'll die. I suggest we roast Captain Ride. I'm sure no one will miss him.'

Sir Philip laughed. 'That sounds like a great suggestion. Please don't tempt me.'

They continued riding.

After midday, the crops became grasses. The first was acres of rye and then corn and finally miles and miles of wheat. Sir Philip thought it interesting that there seemed fewer hamlets and people in this area of The Field.

The road had been good all day and they moved at

a fast pace, but even so it was close to dusk when they finally left The Field. The road exited through a gap between the Great Forest and the thousands of acres of wheat. Captain Ride pointed to the northeast. 'Keep going that way and you can't miss Harbourtown. Magic users are not welcome there you know. They'll arrest you even if I couldn't. Stay out of The Field.'

The captain and his men then turned to ride away. As they did so, two of Captain Ride's men started to gallop towards Rose while lowering their short lances. The captain shouted, 'Stop, what are you doing?' Some of his men went to ride after them but the captain shouted, 'No one else moves.'

Sir Philip shouted, 'Protect Rose,' and rode to intercept the two The Field soldiers.

Roget lifted his hand and blew one of the attacking soldier's head off. The headless soldier didn't miss a beat and continued to attack. Captain Lipson intercepted the headless man and chopped off the arm holding the lance. This caused the headless man to slow while he attempted without success to draw his sword with his left hand. Roget pointed at the horse's front legs and it stumbled, throwing the headless man to the ground. Captain Lipson and two of his men dismounted and proceeded to chop The Field soldier to pieces.

The other rider was knocked off his horse when Jason, the giant black wolf from the silver ring Rose was wearing, leapt past him, tearing out the rider's throat as he passed. The rider immediately got up, drew his sword and started to run towards Rose. Sir Philip and Cherry rode over him from behind and then Sir Philip dismounted and was joined by Prince Rudolf and another of Captain Lipson's men. The attacking soldier got up, drew his sword and staggered towards them trying to reach Rose, who, still mounted, had turned white as the other three magic users and three soldiers stayed with her to protect her. Jason, blood dripping from his mouth also stood growling, protecting Rose while Great Wing the black eagle circled above.

The Field soldier, outnumbered as he was, didn't last long before he also was chopped to pieces. Captain Ride, after the fight was finished, ordered his men to stay where they were and rode towards Sir Philip with his right hand in the air well away from his sword. 'I know nothing of this. They were two of my best men. I don't know why they attacked you.'

'I believe you,' Sir Philip answered. 'This was evil magic, and I don't think you would have anything to do with it.'

'Thank you, Your Majesty. But I must say that those who live with magic will die by magic. I will leave you now.' Captain Ride turned and proceeded to lead his men back to The Field.

Sir Philip called everyone to him. 'We must take this as a warning that we cannot trust anyone, and Rose and Roget must be protected at all times.' He turned to Roget. 'Any ideas on what happened?'

Roget answered, 'Obvious someone powerful in the magic doesn't want us to succeed in our quest and took possession of the two soldiers who attacked us.'

'Wouldn't it have been more successful if whomever this person is, took possession of two of us?' asked Liam.

'We are a quest of thirteen. We can be killed but not possessed while we travel on a magical quest for a god,' Roget answered. 'We must be very careful in future and not trust anyone.'

'Everyone mount up and let's get going,' Sir Philip ordered. 'The sooner we finish this quest the better.'

After a short while, the prince rode up to Sir Philip. 'That was very scary. I wish we could get to Harbourtown faster, but unfortunately the larger the group the slower the travel.'

'Which reminds me,' Sir Philip answered, 'what was that comment about five hundred men?'

'I asked Grandpapa to send troops to Falconia, in case of a war between you and your myriad of enemies.'

'Thank you, they could prove useful.'

'You're welcome. Imagine having the Duchess in charge of Falconia. It would be the end of the independent towns and a constant armed mass on our border with Harbourtown.'

Sir Philip smiled. 'True, it looks like we'll have a hungry camp tonight and we're not taking anything from The Field.'

At that moment Lizzy rode up to them. 'Edgar has spotted several wild pigs just inside the forest, we could catch one of them for supper.'

'Captain Lipson,' Sir Philip shouted.

'Yes, sir?'

'Follow Lizzy and Edgar with your men and bring us a pig or two for supper. Leave Graham.'

'My pleasure, Sir Philip.' Captain Lipson and his men followed Lizzy towards the forest.

'Rose.'

Rose rode up looking grim. 'Do I call you sir or father?'

'This is a military mission so I'm your senior officer. Work it out for yourself.'

Rose gave the Falconian salute of her fist over her heart. 'Yes, sir.'

'You look after Graham.' Rose nodded; Sir Philip's voice softened. 'Rose, how is he?'

'He's better than expected. I think if we can get him a crutch in Harbourtown, he would be hard to leave behind. We should really get him a special stirrup for his horse though.'

'Good, thank you Rose.' Rose went to look after Graham. 'Rudi, you and erm, Evan,' Sir Philip finally remembered Prince Rudolf's wyvern rider's name, 'prepare a fire ready to cook up some pork. I think you'll have to make a spit. Liam will help you.'

Prince Rudolf asked, 'What are you doing?'

'I'm going to have a chat with Roget. Just think, if magic users aren't popular in Harbourtown, what are they going to say about a high priest of Braidos?'

Prince Rudolf nodded and went to help prepare a fire.

In the small, black brick, windowless room, the small woman in a black, hooded gown sat on her stool staring at her crystal ball on the stand in front of her and cursed. She had failed. Her master would not be happy. She could not try again for at least a week, if then. The magic she used had weakened her. She dreaded telling her master what had happened. She could only hope she would not be punished.

Lizzy, Captain Lipson and the guards caught two pigs and the group had a magnificent meal of pork that night. Graham ate his share and seemed to be in good spirits despite the loss of his foot. After they had finished eating Sir Philip called everybody to listen to him. 'We will be at Harbourtown tomorrow. The authorities there have banned magic and strange creatures, so no one is to use magic without my express permission and Edgar there is just a pet.' He paused while he gave each of the magic users a stare. 'Our friend Roget is a monk from the Abbey of the Northern Desert, which is a real place to the south of Melita. Most, if not all the population of Harbourtown will never have heard of it. The monks there worship the sand, don't ask me why but they do.' He looked at Roget and smiled. 'I think you'll make a great sand worshipper, Roget.'

Roget said nothing but Sir Philip thought that if he could see Roget's face he would be scowling. 'Queen Charlotte is known in Harbourtown as Charlotte Silver and many there are her friends, so behave yourselves. There is also a warrant for her arrest there for consorting with monsters.'

Rose interrupted, 'They don't really want to arrest mother, do they. What monsters were they?'

'Well, she had received a warning before, but the monsters she was actually arrested for consorting with, were Slinky and Speedy.' Rose's hand went to her wrist where the double dolphin-headed bracelet was. 'They had just rescued your mother from a pair of harpies and some sharks, Burgher Jackson who hates your mother said because they had rescued her, she was consorting with monsters. The charge has never been dropped.'

'I'd like to meet this Burgher Jackson,' Rose growled while folding her arms.

'If you do you will be polite and make no mention of your mother.' Sir Philip glared at her. 'And that's an order!'

Sir Philip once again addressed everyone. 'We are going to be polite and friendly. Charlotte Silver is still a rich person in Harbourtown and we will be using some of those riches to hire a ship. We will cause no trouble, just find a ship and leave. Is that clear to everybody?'

Everybody nodded or murmured agreement, even Rose. 'Alright we've eaten well, there's plenty of pasture for the horses which have been hobbled. By the way, I will expect everyone to give their horse a good rub down after we get to Harbourtown. We have been rather remiss in this, but it couldn't be helped. You all will make up for it tomorrow. Captain Lipson, please organise the watch and whoever is on watch, make sure none of the horses go anywhere near that wheat.' Sir Philip pointed at the wheatfields. 'If they do the cost of whatever they eat will come out of his pay. Now get some sleep. We've another busy day tomorrow and remember, be polite!'

CHAPTER TWENTY-ONE

The next morning, they breakfasted on the remnants of the pork. Sir Philip repeated what he told everybody the night before to make sure nobody would cause any trouble when they got to Harbourtown. Rose and Lizzy replaced the dressing on Graham's leg and made sure the green crystal was set in place. They then all mounted up and set off for Harbourtown.

As they had no supplies, Sir Philip decided they would keep riding until they reached their destination. Just after noon, Lizzy rode up to Sir Philip and Prince Rudolf. 'Edgar says there's one of those funny flying things flying up ahead with a rider on it.'

'What?' Sir Philip looked up at the sky but couldn't see anything. He asked Prince Rudolf, 'Do you have any more of those crossbow bolts that shoot stars?'

'Some.'

'Fire one into the air and see if we attract a wyvern.'

'Certainly.' He picked up his crossbow from its holder on his saddle and chose a bolt from the adjoining sheaf. He turned to Lizzy, 'May I have a light?'

Lizzy put her hand on the bold and it started to burn. Prince Rudolf immediately fired the bolt into the air. Once again, the bolt soared into the sky, leaving a smoke trail behind it and when the bolt reached its apex, it burst into a cloud of bright stars. They then waited. Liam saw the wyvern first when it was still a tiny spot in the distance. It got larger quickly and soon everyone could see it become a wyvern and rider. The horses became nervous, and everyone had to work to keep them calm. The wyvern landed fifty yards away and Prince Rudolf and Sir Philip dismounted and walked over to it.

'Sergeant Alexander, I didn't expect to see you here. What news do you have?'

Sergeant Alexander touched his forehead with the back of his hand in the Concordian salute and stayed mounted on the wyvern. 'How much time do we have, sir?'

Prince Rudolf grinned. 'Very little, so keep it as short as possible.'

Sergeant Alexander had a frown on his face. 'Where to

start? Well, there are over five hundred men about two days' ride from Harbourtown on their way to Falconia. They're being led by your brother, Sir Philip.'

'It would be nice to see Matthew, but I hope we'll be at sea by then,' Sir Philip commented.

'There is an advance party almost at Harbourtown to organise supplies for the troops as they march past. They're led by Sir Damian.'

'A good man,' Prince Rudolf noted.

'When the message from Prince Rudolf got to Falconia, the queen sent a message to the mines to arrange a meeting with Malgon Steelhammer to talk to him about Balor Hardfall and Iggord. We left before she did, so we don't know how the meeting went.'

'Who's we?' the prince asked.

'Me, John and Martin.'

'I sent Martin to talk to my grandfather.'

'He got back. Your letter did the trick. He sent more than five hundred men, three more wyverns which two are now just outside Passville to patrol Duchies Pass and the third is at Townsville in case of an attack from the Redcap Goblins and their allies, and six more riders just in case they're needed, travelling with the army.'

'Grandpapa always knew how to react in a crisis.' Prince Rudolf smiled.

'There does seem to be one slight problem however.'

Prince Rudolf's smile disappeared. 'What?'

'Every time we try to land outside Harbourtown, troops come out and try to attack us. We've landed there three times and it's happened three times. Fortunately, the border with Concordia is pretty close to Harbourtown, so we've been able to land not too far away, but we'd rather be closer so we can report back to Falconia when we need to.'

There was silence for a few seconds then Sir Philip spoke. 'I've got an idea. It may or may not work, but it's worth a try. Sergeant Alexander, can you arrange for Sir Damian, you and the other wyvern riders and ourselves to arrive at Harbourtown at the same time?'

Sergeant Alexander looked puzzled. 'Yes, sir.'

'How far away are we from Harbourtown?' Sir Philip asked.

'Hmm, about two and a half to three hours.'

'We'll ride fast so make it two and a half hours. I want you to arrange for Sir Damian, you and us to arrive at the same time. Do you understand?'

'Yes, sir.'

'Well, what are you waiting for? Get going.'

Alexander waved and took off. Shortly he and his wyvern were just a fading dot in the distance. Sir

Philip and Prince Rudolf walked back to the group and remounted. 'We'll be at Harbourtown in about two and a half hours. If necessary, follow my lead, otherwise, remember what I told you this morning. Let's get started.'

They started out for Harbourtown.

About two hours later they started to see seagulls and shortly afterwards they could smell the sea. Sir Philip's group timed it perfectly. Just as the two and a half hours were up, they were approaching Harbourtown. It was surrounded by a ten foot wall without a glacis or moat as it had not fought with anyone, ever. Three wyverns came into land at the same time and approaching fast was about a dozen riders from the north. As Sir Philip's party approached, the wyverns landed near the forest. Sir Philip ordered all visors to be left open to show they didn't want to fight. The gates to Harbourtown opened and three dozen men rode out. Thirty of them were Harbourtown constables. They all wore an open helmet, and breast and back plates and carried short lances and swords and bucklers. All were dressed in the black uniform of Harbourtown constables. The other six wore red and gold over their armour which showed they were burghers. They didn't carry short lances but except for that, their weapons and armour were the same as the constables.

Sir Philip's party rode so as to put themselves between the wyverns and the Harbourtown constables. They spread out into a line with Sir Philip and Prince Rudolf a little way in front of them. The constables and burghers also spread out and halted about fifty yards away, except for one who kept riding straight at Sir Philip. Just before he was about to collide, he halted right next to Sir Philip and there was a loud crash of armour as he attempted to put his arms around Sir Philip. 'What are you doing here and how's my goddaughter and the children?'

'Burgher Rowles, it's good to see you. It seems the news from Falconia hasn't got here yet. We are on a desperate mission to save Stephen and Julie and Charlotte is trying to prevent a war with the dwarfs.'

Burgher Rowles was an older, handsome, tall and slender man, with long, blonde, wavy hair. He had blue eyes and a broken nose and looked shocked. 'That is not good news, if there is anything I can do to help, please ask. But first, are those creatures anything to do with you?'

'I know my party is a bit bedraggled but calling them creatures is going a bit far,' Sir Philip answered smiling.

Chapter Twenty-one

While they were talking, Sir Damian's men arrived and joined the line.

'So, they are yours, I should have guessed. You know who's leading our men behind me?'

'Burgher Jackson?'

Burgher Rowles nodded and turned to look at the Harbourtown troops. As he did so one of the constables rode back to the town. 'He's going to fetch the rest of the constables and burghers. I hope this isn't going to turn into a fight.'

'I hope so too. Let me introduce you to Prince Rudolf, the son of the Crown Prince of Concordia, the second in line to the Concordian throne.' Sir Philip nodded towards Burgher Rowles. 'This is the Burgher Harold Rowles, Charlotte's godfather.'

Prince Rudolf nodded towards Burgher Rowles. 'Nice to meet you. If you're Charlotte's godfather, it means we're almost related.'

The burgher nodded back. 'Nice to meet you also. So, we have the King of Falconia and the second in line to the Concordian throne here, and Burgher Jackson, who is now the Deputy Head Burgher, is planning on arresting you.' Burgher Rowles shook his head.

'The best part is there are over five hundred Concordian troops less than two days away,' Sir Philip told the burgher.

'Why, are you planning to attack us?'

'No, of course not. They're on the way to Falconia in case a war breaks out either with the dwarfs or the duchies. But I don't think they'd take it too kindly if the prince or myself were under arrest. When the rest of the burghers arrive, have them ride out halfway between our groups and Prince Rudolf, Sir Damian and I will meet them and we will try to come to some sort of agreement.'

'Good luck with that, you know Burgher Jackson's still got that warrant out for Charlotte even though she's now Queen of Falconia.'

'I hope to show him the error in that.'

Burgher Rowles laughed and shook his head and was about the ride away when he noticed one of the soldiers behind Sir Philip was rather small and had red hair. 'Rose?' he rode towards her. 'Rose, is that you?'

'Uncle Harold, how are you?' Rose asked as she took off her gauntlet, broke ranks and rode forward.

'Good, I hope you are too.' They touched hands and smiled.

'Stay safe, I must leave,' Burgher Rowles said as Rose replaced her gauntlet and took her place in line. He rode past Sir Philip and gave him an angry look. 'She shouldn't be here. What were you thinking?'

Sir Philip stared back at the burgher. 'Not my idea, I assure you. I wish she wasn't here.'

Burgher Rowles nodded and rode back to his men.

While the group waited for the delegation from Harbourtown, Sir Philip, Prince Rudolf and Sir Damian talked and decided on their strategy. It was over half an hour before almost fifty men rode out of the Harbourtown gate and went to join the others. Then another half hour while the burghers talked.

Eventually, fifteen riders rode to a spot halfway between the two groups. There were fifteen burghers in Harbourtown and they were elected for life or until they wished to retire. Sir Philip, Prince Rudolf and Sir Damian rode out to meet them.

Burgher Rowles just stared at them as they rode up but one of the other burghers and several of the constables gave Sir Philip a friendly wave. The burgher who waved was Burgher Thompson, he was a large rotund, dark-haired man of about five feet eleven inches tall and his horse looked as if it was under a great strain. Burgher Thompson had acted as Charlotte's lawyer when Burgher

Jackson had arrested her fourteen years before.

One burgher, an old, grizzled, grumpy, white-haired man who was tall and lanky pointed a bony finger at Sir Philip. 'What are you doing here? Are you planning to return that criminal Charlotte Silver back into our custody? Are you going to remove those evil flying monsters? And why do you travel with a monk?'

There was a lot of murmuring at this. Charlotte had been an extremely popular citizen of Harbourtown and had helped and cured numerous of its citizens. Her arrest, even amongst burghers and constables had not been popular.

Roget spoke, 'I am a monk from the Abbey of the Northern Desert, and I come with Sir Philip to find a new place to found a new abbey.'

Before Sir Philip could answer Burgher Jackson, Burgher Thompson spoke. 'Charlotte Silver has never been convicted of anything and the charges against her are just figments of your imagination.'

Burgher Jackson turned on Burgher Thompson with a snarl. 'Can you deny she's a magic user? We've all heard of her exploits with magic since she became the Queen of Falconia. Can you deny our law that magic users are banned in Harbourtown?'

Burgher Thompson smiled. 'I've been waiting for the

right moment to use this information for a long time. The original law, which is in the founding documents of Harbourtown, which were written over three hundred years ago and which are now in my keeping, does not state that magic users are banned, but the use of magic is banned and there is no evidence that Charlotte Silver ever used magic while living here.'

Burgher Jackson was left spluttering. Meanwhile, another burgher had ridden forward. 'My name is Burgher Robson. I am the Head Burgher of Harbourtown. Please explain your presence.'

Sir Philip turned to Sir Damian. 'You first.'

Sir Damian and Burgher Robson were much alike. Both were about six foot two inches tall, had long brown hair, one straight and one curly, and had brown eyes and both were slender.

Sir Damian took a sealed letter with the name Harbourtown on it from his saddlebag and handed it to Burgher Robson who opened it, read it and passed it to the other burghers to read. Burgher Robson stopped and thought for about a minute. 'Well, it wasn't a bluff to scare us. There are really over five hundred Concordian troops on the way here.' He spoke loudly so that all the burghers could hear him. 'That letter bears the seal of King Regis of Concordia and asked us to supply them with food so they can continue their journey to Falconia with all speed. Sir Damian just leads an advance group to organise our help beforehand and will head off to Thrackstown to organise the same thing there.' He turned to Burgher Jackson. 'What do you think they will do if we arrest King Regis' nephew and grandson?'

'But they have brought monsters here.' Burgher Jackson glared at Burgher Thompson. 'And there's no denying they are illegal.'

Sir Philip rode forward. 'What monsters?' He looked behind him at the wyverns and turned back. He pointed at them with his thumb over his shoulder. 'You don't mean those domesticated pets surely. They're really nothing more than the equivalent of flying horses. If they're monsters you are going to have to declare horses monsters.'

Burgher Robson rode close to Sir Philip and spoke in a quiet voice. 'Why are you here?'

Sir Philip spoke just as quietly. 'There have been some serious attacks on Falconia. You will hear the details soon, no doubt. I'm surprised the news hasn't yet gotten here. The people with me must get to the Eastern Isles as soon as possible, so all I wish to do is hire a ship and leave. I would like to leave one of the wyverns here under heavy guard by our men so that news of our return can be sent to Falconia as soon as we get back. Other than that, as I said, we just wish to hire a ship and leave. Keep this in mind, if Falconia loses, our enemies will not stop until they control all of Strasia.'

Burgher Robson spent some time in thought and then turned and addressed the burghers. 'Sir Philip, Prince Rudolf and Sir Damian are here as friends and customers for our trade. I find there are no legitimate charges that can be brought against them. I suggest we all go back and prepare to do some profitable business.'

This caused some muttering amongst the burghers with Burgher Jackson turning a bright red before he turned and rode back with all the other burghers and constables to Harbourtown. Before he rode back with them, Burgher Robson spoke again to Sir Philip. 'After you get back, we don't want to see any more of your flying pets. Understand?'

'Yes, Burgher, thank you.' Sir Philip then spoke to Prince Rudolf and Sir Damian. 'Rudi, go and see Liam and get the ingredients for the potion from him and write a letter to Charlotte about what is happening. Keep it brief, I want us all at the docks before anyone changes their mind.' Prince Rudolf went to see Liam while taking writing implements out of his saddlebags.

'Sir Damian is to stay and defend the wyverns.' Sir

Damian looked at Prince Rudolf who nodded. 'I don't trust Burgher Jackson and when Sir Matthew arrives, have him leave a strong force with the wyvern that is staying.' Sir Damian went to obey. 'Wait until Prince Rudolf has finished his letter then your men can take it to the wyverns.'

Five minutes later, Prince Rudolf had finished the letter and he, Sir Philip, the rest of the group, Sir Damian and two of his men rode towards the gates of Harbourtown, the rest of Sir Damian's men went to join the wyverns.

CHAPTER TWENTY-TWO

When they passed through the gates of Harbourtown they found three burghers and several constables waiting for them, all mounted. One of the burghers was Burgher Rowles. Burgher Rowles rode up to them. 'You and your group follow me and two of the constables to the docks. Sir Damian, please follow these two others and they will start to organise supplies for your army.'

As the two groups split up, Sir Philip spoke to Burgher Rowles. 'Would it be possible to ride past Charlotte's apothecary?'

'Certainly, it's almost directly on our way,' Burgher Rowles said as he led the way.

Burgher Rowles and Sir Philip were riding together

when they saw the apothecary. 'The last time I saw this, the front was almost fully covered by a climbing white rose.'

'I was told it suddenly shrivelled up and died about the time you were dying from being stabbed with that poisoned knife in the forest.'

'Yes, and the silver rose pendant Charlotte gave me melted at the same time. We gave the children a silver rose pendant each, I hope they work just as well. I've told you this, but you must keep it a secret. Do Pat and Jayne still work there?'

'Pat still runs the place, Jayne left to get married.'

'I'll be five minutes,' Sir Philip announced to the group as he dismounted outside the shop.

As he entered, he looked around. It was late in the day so there were no customers, otherwise it looked just as he had seen it last. Lots of bottles and jars on shelves behind a counter which had a door behind it and several tables and chairs in front. The walls were painted white with various wildflowers dotted around. Pat, a plump older lady with hair that was greying, had looked after Charlotte after her adoptive parents had been murdered, saw Sir Philip gave a little scream and cried, 'Sir Philip,' and rushed over and tried unsuccessfully to give him a hug around his armour. 'How are Charlotte and the children? Is she with you?'

'Charlotte is still in Falconia and the news of the children will be all around the town by tomorrow. I can't stop, I'm on an important mission. I just stopped to tell you that Charlotte misses you and this place and if my mission is successful, we expect you to visit us again very soon. Also, I need to get a crutch.'

Pat looked concerned. 'You're not injured, are you?'

'No, but one of my men is.'

'Wait here.' Pat disappeared into the back room and about half a minute later came out with a crutch. 'Will this do?'

'Pat, you're a marvel. Thank you, it will do perfectly.'

Pat gave Sir Philip the crutch. 'No charge. I hope you're up to nothing dangerous. Charlotte would be devastated if anything happened to you.'

'I wouldn't be too happy either.' Sir Philip smiled. 'I must go. I could only stay a minute. Please stay well. Thank you for the crutch. Goodbye.' Sir Philip gave Pat a kiss on top of her head.

Pat, with a tear in her eye, sobbed, 'Goodbye. Stay safe,' as Sir Philip left the shop.

Shortly afterwards, they arrived at the docks which were still busy even though it was late in the day. Sir Philip asked Burgher Rowles where they could find a stable that would look after the horses that was near the docks. The burgher recommended one which Sir Philip and the others were extremely impressed with, although it was expensive. 'Some quite wealthy people come through the docks here and they want the best,' the burgher had told Sir Philip and told the owner that he would guarantee payment. Sir Philip and all of the group, even Roget, then groomed and brushed the horses down and made sure they were left with top-quality corn and water.

While they were doing this, Burgher Rowles told Sir Philip he would go and find a good ship and crew to transport them to the Eastern Isles. He would also arrange for the constables to purchase clothes for the group. The burgher commented that they really couldn't wear their armour for the entire trip. They arranged to meet at the tavern that was next to the stables. When Sir Philip and his companions got there, they were all totally famished as none of them had eaten since they had the remnants of the pork for breakfast. They all ordered ale and a steak with potatoes, steak being plentiful as Harbourtown was next to Concordia which had massive cattle herds. Prince Rudolf tried to order carrots for everyone, but unfortunately for him, Sir Philip heard and cancelled the order. Burgher Rowles came in with the two constables and they ate also.

After they had finished eating, Sir Philip, Prince Rudolf and Burgher Rowles sat together. Sir Philip asked Burgher Rowles whether he had found a ship. 'Yes, of course, a really good one, *The Flying Porpoise*. The captain, a man called Jason Wright, has been sailing for almost thirty years, I know him well. You were fortunate that his ship is only half-filled with cargo so there is plenty of room for your party. He was going to finish loading tomorrow and then sail on the next morning's tide, but now he will sail early tomorrow. He and most of his crew are right now at the Temple of Coralie praying for a safe journey.'

'Coralie. She's the goddess of the sea, isn't she?' Sir Philip asked.

'Yes, most sailors go there before they sail.'

'If they're leaving early without a full cargo, I suppose they are going to be expensive to hire,' Sir Philip mused. 'Could you arrange for some of Charlotte's money to be paid to Captain Wright to secure his services?'

Burgher Rowles shook his head. 'No, I'm afraid not.'

Sir Philip and Prince Rudolf looked at him in surprise. 'Why not?' they both asked, almost in unison.

'Burgher Jackson may not have been able to arrest Charlotte, but he has frozen her money with the bankers.'

'Can he do that?' Sir Philip asked angrily.

'He's done it,' the burgher answered.

'Damn, this means postponing our sailing until Rudi and I can arrange credit. That won't be a problem, but I didn't want the delay.'

'I'm sure you can make some arrangement with the owner of the ship. He's a very reasonable man.'

Both Sir Philip and Prince Rudolf stood. 'Well, let's be off to see him.'

'I'm sitting here.'

Both Sir Philip and Prince Rudolf looked at the burgher in surprise. 'Harold, we don't have time to waste. We must go and see him at once. I want to sail in the morning.'

'We will. I own the *The Flying Porpoise* and I haven't had a proper sea voyage for a long while.' Burgher Rowles smiled.

'I'm sorry but our party must remain at the number thirteen. You cannot come.' Sir Philip's tone was stern.

'I'm not part of your party. I'm just taking a trip on a ship I own. I do that occasionally to make sure my captains aren't up to anything they shouldn't be. You can't get the money to hire another ship until tomorrow and I'm not going to charge you anything. Well?' Burgher Rowles threw his arms wide.

'I'm going to have to talk about this with someone else.' Sir Philip looked around for Roget who had been sitting by himself but was now being harassed by half a dozen sailors. Sir Philip and Prince Rudolf walked over to Roget's table.

'So, you're a monk from the Abbey of the Northern Desert and you worship sand. Do you eat it too, you freak?' one sailor was asking. Someone in Harbourtown had obviously heard of the Abbey of the Northern Desert and how they worshipped.

Roget didn't move. Another sailor said, 'Let's find out. I've still got some sand in my boot.' He went to take his boot off but stopped when he found Sir Philip's sword at his throat. He moved away from the sword. 'You reckon you two can beat all six of us? I don't expect the sand eater will help you.'

'We don't need *the sand eater*. Captain Lipson,' Sir Philip called loudly.

Captain Lipson and all his men except Graham rose from seats and drew their swords. All were still in their armour.

The sailor who had threatened Roget with the sand from his shoe smiled and held up his hands. 'I'm sure you realise we were only joking with the monk and you. We meant no harm.'

'I think you should apologise to him.' Sir Philip smiled.

The sailor gave Roget a slight bow. 'We're really sorry, Your Reverend, we meant no harm. Please forgive us.'

Roget did not speak but waved the sailors away with his hand. They left the inn. Sir Philip and Prince Rudolf joined him, and Captain Lipson and his men resumed their seats.

'We have a ship, Roget. It sails early tomorrow,' Sir Philip said.

'That is good.'

'The owner wants to sail with the ship.'

'That is fair. It does not make him one of us.'

'In that case, it's all arranged. I suggest we finish here and board the ship as soon as possible.'

'That seems a good plan,' Roget intoned. 'Tell me when we are ready.'

Sir Philip and Prince Rudolf went back to Burgher Rowles. Before they got there, Prince Rudolf asked Sir Philip in a whisper, 'Don't you think we should have told him that the owner is Charlotte's godfather?'

'Probably, but I'm more worried about telling Harold that the monk from the Abbey of the Northern Desert is Roget, High Priest of Braidos.'

'Hmm.' Prince Rudolf nodded. 'Rather you than me.'

Chapter Twenty-three

They all went down to the dock where they found that Captain Wright and his men had returned from the Temple of Coralie. Captain Wright, about five feet ten inches tall with brown hair and brown eyes, wearing a navy-blue sailor's jacket and trousers and heavy boots, gave a warm welcome to Burgher Rowles and the two constables as they boarded *The Flying Porpoise*, and a slightly less warm one to Sir Philip and his group. However, he fawned over Rose and Lizzy. He gave a much cooler welcome to the monk from the Abbey of the Northern Desert. Captain Wright, as Burgher Rowles went aboard, told him he had arranged for extra rations to be taken on board to account for all the extra personnel.

The Flying Porpoise was a barque, a three masted

ship, but unlike most barques, it had an aft castle but no forecastle. It was thirty yards long and had a crew of twenty.

Burgher Rowles had a permanent cabin on board reserved for him as owner, although it got used by others when he wasn't aboard. There were three other cabins on the ship. The largest was the captain's, the next largest was for the three ship's officers and the smallest, which was used by the occasional passenger, was offered to Sir Philip and Prince Rudolf who declined the offer, instead giving the cabin to Rose and Lizzy. All the men would find space in the hold that had no cargo. Roget did not seem happy with this and offered to sleep on deck. He was found a small space near the stern of the ship.

Before he went there, he asked to talk to Sir Philip. He spoke quietly. 'You did not tell me the owner of the ship is Queen Charlotte's godfather.'

Sir Philip spoke just as quietly. 'He is not part of our group and we'd still be looking for a ship if it wasn't for him. He will leave us at Danziger, so he's not a worry.'

'I hope you are right,' Roget hissed. 'It could affect the outcome of our quest.'

'Just hope when he finds out who you are, you don't get thrown overboard,' Sir Philip answered. 'Just get yourself organised and hope we have a fast voyage. Burgher

Rowles said it should take a week to ten days, but he'd order Captain Wright to do everything he could to make the trip faster. Good night.' Sir Philip went down to the hold to join the other men.

When they awoke the next day, the ship was speeding over the water. Burgher Rowles told Sir Philip that with the speed they were travelling they may even make Danziger in six days. 'We're lighter because we don't have a full cargo. You lot weigh much less. I want you and Prince Rudolf to come to my cabin for breakfast. There's a lot we have to talk about.'

Sir Philip went to find Prince Rudolf with some dread.

A couple of hours later an extremely angry Burgher Rowles emerged from his cabin. As luck would have it, the first person he saw was the monk from the Abbey of the Northern Desert. He used all his self-control so he wouldn't throw a tantrum at the monk. Instead, he turned and re-entered his cabin to continue the conversation with Sir Philip and Prince Rudolf.

While they were still in Burgher Rowles's cabin, they heard the ship's bell ringing frantically. Burgher Rowles jumped up. 'That's the alarm!' Everyone stopped what they were doing and dashed out onto the deck. About half a mile in front of them and approaching slowly, looked to be a giant squid. It was about the same size as the ship and was coloured a light grey. Its legs kept moving so the crew were unable to make an accurate count. Some of the crew fell to their knees to pray to either Craidos or Coralie, while others helped to turn the ship's wheel and adjust the sails to try to avoid the monster.

The ship started to turn but it was too slow. The giant squid could not be avoided. The magic users rushed to the bow of the ship and Liam, Rose and Lizzy sent lightning bolts to hit the monster. Although Liam's were the strongest, it did not matter as none of them seemed to have any effect, but just seemed to bounce off the squid. Roget sent a fireball, which did as much damage to the squid as the lightning bolts.

Two large black dolphins appeared beside the squid, nibbling at its legs, distracting it. 'Go Speedy. Go Slinky!' Rose couldn't resist shouting. The squid hesitated so it could defend itself from the dolphins and then started to move away from the ship. The water next to the squid started to grow upward into the air. When the mass reached a height of twenty-five feet it started to take the upper shape of a female. She appeared to have green skin and long green hair which covered most of her unclad body. The face was quite beautiful, and she had green eyes. She shooed the squid away with her arms, moved towards the ship and then spoke with a bubbly voice. 'Charlotte Silver, are you there?'

No one answered. 'Speedy and Slinky are here. Who has the bracelet?'

Rose spoke up. 'I do. Charlotte Silver is my mother.'

The water creature moved to the edge of the ship and looked down at Rose. 'I am the Goddess Coralie, and I gave the dolphin bracelet to your grandmother Julie after she saved the life of one of my favourite servants and instructed her on how to make other animals for the protection of your mother.'

'My grandmother used that knowledge well. She made three other animals but alas one was destroyed.'

'I have heard that Charlotte is now Queen of Falconia. Why is it that her daughter is here with an agent of Chaos?' At the mention of an agent of Chaos, most eyes turned to Roget.

Roget bowed to Coralie. 'It is true, I am here at the orders of my master. But we are probably on the same side in the matter that brings me here. Rose and I must take the Chalice of the Dawn together and get it back to Falconia to save the lives of the other two of Charlotte's children.'

Coralie looked at Rose. 'Is this true?'

Before Rose could answer Sir Philip stepped forward. 'I am Sir Philip Concord, the King of Falconia, husband to Charlotte Silver and father to all three of Charlotte's children. And while I must admit that Roget and his master are nowhere near my favourite entities, what Roget says is the truth.'

While the conversation was taking place, the squid had disappeared and Speedy and Slinky were swimming around Coralie. Coralie was quiet for several minutes and no one aboard the ship dared say anything or even move. Coralie looked down at the dolphins and smiled, she then looked up. 'Leggy, my squid friend, was attracted to your ship by one of your passengers. She was planning to destroy you all and I was going to let her. It seems though, that the agent of Chaos may be on a worthwhile quest, so I have told Leggy to let you be. However, I would like to have my friends Slinky and Speedy re-join me. I would make a bargain. Give me back the dolphin bracelet and I will guarantee you all a safe passage to Danziger and back to Harbourtown from whence I know this ship comes. I cannot help you past Danziger, as the island where the Chalice is, is outside all of we gods' influence. But give me the bracelet and as I said I will assure a fast and peaceful passage across the sea.' She looked at Roget. 'And I don't expect to see you ever again after you return to Harbourtown. I will let Leggy greet you next time.'

Roget bowed. 'Your mercy is legendary, my lady.'

Rose took the dolphin bracelet from her wrist and looked at her father who nodded.

'I cannot hold the bracelet in this world. Please throw it just in front of me,' Coralie told Rose, who did as she was bid. Coralie smiled and said, 'Good luck in your quest. I hope you all return safely.' She then sank down back into the sea.

Burgher Rowles approached Sir Philip. 'Well, I must admit, there's never a dull moment when you're around.'

Everyone went back to their duties aboard ship, and they made it to Danziger in five days from when they left Harbourtown.

While Sir Philip, Rose and Roget were talking to the Goddess Coralie, Queen Charlotte was at the fort at the mines talking to Malgon Steelhammer, a week after she had received the letter from Prince Rudolf. They were in the main mine hall which was big enough to hold over a hundred miners. It was made of stone that was brought up from the mines and had openings with shutters in the walls which functioned as windows. The roof had long beams of wood that held tree branches to keep out the weather. There were no tables in the hall and only six chairs, in three of them were Malgon Steelhammer and two of his most trusted aids, in the other three were Queen Charlotte, Sir Robert the mine manager and Captain Davies who had taken over from Colonel Blayton as the commander of the mine's troops. None of the six were armed, although the dwarfs and Captain Davies wore armour. There were four armed guards just outside the hall door, two dwarfs and two of Captain Davies' men.

Malgon was speaking. 'While I've heard of Balor Hardfall making an alliance with Iggord of the Redcap Goblins, I have been informed that it has nothing to do with you or Falconia. It is to fight the werewolves. In fact, that's what they were doing when your troops attacked them. Not the other way around, they did not attack your men. I have been told that your flying creatures and cavalry killed numerous dwarfs and Redcap Goblins with no loss. That doesn't sound like Balor starting anything against Falconia, but just the opposite. Falconia attacked him.' Malgon used his finger to emphasise the point.

Queen Charlotte gave a grim smile. 'We were informed that Balor Hardfall was making the alliance with Iggord in order to attack Thomastown.'

Malgon Steelhammer laughed. 'And who told you this? It wouldn't have been one of the werewolves, would it?'

Queen Charlotte was silent.

Malgon Steelhammer continued, 'As a matter of interest, did the werewolves tell you these lies before or after your Falconians attacked the dwarfs and the goblins?'

Queen Charlotte remained silent.

Malgon softened. 'I have heard of what has happened at Castle Falconia and the harm your children have come to. These things can make a mother overwrought. Mistakes can be made. We have been at peace for thirteen years. I know what power you can fight us with, and a war would be disastrous for both sides. I will ignore your attack on my men, *this time,*' he emphasised the last two words, 'and guarantee no dwarf I command will attack the mines unless we are attacked first. As well as this, I offer to give you any assistance I can, to help you recover the full health of your children, just promise no more attacks on dwarfs.'

Queen Charlotte nodded. 'I thank you for your offer of assistance. I must remind you that Falconia and the Redcap Goblins have been at war since I became Queen, as they tried to murder me. I will promise to give the order that no dwarfs will be attacked that are not in the company of Redcap Goblins and that if they are, the dwarfs are to be taken prisoner and brought to you for retribution rather than being killed.'

Malgon Steelhammer interlocked his fingers and looked down in thought. There was silence in the hall for about thirty seconds until a soldier burst through the door. He ran up to the chair that held Queen Charlotte. He dropped to one knee. 'I'm sorry for the interruption, Your Majesty. An urgent message from Sir Philip, Your Majesty.'

Queen Charlotte stood. 'Please excuse me, Malgon, but this involves my children.'

Malgon Steelhammer and his assistants stood and bowed. 'I understand, Your Majesty. We will wait outside until you have received this message.'

The soldier stood. 'Please wait, part of the message could concern you.'

Malgon's face looked puzzled as he and his men waited.

'Most of the message awaits you at Castle Falconia, but Sir Philip has found a way to save Prince Stephen and Princess Julie. It involves a potion, of which one of the ingredients is the berries of the red mountain ash.'

'Ah-ha,' exclaimed Malgon. He turned to one of his men. 'I want two large sacks of the berries here within the hour. Now go.' The dwarf he spoke to ran from the hall. Malgon turned to Queen Charlotte. 'It would be my honour to play even a small part in helping your children.'

Queen Charlotte smiled at him. 'I thank you. I hope we can have at least another thirteen years of peace between our two nations.'

'So do I,' was Malgon Steelhammer's answer. 'I also accept your suggestion. I will order Balor Hardfall to stop associating with the Redcap Goblins and I will expect any who do will be brought to me by your men and I will decide the punishments.'

Queen Charlotte smiled. 'It is agreed.' She turned to Sir Robert. 'Bring a table, refreshments and wine for our guests. Water for me.' She turned back to Malgon. 'Thank you.'

Malgon smiled.

It took almost two hours for Malgon Steelhammer's assistant to return and he only had one sack, but it was almost as large as he was and needed three dwarfs to carry it. Queen Charlotte once again thanked the dwarf leader for the berries and stated that because of the size of the sack, there should be more than enough berries. Malgon told her that if any more were needed she just had to ask. Queen Charlotte then left the fort with twenty soldiers, two of them carrying the sack between them, to make the walk to the haze and back to Castle Falconia.

When Queen Charlotte got back to Castle Falconia, she was told that Colin, Sir George, Fabian Hastings and Sergeant Alexander were waiting for her in the royal reading room. She dismissed the soldiers with her except the two carrying the red mountain ash berries who were told to take it to Colin's laboratory. Colin later remarked in jest whether Queen Charlotte was sure she had enough berries. The Queen had answered, 'better too many than too few.' Colin had to agree.

When Queen Charlotte reached the royal reading room, Sir George gave Queen Charlotte the letter and the instructions for the potion. Queen Charlotte read the letter, her eyes growing wider the more she read. 'What is Philip thinking, making a bargain with Braidos? And he has Rose with him. Aengus' message didn't mention this.' (Helmut who had passed the message on had decided it was probably not a good idea to tell Queen Charlotte about the bargain.) She turned to Sergeant Alexander. 'Go straight back to Harbourtown and tell him to come back immediately. We will find another way.'

Sergeant Alexander looked embarrassed. 'I fear they have already sailed, Your Majesty. Prince Rudolf told me that they all expected to complete the quest for the Chalice of the Dawn and be back here in Harbourtown in about three weeks and could we set up a communications link using Colin's crystals so as to stay in touch with the men outside Harbourtown.'

'Outside Harbourtown? Why outside?'

'They won't let the wyvern inside.'

Queen Charlotte gave a wry smile. 'Of course, my old friend Burgher Jackson. Is there anything else you can tell us?'

Sergeant Alexander told them what happened outside the Harbourtown walls. After he had finished, Queen Charlotte dismissed him. She then turned to the others in the room. 'Well, give me your opinions.'

Both Sir George and Fabian Hastings stated that they both had immense faith in Sir Philip's judgement. She then turned to Colin. 'How hard will the potion be to make?'

'Well, we have more than enough berries,' Colin said with a smile. 'I'll send two of the students out tomorrow to get the red petals of the lace leaf flower. I'll warn them to be careful as it's very poisonous and we'll also give them a military escort as things are beginning to get pretty strange in the forest with the Redcap Goblins.'

'I hope my visit with Malgon Steelhammer has sorted that out. But it's best to play safe. What about the crushed rubies?'

'You, Liam and Jacky could do that easily, but it will be

good practice for some of the others to try. They should succeed. We have lots of dragon's blood, both liquid and powdered, which we inherited from when Queen Katerina had the lab.'

'So, we just have to wait for Sir Philip to get back. Have the communications groups moved and have new ones set up for the communications link to Harbourtown. Give them plenty of protection. Start to build a track so that Sir Philip and the others can get back here quickly. Is there anything else?'

'We're starting to run short of magic users with all the extra duties they are getting,' Colin noted.

'We will sit down tomorrow and reorganise their duties. We still need to keep the school going.' Colin nodded. 'I am now going to see my children. Good day gentlemen.' Queen Charlotte got up and left, leaving the others to get the plans organised.

CHAPTER TWENTY-FOUR

t was the first time any of the group of thirteen had ever seen Danziger, the capital and main port of the islands. The island it was on was called Forkley. It looked utterly stunning in the late afternoon light. Burgher Rowles and the two constables had been there before. The port was not large but even so, extremely busy, being the only major port on the Eastern Isles. There were six large, seagoing ships in the port, two of which were larger than the others, brightly painted with yellow sails and five masts and numerous smaller ships that carried goods between the islands and Danziger. Burgher Rowles told the group that the Eastern Isles traded herbs, spices, hardwoods and various other exotic items to Harbourtown, Thrackstown and to the lands south of Thrackstown and to lands that were even further east than the islands. Lands that he personally knew nothing about except that the two five-masted ships came from there.

As *The Flying Porpoise* came into its berthing spot, helped by a harbour pilot that had come on board as they entered the harbour, the dirtier side of the port became more obvious. The water near the docks was full of filth and rubbish. Some of the warehouses that could be seen were starting to fall down, they were in that much disrepair. There were beggars everywhere. Captain Wright told his passengers, 'We're here earlier than we were expected. The better berths are already in use, and we've been put here temporarily until one of those five-masters leave, which should be in the morning.'

'We'll disembark now. Is there a reasonable inn near here?' Sir Philip asked.

'I know of one,' Burgher Rowles stated. 'It's about a quarter of a mile from here, nearer the better part of the port. We can go over there now, and I'll send the constables to the palace to arrange a meeting with the Potentate. In fact, we've known each other for years and I'm sure he'll arrange a guide for us in the morning.'

'A guide to where?' Sir Philip asked.

'To wherever we need to go. If he doesn't know, one of his seers will.'

'All right everybody grab your equipment and we'll head off to the tavern.'

No one was wearing their armour at the time, but even though they all still carried their weapons, they had a lot to carry, so Burgher Rowles arranged with Captain Wright to get some of the crew to help them. They made quite an interesting procession on the way to the inn. They caught the eyes of everybody they passed. Two sets of eyes especially.

'What a magnificent head of red hair.'

'I know of someone who would pay a lot of gold for a female with that coloured hair.'

'You mean the Satrap of Kalam?'

'Yes.'

'There's a lot of them though.'

'I've an idea. Go and tell the thief master I need to talk to him immediately.'

'Of course, with his help, she's in the bag.'

'Literally.' They both laughed.

They all had managed to find rooms for the night at the inn. The two constables still hadn't returned when they ordered meals. There were few others eating at the inn.

The menu had more choices than most inns in Strasia, but most sounded awfully strange, so most of the group ate cold meat, cheese and bread. Roget ate an exotic concoction of insects cooked in a treacle sauce, which made many of the others feel slightly nauseous. It was after they had finished eating when a man dressed in the white uniform of a harbour official burst through the inn door.

'Help! Pirates are attacking *The Flying Porpoise*. The crew need help immediately.'

Burgher Rowles leapt up immediately. 'We must help them.'

Sir Philip stood. 'Everyone with me now!' He turned and looked at Rose and Lizzy. 'You two stay here with Graham.'

Rose stamped her foot and crossed her arms. 'Why?'

'Because your commanding officer said so,' was the answer.

Everyone, even the other customers, except Rose, Lizzy with Edgar on her shoulder and Graham, followed the harbour official out of the door.

Thirty seconds after the last man had left, a dozen of what could only be called scruffy ruffians carrying various weapons entered the inn. The leading ruffian, who was bigger than all the others, bald and had a scarred face and carrying a machete, sauntered over to the table where Rose, Lizzy and Graham were sitting, followed by the others. He spoke to Rose. 'You can come with us the easy way, or the hard way, little missy. What's it to be?'

One of the other ruffians said over their leader's shoulder, 'We should take the other girl too.'

'Good idea.' The leader took a step back. 'All right you two, get up. The cripple stays.'

The cripple then saved the ruffian leader's life. He did it by attempting to hit him with his crutch, which made the leader duck, so Rose's lightning bolt missed him by inches but took the ear off the man behind him. The man screamed and put his hand to where his ear used to be, blood poured through his fingers. Lizzy's bolt did better, it hit a man carrying a carving knife in the shoulder, leaving it a smouldering hole and he crumbled to the ground. Edgar pecked at the eyes of another of the ruffians, who, while attempting to get rid of Edgar, cut his own face with the razor he had in his hand, Edgar having flown away to avoid the razor. What really took all the ruffians by surprise though was the giant black wolf who tore out one throat while clawing simultaneously at two stomachs. The three dropped to the floor.

Graham's backswing had hit another in the forehead, and he joined the others on the floor. The seven surviving ruffians, which included the one with blood pouring from his face and the one with one ear, backed away and then turned and ran for the inn door. As they ran for the door, Jason took down another ruffian, then stopped and looked at Rose as if asking whether to kill some more or not. Rose said to Lizzy, 'I wish Colin would teach us how to understand the animals.' Jason stayed.

The ruffian leader was the first out of the door and he screamed as he suddenly found himself flying. He had dropped his machete and looked up to find himself in the claws of a giant black eagle. The eagle flew out over the water before tearing the man in two and dropping him and his various bits in the harbour as fish food.

Sir Philip and the others had hurried back to the inn after finding out the attack on *The Flying Porpoise* was a hoax, with the harbour official disappearing down an alley never to be seen again. They found the front door being guarded by a giant wolf and a giant eagle. They let Sir Philip enter but none of the others. He looked at the bloody carnage in the inn and immediately ran to Rose, who was shaking, and held her tight. While holding her, he asked Lizzy and Graham what happened. They told him about the fight and how it had been Rose the men had really been after. Sir Philip gave Rose a kiss on top of her head and then ordered Jason and Great Wing to let everyone else back into the inn. Rose went to the animals and touched them with the ring and the brooch, and they disappeared.

'This one's still alive.' Captain Lipson lifted the ruffian who had been hit by Graham's crutch.

Sir Philip strode over to him. 'Why did you want Rose and who sent you?'

The ruffian spat in Sir Philip's face and Sir Philip hit him in the stomach and the ruffian doubled over. Roget came over. 'Let me. Someone hold him.'

Captain Lipson held the ruffian's arms behind his back as Roget placed his hands on the ruffian's head. Roget started to quietly chant, but none of the others could make out or understand the words. The ruffian gave a loud scream and went limp.

'You can drop him, Captain. His brain, what there was of it, has now burnt away.' Captain Lipson let go and the ruffian slid to the floor. 'He knew nothing of importance. The leader of the gang was a lieutenant of someone who calls himself the thief master and the plan was to take Rose to him. Unfortunately, only the lieutenant knew where the thief master would be.'

Sir Philip looked down at the ruffian's body. 'Thank you, Roget. That's an interesting talent you've got there.'

Roget nodded. Just then the two constables returned

and looked around the inn in amazement. They informed Burgher Rowles that the Potentate of Danziger would see them first thing in the morning and was honoured that the King of Falconia and the son of the Crown Prince of Concordia were here to meet him. He had cancelled all his other appointments that he had for the morning. Sir Philip then addressed the group.

'Everyone will now go and get some sleep except the first watch. Captain Lipson, please organise that.'

Captain Lipson saluted. 'Yes, sir.'

Burgher Rowles spoke, 'Include me and the two constables in the roster.'

Prince Rudolf added, 'Me and Evan also.'

'And me,' added Liam.

'Put me down for the last watch,' Sir Philip told the captain. 'And make sure there is a guard outside Rose and Lizzy's room all night. Goodnight, everyone.'

Sir Philip escorted Rose, whom he had spent some time comforting, and Lizzy to their room and stood outside it until one of Captain Lipson's men came to take over. He then went to bed. Burgher Rowles gave the innkeeper two gold pieces to compensate him for the mess.

The next morning Sir Philip ordered everyone to be armoured to be able to leave at the first possible moment. Burgher Rowles said that he would arrange to buy sixteen good horses. This caused an argument as Sir Philip told Burgher Rowles he couldn't come.

'But I got you here,' the burgher shouted.

'I told you before we started, we have to start the journey as thirteen. Besides, I have a job for you.'

'What?'

'I need you to find this thief master and find out why he wants Rose. It is important.'

'All right, I agree, on one condition.'

'What?'

'You don't expect me to keep him alive.'

Sir Philip smiled. 'I'm not Charlotte, take your time with him, but get the information.'

Burgher Rowles nodded. 'Only thirteen horses then.'

Sir Philip nodded back and held out his hand to shake the burgher's. 'Yes, thank you.'

The Potentate of Danziger's palace was immense. It was not built for defence but for luxury. Everything was red marble with white veins, the walls, the floors and the ceilings. Only Sir Philip, Prince Rudolf and Burgher Rowles were admitted to see the Potentate, and the fact they were wearing armour was frowned upon by the officials that greeted them. They were asked to leave their swords at the entrance. They also left their helmets. Captain Lipson and the two of his men who had accompanied them, waited at the entrance to the palace. Everyone else was at the inn. Burgher Rowles had told the others he got on really well with the Potentate and in fact, the burgher was the Potentate's second son's father-in-law.

They seemed to walk for almost a mile along winding corridors with many other corridors and rooms branching off before they came to a great hall. It dwarfed the throne room at Castle Falconia and had several doors that entered it. At the end of the hall, there were steps that led to a stage. On the stage was an immense throne that looked as if it was made of solid gold. On the throne was the Potentate. He was an older man who looked past his prime. But in his prime, he must have had a superior physic. He was only about five foot six inches, and he looked like a barrel slightly going to fat. He had short grey hair and beard and grey eyes. He wore a blue silk shirt and pants and blue slippers. Also on the stage were a dozen huge men wearing white silk shirts and pantaloons.

They were all armed with large, heavy-looking, studded clubs and were all expressionless. There were also four red-clad officials.

The official who had guided them waited at the main hall door as Sir Philip, Prince Rudolf and Burgher Rowles approached the throne. When they were about six yards away from the steps they stopped and gave a small bow. The Potentate stood and gave them a small bow in return. He then exited the stage down steps at the front and went to give Burgher Rowles a hug, surprised that he was wearing armour. He then said in a deep voice, 'We are all rulers here. Let us dispense with formalities. Welcome to my friends from Falconia and Concordia. What brings you to my islands and do you expect to be attacked so that you come to me wearing armour?' He then climbed back up the steps and sat back down.

They had decided to let Sir Philip do the talking. 'We are honoured to be in your presence. It is unfortunate that we are here because of troubles in our own lands, but as soon as the troubles are over, we wish to visit you again in happier times and also offer an invitation to visit us. As for our armour, of course, we didn't expect you to attack us. However, there was an attempt to kidnap my daughter by the thief master last night.'

This news caused gasps from the Potentate and his

officials. The guards remained expressionless. 'This thief master has been a blight on these islands for years. We have tried to catch him numerous times without success. I apologise for this occurrence on my islands. How can I help with your troubles?'

'We need a guide to help us get to the island that contains the Chalice of the Dawn.'

'So, you're after the Chalice.' The Potentate rubbed his beard. 'That will not be easy.'

'This is known, and we are prepared.'

'I will give you a guide to cross this island after we have talked for a while.' The Potentate whispered something to one of his officials who then left the hall.

The three of them then talked about their various nations for almost an hour. The official then returned. 'Your guides are here. They will take you across the island to someone who can supply you with a boat that will take you to the island containing the Chalice. It cannot be approached from here as there are creatures that surround most of the island to stop ships from here approaching. There is only one approach from this island, and you will need to go there. There are also creatures on the island with the Chalice. You will have to get past them. I have had a letter prepared to order my vassal to give you help to get to the island. I wish you every success.'

Chapter Twenty-four

Sir Philip asked, 'Who is the vassal?'

'The Satrap of Kalam.'

255

Chapter Twenty-Five

The same night that the kidnap attempt on Rose was made, but several hours later at two o'clock in the morning, six shadowy figures exited a large merchant's house near a small postern gate in Castle Falconia's wall. The postern gate was near Colin's laboratory which used to be Queen Katerina's laboratory. It was one of the ways Queen Katerina used when she wanted to exit or enter the castle without being seen. It was hidden by a couple of large bushes and the door itself was locked and barred with two guards behind it.

The six shadowy figures waited while a smoky figure floated straight through the door. About three minutes later the door opened and the six entered the castle and made their way down the corridor. The leading figure put out his left hand and a flame appeared there so the group could see the way. All of them could not help but notice the two bodies on the ground. Both had holes in their chest with blood pooling there. Two human hearts lay next to them.

The six figures came to a junction in the corridor. The leading figure pointed down the left-hand corridor, 'That way leads to the laboratory. The cells are this way.' The intruders turned right. There were now torches in sconces every ten or so yards, so the leader extinguished the flame on his hand. They all moved silently down the corridor, none of them wore any armour as armour can make a noise, and all wore black. They turned another corner and the leader almost tripped over another body that looked much like the ones at the gate.

The corridor terminated in a small hall that had half a dozen other corridors leading from it and a staircase going up to a landing where it turned. There were many more torches in the hall so that there was plenty of light. The leader whispered, 'This way,' and started to head towards a corridor on the other side of the hall.

'Who are you and what are you doing.' A boy who looked no more than ten stood on the landing.

The leader looked up and smiled at the boy. 'We are performing a security exercise to make sure all the guards are on their toes.'

The boy looked sceptically at the leader, shouted, 'Liar,' and sent a weak bolt of lightning at the leader which missed by a yard.

The man behind the leader sent a bolt of lightning back, which was neither weak nor inaccurate. The boy screamed as he was blown to pieces. The leader muttered an expletive. The wraith which had been scouting ahead down the corridor that led to the cells reappeared. It hissed at the leader, 'Do we go on?'

'Of course, we have to get Scarlett,' Sir Peter answered. 'He may not have been heard.'

Just as he spoke one of his men fell with a crossbow bolt in his chest. A guard with a crossbow had appeared at one of the corridor entrances. Sir Peter sent a lightning bolt at him, and the guard disintegrated. From the landing of the stairs, another lightning bolt happened. This one also was not weak or inaccurate and another of Sir Peter's men died.

On the landing, Queen Charlotte, who had fired the bolt, shouted, 'Stop or you will die!'

One of Sir Peter's men shouted, 'It's Charlotte,' and aimed a lightning bolt at the landing. Queen Charlotte screamed as she slowly disintegrated. Everyone stopped in shock. The man who had fired the bolt shouted, elated,

'I did it. I killed Queen Charlotte.'

Sit Peter turned and looked at his man. He then started to walk towards him. As he did so he aimed a bolt of lightning at the man's right hand. The hand turned to dust. 'You,' this time the bolt hit the man's left leg and he fell to the ground, 'killed,' the third bolt hit the man in the lower stomach, 'my,' the last bolt destroyed the man's head, 'cousin.'

More guards with crossbows appeared in the hall and Sir Peter's arm was grazed with a bolt. Sir Peter shouted, 'Run' and the last two of his men went to follow.

Sir Peter also shouted at the wraith who had another one of the guard's hearts in one of its claws, 'Guard our retreat!'

Sir Peter and one of his men made it to the corridor that led to the postern gate, the other fell with five crossbow bolts protruding from his back. The wraith did a good job of defending the entrance to the corridor and soon there were half a dozen guards without hearts lying on the floor. Captain Clough who had arrived from one of the corridors and was the next man who attempted to attack the wraith stood back in surprise as a knife flew past him and hit the wraith between the eyes. The wraith dissipated. He looked around to see Stuart the magic user smiling. 'I admit I did use magic to guide the knife.'

Captain Clough gasped, 'Thank you. They killed Charlotte.'

The smile immediately fell from Stuart's face. 'What?'

'Get a message to the wyverns. They will try to leave the town.'

Stuart immediately started to run down one of the corridors.

The wraith had bought Sir Peter and his surviving man enough time to get to the postern gate. They reached the merchant's house from where they started the night mission out of breath and shaking. There was another of Sir Peter's men there waiting in the house courtyard with seven horses and a large frame made of wood to protect a painting. 'Forget the frame and let's mount up and go. The mission's failed. We have to run.' All three mounted a horse and headed to the town gate.

The town gate was closed at two thirty in the morning and protected by four sleepy guards. There were four more guards on the wall over the gate who were supposed to be looking outwards for an attack who were also sleepy.

The sound of galloping horses startled the guards awake and they stood their pikes into the ground in a defensive position. It didn't help them though as Sir Peter aimed a lightning bolt at them and they were blasted out of the way. He then sent a second lightning bolt at the gate. But this bolt was weaker, and he had to let one of his men dispose of the gate. Sir Peter realised that his power was running out and he needed rest to recharge. The three men rode through the remnants of the gates on their thoroughbred horses and the four guards on top of the gate fired crossbows at them. The horse of the man who had entered the castle with Sir Peter was hit and fell with the man's leg under it. They were both left unmoving.

Shortly after the gate had been blasted open, numerous guards and magic users arrived there. Some of the guards had saddled horses and were prepared to ride after the fugitives. Captain Clough ordered one of the guards to give him his horse and he led over a dozen guards in the chase. Stuart the magic user rode with them.

The two wyvern riders ran through the gate heading for the field where the wyverns were tethered. There were two major roads south of Town Falconia. One headed for Passville and the other towards Duchies Pass. They decided one would follow each road and the one who spotted the fugitive would fire a signal bolt.

⚘

Colin and Sir George stood next to Charlotte's ashes. Colin had arranged for a message to be sent to the fort at Duchies Pass and Passville ordering troops to start up the roads to Town Falconia in the hope of intercepting the two fugitives. Fabian Hastings with some guards was searching for where the intruders had been hiding in the area near the postern gate.

'This of course means war with the Duchies,' Sir George growled. 'How dare they kill Charlotte. I'll kill the Duchess with my bare hands.'

'I'll have someone collect the ashes for burial,' Colin whispered while trying to hold back tears. 'I will start a new search in the library.'

'For a way to beat the Duchess?'

'No, for a way to kill Scarlett.'

❧

It was the wyvern rider following the Fort Philip road who spotted the riders. He took out his tinder box and lit one of his signal bolts. The other wyvern rider followed the stars to join him. The two wyvern riders decided to make things warm for the fugitives. The first flew down and incinerated one of the horses and its rider. The second started to get ready to stop the other, when Sir Peter turned and fired a lightning bolt at the wyvern and its rider. Fortunately, Sir Peter still hadn't completely recovered from the battle in the small hall. He still managed to hurt the wyvern enough to force it to land immediately without using its flame.

Sir Peter did not slow his horse for the next two hours with the unhurt wyvern following him all the way. The wyvern rider sent two crossbow bolts towards Sir Peter, but the range and the fact Sir Peter was travelling quickly meant that they missed easily. Then Sir Peter stopped his horse and looked at a spot just off the road, waved his hands twice just in front of his face and a travelling haze appeared. He looked up at the wyvern and its rider and gave them a wave. He then led his horse through the haze and moments later the haze disappeared. The wyvern rider landed and marked where the haze had been and then waited for the other Falconians to arrive.

Back at Castle Falconia, Sir George was in the courtyard looking at the man the guards had dragged in from under his horse outside the main gate. The man had his hands tied behind him and there were over a dozen crossbow bolts aimed at him. 'Don't forget, if he tries anything aim for below the waist,' Sir George ordered his men. 'We don't want to kill him, yet.' Sir George walked up to the man and pushed his face close to the man's. 'Are you a Mayflorian? What were you planning to do? Who led you?'

The man spat in Sir George's face. Sir George wiped away the spittle and stepped back. 'You are going to be honoured and make history.' The man looked puzzled. 'You are going to be the first official prisoner to go to the torture chamber in over thirteen years.' He turned to the sergeant in charge of the guards. 'I suggest you chop off his hands first, that should make it hard for him to perform magic. I will be down later to help.'

The sergeant saluted and the man was dragged away with the crossbowmen watching him all the way. Just as the guards and the men left, Fabian Hastings and his guards entered the courtyard. They were dragging a merchant who obviously didn't want to be there. 'This man owns the house the intruders used as their base,' Fabian told Sir George.

'I didn't know anything. I thought they were just travellers looking for a place to stay.' The merchant had fallen to his knees in front of Sir George.

Sir George smiled. 'A second official prisoner. We are going to be busy.'

Later that day but half a world away, Sir Philip and Prince Rudolf finally got away from talking to the Potentate. They got back to the inn just before noon. Burgher Rowles had done an excellent job finding thirteen well-bred horses and was waiting for them with his two constables, Captain Wright and several members of the crew of *The Flying Porpoise*. The captain told them that the rest of the crew under the first officer was moving the ship to the better berth now that one of the five-masters had left. Burgher Rowles and the constables were going to stay on the ship until Sir Philip and the rest returned so that they could sail immediately when they did.

They waited for two hours for the Potentate's guides to arrive, who were two of the Potentate's soldiers. They didn't wear plate armour but were dressed in long chain mail, a half helm and wore scimitars. It was another half an hour before the guides were ready to leave. Sir Philip and the rest did their best to hide their impatience to start. The guides travelled slowly on a good road through grassy rolling hills, taking no notice when Sir Philip tried to get them to hurry, but when the guides wanted to stop for the night when there was at least three hours of daylight left he got Liam to fire a bolt of lightning over their heads. When they camped for the night two hours later Sir Philip told Captain Lipson to double the guard. Half were to watch the guides.

After Sir Philip's party left the inn, Burgher Rowles arranged with Captain Wright to send the crew members that were with him out to gather information. They were not to directly ask about the thief master but to go to some of the less salubrious inns and keep their ears open. Also, to keep an eye out for someone with their left ear missing or someone with a new slash mark down their left cheek. After the crew members had left, the burgher, Captain Wright and the two constables walked to the new berth of *The Flying Porpoise*. Captain Wright asked the burgher, 'What makes you think we'll do any better catching the thief master than the Potentate's men?'

Burgher Rowles answered with a determined look on his face, 'There's one enormous difference. The Potentate's men are just going through the motions. We're going to make it a war.'

CHAPTER TWENTY-SIX

The next morning at Castle Falconia saw Sir George Potts sitting on the dais in the throne room with most of Falconia's important advisors in the hall. It had been decided by most of the people in the hall that, as he was the closest functioning relative of Queen Charlotte, he should take charge until Sir Philip returned. He wasn't sitting on either of the two thrones but had had a well-upholstered wooden chair put up there for him. To say he was in a bad mood would have been an understatement. He had had hardly any sleep and on top of that, when he had gone to help in the torture chamber, he was told that both the prisoners had given all the information they could without being tortured.

The merchant who traded extensively with Mayflor

had been offered three gold pieces a day in advance to rent most of his house for a week. There were still three days left. He himself had moved into the servant's quarters which was where the guards had found him sleeping.

The man who was one of the intruders had decided that he really didn't want his hands cut off as a prelude to torture. He told his captors that he had been one of a group recruited by the Marquis Sir Peter Mayflor to rescue Sir Peter's cousin, Princess Scarlett. All of the group had been magic users and they also had a wraith with them, so they thought the rescue wouldn't be too difficult. They were wrong, although he thought that if the boy hadn't discovered them, they could have succeeded. They had spent the previous four days scouting and finalising their plans. He also told the guards that the other side of the haze that Sir Peter had entered came out near Mayflor Castle.

Sergeant Alexander was addressing the assembly. He told them of the chase the previous night and how one of the intruders had escaped and waved to him as he did so. Sir George commented that it was probably too much to hope that the one who escaped wasn't Sir Peter. He also told them that Captain Clough and Stuart had marked the exact spot the haze was, from the disappearing hoof prints, and had started to organise the building of a wall on both sides of it to stop any further incursions from Mayflor. Captain Clough and Stuart asked that equipment and stone masons be sent to them to start cutting stone blocks from the nearby mountains, plus more soldiers and magic users to help with the walls and to tend the wounded wyvern. Sir George told Colonel Blayton and Colin to organise it immediately. Colin agreed but grumbled that there was going to be a shortage of magic users and he was going to have to spend time trying to locate more.

They then went through the casualty list. Besides the death of Queen Charlotte and the young magic user, who was an eleven-year-old boy named Simon, there had been fourteen guards killed. Sir George ordered that all the guards or their remains be buried with honours and a special funeral for Simon as he had been the one who had raised the alarm. Queen Charlotte's remains would not be buried until Sir Philip got back.

'We now have to decide our response to this attack on our nation and the murder of our Queen. What say you all?' Sir George asked the assembly.

He was greeted by numerous shouts of 'War!'

'Much as I agree with you, unfortunately only our sovereign can declare war and at the moment that should be King Philip. At the moment as Regent, I can only ask that Sir Peter be sent here from Mayflor for execution, as he may have been acting without the Duchess of Mayflor's knowledge. However, if they refuse to give him to us, we can interpret that as a declaration of war on Falconia by Mayflor. I propose a messenger be sent to Mayflor immediately demanding his expulsion back here.'

There were general murmurings of agreement.

Just then one of the magic users ran into the throne room. He called out, 'Sir George, a message from Duchies Pass.'

Sir George ordered the magic user to the bottom of the dais. 'Is it secret or can you tell everyone?'

Gwaine, a young, tall, gangly, dark-haired magic user looked confused. 'I don't know, sir.'

Sir George gave a small smile. 'Well, even if it is a secret soon everyone will know. Spit it out boy.'

'The Duchess of Mayflor demands a meeting with and I quote "whoever is pretending to rule Falconia," in four days' time at and I quote again, "your ridiculous wall in the pass." It just came by crystal.'

'So, she knows what happened,' Sir George mused. 'This means we can make our demands face-to-face.' There were shouts of "Yes" and "You tell her". 'Send a message back saying we agree, and we would like her to bring Sir Peter with her.'

Gwaine nervously answered, 'Yes, Sir George,' and ran from the hall.

'There will be a meeting of advisors in one hour in the Queen's consulting room,' Sir George ordered. 'I want Colin, Colonel Blayton, Fabian Hastings, Sir Gillian Stevens and is Captain Clough back yet?'

He was informed that Captain Clough and Stuart were still working at blocking off the haze. 'Have one of the wyvern riders fly and find the Concordian troops that are coming here and have them diverted to Duchies Pass. Ask them to make all speed. Can a wyvern still be controlled without a rider?' No one in the hall knew as Sergeant Alexander had already left to help with organising the assistance to be sent to the wounded wyvern. 'If they can, have them flown down to Fort Philip so that the new riders can use them. Let us get prepared.' Sir George left by one of the doors at the back of the dais.

Sir Philip was beginning to find it extremely hard to keep his temper with the guides. They obviously weren't used to getting up at the crack of dawn and were horrified at only having a quick, cold breakfast. When they eventually got started, the guides had to be chivvied so that they would travel faster than a walk.

After they had travelled for about two hours, the rolling hills started to get steeper and steeper. The road was still good, but they were entering a mountainous country. The guides called a halt which Sir Philip didn't want, but they informed him that they had to warn the group they were entering bandit country. The guides told them that their group probably looked too strong for the bandits to attack but they should keep their eyes open just in case.

As they travelled further into the mountains, Sir Philip and the others noticed that they were being watched. Sir Philip called Liam to join him. 'Can you give one or two of them a scare without actually hitting them? I want to make it clear we are too strong to be attacked without them deciding to attack out of vengeance.'

'Not a problem,' was the answer.

A little while later, Liam sent a couple of lightning bolts near two of the watchers. After that, they were still watched, but the watchers were fewer and better hidden.

The guides were unhappy with the short time that was taken for the midday meal but did not complain when Sir Philip called a halt about three hours before nightfall as they had come across a grassy plateau, and it made a good place to camp. The guides informed him that they should reach Kalam by the end of the next day.

As it was still hot, Sir Philip and the others took off their helmets, although they kept wearing their other armour. About an hour before dusk three men strolled down the road from the direction of Kalam. They were all wearing thobes and keffiyehs and looked unarmed. Sir Philip, Prince Rudolf, Liam and one of the guides walked out to meet them. As they did so, the guide informed the others that the three were probably bandits. As the two groups closed, the man in front threw his arms wide and greeted Sir Philip's group, 'Welcome to my mountains. I am Raj Arjun Reddy and I rule these mountains. What brings you to my domain?'

The guide answered, 'We travel under the protection of the Potentate of Danziger, the ruler of these islands and we are on the way to Kalam. What do you want?'

Raj Arjun, a tall man with grey eyes and a scar along his forehead, laughed. 'He may rule the islands, but I rule these mountains and travellers must pay a toll to travel through them.'

This time Sir Philip answered, 'Didn't you get the hint when we sent lightning bolts to warn you off?'

The Raj laughed again. 'Two small flashes do not scare me or my men, all five hundred of them, many with bows and they know how to use them. Shall we now discuss the toll?'

While they were talking, Captain Lipson had jogged up and spoke to Sir Philip in a whisper, 'Lizzy just told me that Edgar has returned from flying around the area and he said, "I saw about ten times ten men and about two times ten of them with small, those funny things that shoot the pointy things."'

Sir Philip laughed, which somewhat disconcerted Raj Arjun. 'What is so funny? We should be discussing the toll, or shall I order my men to attack?'

Sir Philip grew serious. 'If you want to sacrifice your men that's up to you. What do you suggest the toll should be?'

'The redheaded female should be payment enough, she's——'

He never got to tell anyone what she was as he suddenly found the point of Sir Philip's sword at his throat. The Raj put up his hands. 'Too much? Don't forget we are still bargaining.'

'You even look at "the redheaded female" and you will die a very slow and painful death,' Sir Philip snarled.

Raj Arjun took a step back and twirled his hand as he gave a small bow. 'A thousand apologies, sahib. I should have realised that she would be your gift to the satrap.'

Sir Philip took a step forward and left his sword at the Raj's chest. 'What do you mean?'

'It is known that the satrap likes redheads, most of his wives are redheads and he will pay a lot of gold for one,' the Raj answered nervously. 'I will change the toll. One gold piece for each one of you. That is fair.'

'I will pay you five gold pieces,' Sir Philip informed the Raj. 'That is not for a toll, but as a thank you for your information about the satrap. Take it or die.'

'Ten?' countered Raj Arjun.

'Eight and that's it and if you and your men try to attack us, the next lightning bolts won't be a warning.'

'Thank you, sahib. I accept,' Raj Arjun settled. 'We have an agreement. My five hundred men and I will not disturb you again.'

Sir Philip took two gold pieces each from Prince Rudolf, Liam and Captain Lipson plus two from his own pouch and gave them to Raj Arjun Reddy.

The Raj bowed as he backed away. 'I wish you all a pleasant and safe journey.' He then turned and walked away, followed by his two men.

Sir Philip turned to the guide. 'Did you know about the satrap's liking for redheads?'

'No, Sir Philip. What the Satrap of Kalam does on the other side of the island is not well known in Danziger,' the guide answered.

Sir Philip walked up to his daughter who was with the

others. 'We may now know why there was an attempt to kidnap you. The Satrap of Kalam might have been behind it. He likes his wives to have red hair.' Rose looked shocked. 'While we are there you are not, I repeat, you are *not* to take your helmet off! Understood?'

'Yes, father.'

Sir Philip gave Rose a kiss on top of her head and turned to Lizzy. 'Please don't let her out of your sight for a second. Please.'

'I won't, Sir Philip.'

'Captain Lipson double the guard for the night. Everyone except the girls and Roget is to take a turn and that includes Prince Rudolf and myself.'

'Yes, sir.'

'I will also take a turn. We are a company now.'

'Thank you, Roget,' Sir Philip replied.

CHAPTER TWENTY-SEVEN

I n Danziger, Burgher Rowles had visited his daughter and son-in-law, Prince Azul, a tall, muscular dark-haired man with deep brown eyes and, fashionable for the islands, a goatee beard, and his two grandchildren, a boy and a girl, for the midday meal. They were all pleased to see each other as their last meeting had been several months before. After the meal, his grandchildren were sent out to play and his daughter and son-in-law listened in amazement as the burgher told them the story of why he was there. He only left out that the monk from the Abbey of the Northern Desert, was in fact Roget, High Priest of Braidos. His son-in-law, who was one of the most powerful men in Danziger, promised to arrange for some of the Potentate's best soldiers to be at the burgher's call.

He told the burgher that he owned a warehouse a street back from where *The Flying Porpoise* was docked and he would have them disguised as warehouse workers, but they would be on call twenty-four hours a day. The burgher thanked him and, after they had eaten, made his way escorted by the two constables, six sailors and now ten soldiers back to the ship.

When he got back to the ship the soldiers set up a guard on it. When he boarded, he was greeted by good and bad news. The good news was that the man who had lost an ear had been spotted and had been grabbed by several of *The Flying Porpoise's* crew and was now below deck waiting to be questioned. The bad news was that there were now groups of beggars, wharfies and other persons numbering over three dozen watching the ship. The burgher was glad of the Potentate's soldiers guarding the ship. All the crew were also armed with various weapons. The burgher went below deck with Captain Wright to see the prisoner who was guarded by four of the crew.

Burgher Rowles looked at the prisoner who was short, balding with thin brown straggly hair and a bandage around his head covering the spot where his left ear used to be. The burgher walked up to the man and hit him in the stomach.

'Why were you trying to kidnap Princess Rose and where can we find the thief master?'

The man spat at the burgher who hit him again.

'There's no way you're going to make me talk. The thief master can do much worse than you.'

The burgher sighed. 'I never thought I'd say this, but I wish Roget was here.'

'I've got a confession to make.'

Burgher Rowles turned to Captain Wright in surprise. 'What?'

'I've been very unprofessional.'

The burgher's eyebrows went up. 'Can't this wait?'

'I didn't get the ship's hull scraped this month.'

All of Burgher Rowles's ships had their hulls scraped at least every two months to keep the barnacles off. These small crustaceans with their sharp shells slowed the ship down.

'That's against my express instructions for the maintenance of my ships.' Burgher Rowles turned on the captain. 'When this is over, I will fine you for incompetence.'

The captain looked surprised but added, 'It does, however, make the idea of keelhauling him more interesting.'

The burgher thought for a moment. 'Hmm, I might

actually forgive you.' He turned to the prisoner. 'Do you know what keelhauling is?'

The prisoner shook his head. 'Well, it's when a long rope is threaded under the ship and one end is tied to your wrists and the other end is tied to your ankles. It is then pulled under the ship. A person, when they are keelhauled, usually comes back half-drowned and with his skin shredded with many small cuts made more painful by seawater. I am told it's not very pleasant and sometimes the person being keelhauled dies. Can the thief master do worse than that?'

The prisoner shrank back. 'No, that's inhuman. You wouldn't.'

'I've known Princess Rose since she was a baby,' the burgher snarled. 'There is nothing I wouldn't do to protect her.'

The prisoner started crying. 'There's nothing I can tell you.'

'Captain, get a rope ready,' Burgher Rowles ordered.

Just as the burgher had said this, the first officer entered the hold. He touched a finger to his forehead in a kind of salute. 'Burgher Rowles, sir, there's a beggar at the gangplank asking to speak to you in private. He says he can answer all your questions.'

'Let him on board. I will see him in my cabin. Captain

Wright, continue to question the prisoner. If he doesn't give the answers we want, we'll keelhaul him after I've talked to the beggar.' The burgher went up on deck.

On deck, there was a bent-over man dressed in rags with a crutch under his left arm. He had straggly black hair and a rag tied over one eye. He used his right hand to touch his forehead. 'Good afternoon to ye master. I believe ye want to know about the thief master. For a small reward, I can answer yer questions.'

'I'm listening.'

'So is everyone else on this ship. I would speak to ye in private.'

'Follow me.' The burgher led the beggar to his cabin and closed the door. He went to his desk and took out his sword and dagger and laid them on the desk in front of him within easy reach if they were needed. He then sat. He didn't offer the beggar a seat. 'Well?'

'Ye are looking for the thief master?'

'Yes, you know that. What do you have to tell me? Hurry.'

The beggar dropped his staff, stood up straight and removed the bandage from his eye, revealing two bright blue eyes. 'Well, here I am.'

The burgher started to stand and grabbed for his sword. Before he could grab it, the thief master had a throwing knife in his hand. 'I never miss at twice this range. I suggest you sit and listen to what I have to say.'

The burgher sat.

'I firstly must apologise. The society of which I am the head does not as a rule cause trouble for the Potentate, his relatives or friends. That way he doesn't make too much effort to catch us. So, if we had known that your group contained not only Prince Azul's father-in-law, not to mention the King of Falconia and the son of the Crown Prince of Concordia, and there's even a rumour that you had the High Priest of Braidos with you, there is no way we would have accepted the commission against you.'

Burgher Rowles asked, 'Commission?'

'Yes, we were hired to kidnap the red-haired girl.'

'You mean Princess Rose of Falconia?'

The thief master shook his head. 'A princess of Falconia? That's why she is a magic user. I should slit their throats myself. I would make a deal. I will tell you the names and where to find the ones who gave us the commission and in return, you will tell the Potentate you no longer wish to pursue me or the society. He is already causing us more trouble than he has for a long time.'

Burgher Rowles thought for a short while. 'What is to stop me from agreeing and then having you seized by my men as soon as you leave this cabin?'

'You could, but then the members of the society would attack this ship which would result in not only my death but the deaths of you, the captain, all the crew and the soldiers on the dock. It is true the Potentate would cause great damage to the society but eventually there would be a new thief master and the society would go on. It would be a pretty drastic decision; I suggest you take my offer.'

'It is agreed. Who commissioned you?'

The thief master took a sheet of parchment from his rags and gave it to the burgher who read it quickly. The burgher, after reading the parchment, said, 'I will not shake hands with you but we have a bargain. I assume these people will not be warned.'

'I hope you torture them long and slowly. They cost six good men. Which reminds me, how is Ned?'

'You mean the man with one ear?'

'Yes.'

'We even threatened him with a keelhauling and he wouldn't talk.'

The thief master smiled. 'He's a good man. May I take him with me?'

'I will have him released.'

The thief master said, 'Thank you,' as he resumed his disguise.

They both left the cabin, with Burgher Rowles ordering

that the prisoner was to be brought back on deck. The burgher then ordered his release and the beggar and the man with one ear left the ship. As they left, with the burgher and the captain watching them, Burgher Rowles turned to Captain Wright and asked him, 'Did you really forget to have the hull scraped?'

The captain didn't answer but gave the burgher a withering look.

∞

Back at Castle Falconia, Sir George Potts, Colin, Colonel Blayton, Fabian Hastings, and Sir Gillian Stevens had resumed their meeting. Sir George was speaking, 'So, it's decided, Colin. Stuart, being our most powerful and available magic user, Captain Clough and myself will meet with the Duchess.'

'I mean no offence to Stuart, but I'd feel happier if we sent Jackie,' Fabian remarked. 'She is a much stronger magic user.'

Colin answered, 'True, but Stuart is quite capable and since Malgon Steelhammer has just sent us a message that he wishes to renegotiate the mine agreement with us now that Queen Charlotte is dead, we really need her at the mines together with one of the wyverns in case he tries to take what he wants by force.'

'We'll have three wyverns at the pass because we need to leave two wyvern riders here. One to patrol around Thomastown and one to look after the other wyverns.' Sir George looked at Colonel Blayton. 'What news of the Concordians?'

'They should reach Melita today and be at the pass in two more, they'll be there in time for our meeting, which means that it may be a good idea to ask Sir Matthew to join you at the meeting. The wyvern riders are riding ahead with an escort but still won't be here in time to be at the pass.'

'I've an idea.' Everyone looked at Sir Gillian Stevens. 'Why don't we ask Mythias to join you.'

'Surely you don't mean the high priest of Craidos?' Colin exclaimed. 'He would never agree. He makes a point of not getting involved in politics of any kind.'

'Precisely,' Sir Gillian continued. 'But as an independent observer he wouldn't allow any trickery from the Duchess, and he would also give an honest report of what happens.' Sir Gillian paused to let the idea sink in. 'We're not going to try anything underhanded, and he may stop the Duchess doing so.'

Colin nodded. 'I like it, excellent idea Sir Gillian. I will go and see him as soon as we finish here.'

'I knew it was a good idea when we made you the new Royal Chamberlain.' Sir George smiled. 'Well, I think that's all for now. We will get prepared to leave first thing in the morning and pick up Captain Clough and Stuart on the way. Colonel Blayton, please organise an escort.'

'Yes, Sir George.'

'Well, until the morning. Good luck with Mythias, Colin.'

'Thank you, Sir George.'

'Oh, and you'd better organise a replacement magic user at the haze.'

'If I can find one,' Colin muttered to himself.

The next morning Sir Philip and his party were up with the dawn. Even the guides didn't complain. They were both looking forward to the pleasures of Kalam that evening. Sir Philip was pleased to see that Rose was wearing her helmet even before she appeared for the quick, cold breakfast and didn't even take it off as she ate, just raising the visor. After about an hour of riding, they were no longer climbing, even though they were still in the mountains, but now they were on the downhill side. Just before noon, Lizzy rode up to Sir Philip. 'Edgar says there a lot of men hidden about two miles down the road.'

'Let me know when we get close. I want to talk to you, Liam and Roget. We'll prepare a surprise for our friend the Raj.'

'What about Rose? She's a magic user too.'

'Not a very good one yet.'

'She's better than you think.'

Sir Philip thought for a while. 'And Rose.'

It was less than ten minutes later that Lizzy told Sir Philip that the men were hiding on both sides of the road in the rocks ahead. Sir Philip called a halt and called for the magic users. 'Liam and Lizzy, when I give the order, start blasting the rocks on the right-hand side of the road. Roget and Rose the left.'

Roget said, 'Rose should take the right also. I will take care of the left. Give me five minutes to prepare and have your magic users ready.' Roget dismounted and sat cross-legged.

Sir Philip ordered the others, 'Dismount as if we're going to eat. Liam, Lizzy and Rose eat near me.'

They all dismounted and got food out of their saddlebags. Rose took her gauntlets off so she could use her hands.

After five minutes, Roget got up and put his hands on his cowl where the sides of his forehead should have been and there were numerous screams from the left-hand side of the road. 'Magic users fire,' Sir Philip shouted and each of the magic users sent three bolts of lightning in succession to blast the rocks on the right-hand side of the road and screams started to come from there too.

'Mount up and follow me,' Sir Philip shouted.

Everyone mounted except for Roget who had bowed his head and not moved. 'Lizzy, Rose, Graham, look after Roget, the rest with me,' Sir Philip ordered and the nine charged down the road.

When they arrived at the spot where the ambush was supposed to be, they found no resistance. Only men running for their lives. Liam fired an extra bolt of lightning to encourage them to keep going. Prince Rudolf complained that the magic users should have left a few for him to fight. On the right side of the road, there were many crushed bandits who had been hit by the exploding rocks. Some had survived but were injured and Sir Philip ordered that the bodies be checked for the bandit leader and the injured be put out of their misery. On the left were over thirty bodies, all dead and all with blood pouring from their ears. The body of Raj Arjun Reddy wasn't found.

While they were checking the bodies, Lizzy, Rose, Graham and Roget rode up. Sir Philip walked up to where Roget was sitting on his horse. 'Thank you, Roget. That was some display. How did the Duchess of Mayflor manage to force you and Braidos out of Mayflor? That's some power you have.'

'That is not my story to tell,' answered Roget.

'Well, if she's that strong, I hope Falconia never has to go to war with her.'

'If Queen Charlotte learns to use the Great Ring of Falconia, she would be stronger.'

Sir Philip blinked in surprise. 'Really?'

'Yes, but she must lose her compassion for her enemies.'

'That could be harder than it sounds.'

'The ring can make its wearer as strong, if not stronger than a god.'

'It didn't help Queen Katerina much,' Sir Philip remarked.

'She was not wearing it when she was destroyed,' Roget answered. 'But I have said enough.'

Sir Philip and the rest of his men remounted and started back on the road, which became quite steep and winding. About an hour before dusk, they entered Kalam.

CHAPTER TWENTY-EIGHT

Kalam was a completely walled town and they entered via the main gate which was manned by two very alert mail-clad guards. As soon as the group was spotted, one of them ran inside the gate and shortly returned with six more guards and someone who looked like an officer. He was also mail-clad but, whereas the guards all wore plain half-helms, his had a black feather. The guides handed the officer the letter they had been given by the Potentate of Danziger. They were shown to a small room which was much too cramped for the fifteen of them. While they were waiting Sir Philip noticed one of their party was missing. He asked Lizzy, 'Where's Edgar?'

Lizzy answered, 'He decided to roost somewhere

rather than be stuck inside. He'll join us when we go to the island.'

Two hours later the officer reappeared and told them all to follow him except the two guides. None of the group had removed their helmets. They were escorted by twenty guards all of whom, besides wearing swords, carried short bows at the ready with an arrow attached. They walked through narrow streets to the satrap's palace.

This palace was much smaller than the Potentate's and was built using the grey stone of the nearby mountains. The palace doors opened into a large hall lit by many candles and torches. The hall was lavishly decorated with tapestries and silks everywhere. The ceiling could not be seen because of the multicoloured silk sheets that covered it. At the end of the hall was a dais that had a solid gold throne on it. Sitting on the throne was a tall man who had black hair and a black goatee beard, his robes as multicoloured as the silks and sheets that surrounded the hall. His skin was smooth, and he wore several golden necklaces, chains and rings with gems on his fingers. In front of the dais were ten guards all carrying halberds. Behind him on the dais were twenty extremely beautiful women also dressed in multicoloured robes but what was most interesting about them was that all bar three had red hair.

The man on the throne stood and flung his arms wide.

'Welcome, rarely do we have such distinguished guests. The King of Falconia, the son of the Crown Prince of Concordia and I am told even a monk from the Abbey of the Northern Desert. I wish you all welcome.'

Sir Philip and Prince Rudolf took a step forward. Roget didn't move. Sir Philip said, 'Thank you for your welcome. We are on an urgent mission, and we would like to be on our way first thing in the morning. With your leave.'

The satrap looked offended. 'Are we not supposed to be talking face-to-face? Equal-to-equal? Take your helmets off and be civilised.'

Both Sir Philip and Prince Rudolf took their helmets off. Sir Philip addressed the satrap, 'My apologies, we have had a hard long journey and frequently on our way it has been too dangerous to take off any of our armour. It has become like a second skin.'

The satrap smiled. 'Your apologies are accepted. I understand dangerous journeys.' He looked at Prince Rudolf. 'Prince Rudolf, your hair puts many of my wives' hair to shame. It is a most beautiful red.'

'Thank you, I was born with it.'

The satrap clapped his hands and the women behind the throne split into two and moved to the front of the dais, half of whom were on either side of the throne. 'Prince Rudolf, which do you think has the best red hair?'

'I think that anyone with red hair is magnificent,' the prince answered.

The satrap gave a sly smile. 'Very diplomatic. As none of you will be able to leave before the morning, I insist you all join me in a feast. Tables, chairs and refreshments will be brought at once.' He once again clapped his hands and servants started to bring in tables and chairs. The women went to the back of the dais. The guards with bows moved to the sides of the wall.

'Please everyone, sit. We will eat shortly. King Philip and Prince Rudolf will sit either side of me.'

Sir Philip had decided he would let the satrap call him King as a king had more status than a knight. He had ordered everyone to do so also while they were with the satrap. Everyone went and took a chair at the table. Prince Rudolf and Evan placed their crossbows and bolt holders next to their chairs. Rose and Lizzy sat at the far end with Rose sitting on the opposite side of the table to her father.

The satrap stood. 'Come now, you don't expect to eat wearing your helmets. You are safe now. Honour my table and take them off.'

All the group looked at Sir Philp, who nodded. They all removed their helmets with Rose doing it last. Rose shook her head to loosen her hair and all of the others in Sir Philip's party started grinning except Sir Philip who just let his jaw drop as Rose smoothed her long, black, hair.

'Do your men always grin when they take their helmets off?' asked the satrap.

'Er, no.' Sir Philip thought quickly. 'They all thought we would be sleeping on the ground and eating rations tonight. They are pleased that they are wrong.'

The satrap shook his head and mumbled, 'Strasians.'

The meal went well. The satrap promised a boat to take them to the island the Chalice of the Dawn was on, first thing in the morning. He informed them that the island was only about two and a half miles around in a rough diameter. He warned them that almost everyone who had gone inland from the beach had never returned and the few who had, returned with their brains addled. The survivors had talked about huge, strange creatures that looked human except they didn't have heads. Their eyes, nose and mouth were in their upper chest, and they had hair growing out of where their neck should be. They were called Blemmyes. The satrap said none of his people were strong in the magic, but even that little didn't work on the island. No one had ever been able to make a map of the island, but it was thought that the Chalice of the Dawn was in the centre of the island.

Roget had told Sir Philip that he had to ask for a one foot square wooden, lead-lined box with a hinged lid and handles. Roget had also told Sir Philip to tell the satrap that they expected to take two days and that the boat should wait just offshore for them to return. Sir Philip also asked for chain mail, helmets and swords for Liam, Lizzy and the monk from the Abbey of the Northern Desert. The monk from the Abbey of the Northern Desert said he didn't need the chain mail, helmet and sword. The satrap promised all would be ready for the morning and ordered one of his men to go and get it organised.

The satrap then told them that rooms had been prepared for King Philip and Prince Rudolf and a barracks with eleven beds had been prepared for the rest of the party. Sir Philip told the satrap that they would all sleep together and two of his men would sleep on the floor. 'It'll be better than sleeping on the ground which has been our beds for the last two weeks.'

When they got to the barracks, Sir Philip told Captain Lipson to organise a watch so two people would stay awake at a time and then get a bed. He then ordered Rose to come and speak to him.

'What were you playing at, not telling me you'd changed your hair and how did you do it?'

Lizzy answered for Rose, 'We used black saddle polish and some magic, we decided not to mention it in case it didn't work.'

Chapter Twenty-eight

'Rose can answer for herself,' Sir Philip snarled.

Rose stepped forward. 'I'm not a child anymore. You should treat me as an adult, like the rest of our group.'

'I'm treating you as a subordinate. Which is what you are, and you should obey orders. Even Prince Rudolf obeys orders without grumbling.'

'Except when it comes to carrots.' The prince smiled.

The look that Sir Philip gave the prince would not have shamed Medusa.

In a small room under the palace were the satrap, the captain of his guards, two burly guards and a man tied to a chair. The satrap hit the man tied to the chair in the face. 'You lied. The only person there with red hair was Prince Rudolf. There was one girl with dark brown hair and a younger one with long black hair.'

'She must have dyed it when they learnt you liked redheads. Why would I come here and lie to you when I know what would happen if I did?'

The satrap looked down at Raj Arjun Reddy. 'You're right. I believe you. Even you are not that stupid.'

'Would you like me to take some men and grab the redhead and kill the others?' the captain of the guard asked.

The satrap stroked his beard. 'No, I think this group may have a chance to procure the Chalice. The monk intrigues me. Why would a group of warriors bring a monk with them? They have something planned for when they get to the island. Their armour is better than anyone else who has gone there had. I think we should let them go and get the Chalice and then we'll grab it and the girl when they get back.'

'But the girl could be killed.'

'The Chalice is much more important than one girl. If she gets killed,' the satrap shrugged, 'so be it. I have decided.'

Raj Arjun Reddy looked up. 'What about me?'

'Yes, what about you?' The satrap thought for a second and turned to his captain. 'Kill him slowly and painfully.'

Raj Arjun Reddy screamed. 'No, you can't do that. You promised me a reward.'

The satrap fingered his beard for a few seconds and then put his hand to his chest and gave a little bow. 'You are right. I apologise. I'm a man of my word. Make it quick.' He turned to leave.

CHAPTER TWENTY-NINE

The same day Sir Philip arrived at Kalam, in Danziger Burgher Rowles, Prince Azul and twenty of his men smashed in the door of a house a quarter of a mile from the docks. They found five men in the house, three of whom were obviously guards for the other two. None of the five were handled gently. The three guards were locked in a room that looked like it had been used as a prison in the past. The other two who were obviously brothers as they both had the same green eyes, large nose and brown hair and looked much alike, were tied to chairs in the main living room of the house.

The prince told Burgher Rowles that he would allow the burgher to question the prisoners as it was his friend they tried to have kidnapped, but if any violence was needed to leave it to his men as they were, "Bigger and stronger than you".

'Why did you commission the thief master to kidnap Princess Rose of Falconia?' the burgher asked.

The two prisoners looked aghast and then looked at each other. One groaned. 'That's why all this trouble has been taken.' He shook his head. 'What do you offer us to talk?'

Burgher Rowles looked at the prince, who smiled. 'I offer you and your men a quick death rather than a slow and painful one. There are men who have been in constant pain in my father's torture chambers for over two months.'

The prisoners looked frightened at this comment. The same one who had spoken before asked, 'Could you not exile us instead? We can give you a lot of information, not just about the kidnap attempt, but about a lot of the crime that takes place in Danziger.'

The prince spent several minutes in thought while everyone was silent. 'Agreed, but you both must be punished. I propose two hundred lashes then you will be exiled. Provided of course that your information is useful.'

'It is, I promise you. But make it one hundred lashes.'

'One fifty. No less. You will tell us now about the kidnap attempt and then we'll take you to the palace for the extra information.'

'We agree, the kidnap attempt was made on behalf of the Satrap of Kalam.'

Burgher Rowles and Prince Azul gave each other an extremely concerned look. The burgher said, 'But that's where Sir Philip has taken his daughter. We must do something.'

The prince answered, 'I will have my personal bodyguard made ready to ride at once, once these men have been taken to the palace. Your daughter will also go there as my home will be unprotected. I have the fifty best fighters on the islands and the best horses. We should be there in less than two days.'

'I'm coming too,' Burgher Rowles insisted.

The prince shook the burgher's forearm. 'You are very welcome.'

The same morning almost half a world away at Castle Falconia, the royal carriage was being made ready. The carriage was fully enclosed except for six windows, of which two were in the doors, and a flap so the inhabitants could communicate with the driver. It was made mainly from dark hardwood grown in the Great Forest. The dark wood was beautifully, ornately carved with curved patterns all over except for the roof and floor. The roof was flat but had rails all around it which enabled it to carry luggage. All the windows had thick white curtains attached, which at the moment were tied back. It was big enough for six normal-sized passengers and two on the driver's seat and it was drawn by six horses.

There were three men boarding the carriage and one of them looked like he could fill the carriage all by himself. He was six foot nine inches tall, very heavily built, with thick black hair, a very thick, long, black beard, and had dark eyes without any colour except for the whites. He wore a white monk's habit and cowl but unlike his counterpart, Roget, he wore his cowl down. This was Mythias, High Priest of Craidos the God of Order. He climbed the steps to enter the carriage and had a short problem entering the door and when he did, he flopped down on one side of the carriage's well-upholstered, brown leather seats. Sir George Potts and Colin then entered the carriage, having tied their horses to the back of it. They managed to squeeze in opposite Mythias on either side of his meaty legs, facing the front of the carriage. The inside of the coach was decorated with red silk cloth, and on the doors were holders for wine and water together with glasses.

'I hope you don't mind taking the carriage. I always think it's unfair on the horse that has to carry my weight.' Considering the size of him, Mythias's voice was a high falsetto.

'Not at all,' answered Sir George. 'We're just happy that you agreed to be an independent observer to our talks with the Duchess of Mayflor.' While he was saying this he signalled out of the window for the driver and his companion to start moving. They were being escorted by thirty soldiers and two magic users. One of the magic users was going to swap with Stuart when they reached the blockage at the haze. There was also a wyvern flying above them to watch for any hazards.

'That is, of course, all you wanted me for.' Mythias smiled.

Sir George answered, 'Of course, we wanted an irreproachable person to witness what will happen in our talks with the Duchess.'

'Naturally.' The high priest of Craidos smiled. 'And who could be more irreproachable than myself?'

'Naturally,' Sir George and Colin answered in unison.

'You know that I know your secret.'

'What secret would that be?' asked Sir George.

Mythias, still smiling, said, 'True, you have many, but Craidos watches.'

Colin asked, 'More importantly, have the gods told the Duchess any of our secrets?'

'Since the Duchess banished Braidos her information has been somewhat limited. Atlitica, the God of the Mountains doesn't really want anything to do with her, but has to talk to her occasionally, so the only god she can really call on is Callica the god of the Eastern Plains, which is the land the Seven Duchies is on. Callica is only a minor god and therefore cannot inform the Duchess of what is happening in most of the world or even Strasia.'

'Well, that's good news,' Sir George replied. 'We were worried that the Duchess would know too much of our plans.'

'I have been given permission by Craidos to give you more good news.'

Both Sir George and Colin moved forward on their seats.

'Sir Philip's party are about to embark on the most dangerous part of their journey. At this moment they have landed on the island that contains the Chalice of the Dawn. They have had only one serious casualty and he is still able to function. Craidos is not happy that Roget is with them but understands their mission can only be completed with him. I can tell you no more.'

Colin leaned forward. 'I have a question.'

Chapter Twenty-nine

Mythias waved his hand as if to say, what.

'Why was Rose chosen to be Craidos's representative to get the Chalice of the Dawn?'

'Does it matter? The gods do strange things.'

'Yes, I would like to know.'

'I cannot tell you the answer to that question. One day you may find out. And now I think I shall go to sleep. It is a long journey.' Mythias lifted his cowl over his head and soon began to snore.

Sir George took a flagon of wine and two glasses from the compartment on the door. He gave a glass of wine to Colin and kept one for himself. 'Here's to lots of luck for Sir Philip and his company. It sounds like they're going to need it.' Both Sir George and Colin emptied their glasses. 'Now, I'm going to join Mythias and I suggest you do also.'

Both Sir George and Colin slept.

At Kalam in the morning, Sir Philip and his group didn't see the satrap but were escorted to the harbour by the satrap's captain of the guard and six of his men. The equipment, food and water Sir Philip had asked for was on the dock. The satrap had also included a sheaf of spears for each of Sir Philip's group. Roget surprised everyone by accepting his sheaf. Roget then examined the wooden box. 'The lead is only a quarter of an inch thick and the box weights just under one hundred pounds.'

'That will make it easy to carry on one of my men's backs,' Sir Philip told him.

'I would rather it weighed more than twice as much. It would make us safer.'

'Why?' Sir Philip asked.

'You will find out soon enough,' was Roget's reply.

The captain of the skiff that was to take them to the island saw Edgar on Lizzy's shoulder and immediately began to object and wave his hands. 'The bird is unlucky; it cannot come aboard.'

Edgar took off from Lizzy's shoulder and started to fly the five miles to the island. Lizzy spoke to Sir Philip, 'Edgar will fly the five miles easily and will wait for us on the island.'

Sir Philip answered, 'Ask him to scout around and warn us of any strange or hostile creatures.'

'He was going to do that anyway.'

'Good bird that,' Sir Philip replied.

Sir Philip turned to Roget. 'We should leave Graham behind. If we have to run there's no way he can keep up.'

'There must be the thirteen of us that land on the island.'

Sir Philip shook his head and went to make sure everyone was organised as they boarded the one-masted sailing ship. Besides Sir Philip's group was the captain and four crew. The captain, an old, bald, craggy-skinned man with most of his teeth missing, told them it would take about two hours to sail to the island. On the way, on either side of the strait they were sailing across, there were rocks that seemed to stretch from the edge of the island they were sailing to and the island they had just left. The captain told Sir Philip that there were large sea creatures on the other side of both sets of rocks and the rocks prevented them from getting into the strait. Smaller fish could get in and in fact, the strait was an extremely good place for fishing.

As they approached the island, they could see a wide path that made its way between the trees that seemed to completely surround the island. Sir Philip remarked to Prince Rudolf, 'Looks like there's only the one way in.'

'Not unless we want to chop our way through all those trees. I can't see us doing that quietly.'

Sir Philip called Lizzy over. 'Has Edgar seen anything?'

'The path leads to the centre of the island where there is a hill with a funny building on top. The trees form a border all around the island and after that it's mainly grassland with some large clumps of trees here and there.

Just past the first ring of trees there are about six times ten funny men without heads waiting. Some have long pointy sticks but most have large clumps of wood. There are more of them around the island. There is a large village near the hill about two hundred paces from this path. That's all Edgar told me.'

'Remind me to buy Edgar several sacks of his favourite seeds. He deserves it,' Sir Philip told Lizzy.

Just before they reached the island, Prince Rudolf had an idea. He paid the captain two silver pieces for a large container of lantern oil and a large piece of old sailcloth.

Sir Philip asked the prince why. 'We may need torches before this is over. Don't forget Roget said we may not get back here until tomorrow.'

The captain sailed his boat up close to the beach which left it in about two feet of water. The thirteen disembarked onto the beach and the boat's crew pushed it back into deeper water. The captain shouted as the boat left, 'We'll be here until tomorrow dusk. Then we leave.'

Roget shouted back, 'Wait one more day if necessary and there will be gold for each one of you.'

'One more day it is then, but offshore.'

'Agreed,' shouted Roget.

Sir Philip approached Roget. 'I thought you said we'd be back within two days.'

'We should. But it doesn't harm to have an extra day in case of emergencies. Besides, it's your gold, not mine.'

Sir Philip laughed. Prince Rudolf started to get most members of the group making torches using wood from the few dead trees around the beach. Three of Captain Lipson's men stood guard. Edgar had returned to Lizzy's shoulder and Sir Philip bowed to him. 'You are undoubtably the best scout I have ever had.'

Edgar gave a chirp and bowed back.

Prince Rudolf ordered one of the torches lit and asked Lizzy to carry it. 'But there's still plenty of daylight,' Sir Philip remarked.

'We do not know what will happen once we get through these trees. I'd rather have one lit now than have to try to light one if we suddenly had to.'

Sir Philip shrugged. He called the group together. 'Edgar has informed us that there is a mass of those headless things waiting for us beyond the trees. We will move in a group with Roget, Liam and Lizzy in the middle as they have the worst or no armour. Lizzy will carry the torch. Rose and one of Captain Lipson's men will be our rearguard and have the box tied to his back. Graham will wait for us on the beach.'

Graham objected. 'I've kept up with you all this far. I'm not going to miss the ending.'

'If that's what you want. You can help with the rearguard. Edgar will also watch our rear after checking on the things on the other side of the trees. Prince Rudolf and Evan will be on our flanks with loaded crossbows. Captain Lipson and I will be in front with Captain Lipson's men on either side of us. Does everyone understand?'

There were nods and murmurs of, 'Yes, sir.'

'Lizzy, if Edgar sees anything different inform me immediately.'

'Yes, Sir Philip.'

Rose spoke up. 'We also have Jason and Great Wing. They should be able to help us get through the Blemmyes.'

Sir Philip looked at his daughter. 'Jason and Great Wing are creatures of magic. I don't think they'll be able to appear.'

Rose looked downcast. 'They would have been a great asset.'

'Yes,' answered her father. 'Now we go. Good luck everybody.'

The entire group cheered him and then moved off through the trees. They had gone less than twenty yards when Lizzy tapped Sir Philip on the shoulder. 'There are several of the funny men in the trees on either side of us.'

'Thank you,' Sir Philip answered. 'Liam, Roget, do you still have magic? If so, blast the trees.'

The bolts that Liam and Roget fired were much weaker than their normal bolts. Even so they were enough to leave several Blemmyes dead and have the few that were left attack the group with clubs. Both Prince Rudolf and Evan fired a bolt at two of them leaving only four which were quickly dispatched by Captain Lipson's men.

'Well, that was easy,' one of Captain Lipson's men said.

'There's a lot more beyond the trees,' Sir Philip told him. 'It's going to get a lot harder.'

Rose called a halt. She asked for a scrap of sailcloth. She lifted her visor and wiped a mass of black saddle polish off her face. 'The magic isn't holding the dye anymore,' she complained, which brought a smile to her father's face.

'Edgar says the number beyond the trees has more than doubled,' Lizzy told the group.

'Everyone get a spear ready. They've longer range than swords,' was Sir Philip's order, 'but be ready to throw one. Everyone wearing plate armour, except Rose and Graham, move to the front in a V formation.'

They got near to the end of the path that was still in the trees. 'Once we start moving out there, we keep moving until we get to the building in the centre of the island. Don't stop for anything. If you fall, I'm sorry.'

They emerged from the trees to find a semi-circle

of the strange eight foot tall creatures without heads. They were naked from the waist up. Where their chests should have been were their faces. Most were not holding weapons but had their hands at their mouths. There was a sudden loud noise of dozens of darts hitting plate mail. None penetrated.

'They're trying to use blowpipes. Throw spears and charge,' Sir Philip shouted.

The group, except for Roget and Lizzy who was carrying the lit torch, threw their spears at the group in front of them. Most hit their targets and nine Blemmyes fell. Everyone drew the swords and charged the now weakened section in the centre. Most of the Blemmyes tried blowing another dart and only a few picked up the clubs and spears at their feet. Sir Philip's men went through them like a knife through butter, slashing the Blemmyes unmercifully, leaving dead and wounded, bleeding Blemmyes everywhere.

'Keep running, we'll try to outdistance them,' was Sir Philip's new order. Most of the Blemmyes, now realising that their blow darts weren't working, picked up other weapons and started to chase them. Graham started to fall behind and was tripped by a Blemmyes's spear. Most of the Blemmyes stopped and picked up large rocks which they threw down at Graham slowly smashing his armour with him in it. Rose stopped and started to go back to help Graham and was about to be grabbed by two Blemmyes when Roget, using his spear as a staff, leapt and used both feet to kick one of the Blemmyes in the chest where its nose was and then used the spear to slash down the other's *face*. 'Keep running you fool. If you die then this is all for nothing.'

Rose started running with Roget following her. They could now see the small hill with what looked like a round temple on top of it. The building was made from what looked like white marble and had steps leading up to it from the path. It had an open doorway flanked by white columns. Unfortunately, they could also see the village which had dozens more of the strange creatures running from it to get between them and the temple. They succeeded and one of Captain Lipson's men was downed by a club to the head and suffered the same fate as Graham. The ones chasing them also caught up as running even in the lighter, stronger armour slowed them down. 'Spears everyone,' Sir Philip ordered. 'Form a circle.'

Prince Rudolf called to his fellow wyvern rider, 'Evan, flash bolt, half-power, you take the rear. Lizzy your torch please.'

Lizzy lit the two bolts which were then fired into the air so that they came down over the Blemmyes.

They exploded, sending explosive sparks amongst the Blemmyes causing serious burns to many of them and leaving them in confusion. 'One more Evan, both to the front,' Prince Rudolf shouted.

Sir Philip added, 'As soon as the bolts come down, throw spears and run the rest of the way to the temple.'

This time as the flash bolts exploded the Blemmyes began to scatter. The spear-throwing killed less this time as the enemy was no longer bunched up and the group managed to cut their way through the few that were still in front of them. They made it to the steps, climbed them and entered the temple. Some of the Blemmyes followed them cautiously to near the bottom of the steps and started to use their primary weapon which were the blowpipes. Unfortunately, not all of the group was wearing plate armour and Liam was hit in the back by one of the darts. He collapsed immediately and was dragged into the temple. Fortunately, the temple opening was small, and Sir Philip set three men to guard it while they took care of Liam.

Roget took the dart out of Liam's back and sniffed it. 'Poisoned. He will not live long.'

Lizzy held Liam as he spasmed and his eyes glazed over. 'I can see Jackie, she's holding her hands out to me. I'm coming Jackie, I'm coming.' And with that final comment, he died.

The survivors looked around the room. It was made completely from white marble and had a domed roof which was split by a marble wall. There was not a speck of dust anywhere. In the marble wall was a pair of tall golden doors that stretched almost to the roof. One of the guards at the door shouted to Sir Philip, 'We could be safe while we're in here. None of those things are coming within ten feet of the steps, but there are more coming from the village.'

'Thank you, tell me if anything changes,' Sir Philip answered. 'Prince Rudolf, Roget, let's look behind those doors.'

The three of them walked to the doors watched by everyone except those watching the opening to the temple. There were handles in the doors. Both Sir Philip and Prince Rudolf grabbed one each and pulled. They opened silently and the three entered. The room finished the dome that was on the other side but instead of being white marble everything inside was golden. There was a long narrow slit low down along the entire length of the outside wall and in the room's centre was a golden plinth, on top of which was the golden Chalice of the Dawn.

The Chalice looked solid gold and was about nine inches tall, which included a five-inch stem and four inches in diameter. It had two golden handles of about three inches. At its front was a dawning sun with its rays surrounding the entire Chalice.

Sir Philip shouted to Roget who had followed them into the room. 'Go and get Rose. Grab the Chalice and then we'll fight our way out of here.'

Roget answered, 'We cannot. We can only take the Chalice at dawn.'

Sir Philip sighed. 'I should have known.'

Chapter Thirty

The next morning a large number of Mayflorian troops appeared at the pass. They halted about half a mile from the wall that defended the pass. At the Duchies Pass Fort everyone who could watched as a large cloth gazebo with four poles floated towards the gate in the wall from amongst the Mayflorian troops. Under it strode a woman with silver hair wearing a plain black dress. Behind her floated a well-padded black chair. The gazebo and chair settled to the ground just under one hundred yards from the gate and the woman sat down and waited.

'She's showing off,' Colin remarked to Sir George who, together with Captain Clough, Stuart, Mythias and Sir Matthew, were watching from the wall's ramparts.

Sir Matthew was three inches taller than his younger brother, but like him had long blond hair and blue eyes. Unlike him, Matthew was clean-shaven.

'Well, I guess we'll have to carry our own chairs,' muttered Sir George. 'Let's go.'

Two minutes later the gates in the wall opened and the six men emerged. Five of them were carrying chairs. Mythias had decided to show-off also and his floated behind him. They reached the gazebo and they all took seats opposite the woman in its shade, except for Mythias who had his chair place itself at the side halfway between the woman and the men.

The tall woman, about six foot two inches, who had smooth pale skin and looked strikingly handsome despite what must have been a great age, looked at each of the six with her blue eyes, hooded under her eyelids. She wore no jewellery except for a golden clasp on her right wrist, with a large, round, azure stone embedded in it. She started counting using her right forefinger to point. 'One, two, three, four, five and the exulted High Priest of Craidos. I must inspire great fear in you.'

Mythias answered, 'Your Grace, I am only here as an observer and to make sure of fairness.'

The Duchess of Mayflor nodded to Mythias. 'Thank you, Your Eminence, an independent witness could be quite useful. Now let's see …' She looked at the centre of the group. 'You are Sir George Potts, a useless, retired meddler.' She then looked at Colin on Sir George's right. 'You are Colin, someone who would like to be a magic user but doesn't have the talent.' She then looked at Sir Matthew on Sir George's left. 'Hmm, you are harder. You look a little like the late King Philip before he grew his beard. Would you be his brother, Sir Matthew Concord, leading that pathetic rabble of troops who have just arrived?'

Sir Matthew didn't answer but gave the Duchess a nasty look.

'The two pathetic creatures sitting at either end of your group have no relevance.'

Neither Stuart nor Captain Clough moved or gave any indication they had heard.

Sir George gave a small cough. 'There is no late King Philip. He is alive and well. But enough of this. We want you to give us Sir Peter Mayflor, who is to be charged with regicide, tried and beheaded.'

The Duchess gave Sir George an angry look. 'I am Your Grace, especially to lesser mortals such as you. I can honestly say that I have no idea where he is right now, nor know how to get in touch with him. Although, I personally cannot blame him for wanting to save his cousin from the torture you are putting her through. But forgetting him,

I hate to have to tell you this. It makes me sad,' a tear fell from her left eye, 'to have to inform you that King Philip, Prince Rudolf, Princess Rose and all the others except for Roget, the High Priest of Braidos who only just escaped with his life, died on the island of the Chalice of the Dawn. I swear this by er … whoever our god is now.' She looked at Mythias who mouthed, "Callica." 'By Callica. They died bravely fighting the Blemmyes but there were just too many of them.' She looked at Mythias. 'Roget survived, just, which is why you haven't noticed his demise.'

The five men looked shocked. 'My bother dead, I can't believe it,' Sir Matthew sobbed.

The Duchess also looked sad. 'I know, but I can tell you he died bravely. But with both Queen Charlotte and King Philip dead, also, Rose. And with Stephen and Julie in a state of coma from which they will never recover, now that the Chalice of the Dawn is lost, you, Sir George, have already renounced your claim to the throne thirty years ago.' Sir George nodded sadly. 'This means there is only one candidate for the throne of Falconia. Princess Scarlett!' The Duchess added the last words with a note of triumph in her voice.

Colin was shaking his head. 'This is hard to take in. But there is a problem. Princess Scarlett doesn't have a body.'

'I have a body prepared in Mayflor for Princess Scarlett. Just bring me the portrait and I will return you a Queen.'

The five men started to nod in agreement. Mythias stood and waved his arms in a circle in front of his face. 'This has gone far enough. Using mesmerism on these men is not what I or Craidos would call fair and in the interests of fairness you must stop at once.'

'Why you,' the Duchess, standing, snarled. She started to move her arm back as if to fire a lightning bolt.

'You would risk the wrath of Craidos, whom I assure you is watching. You will die too,' Mythias warned.

The Duchess sat. The five men were shaking their heads. Colin spoke first, 'We almost agreed to give her Falconia.'

'So, that's how you got my nephew, King Edmond to marry your daughter Katerina. I knew it must have been magic.' Sir George gave the Duchess a hateful look.

'This is not over yet,' the Duchess spoke calmly. 'You may be interested to know, now that Queen Charlotte is gone, Malgon Steelhammer is right now at the mines demanding that all the mines to the east be conceded to him immediately or he will take them by force. I am sure you are thinking that your wyverns will stop him but the northern tribes in Concordia are starting to cause trouble again and King Regis is, as we speak, sending a message asking for at least three of his wyverns back. Balor Hardfall and Iggord are collecting a force of dwarfs, goblins, slime tunnellers, renegade humans, werewolves and whatever other creatures they can get for an attack on Thomastown. And here I am with my army, ready to smash your puny wall. Mythias, isn't it true that you and Craidos always remain neutral in wars?'

Mythias nodded. 'We will help neither side.'

The Duchess gave the five men a smirk.

Colin stood. 'There is one more thing.' Everyone looked at him. 'Since your grandson, Sir Peter, killed Queen Charlotte I've been looking for revenge. Not so much as against him, but how to kill Scarlett.'

'You wouldn't dare and you're not able to,' scowled the Duchess.

'That was true,' Colin continued. 'But we are fortunate that your daughter had, and it still is maybe the best, library on magic on the continent. I wouldn't be surprised if it wasn't better than your own.' He nodded towards the Duchess. 'As you know, I have no magic as such, but I am a master of crystals. Your daughter's library has an amazing section on crystals which I don't imagine she used very much. However, there are some brilliant books in that section. I discovered how to make a crystal that can absorb a person's essence such as the one now trapped in the portrait, Scarlett. It can drag the essence out of the portrait and into itself, trapping the essence until released. Once the essence is in the crystal, the crystal itself can be smashed into many pieces and the essence smashed with it, unable to be released until all the pieces are put together again. I hope the crystal will have finished growing within the next forty-eight hours, after which I will trap Scarlett inside of it, smash it and have the wyvern riders drop the pieces all over Strasia. In the Infinity Mountains, in the Great Forest, in the Southern Desert and even some in the Eastern Ocean. You'll never be able to find all the parts.'

'You dare and I will torture you to the end of time,' was the Duchess's answer.

Mythias, standing, raised his hands. 'May I make a suggestion?'

Everyone now looked at him. 'While it is true that Craidos and I remain neutral in wars, there is an exemption. It is when both parties have sworn by Craidos that they will or will not do something and then do it. I suggest that the Duchess swear to take her army away and not return for two months and Colin promise not to put Scarlett in a crystal. Can we agree?'

'One month,' scowled the Duchess.

'Six weeks,' answered Colin.

Mythias smiled. 'So, it's agreed. Five weeks. If either of you break the agreement you will have Craidos to contend with. Now swear by Craidos.'

Colin already standing put his hand over his heart. 'I swear by Craidos I will not put the essence of Princess Scarlett into a crystal for at least five weeks.'

The Duchess then stood and put her hand over her heart. 'I swear by Craidos that I will take my army back to Mayflor and will not attack Falconia for at least five weeks.'

A clap of thunder split the air. Mythias told the assembly, 'Craidos has heard and will punish whoever breaks this promise made in his name.'

The Duchess announced, 'This meeting is over.' And started to walk back towards her men, leaving the gazebo and her chair behind.

As the others started to walk towards the gate, also leaving their chairs, Sir George suddenly stopped and spoke privately and quietly to Colin, 'We didn't get Sir Peter.'

Colin answered just as quietly, 'I think Sir Peter will have to wait for another time.'

'And why didn't you tell me you had a crystal that could trap Scarlett's essence.'

'I said I hoped to have it ready within forty-eight hours,

the way it's going I'm going to hope to have it ready within forty-eight years.'

Sir George laughed.

It was still late evening on the island of the Chalice of the Dawn. During the rest of the previous day and the night, the Blemmyes had not approached within ten feet of the steps to the temple. There were a lot more of them now though and their mass stretched for two hundred yards down the path that led back to the beach. Even though they had not attacked there was the steady ping of blow darts wasting themselves against the guards' Concordian plate armour and the occasional spear thrown. The spears were collected by the defenders as they would be useful to throw back when they tried to escape.

Sir Philip had asked Lizzy to get Edgar to scout the village, especially the extra-large, thatched building in the centre. Edgar had reported back that most of the buildings were just the wooden huts that the Blemmyes lived in. The large building had a large wooden thingy in it. There were headless men around it, bowing and kneeling to it. Sir Philip, Prince Rudolf and Roget discussed the building.

'If it is their temple, and it sounds like it is, if we can set it on fire, they may leave to save it,' Roget told the other two.

'Will your exploding bolts do the job?' asked Sir Philip of Prince Rudolf.

'An ordinary bolt might, and I say *might*, just reach the building, but the exploding ones are heavier than ordinary bolts and there is no chance of one reaching it,' was his reply. 'Evan and I have only three exploding bolts left which I don't think will be enough to shift all that mass out front.'

'In the morning when Rose and I put the Chalice of the Dawn in the box a little of our magic will return as it is the Chalice that prevents magic from working on the island. Unfortunately, the box has only a quarter of an inch of lead in it so it will still make our magic much weaker,' Roget told them.

'Why is that?' asked Sir Philip.

'The Chalice prevents all normal magic from working for up to a mile in diameter. Lead stops its power, but it must be much thicker than a quarter of an inch to prevent it completely,' replied Roget.

'So, what's our plan for the morning?' asked Sir Philip.

They were all silent for several minutes.

Prince Rudolf called Lizzy over, 'How much weight can Edgar carry?'

'I'm not sure. He can pick up rocks and use them to drop on possible prey.'

'Evan come here,' Prince Rudolf ordered. Evan came over. 'How much of that lantern oil do we have left and how much does the container weigh?'

'Not very much, sir, and the pottery container is quite heavy.'

'Get me a small water pouch.' Evan did so. The pouch would hold about a pint of water and was made of leather and had a handle. The prince emptied the pouch by drinking the contents. He then turned it with the open top towards the ground in order for any leftover dregs to dry out. 'If we filled this with lantern oil and used a scrap of burning sailcloth in the opening, held there by some of the saddle polish that's still in Rose's hair, could Edgar drop it on the big building in the village?' Prince Rudolf asked Lizzy.

Lizzy was quiet for a few minutes then laughed. 'Edgar wants to know if the prince is thinking of developing a taste for roast raven?'

The prince also laughed. 'We could tie some rope to the handle to keep the fire away from Edgar. But could he fly it to the building?'

'Edgar will try.'

'Good, hopefully, a fire in their temple will draw

most of those creatures away and we'll just have to fight our way through any that stay. Evan and I will have an explosive bolt ready to fire as we go. A volley of spears to start would help and if our magic users are able to use magic again, we should succeed.' The prince couldn't hide his enthusiasm.

'Were you listening when I said the thickness of the lead will not be enough to give us most of our magic back?' asked Roget.

'But you'll have some,' Sir Philip asked.

'Blemmyes have only rudimentary brains. Even if I had all my power, I would not be able to do to them what I did to the bandits. I fear that Lizzy, Rose and I will only be able to fire weak lightning bolts.'

'Well, that's better than nothing, I suggest we sleep. Captain Lipson, organise a strong watch. Roget and Rose are to be excused and I'll take the one before dawn. Goodnight, everyone.'

Sir Philip watched the false dawn as he had Evan wake everyone up. The lead-lined box had been placed in front of the plinth ready to receive the Chalice of the Dawn. The mass of Blemmyes out the front looked like they had not moved at all during the night, but the good news was none had approached the temple. Roget and Rose moved towards the golden doors. Rose was not wearing her helmet or her gauntlets and even now Sir Philip could not stop himself from smiling when he saw his daughters black-streaked red hair.

'Rose and I must enter the room by ourselves,' Roget told them. 'When we have the Chalice boxed, we will come out.'

Sir Philip had learnt not to argue and stood silently as the two entered the room and closed the doors. He turned to Prince Rudolf. 'Get the fire container ready.' Prince Rudolf picked up the materials. 'How's Edgar this morning?'

'A little nervous but determined to succeed,' Lizzy answered for Edgar.

'Everyone get ready to move on my order.' Then they waited.

In the golden room, Roget and Rose stood on either side of the Chalice of the Dawn. 'As soon as the sun's rays touch the Chalice take one of the handles with one hand and put it in the box. I will have the other handle. Prepare to be dazzled,' Roget told Rose.

Rays of light started to enter the room through the long gap near the bottom of the outside wall. They bounced off the golden walls. Then they started to move near the plinth. When one finally reached the Chalice, the Chalice burst into a bright light, dazzling both Roget and Rose. 'Into the box quickly,' shouted Roget and both he and Rose grabbed a handle and lowered the Chalice into the lead-lined box, which Roget slammed shut.

'Let's get out of here. Grab one of the handles.' Rose did so with Roget grabbing the other one. The original box weighed just under a hundred pounds but now it weighed almost one hundred and fifty pounds. They pushed the golden doors open and Roget informed the group, 'We've got it.'

One of the guards watching the door shouted, 'That must be why they're becoming agitated.'

It was true, the Blemmyes that had been almost motionless through the night and morning were starting to move about, pointing at the temple. Darts and spears started to be blown and thrown at the temple opening.

'Well, it's now up to Edgar. I hope he can save us. Light the sailcloth,' ordered Sir Philip.

The sailcloth plug was lit and Edgar, with the length of rope that was tied to the handle of the water pouch now filled with lantern oil in his claws, took off through the temple opening. Everyone watched the bird as it flew towards the village except Captain Lipson, Roget and Rose who were tying the box containing the Chalice of the Dawn to Captain Lipson's back. Several Blemmyes either blew darts or threw spears at Edgar but none hit him. The fire from the plug was stronger than any of the group expected and started to burn the rope Edgar was holding. Everyone held their breath as Edgar got closer to the Blemmyes's temple and a number of the creatures started to run towards it. Edgar finally landed on the thatched roof of the building and let go of the rope. The water pouch immediately started to slide off the roof. Edgar seeing this grabbed the burning rope in his beak and started to pull the pouch back up. The plug came loose and the oil in the pouch poured out onto the burning rope. There was a loud whoosh that could even be heard by Sir Philip's group as the lantern oil began to burn. Edgar was not to be seen.

Lizzy screamed. 'I can't feel Edgar!'

The fire on the thatch on the Blemmyes temple started to spread even to other buildings. Most of the creatures started to run towards the village. Sir Philip gave them time to move away. There were now less than a quarter of the Blemmyes that were there before. 'Now charge,' shouted Sir Philip and the group poured out of the temple. Everyone including Roget threw spears at the remaining Blemmyes. Prince Rudolf fired an exploding bolt which burnt a significant number as well, leaving him and Evan one more exploding bolt each plus their normal ones.

Sir Philip and Captain Lipson led the charge. 'I'd rather fight the snake,' quipped the captain which brought a smile to Sir Philip's face.

'I'll try to arrange it when we get back, Captain. I wish I had my battleaxe.'

'Me too,' was the captain's reply.

The remaining Blemmyes had started to scatter as more of them died from the almost berserker attack from all of the group, especially Sir Philip and Captain Lipson. Some, but not many, stopped running towards the village to fight the fires and turned back to chase Sir Philip's party. Prince Rudolf called to Evan and pointed at them. Evan fired his last exploding bolt at the returning group and the burnt survivors stopped chasing them. The guard that was acting as the group's rearguard was brought down by several Blemmyes, and they crushed him to death with rocks. Three of the Blemmyes, noting that Roget had no armour, tried to cut him off from the rest of the group. The three all had spears and stabbed them at him. Roget used his spear to knock one aside and stabbed the Blemmyes instead. The other two were about to stab Roget when Sir Philip knocked their spears aside with his sword and slashed their strange faces with his backstroke, leaving their faces covered in blood. Both Blemmyes fell holding their bloodied faces. Sir Philip and Roget continued running, with Sir Philip running back to the vanguard.

A final group of Blemmyes stood across the path in front of the trees that led to the beach. Prince Rudolf fired the last exploding bolt at them and, as they burnt, Sir Philip and Captain Lipson hit them. The Blemmyes went down like ninepins and started to run away from the band. Evan fired a last normal bolt at them as the Blemmyes ran. They then entered the trees and started to slow down. Sir Philip shouted, 'We're almost there, keep going,' as several Blemmyes appeared from the trees. Most were immediately cut down, but Evan fell and was about to have a rock smashed down on him when Lizzy tried to fire a lightning bolt at his attacker. The bolt was weak, but it was enough to cause the Blemmyes' strike that would have hit his head to hit his shoulder instead. Prince Rudolf finished the Blemmyes with his sword. Roget and the prince lifted Evan, with Roget grabbing his crossbow, and helped Evan to join the others on the beach.

The boat was already heading towards the beach to

pick up the survivors. The boat beached and the nine climbed on board. Roget spoke to Sir Philip, 'Thank you for saving my life.'

'Forget it. It's what comrades do.' Sir Philip smiled.

The four crew pushed the boat back into the sea as several Blemmyes appeared at the edge of the trees but did not advance onto the beach. They could see beyond the trees smoke billowing from where the village was burning.

From that direction a bird, flying quite erratically, headed towards the boat. It slowly caught up and landed in Lizzy's lap. It was badly burnt, and Rose told Lizzy that she had some of her mother's balm in her pouch to help Edgar.

The captain of the boat started to shout. 'No, no, the bird is unlucky.'

Sir Philip flipped him a gold coin. The captain of the boat gave an almost toothless smile. 'What a pretty bird.'

CHAPTER THIRTY-ONE

t was decided for everyone who had met with the Duchess to head back to Castle Falconia at once, except for Sir Matthew, who would ride there with his men. It had also been decided that just over twelve hundred men all of whom had been there already should stay at the Duchies Pass Fort and guard the wall. Not far away were three hundred men at Fort Philip and just over a hundred at Passville. The hundred men who were patrolling the road between Duchies Pass and Town Falconia were now helping to block the haze so that no Mayflorian troops could suddenly appear from there. The hundred men who had been watching the forest had been sent to help protect the magic users and their crystals that made the communications link between Castle Falconia and

Harbourtown. There were over almost nine hundred men at the mines with another four hundred at Fort Charlotte and Minesville. Townsville had a garrison of three hundred and fifty men and Castle Falconia itself had over four hundred men.

It was after dark when Sir George and the others arrived at Castle Falconia. As Sir George, Colin and Mythias, who had slept the entire way back, exited the royal coach Mythias thanked them for the adventure. 'That was the most interesting time I've had for a long time. I'm still unsure who told the most lies.' Both Sir George and Colin gave him blank looks. 'A crystal that can capture a person's essence to be ready within forty-eight hours.' Mythias smiled as he shook his head. 'That was one of the best stories I've ever heard.'

Colin answered, 'I assure you I have started work on the crystal and its completion could occur at any time.'

'Tell my next reincarnation when it's finished. By the way, do you have plenty of dragon's blood?'

Colin answered, 'We have lots, dried and liquid from when we inherited Queen Katerina's laboratory.'

'Hmm, and when was Katerina the Queen? I must go now. Give my regards to Charlotte.' He smiled, winked, and turned to go back to the Temple of Craidos.

Mythias's comments left Colin in deep thought

but they were forgotten as Sir George and Colin went straight to the Queen's consulting room and ordered that any news was to be brought to them immediately. Soon, Fabian Hastings, Sir Gillian Stevens and Colonel Blayton entered. Sir George spoke first. 'Our discussions with the Duchess went reasonably well. We didn't get Sir Peter, but we have peace at the pass for the next five weeks. She told us some things I hope were lies, but first, the news from Harbourtown.'

Sir Gillian answered, 'There is no news from Harbourtown. At least one of our communication bases has been massacred by dwarfs, goblins and their allies. Helmut is trying to regroup his werewolves inside the forest but some of the enemy are werewolves also. Sharag and his companions also have been killed trying to defend the bases.'

'Sharag dead?' sobbed Colin. 'I thought he'd live forever.'

'That's not all the fun, it looks like the dwarfs, goblins, renegade humans and other creatures are grouping for a possible attack on Thomastown.'

'So, the Duchess wasn't lying,' commented Sir George. 'I suppose Malgon Steelhammer is going to attack the main mines and the ones to the east tomorrow.'

'Dawn the day after,' Fabian Hastings answered. 'And

Jackie seems to have disappeared from the mines. We've sent two lesser magic users up there.'

Colonel Blayton then spoke, 'I have ordered the troops at Minesville to reinforce the men at the main mine's fort and half of the men at Fort Charlotte to Minesville and fifty to here. We should have at least one hundred longbowmen there but there is a shortage of arrows. All the people and troops in the outlying mines to the east have been withdrawn to the main mine fort. We think that Malgon Steelhammer may have as many as two and a half thousand dwarfs at his command.'

'And Balor Hardfall has at least five hundred,' added Fabian Hastings, 'plus a few hundred Redcap Goblins and other assorted allies. Strangely, none of the Bluecap or Yellowcap Goblins have joined them. At least, thanks to the forest, the archers at Thomastown have no shortage of arrows.'

Sir George, shaking his head, asked, 'And which of you are now going to tell me that King Regis wants his wyverns back?'

Fabian Hastings, Sir Gillian Stevens and Colonel Blayton looked at each other in puzzlement. It was Sir Gillian Stevens who answered. 'We did receive a message from King Regis letting us know that the Northern Tribes are getting restless again. He wrote that Concordia had been able to look after the Northern Tribes for decades without wyverns and they can do so again. He feels that our need at the moment is more urgent than his and to send them back when we no longer need them.'

Sir George let out a loud laugh. 'Well, that's one thing the hag got wrong. The other things she got wrong was that we can't handle these problems. Gentlemen, please keep yourselves available. We will have orders for you all later this evening. Now Colin and I have to go to his laboratory.'

There were ten bunks which had been put into the laboratory and nine of them were being slept in. The twelve guards protecting Queen Charlotte's children may not have been the best in the castle, but they were the most trusted. Neither the guards nor the magic users in the laboratory had left it for five days and the only people they had seen were Sir George, Colin and the servants who brought them food. Only three magic users had been allowed in the laboratory, the others had taken their lessons elsewhere. As they entered, Sir George saw a glass jar bubbling away over a flame with a rainbow crystal in it less than the size of a small marble. 'Is that your famous new crystal?'

'It takes time,' was the curt answer.

They walked to where two guards and a small brown-haired magic user were sitting outside the large iron door. 'Hi, Noah, who's downstairs?'

'Cooper.'

'Let him know we're coming down.'

Noah whispered into one of Colin's communication crystals and magicked a large key from the air. Sir George, Colin, Noah and the two guards chatted the twenty minutes that they had to wait for an answer. Noah then opened the door and relocked it behind Sir George and Colin and disappeared the key. At the bottom of the steps was the yellow screen that Colin had set up to protect Prince Stephen and Princess Julie. After descending the stairs, they spent several minutes moving through the screen. In the room were two beds containing the prince and princess and several chairs. In one sat Cooper the magic user officially on duty, in two others were two guards, in another looking very much alive, Queen Charlotte.

Charlotte got up and gave both her uncle and Colin a hug. 'What news do you have?'

After nodding greetings to Cooper and the two guards both Sir George and Colin sat down and told Charlotte what had happened at the meeting with her grandmother and of the threats that troubled Falconia.

'No news of Sir Philip or Rose?' asked Charlotte.

Colin answered, 'The communication system we set up between here and Harbourtown is destroyed, but it's still too soon for them to have got back from the Eastern Isles. We know your godfather is with them and he has a lot of influence with the Potentate so they should be safe. Our troubles here at the moment are more important. Your grandmother will remain quiet for five weeks, so our real problem is the dwarfs. Remove them and the rest of the enemy alliance is weak. We think you'll have to become alive again and confront Malgon Steelhammer. He'll probably back down if he sees you and we can punish him after we remove the threat to Thomastown.'

'But what if they attack Thomastown before we talk to Malgon?'

Sir George answered, 'I think that's a risk we're going to have to take. Malgon knows that the magic user we have isn't strong enough to stop him and although Captain Harrison the new mine commander is competent, he's no Colonel Blayton. I think, but I could be wrong, that Malgon will expect to take the main mine fort without too much trouble and then send reinforcements to Balor Hardfall to attack Thomastown. So, if we can stop Malgon, the attack on Thomastown may not even happen. To be safe though, I'm going to send two hundred men from here commanded by Captain Clough to Thomastown tomorrow. Sir Matthew will arrive here tomorrow also with his four hundred and fifty men but they have had an extremely long trip, so we'll put them on garrison duty for a day or so to recover.'

'So, tomorrow I become alive again.'

'Tomorrow night, so you can be at the mines with one hundred men and several magic users by dawn.'

'I miss Jackie,' Charlotte sobbed.

Colin answered, 'Jackie would have been killed even if she hadn't been using her confusion spell to make people think she was you. She was proud of that spell, she developed it all by herself. We'll bury her when Liam gets back. Jackie would have hated it if Falconia fell or was seriously weakened. We must win even if it's just for her.'

'We should have smashed the dwarfs thirteen years ago,' Sir George said angrily.

'They had a fair grievance then, but now they go much too far,' Charlotte answered. 'Until tomorrow, gentlemen.'

Colin and Sir George spent over twenty minutes leaving.

Shortly before the boat landed, Sir Philip gave the captain and the crew a gold coin each for their trouble. They were all extremely grateful. As they came into land, they could see the satrap, the captain of his guard and about twenty soldiers all holding short bows with arrows notched. As Sir Philip and the others climbed onto the dock carrying the box holding the Chalice of the Dawn, the captain of the boat and his crew stayed on board. The satrap walked towards Sir Philip with arms held wide in welcome. 'Congratulations, you succeeded. I would never have thought it possible.'

'We lost good men and it wasn't easy. But yes, we got it,' Sir Philip answered.

'May I see it?'

Sir Philip looked at Roget who nodded.

Roget and Rose opened the box and the satrap walked over and looked down at it. 'It's beautiful. May I hold it?'

'Not a good idea,' answered Roget. 'You could lose your hand.'

The satrap, startled, stepped back. 'Surely it cannot be that dangerous?'

Roget smiled. 'It is one of the most dangerous things in the world.' He closed the box.

The satrap fingered his beard. 'Is that why the box is lined with lead?'

'It should be a lot thicker, but it helps,' one of Captain

Lipson's two surviving men answered, which angered Sir Philip and the rest, but no one said anything.

'I will have a new box made immediately with a much thicker lead lining,' announced the satrap.

Sir Philip stepped forward. 'We thank you for your offer, but we don't really have time. If you could please return our horses and give us some food and water, we would be on our way back to Danziger immediately.'

The satrap nodded to his captain of the guard who pointed at Sir Philip's group. The archers all brought their short bows up to the ready, all aimed at Sir Philip's group. Sir Philip, who knew that all his group was wearing the best Concordian armour, that although stopped the Blemmyes darts easily, would have no chance against arrows fired at such a short range, asked, 'What is happening?'

'My dear King Philip, the Chalice of the Dawn will never leave Kalam. I plan to keep it for myself.'

'But we are under the protection of the Potentate of Danziger. He will avenge us.'

'My dear King Philip, you are just more poor souls who went to the island and never returned. It's happened to so many. But before you die, I want all of you to take off your helmets.'

Everyone took off their helmets except Rose. The satrap addressed her. 'My dear girl, that order includes you or shall I have it dragged off you.'

Before Rose could do so Roget stepped forward. 'I am not who you think I am. I am not a monk of the Abbey of the Northern Desert, but Roget, the High Priest of Braidos and I assure you Braidos will avenge me.'

'As long as I have the Chalice of the Dawn, I feel I do not have to fear Braidos. If he was going to help you, he'd be here now.' The satrap looked around. 'I don't see him anywhere. It looks like he has abandoned you.' He turned back to Rose. 'Take your helmet off.'

Rose took her helmet off and her mix of black and red hair cascaded down her back. 'That's an interesting colour.' The satrap smiled. 'It should look amazing when we wash the black out of it. You will be my next wife.'

'I'd rather die.'

'I'm sure I'll manage to keep you alive somehow.'

Just then a bell started to toll from the direction of the front gate of Kalam. The satrap turned to the captain of his guard. 'Find out what that's about.'

The captain never got the chance as over fifty men rode onto the dock, most holding short bows with notched arrows. 'What is happening here?' Prince Azul demanded angrily.

The satrap approached the prince and bowed. 'I fear there has been a misunderstanding,' the satrap told

Prince Azul. 'We were about to fire an arrow salute to congratulate King Philip on his success in gaining the Chalice of the Dawn.' He turned to his captain. 'Captain, arrows into the sea.'

The twenty Kalam archers fired their arrows into the sea, some only just missed the boat that Sir Philip's group had sailed in.

Prince Azul watched the salute. 'Nice,' then ordered, 'Now every one of you drop your bows.' They all did except one who reached for another arrow from his quiver. He was rewarded with three arrows in his chest, and he fell to the ground bleeding profusely. Two of the satrap's men moved to help him.

'Leave him, he disobeyed my direct order,' Prince Azul ordered. The two men left him to bleed to death.

'And I've just proposed to the lady in armour. She has not yet answered my proposal,' the satrap told Prince Azul.

'Why would Princess Rose of Falconia want to marry you?' asked Prince Azul. 'I think you may be lying.'

'She may have misunderstood my intentions.'

While this last bit of conversation was happening Burgher Rowles took a look at Rose and burst out laughing. Rose turned as red as her hair and put her helmet back on.

Prince Azul then turned to Sir Philip. 'My congratulations King Philip on your success. We will get fresh horses and head back to Danziger immediately. I must admit, travelling through the mountains could be dangerous as there are bandits there.'

Sir Philip answered, 'We have already met the bandits in the mountains, Your Highness. They won't be bothering anyone for a while.'

Prince Azul laughed. 'I should have known, from what Burgher Rowles told me about you, that you were unstoppable.' He then spoke to his captain. 'Disarm all of the satrap's men. Ask the populace who are the good ones and who are the bad ones and put the bad ones in the cells. Also, imprison the satrap and the captain of his guard. I will have my father send a lot more men to take them to Danziger for trial.'

The satrap asked, 'On trial for what? We have broken no law.'

'I'm sure my father's jailors will find something for you to confess to.' He then addressed his own captain. 'You will stay here with forty men. You will be in total charge until my father appoints a new satrap. I cannot promise but I will put in a good word for you.'

'Thank you, Your Highness,' the captain answered.

'One more thing, make sure the satrap's *wives* get back to their families. Now, let us get fresh horses and be on our way. I'm sure King Philip is in a hurry.'

'Thank you, Your Highness. The sooner we can back to Danziger the better. But one more thing ...' Sir Philip walked up to the satrap and hit him as hard as could with his gauntleted fist, breaking his nose and front teeth, knocking him down with blood pouring down his face.

'That's all. Thank you, Your Highness.'

Prince Azul laughed. 'Nice punch, King Philip. If you hadn't the pressing need to return to Falconia I'd let you do the questioning of him.'

'That would have been a pleasure.'

Prince Rudolf spoke to Evan, 'You'll have to stay here until the Potentate's men come. You're injured so will slow us down.' Evan protested. 'Sorry Evan, but speed is essential. Give Rose your crossbow, I will teach her to use it. She's just about the right size to become a wyvern rider.'

'I don't think so,' Sir Philip commented. 'She's able to get into enough trouble without riding one of those things.'

Prince Rudolf laughed. 'I will not argue with her father, but let her learn the crossbow, Lizzy also.'

'All right, let's get the horses.'

Soon, Prince Azul with ten men and Sir Philip with seven companions and one pack horse carrying the Chalice of the Dawn, rode out of Kalam.

CHAPTER THIRTY-TWO

Before dawn the morning Malgon Steelhammer was going to attack the mines, Queen Charlotte with one hundred men, almost all the men left at Castle Falconia, half of them with longbows and four full quivers of sixty arrows each, exited the haze near the mines. Queen Charlotte had stayed hidden until the last minute with Sir George organising the men, who were surprised to see her as they all thought she was dead but cheered her return. They were told that everything would be explained when they got back. She used the most powerful shimmering charm she could, so that none of them would be seen as they approached the mines. The previous day Sir Gillian Stevens had gone through the haze with fifty men to the mines to negotiate with Malgon Steelhammer; Malgon not knowing Queen Charlotte was alive. When Queen Charlotte and her men reached the solitary entrance that led into the small valley between the three mountains containing the fortified mine camp, she surveyed the situation. Some of the dwarfs had bows. They were stationed just under a small overhang that would help protect them from the wyverns. There were several hundreds of them. Most of the other dwarfs were arranged in lines in front of the fort's palisade and the first two lines had shields. They were made of wood with iron bands that would help to deflect arrows and for them, hopefully, some of the wyvern's flames. In total there would have been close to three thousand dwarfs.

Just as the sun started to break over the mountains, Malgon Steelhammer with half a dozen of his men walked towards the fort with a white flag of truce. The group stopped when they were about thirty yards from the palisade. The dwarven leader's loud booming voice could be heard throughout the valley. 'Who is in charge here?'

Sir Gillian Stevens, standing on the ramparts, shouted back, 'I am Sir Gillian Stevens, the Royal Chamberlain of Falconia and I am in charge here.'

'Sir Gillian,' Malgon's voice boomed, 'I have heard of

you. You are said to be a sensible man. Look about you at my army and quake in fear. As you can see, we now have archers to attack your wyverns and the overhang they are under makes them hard for your wyverns to attack. We have shields to protect us from your arrows and your wyvern's flames, which I am told take more than two hours for them to use again, not that you can have many, as I believe King Regis has recalled some and there is at least one injured. My dwarfs thirst for blood and the return of the mines, which are ours, and when they attack it will be hard to refrain them from killing everyone they are able. I personally do not wish for bloodshed. Lead your men out of the fort and back to Minesville. You may take your weapons and I will guarantee your safety until you reach Minesville. We will take the mines anyway. At least save your men.'

Sir Gillian didn't answer but instead looked at the valley opening where he hoped Queen Charlotte would be. Queen Charlotte looked at the Great Ring of Falconia on the ring finger of her right hand and gave it a quick rub. She then dissipated the shimmering spell that hid her and her men and used the ring to blast an area of the mountain near the overhang that protected the dwarven archers. This was also a signal for the five wyvern riders to take to the air.

Malgon, startled, looked around and saw Queen Charlotte and her men. He turned white and pointed at her, 'But ... you're ... dead ...' he stammered.

Queen Charlotte magically amplified her voice. 'Maybe I'm a ghost, Malgon. You soon will be. Let me tell you how this battle will go. My first bolt will bring down that overhang your archers are hiding under. My second will take a large section of your first two lines that have shields, making it easier for the wyverns to roast more of your dwarfs. My third will blow you into little pieces.'

'But my safety is guaranteed. I have a flag of truce.'

'I will treat that guarantee the same way as you treated your guarantee not to attack the mines. My next bolts will blow more holes in your lines while my archers use your men as pin cushions. Then my not insubstantial cavalry and infantry will hunt down any survivors as what's left of your army flees. And finally, I promise you there will not be another dwarf seen in these mountains for at least another two hundred years.'

Malgon Steelhammer dropped to one knee and held his hands out as if in prayer. 'I'm sorry, Your Majesty, please forgive me. I will withdraw my army at once and I will never threaten the mines again. I guarantee it.'

'I have heard too many of your guarantees.'

'I will leave you my first-born son as a hostage. I love

him as much as I love the mines, if not more. If I threaten the mines again you may kill him as well as destroy my army of which you are quite capable. We have gained much during our years of peace and would gain more. Please, please forgive me.'

'You are not forgiven, but I will take the risk that you have learnt an important lesson. Send your son into the fort.'

Malgon stood and spoke to one of the men who was with him. 'Dulgon, go into the fort and obey everything you are ordered.'

Dulgon, a dwarf of about three feet four with brown hair but no beard started to object. 'You will obey my orders,' Malgon declared. 'We are now at peace with Falconia.' Malgon looked at Queen Charlotte and shrugged. 'Children.' Dulgon left to enter the fort.

Malgon then sent another of his men to order his army to leave the valley. He then turned to Queen Charlotte. 'Balor Hardfall takes just about no notice of my orders anymore. I will try to stop his attacks on Falconia, but I cannot be held responsible for what he does.'

Queen Charlotte thought for a few moments. 'I will not hold you responsible, but I assure you right now, that any dwarf that takes arms against Falconia will die.'

'That is fair, I wish you luck against him. He has defied

me too many times.'

Malgon Steelhammer waited where he was until his entire army had left the valley, then started to leave himself. Queen Charlotte called to him, 'Malgon, watch this.' She sent a blast that brought down the entire overhang that his archers had sheltered under. They would have all died.

Malgon turned and bowed. 'I wish Your Majesty a long and happy life. By the way would you like some more berries?'

Queen Charlotte smiled. 'Thank you, but no. You gave me plenty before. I hope we can spend many years in peace.'

'As do I.' Malgon followed his army out of the valley.

After Malgon had left, Sir Gillian Stevens came to speak to Queen Charlotte. 'I didn't want to bring this up until the dwarfs had left, but Thomastown is under attack from dwarfs, goblins, renegade humans, slime tunnellers, giant salamander-like creatures and others.'

'Send all the wyverns bar one there immediately. Also, ask Sir Damian to go and reinforce it with all his men. I will be there as soon as possible. You take your fifty men and Dulgon and ride straight to Castle Falconia. I do not want to reduce the garrison here as I still don't trust Malgon Steelhammer. His guarantees are not worth much.'

Chapter Thirty-two

'We have his first-born son.'

'He may hate him.'

'I think not, dwarfs are reputed to love their families.'

'We must play safe, however. I and my men will leave immediately. I hope to be at Thomastown before dark. I hope I won't be too late.'

In the Eastern Isles, Prince Azul, Sir Philip and their group had ridden their horses hard. They only stopped when it became too dark to ride and were up at dawn. They ate in the saddle, and they arrived at Danziger just before dark on the second day. They immediately boarded *The Flying Porpoise*, but the harbour pilot didn't want to see them out in the dark. A gold piece and the threat of visiting the Potentate's jail changed his mind. When Burgher Rowles and Prince Azul said goodbye, the Burgher promised the prince that his next visit wouldn't be so dramatic, to which the prince replied he hadn't had so much fun in ages, but he had to go and see his father to arrange who would be the next Satrap of Kalam.

As they sailed away back to Harbourtown, Roget asked if they could make a stronger box for the Chalice of the Dawn. When asked how big a box would be needed to completely nullify the Chalice, Roget answered that it should be at least six inches of lead all around. Captain Wright told them that they had plenty of lead ballast aboard, but the box would weigh almost three tons and they would need a good strong wagon to carry it when they got to Harbourtown. They decided to make the heavy box on board *The Flying Porpoise* in case magic was needed and then have the larger box carried by wagon to Castle Falconia while Sir Philip and his party took the smaller box containing the Chalice of the Dawn the quicker way through the Great Forest. It took almost one and a half days to make the box, the crew being extremely efficient at gluing plates of lead together. When it was finished the smaller box was placed inside and pulleys, which fortunately *The Flying Porpoise* had many being a cargo ship, were used to place the three-quarter of a ton lid on top. Meanwhile, *The Flying Porpoise* travelled faster than it had ever gone before. Captain Wright told the others that if they kept up this speed, they'd be in Harbourtown in less than four days. Everyone gave thanks to Coralie and looked forward to their arrival.

CHAPTER THIRTY-THREE

When Queen Charlotte got back to Castle Falconia, there was a great deal of astonishment as everyone had thought her dead. She told people it was a way to fool Falconia's enemies and she promised to explain what had happened and that when she returned from Thomastown, she would tell everyone the entire story. She was told that Sir George and Colin had ridden to Thomastown with what was left of the more experienced magic users except for the ones in the laboratory and fifty men, and that Sir Matthew had already started to ride there with four hundred men leaving the other fifty to garrison the castle under the command of Sir David Reading, the master of the castle, even though he wasn't a member of the military. By the time all the reinforcements got to Thomastown the defenders should have easily over a thousand men. Charlotte thought that many should be enough to not only hold Thomastown but to beat the enemy back without too many problems.

Before she and her men came into sight of the town they could see lots of black smoke in the sky. When they got there the fighting seemed to have stopped for the day, but parts of the town and town wall nearest the Great Forest were burning. The town gates opened to let Queen Charlotte and her men into the town and she rode straight through to the Town Hall where she presumed the defender's commanders would be so she could find out what had happened. Most of the buildings in Thomastown were made of wood, it being plentiful as the Great Forest was so near. The Town Hall, however, was a two-storey stone building. Two guards at the Town Hall door came to attention as she entered, leaving her men mulling outside where she had told them to wait. She strode down a short passage through open doors into a moderately sized but lavishly furnished hall. Murals of the forest and woodcutters covered all the walls and ceiling. There was a large table in the hall and well-padded, red-clothed chairs for twenty people. Charlotte could not help herself thinking back to when she first entered this hall more than fourteen years ago as

Charlotte Silver with her sister and mother trying to kill her. Mayor Andrews stood next to the chair at the head of the table, indicating the seat was for Queen Charlotte. She said, 'Thank you,' and sat down and the mayor found a seat further down the table.

Queen Charlotte looked around the table. Sitting on her right was Captain Clough, next to him was Sir Matthew and next to him was a sergeant she did not recognise but assumed was the sergeant of Thomastown. On her left was Colin, Sergeant Alexander and Mayor Andrews, they were all dirty and had blood on their clothes or armour. They all had goblets in front of them and before Queen Charlotte could even speak again a servant appeared carrying a goblet of water for her. Queen Charlotte looked around the table. 'Where's Sir George?'

Colin answered, 'We have turned the barracks into a hospital. He is there.'

Queen Charlotte looked concerned. 'Giving aid and wise words to the wounded I hope.'

Colin shook his head sadly. 'Alas, he is quite badly burnt.'

Queen Charlotte exclaimed, 'What happened?'

Colin again answered, 'One of the giant salamander-like creatures was climbing over the town wall when Sir George stuck his hook in its eye. The giant salamanders have short-range flame capability and as it fell Sir George got burnt. He killed it though and he's now in the hospital getting his burns treated. I have used my crystals and he should fully recover but he'll have scars.'

'So, he'll live.' Queen Charlotte sighed.

'They'll be glad to get him out of the barracks we are using as a hospital. All he does is complain about how the salamander took his hook with it as it fell off the wall.' Colin smiled.

Queen Charlotte laughed. 'That sounds like Uncle George. Now, tell me what has happened here today,' she continued seriously.

Captain Clough started speaking, 'They appeared this morning but didn't attack until the sun was well up, almost noon.'

Colin interrupted, 'It's possible that the giant salamanders are at least partially cold-blooded and therefore would need some of the sun's heat so that they can move freely. It is surprising that they're this far north, they usually only live in the southern part of the Great Forest where it is warmer.'

Captain Clough continued, 'Well, a dozen salamanders led the attack and the wyvern we had here tried to burn them but its fire had no effect on them. Even the magic users' lightning bolts bounced off them.'

Colin interrupted again, 'When this is over, we're going to have to give them more intensive training and try to find stronger ones.'

The captain went on. 'They were followed by everything else just about, almost a thousand dwarfs, over five hundred goblins, a couple dozen werewolves, untold numbers of giant rats and there were even a couple of manticores. That's not counting about three to four hundred renegade humans, half of which had longbows. Our arrows just bounced off the salamanders unless they were lucky enough to hit one in the eye or down its throat. Their archers kept our wyvern at bay, unfortunately, and when the other four arrived the first two wasted their fire on the salamanders, although, the other two did do substantial damage. The sad news is one of the wyverns was brought down by the human archers and it and its rider were killed. The manticores made tempting targets for our archers and they soon ran back towards the forest with several arrows in them. The dwarfs had shields, but the goblins didn't and the goblins suffered badly. The dwarfs still lost a sizeable number to our archers even with their shields but there are more of them wounded than dead. The giant rats tried to burrow under our palisade but fortunately, they were easy to kill, although some succeeded and they caused many casualties. They were followed by the dwarfs and goblins and there was a bitter fight to repel them. Our biggest problem was the salamanders as they set fire to the palisade when they tried to climb over it, which started fires inside the town. Swords won't penetrate their hide and if there had been more of them Thomastown would not exist. The dwarfs and the rest were slowed by the fires but had started to break through when Sir Matthew arrived and hit the enemy in the flank by surprise.'

'We took almost one hundred casualties but stopped the attack,' Sir Matthew added. 'Most were from the renegade archers. I'd like to disembowel every one of them.'

'Anyway, the enemy broke off the attack but I'm sure they'll be back tomorrow, especially after our palisade finishes burning,' Captain Clough continued. 'But the attack wasn't our only problem. I'll let Sergeant Roberts of the town guard tell the rest.'

Sergeant Roberts, a tall six foot two with brown hair and eyes and a hard face that was partially covered with soot stood and was immediately waved down by Queen Charlotte. 'There is no need to stand, Sergeant. It's not a parade, this is a council of war.'

'Thank you, Your Majesty.' Sergeant Roberts sat. 'They also have slime tunnellers.'

Chapter Thirty-three

'What!' Queen Charlotte exclaimed in surprise. 'How would they communicate?'

'I don't know, Your Majesty, but they are here.'

Queen Charlotte looked at Colin who just shook his head. 'They are another creature that usually only lives in the southern part of the Great Forest.'

The Sergeant continued, 'Well, they're here. The slime tunnellers have caused numerous casualties amongst the townsfolks. They don't care whom they kill. I've had half the normal garrison and most of the townsmen not fighting the fires carrying torches around trying to kill those we find. They don't seem to like fire or bright sunlight. The problem is most houses have dirt floors so that they can appear almost anywhere. There are also a lot of dark alleyways here, even in daylight. Everyone is frightened. We have moved some of our townspeople to buildings that have wooden floors but there are not many. A lot are here upstairs. The slime tunnellers can break through the wooden floors but it gives time for people to escape and sometimes the slime tunnellers can get killed if a magic user is nearby. They are hard to kill, even by your magic users, who have actually killed some. But as I said, everyone is frightened.'

Queen Charlotte spent some time in thought. 'After I finish with Balor Hardfall and Iggord I will have all the magic users look for them. Colin, have a message sent to

Castle Falconia to search the library for ways to get rid of slime tunnellers and have word sent to the Duchies Pass Fort to send us every man they can spare. We have four weeks until we have to worry about my grandmother.'

'I will do so at once.' Colin got up to leave.

'Oh, and Colin.' Colin hesitated. 'Please tell the men outside the Town Hall to either help fight the fires or search for slime tunnellers.'

'I will do so.' Colin left.

'Now, let us decide our plans for tomorrow,' Queen Charlotte told the council of war. 'They have not yet met me and the Great Ring of Falconia.'

The meeting continued with the Queen telling everyone what had happened at the mines. When Colin returned, they made plans for the next day.

After the meeting had finished Queen Charlotte and Colin went to the barracks to visit her great uncle. Colin started using the green crystal on his staff to cure minor wounds. For more serious wounds he used larger green crystals from his pouch. There were several healers and magic users in the barracks looking after the many wounded. Some of the army companies had their own healers who were now there. She asked Thomastown's healer, a man named Healer Hall, short with long black hair and green eyes, to take her to Sir George. He was sleeping. He had bandages over his face and the upper portion of his body and his left arm. The healer spoke to Queen Charlotte. 'His burns are bad, but your magic user Colin has used crystals I've never seen before which he tells me will help him.'

'Colin's crystals can be miraculous. I wish he had a lot more. It looks like you could use some. Colin is not strictly a magic user but a master of crystals.'

'I believe you are a great healer; my teacher, Healer Woodcraft, told me a lot about you.'

Queen Charlotte smiled sadly. 'Healer Woodcraft was a great healer himself. I was sorry to hear that he died. When the battle is over tomorrow, I will come and help here, but I am needed more to fight the creatures that are causing this problem.'

'Your help would be greatly appreciated.'

As they were talking a loud crack was heard from a spot near them on the barrack's wooden floor. Queen Charlotte and the healer turned and watched several floor planks starting to break open. In just a few seconds it was a hole big enough for a slime tunneller to crawl through. Almost immediately, two large squinty eyes on stalks appeared through the hole. They seemed to see Queen Charlotte and the healer immediately and the rest of the slime tunneller started towards them. It was a large one, about seven and a half feet long with a large round mouth surrounded by teeth. Queen Charlotte pointed at the slime tunneller, and it seemed to retreat back into the hole. It was really just shrivelling up and what was left of it dropped back. There was a shout from the next room and Queen Charlotte and Healer Hall saw Colin pointing his staff towards another slime tunneller that had tunnelled up through the floor, a purple beam holding it still. 'Quick Charlotte, the crystal will not hold it for long.'

Queen Charlotte pointed at the slime tunneller and this one also shrivelled up.

Colin leant on his staff. 'Thank you, Charlotte. I think we need more magic users here.'

Queen Charlotte grimaced. 'I wish we had more.' Charlotte turned to the healer. 'I will help here for about two hours then I must get some sleep. I must be prepared for tomorrow's fight. I will then have one of the senior magic users take over from me in case any more of those vile creatures appear. Get a couple of soldiers to repair that hole and send someone to get my medicinal bag. I have salves and herbs that will help here.'

'Healer Woodcraft always said the Silver remedies were the best,' the healer told Queen Charlotte.

'Most of them were my adoptive mother's. Let's get to work.'

CHAPTER THIRTY-FOUR

There was not much to do aboard *The Flying Porpoise* for those who had taken the Chalice of the Dawn. Prince Rudolf taught both Rose and Lizzy how to use Evan's crossbow but seemed to spend more time with Lizzy than with Rose. It became so, that if you saw Prince Rudolf, you would also see Lizzy. Prince Rudolf even helped look after Edgar. They seemed to spend all the time they could together and on occasion, the jealous Edgar gave Prince Rudolf a nasty peck. On one occasion Prince Rudolf and Lizzy were even caught kissing.

On the third night of the voyage, Prince Rudolf sought out Sir Philip for a private talk at the stern of the ship. Prince Rudolf spoke first, 'Philip, Lizzy is a beautiful girl, isn't she?'

'Yes, Rudi, she is. She is also young and innocent. I would hate to see her get hurt.'

'I would never deliberately hurt her. I think I've fallen in love. In fact, I think I've at least liked her from the first time I saw her.'

'You showed no sign of it on while we were searching for the Chalice.'

Rudi nodded. 'True, but how could I? We were on a quest and a quest is no place for romance. I could have been killed; she could have been killed. In fact, it's miraculous that all of us weren't killed. But it's now over, we just have to land in Harbourtown, quickly get the Chalice to Falconia, put the ingredients in it and save your children. Easy compared to what we have been through. I can now show my feelings.'

'I didn't have that problem. I fell in love with Charlotte the first time I met her and saved her from the manticore when she was still Charlotte Silver, but that was before we knew her mother and her sister wanted her dead.'

'I think I may ask Lizzy to marry me when all this is finally over.'

'Your father may not mind too much, but I'm not sure. Are you planning to assassinate King Regis?' Phillip smiled.

'I admit that being second in line to the throne of

Concordia may cause problems but I'm sure we can think of a way to overcome them.'

'We?'

'You will help me, won't you?'

'Of course.'

'Has Lizzy got any royal blood we can tell my grandfather about?'

Sir Philip rubbed his beard in thought. 'I think if we search really hard we may find a reference that shows that Lizzy is a very distant relative of Sir George. Sir George would be happy to have a new relative.'

'And Sir George is royal blood. Excellent.' Rudi frowned. 'But what if we don't find the reference?'

Philip smiled. 'What? With Colin in charge of the library, it will be found even if Charlotte has to help.'

'Thank you, Philip.'

'I hope you and Lizzy will have a long and happy life together. If she says yes.'

Rudi looked alarmed. 'I'm sure she'll say yes.' He laughed. 'I'll make it a royal command.'

'I don't think that would be a good idea,' Philip said seriously.

'What? I was only joking. I could never force anyone to love me, but I'm sure she does.'

'There's no problem then.' Philip shook Rudi's hand. 'I

wish both of you all the joy in the world.'

'Thank you.'

The voyage continued.

The fires at Thomastown were extinguished. They had left a large hole in the palisade and all of the houses near the hole were destroyed. Queen Charlotte had spent almost three hours helping the healers in the barracks before finding a bed of her own at the Town Hall. Fortunately, no more slime tunnellers entered the barracks but they kept appearing randomly around the town and there were more casualties amongst the town population and patrols looked for them all night. The next morning, Queen Charlotte donned a suit of plate armour and went to the palisade's hole, keeping her visor down so she would not be recognised. She also did not wear gauntlets. Archers had been placed on the platforms near the top of the palisade where it hadn't been burnt and more were behind her and the troops that stood with her. There were over three hundred, all Concordians as denoted by their Concordian plate armour. The rest of the troops were either still looking for slime tunnellers, watching the other walls in case of a surprise attack, or held in reserve. Colin had gone to the barracks to help the wounded as he couldn't really fight with his crystals and staff. With Queen Charlotte were Sir Matthew, Captain Clough, Mayor Andrews and Stuart, all in plate armour, although Stuart also didn't wear gauntlets. Sergeant Roberts commanded the reserve. Sergeant Alexander and the other wyvern riders waited with the wyverns in the square behind the Town Hall.

They watched all morning as their enemy got organised. The green salamander-like creatures, which were ten feet long and three feet wide, seemed to be about five feet high when standing, had feet that could act as suction cups, large green heads with bulbous eyes and large mouths that looked toothless, and seemed to be sunning themselves as the dwarfs, goblins and renegade humans formed up. There seemed to be no other creatures with them and most of the men who had been on the walls the day before were thankful that there did not seem to be any rats.

Just before noon, the enemy began to move. The nine surviving salamanders started to lead the attack but were soon overtaken by thousands of giant rats who appeared out of the trees and swarmed over and around them as they raced towards the town. The rest of the army followed the salamanders and rats. Queen

Charlotte told Sir Matthew, 'Get some men to defend me against the rats. Stuart, you help him. I'm saving myself for those big monsters.'

As the attack started, one of the archers on the wall fired a burning arrow in the air as a signal for the wyvern riders. Two of the wyverns roasted a large number of the leading rats while the other two waited for a chance to attack the dwarfs and the goblins. Queen Charlotte pointed her finger with the Great Ring of Falconia and the head of one of the salamanders exploded. A few seconds later another one died. Then the attack stopped. The rats didn't seem to know what was happening and a few made it close enough to be killed by either Stuart, who was hitting them with lightning bolts, or Sir Matthew and his men, before they ran back to their own lines. There was a loud cheer from the dwarfs and goblins who all started to look to the north. The defenders turned to look there likewise.

Almost three thousand dwarfs had appeared, marching towards Thomastown. They were led by Malgon Steelhammer. 'If we survive this it will be the last time I ever trust that dwarven swine,' Charlotte said to herself. 'I will kill him personally.'

No one moved except the approaching dwarven army. The army stopped twice the distance from Thomastown than the other army was. A dwarf ran from Balor Hardfall and Iggord's army towards the arriving one. Charlotte said to anyone who was listening, 'That's probably Balor Hardfall going to help organise their attack.'

'Could you hit him from here?' Sir Matthew asked Queen Charlotte.

'Probably, but why get rid of an incompetent enemy commander when they may replace him with a better one.'

Balor Hardfall made it to Malgon Steelhammer, and they started to have an extremely animated conversation. When it ended Balor Hardfall ran back to his forces and another animated conversation started between himself, two other dwarfs and a goblin that Charlotte assumed was Iggord. When the conversation was over Balor Hardfall led all of his dwarfs towards Malgon Steelhammer's army. Iggord started to lead the goblins back towards the Great Forest. The giant rats and the salamanders seemed confused, then turned themselves towards the Great Forest. As they turned several werewolves were seen. The renegade humans started to back away as well.

Charlotte took her helmet off and looked towards Malgon Steelhammer who, when seeing her, waved. Charlotte waved back. She then turned to Sir Matthew. 'Get your men on their horses and attack the humans, forget the rest, those humans are traitors to Falconia.'

'At once, Your Majesty.' Sir Matthew started to give orders.

Malgon Steelhammer's army turned around and started to march away with Balor Hardfall's hurrying to catch up. Charlotte told Stuart, 'Get the reserves to watch this gap, but have the others keep searching for slime tunnellers.'

'Yes, Your Majesty.' Stuart left.

Queen Charlotte went back to the barracks to help the wounded. No more slime tunnellers were seen.

On the fourth morning of the voyage of *The Flying Porpoise*, everyone on board was hopefully looking forward to this being the last day. The ship had never moved as fast as it did now. Everyone who was not working took turns to go to the bow and look for land. None of them saw land, what they did see were dark clouds on the horizon which grew larger and darker the closer they got. Captain Wright called Burgher Rowles and Sir Philip to his cabin.

Captain Wright looked worried. 'We're headed straight towards a large storm. I suggest we change course to go around it.'

'How long will that take?' asked Sir Philip.

'Depending on the storm, it could be two or three days.'

'Too long,' Sir Philip told Captain Wright. 'Coralie promised we would come to no harm. I say we sail straight through it.'

'It looks pretty bad. We could sink,' answered the captain. 'As captain of *The Flying Porpoise*, my word is law. This is not a committee meeting. I'm just giving you the courtesy of telling you what I plan to do and why.'

'And if you change course, you'll never captain another ship,' Burgher Rowles told him. 'I'll have you blacklisted everywhere. I also trust Coralie. She made a promise to us, and I believe she'll keep it. I suggest you stay on course or resign your post immediately and I'll find someone else amongst your officers to take over.'

'Ha, they're good but they'd never get through that storm. I know Coralie made us a promise, but that's the worst storm I've ever seen.'

'Captain, why do you go to the Temple of Coralie before a journey if you do not trust her?' asked Sir Philip. 'She herself made the promise. Do you really think she'll break it?'

'It seems we must trust the sea god,' Captain Wright said unhappily. 'I will order our course be maintained.' The three left the cabin.

The storm got closer and closer. All the crew, and

even Sir Philip's group, became increasingly nervous. The waves grew higher and higher. Then Rose, who was standing at the bow, shouted, 'Look!' Two dolphins were swimming in front of the ship. Every now and again one of them would leap out of the water and do a somersault. 'It's Speedy and Slinky.'

The two dolphins led the ship towards the storm and as the ship got close, the storm started to split in two, leaving a path of relatively calm water ahead of the ship. *The Flying Porpoise* sailed into it. Thirty yards off each of the port and starboard sides, the storm raged. Fifty yards off the bow and the stern, the storm raged. But *The Flying Porpoise*, following Speedy and Slinky, sailed quickly in relatively calm water. Over three hours later the storm in front of the bow disappeared. They were through the storm. Speedy and Sleeky leapt out of the water and both did a double somersault and then looked up at Rose who was still standing at the bow. Rose, with tears in her eyes, cried, 'Goodbye Speedy, goodbye Slinky.' And with that, the two dolphins dived down deep into the sea.

Sir Philip walked up to Rose and gave her a hug. Rose told him, 'I'm going to miss them playing in the moat.'

'So will your mother. You've heard how they saved her life?'

Rose started to count on her fingers. 'Once or twice or twenty.'

Sir Philip laughed and gave his daughter another hug.

Captain Wright approached Burgher Rowles. 'I'm sorry about the meeting in my cabin. I should have had more faith.'

Burgher Rowles smiled at Captain Wright. 'What meeting?'

Captain Wright shook the burgher's hand. 'Thank you.'

They made it to Harbourtown just after dark.

CHAPTER THIRTY-FIVE

When *The Flying Porpoise* docked, the top of the large lead-lined box was removed with pulleys and the smaller box containing the Chalice of the Dawn taken out. The first people off the ship were Burgher Rowles, the constables and Sir Philip's group. They were met by Burgher Thompson. Both Burgher Rowles and Sir Philip shook Burgher Thompson's hand. 'Well, we did it,' Sir Philip told Burgher Thompson. 'We got the Chalice of the Dawn.' He pointed to the box that Captain Lipson's two surviving men were carrying.

'Good, good,' Burgher Thompson mumbled with tears in his eyes. 'I have shocking news.'

Sir Philip asked alarmed, 'What?'

Burgher Thompson spoke louder so that everyone

could hear. 'Queen Charlotte is dead.'

Rose burst into tears, everyone else looked downcast, close to tears, except for Roget who seemed unmoved. Sir Philip grabbed Burgher Thompson. 'What happened?'

Burgher Thompson stepped away out of Sir Philip's grip. 'Sir Peter of Mayflor led a raiding party to attempt to rescue Princess Scarlett. They failed, but Charlotte got killed amongst others stopping them.'

Sir Philip fell to his knees with his face in his hands and wailed. After several minutes, as no one dared to disturb him, he got up. His eyes were still red with tears. He walked back to the men who were holding the box containing the Chalice of the Dawn. He put his hand on the box. 'I hereby swear by the Chalice of the Dawn and by Craidos, I will not stop until I catch Sir Peter of Mayflor and give him a slow and painful death.'

Burgher Rowles frowned. 'Sir Peter of Mayflor is a powerful magic user.'

Sir Philip grimaced. 'Not while I've got this box, he isn't and I'm sure I will be much better than him with any other weapon.'

Prince Rudolf interrupted, also with tears in his eyes. 'Did Sir Matthew leave many troops here?'

'There are about fifty who have built themselves a palisade next to the Great Forest. They also have a wyvern there,' was Burgher Thompson's answer.

'We should get our horses and go and join them so we can set out for Falconia first thing in the morning,' continued Prince Rudolf.

Sir Philip nodded and turned to Burgher Rowles. 'Please go with the others and collect the horses and meet me at the town gate. I will send you the money for the payment for tending them after I return to Falconia.'

'I will pay the bill. Forget it. We still need to get our belongings off the ship.'

'Use the spare horses as pack horses.' Sir Philip then turned back to Burgher Thompson. 'I have a favour to ask.'

'Name it.'

'Could you get the armourer next to the constables' barracks to open so I can get a new battleaxe?' Sir Philip bought a battleaxe from there over fourteen years before, after he buried his with Dobbin who had been killed while using it.

'I'm getting one too,' Captain Lipson said.

'Come with me, Jacob and I'll buy you one.'

'If necessary, I'll get the constables to break down the door,' Burgher Thompson told them.

They all went about their tasks.

Just under an hour later Sir Philip and Captain Lipson, both carrying their new battleaxes, met the others at the town gate. Sir Philip put his axe down and went to greet Cherry. He whispered a few words to her and stroked her mane. He then turned to Burgher Rowles who was now wearing his armour. Everyone else's armour was on the spare horses. The burgher had led the others to the gate and Sir Philip offered him his hand. 'Thank you for all you have done, Harold. I'll never be able to repay you for your kindness.'

The burgher looked puzzled. 'You sound like you're saying goodbye. Charlotte was my goddaughter. I'm coming with you.'

'It's a dangerous trip and there could be more danger at the end of it. You should not come.'

'Could it be more dangerous than the last time I travelled through the Great Forest with you? I doubt it. I'm coming. There is no more to say.'

'Glad to have you. I just hope you survive.' Sir Philip picked up his battleaxe and mounted Cherry. 'Let's go and wake up the palisade.'

They rode out of the gate towards the well-built palisade, which had a closed gate. A watch tower had been built next to the gate inside the palisade. The guard was alert and shouted for his commanding officer as soon as he saw the riders. The officer was at the top of the tower when the riders arrived at the gate. 'Who are you and what do you want?' He could not see them clearly in the dark.

'Captain Watson, is that you?' asked Prince Rudolf.

'Your Highness, I'm sorry I did not see you properly.' He saluted the prince by putting the back of his hand to his forehead and then he shouted down. 'Get that gate opened at once and call out everybody for inspection.'

'Forget the inspection,' the prince called back, 'but get them ready to leave at dawn tomorrow.'

'Yes, Your Highness.' Captain Watson started down the ladder to the tower as the gate opened and Prince Rudolf led everyone into the camp.

The Concordians had made a large camp with the wyvern tethered in the centre and the horses corralled near the front gate at the farthest point from the great forest. The men had been living in small tents and these were seen scattered around the camp mainly near the few campfires. They had also made a flagpole and the flag of Concordia, a red fist on a white background, fluttered there. Sir Philip spoke to Captain Watson, 'Could you please find a place to sleep for all those with us and place a strong guard on that box. Then I wish to talk to you.' He pointed to the box containing the Chalice of the Dawn.

Captain Watson, young about twenty, tall, very slender with short brown hair and eyes, looked at Prince Rudolf and nodded. The captain called a sergeant to whom he gave the orders to carry out. Captain Watson then took Sir Philip and Prince Rudolf to the largest of the tents and all three ducked inside. In the tent, there was a bed that could become a stretcher, a travelling camp table with lots of parchments on it and several small stools. Prince Rudolf spoke first, 'Captain Watson, this is King Philip of Falconia who is the leader of this mission.'

Captain Watson came to attention immediately and once again saluted. 'Your Majesty, I and my men are yours to command. I'm greatly sorry for your loss.'

'Thank you, captain, but the time to mourn will come later. Stand at ease and let's sit down on these extremely comfortable looking stools.'

The captain and the prince smiled at the forced joke, and they all sat down. 'What would you like to know, Your Majesty?'

'Well, first, while we're on campaign and this is a campaign, I'm called Sir Philip.'

'Yes, Your Maj … I mean, Sir Philip.'

'It's a nice strong looking palisade you have here, my compliments.'

'Well, we had to do something with all the trees we cut down.' Both Sir Philip and Prince Rudolf looked puzzled. 'We've been cutting a path through the forest so that when you arrived, we could move more quickly towards Falconia and save time.'

Both Sir Philip and Prince Rudolf nodded. Sir Philip spoke, 'You are to be commended, Captain. When did you lose communications with Castle Falconia?'

'Three days ago, sir. The last message said it looked like there could be war between the Falconians and the dwarfs and their allies and maybe Mayflor.'

Sir Philip cursed. 'My wife is murdered, and all the vultures come out. They will regret it.' After a few seconds, he calmed. 'How have relations been between you and Harbourtown?'

'On the whole, not too bad. The men have been working extremely hard cutting down trees and building this palisade. The Harbourtown gates are closed every night as is every town near the Great Forest, so at the start I just let a few men go there during the day on their time off. Well, it seems that some of the townsfolk men started a fight with them and a Burgher Jackson turned up and arrested them all.'

'What?' exclaimed the prince. 'I'll throttle that man myself. Please excuse me while I go and ask Burgher Rowles if he can get them released.' He started to stand.

'They have been released, sir,' the captain told them. 'I went to see Burgher Robson and I promised him that no more of my men would enter Harbourtown except with myself and our wagon to get supplies if they were released. He agreed but Burgher Jackson didn't look happy.'

'So, you've been well supplied?' asked the prince.

'Yes, a lot of the merchants weren't happy that my men couldn't enter Harbourtown. They expected to make a lot of money. As it is, I think prices almost doubled for our supplies. I'm afraid, Your Highness, that Concordia has built up quite a bill.'

The prince smiled. 'That's grandpapa's problem. Ours is to get to Falconia as fast as possible.'

'We will move out at dawn as ordered. My men have cut a long path through the forest, it should save almost a day.'

'Did you have any problems?' Sir Philip asked.

'A few strange creatures and a group of goblins tried to attack us, but my men and our magic user soon saw them off.'

'You'd better tell your magic user he just lost his magic so he doesn't try to use it during our ride. Now could you please show us where Prince Rudolf and I are to sleep.'

'Here, of course, I'll have another bed brought immediately. I'll steal one of my sergeants' tents.'

'Thank you,' chorused Sir Philip and Prince Rudolf.

Captain Watson left the tent.

CHAPTER THIRTY-SIX

At dawn the next morning, sixty-two riders exited the back gate of the palisade. As they couldn't take their wagon with them everything was left except their armour, weapons, food and water. The trees that would have normally made it hard to ride through the forest were gone. There was a passage where it was easy for two riders to ride abreast without a problem, so they were able to ride at a decent pace. The wyvern had taken off at the same time to fly to Castle Falconia with a sealed message for Sir George and Colin from Sir Philip that the Chalice of the Dawn had been acquired and was on its way there. It also instructed them to create a box such as the one that was made on *The Flying Porpoise* on a wagon so that it could be moved. It would have been normally a three-day trip to the ford that Sir Philip, Charlotte Silver and Burgher Rowles crossed almost fourteen years ago but they expected to make it in two. Then it would be less than two more days before they came to Thomastown. On the way, they came across a communications station that had a magic user, ten guards and four werewolves. None of them could tell them anything new. The guards and the magic user joined the column, the werewolves went to find Helmut.

During the ride, Prince Rudolf and Lizzy often rode next to each other. Edgar was regrowing his burnt feathers and was now able to fly short distances. Edgar and Lizzy were still able to communicate even with the Chalice of the Dawn nearby and Edgar made it obvious he was jealous of Prince Rudolf with the prince's hands covered with scars from Edgar's pecks. Prince Rudolf took every opportunity to be nice to Edgar, rubbing some of Rose's potions into his plumage every chance he got and stroking his feathers. Lizzy let Edgar know he had no need to be jealous which, when she told Prince Rudolf, made the prince jealous.

When they made camp just before dusk on the first day, Sir Philip warned Captain Watson that nightwalkers sometimes attacked in this area, and he should set a strong guard. Fortunately for the group, if there were any nightwalkers in the area they decided that the company was too many for them to attack so their night was not disturbed.

They expected to make it to the ford on the River Thracks easily the next day. Late in the afternoon, a much-improved Edgar went for a test flight and to see if the communications station there still existed. It did, but Edgar told Lizzy that there were at least ten times ten goblins and humans near it. Lizzy immediately rode up and told Sir Philip. The travelling that day had been slow. The forest was thicker, and Sir Philip had two riders attempting to cut a way through it. There was a rough path, but it could be only ridden single file. The ford was only about a mile away, so Sir Philip ordered everyone into a single file and to ride as fast as possible.

By the time they reached the river, the attack on the communications station was just beginning. The defenders were one magic user, twenty soldiers and ten werewolves, one of which was Helmut. The defenders had bunched up to make it easier for them to defend themselves. The magic user was attempting to fire lightning bolts at the attackers and couldn't understand why almost nothing was happening.

Following the fight at the werewolf camp near Thomastown prior to their meeting with Queen Lumina,

Sir Philip realised fighting goblins from horseback was ineffective as the goblins were too short to hit from the saddle, so he ordered everyone as soon as they entered the clearing at the ford to dismount and then attack.

Sir Philip was the first to enter the clearing, closely followed by Prince Rudolf and Captain Lipson. Captain Watson with his men and the ten guards from the first camp followed, with the rest of Sir Philip's group guarding the Chalice of the Dawn. Both Sir Philip and Captain Lipson had their battleaxes in their hands and started laying into the goblins and renegade humans as if the two of them were berserkers. The rest of their men followed closely and soon there were bloody bits of goblins and renegade humans flying everywhere. The goblins and renegade humans, even though they had superior numbers, knew they were outmatched and started to panic and flee. They fled towards the forest with everyone, including the werewolves and the men at the camp, chasing them. Less than half made it. Sir Philip called a halt when the goblins and renegade humans entered the forest as he knew his party would lose their advantage in there. He looked around for Captain Lipson. 'You make a great berserker.'

'I'm just copying my commanding officer.' He smiled.

The werewolves had become human and started

looking for their clothes. When dressed, Helmut went over to Sir Philip and shook his hand. 'That's twice now you have saved me.'

'You're still one up on me. But let's hope neither of us needs to be saved again.'

'Yes.' Helmut looked at Sir Philip with sorrow in his eye. 'I'm so sorry to hear about Charlotte. She made a great queen and was a good friend to my pack.'

'Thank you, I've sworn vengeance on Sir Peter Mayflor and will not rest until I have killed him.'

'In that case, I may have to rescue you again. But wouldn't that mean war with Mayflor and the Duchess?'

'I would destroy all the Seven Duchies and the Duchess to get Sir Peter.'

'That would be a massive task. They say that the Duchess even got Braidos to back down.'

Sir Philip gave a grim smile. 'Not as massive a task as you may think.'

Captain Watson joined them. 'The butcher's list, Sir Philip.'

Sir Philip grimaced. 'How bad was it?'

'Four of my men dead, three wounded. Eight of the guards here dead, another four wounded. Two werewolves dead and also the magic user. Lots of dead goblins and renegade humans, no wounded.'

'That bad,' Sir Philip said sadly, looking around the bloody camp. 'We will camp here tonight and bury our dead. Get Rose and Lizzy to help our wounded. We will leave no one here; we will all leave here first thing in the morning. Also, help Helmut prepare two funeral pyres for his pack.'

As they were talking, several of the men started looking up and pointing, soon everyone was. It was a wyvern flying high towards Harbourtown. The rider had obviously not seen them.

Sir Philip called to Price Rudolf. 'Quick, one of your signal bolts.'

Prince Rudolf sighed. 'I knew I should have got some off the rider at Harbourtown.'

'Could Edgar get to it?' Sir Philip asked Lizzy.

'Not yet. He still isn't fully recovered.'

They all watched as the wyvern got smaller and smaller before it disappeared altogether.

Queen Charlotte and Colin had stayed in Thomastown to help the wounded. Sir Matthew had hunted down a lot of the renegade humans, but many had got away. He had also taken thirty-two prisoners. Sir Matthew asked

Queen Charlotte if she would like him to execute them. Queen Charlotte had answered that The Field was always looking for more *workers* and she would have them sent there. Sir Matthew said he would escort them there when the problems in Falconia were over and he went back to Concordia. Queen Charlotte ordered the prisoners to be taken to Castle Falconia and placed in the castle cells as there was nowhere to keep so many in Thomastown.

It was late afternoon four days after the battle when a wyvern rider came to see her while she was checking on Sir George, who was recovering well and still annoying all the healers because he couldn't stand being in bed. Charlotte had just told him that his hook had been recovered and repaired. The wyvern rider handed her the sealed message that was addressed to Sir George and Colin but was told they were at Thomastown. He had thought that Queen Charlotte was dead, but as she wasn't he would give the message to her. Queen Charlotte started to read the message and gave a loud cheer, which attracted the attention of everyone in the barracks. 'They did it! They got the Chalice. I'll order the box made immediately, even if we have to pull the lead off the castle roof.' She continued to read. 'What's this about a royal funeral? What happened to Rose?'

This made Sir George sit up and he winced in pain. 'What has happened to her?'

The wyvern rider nervously answered, 'Your Majesty, Princess Rose was well when I left Harbourtown. We were told you were dead. Sir Philip wanted the castle authorities to organise your funeral.'

'Of course, the dwarfs and the goblins destroyed our communication line.' She turned to the wyvern rider. 'Take the message to Sir Gillian Stevens and have him start to make the box immediately. After you have done that fly back to Harbourtown and tell Sir Philip I am alive and well and I cannot wait to see him and Rose again.'

The wyvern rider replied, 'Yes, Your majesty. I will do so immediately.'

Queen Charlotte then told Healer Hall who had shown the wyvern rider where she was, 'I must leave now. I have to go and find my husband and daughter. I will leave you Colin.'

'I wish you luck. Your help here has saved many lives.'

'I'm coming with you,' Sir George muttered while attempting to climb out of bed.

'You are staying here until you are fully recovered.'

'I am. Just bring me my hook.'

'No, you are not, now get back into bed.'

'I'm not one of your men, I don't have to obey your orders. I'm retired. I can do what I like.'

Queen Charlotte turned to the healer. 'Get me a pen, parchment, ink and sealing wax immediately.'

The healer was back in less than two minutes. Charlotte wrote on the parchment and melted a spot of wax on it using her magic to melt it. She then took the Great Ring of Falconia and pushed it into the wax as the royal seal and showed the parchment to Sir George who had been sitting watching her. 'Do you know what this is?'

'A royal decree,' guessed Sir George.

'You're right, uncle and it says you are to stay here until either I come back or the healers say you are completely healed. To disobey a royal decree is treason.'

Sir George got back into bed grumbling, 'You should have been spanked more as a child.'

Charlotte laughed and went to find Captain Clough.

CHAPTER THIRTY-SEVEN

Sir Philip and his party continued their journey the next day. Helmut and his werewolves did not accompany them. Helmut, before he left, told Sir Philip if he ever needed his help to send a message, although that would be difficult now that Sharag and his companions were dead. Sir Philip told Helmut that he also could call on his help at any time.

Late the next day, Sir Philip and his party came across the clearing where the first communications base had been. Everyone was dead and all of the bodies had been at least partially eaten by forest creatures. The camp itself had been ransacked for loot. Sir Philip called a halt. Most of the bodies looked human and it was impossible to tell which were and which were not werewolves. Sharag and his companion's corpses were easier to tell as they were much taller and had very strange skeletons.

'We will camp here and bury our comrades in the morning,' Sir Philip told the others; he knew his men would not like to bury bodies at night. 'They would have died bravely, and their remains should not be left for forest creatures.'

They moved what was left of the bodies into an area near the edge of the clearing and built fires around them to keep the forest creatures away and set at least ten men at a time to keep watch on the fires and the clearing.

The fires worked and no night creatures entered the camp. The next day, leaving at least ten men on guard at all times, all the other men including Sir Philip, Prince Rudolf, Captain Lipson and Captain Watson helped dig the graves. The only man that didn't help was Roget.

They had almost finished digging the graves. It was slow going as everyone was still wearing their armour. The graves were shallow, most hitting rock at a maximum four feet deep, which was probably the reason the area was absent of trees. There was a cry from one of guards. He spun around with an arrow embedded in his chest. Arrows started to fly from trees all around the edges of the camp. Some were deflected by the superior

Concordian armour but those arrows that hit straight on, killed or wounded their targets. 'Into the graves,' yelled Sir Philip and everyone ran and jumped in, except Captain Lipson who ran and grabbed the box holding the Chalice of the Dawn first. He made it to the grave that held Sir Philip and one of the Concordian soldiers with an arrow protruding from his shoulder and one from his ankle. 'Well done, I should have thought of that. Are you all right?' Sir Philip asked.

'Just a couple of scratches, I'm glad they're lousy shots.' Captain Lipson groaned. 'Who are these swine?'

'I don't know yet.' He shouted out towards the other graves, 'Lizzy are you there?'

Lizzy, who was in the next grave, spoke quietly back, 'I'm here with Rudi and Rose.'

Sir Philip, who was slightly taken aback with Lizzy's familiar term for Prince Rudolf, asked, 'Could you ask Edgar to find out who's shooting arrows at us?'

'He's already doing it. He says that there are about ten times four humans with long sticks that fire the little sticks.'

Sir Philip quickly glanced over the top of the grave and ducked as several arrows were fired at him. He saw several bodies lying around the camp but didn't sight any of the archers. He shouted to the others, 'Keep down and they can't hit you. If they come close, we'll butcher them. Can Roget hear me?'

Roget several graves away replied, 'Yes.'

'Can you do anything?'

'With the Chalice this close the best I could do is give them a minor headache.'

Sir Philip knew that anyone in the open would become a pin cushion immediately, though they would have to wait until after dark and then creep out and attack the humans. Prince Rudolf tried to aim his crossbow at one of the archers but before he could target one, he had to duck back down as several arrows flew towards him. It was stalemate. If the archers approached the graves they could be attacked before they shot down into them and if Sir Philip attacked, a lot of his men would be killed before they made it to the trees. Sir Philip knew that night was a long way away as it was not yet noon, he spoke as quietly as he could, just enough to reach Prince Rudolf. 'Pass it on quietly. We have to wait until dark and then we'll attack stealthily.' The message was passed on.

It was late in the afternoon when Queen Charlotte with Captain Clough rode into the clearing. Queen Charlotte raised her right hand with the Great Ring of Falconia on her ring finger and stopped a mass of arrows that flew towards her. They fell to the ground. She then blasted several trees, sending dead archers tumbling to the ground. Her men spread out, riding into the trees to look for the rest. Several more arrows flew at her, so she raised her right hand again and they also fell to the ground before they reached her. She then targeted another group of trees and more dead archers fell. No more arrows came as the survivors tried to escape her and her men.

Sir Philip and the others hiding in the graves climbed out. Sir Philip took off his helmet as he walked towards Queen Charlotte. Queen Charlotte took off hers. 'I was told you were dead.'

'Do I look it?' Queen Charlotte replied as she dismounted.

The two ran to one another, their armour clashing as they embraced. 'Just having your armour was bad enough, but now we're both wearing it ...' Queen Charlotte left the sentenced unfinished.

A few seconds later there was another clash of armour as Rose, her helmet tossed aside, crashed into Queen Charlotte and Sir Philip. Queen Charlotte looked down at her daughter and kissed her on top of her head. All three had tears in their eyes.

After a while they released each other. Sir Philip told Queen Charlotte, 'I have sworn to avenge you and kill Sir Peter.'

'You may still do that. He or one of his raiders killed Jackie who they thought was me.'

Sir Philip told her sadly, 'Liam is also dead.'

'Let us hope they are now reunited happily,' Queen Charlotte said with a tear in her eye.

'You were lucky none of the arrows hit you when you entered the clearing,' Sir Philip told his wife.

'We were ready for them.'

'How?'

'When a raven starts flapping frantically in your face it's possible to guess something is wrong.'

Sir Philip laughed and looked around for Lizzy. She was with Prince Rudolf, holding hands. Edgar was on her shoulder. Queen Charlotte seeing them, gave Sir Philip a quizzical look. 'I'll tell you later,' he told her. 'Lizzy come here please,' he called.

Lizzy went over to them. Sir Philip looked at Edgar and then back at Lizzy. 'Tell Edgar he's hereby promoted to sergeant.'

A few seconds later Edgar flew onto Sir Philip's shoulder and rubbed his head against Sir Philip's fuzzy cheek. Lizzy laughed. 'He wants to know if he's going to get paid?'

Chapter Thirty-seven

'All the birdseed he can eat for the rest of his life.'

'He says if he eats too much he won't be able to fly.'

Everyone laughed, but suddenly grew serious as Captain Clough came back into the clearing on his horse. 'Your Majesty, we've cleared the area of the archers.'

Edgar flew off Sir Philip's shoulder and headed for the trees. 'Edgar is just going to check,' Lizzy told them.

Queen Charlotte asked Captain Clough, 'How many prisoners?'

'No prisoners, Your Majesty.' He turned his horse to ride away as Queen Charlotte gave him a stern look.

'I have to ask. How did you do it?' asked Sir Philip.

'Do what?'

'Stop the arrows and blast the trees.'

'I used the ring. It covers more area than my magic can. Even after all this time I still have much to learn.'

'But why did it work? The Chalice of the Dawn destroys all magic within a mile. Try hitting that tree with a magical lightning bolt.'

Queen Charlotte lifted her left hand, and an extremely weak lightning bolt didn't even reach the trees. Roget walked over to them. 'There are some things in this world that are more powerful than *The Magic*. The ring is one of them, as is the Chalice of the Dawn. There are also some things that work outside *The Magic* such as Colin's crystals. I have been given permission to tell you a story, but it must be in private, and you must never repeat it.' Both Queen Charlotte and Sir Philip agreed.

Queen Charlotte, Sir Philip and Roget walked to the edge of the camp, leaving Rose behind. As they did so Sir Philip called to Captain Clough, 'Have the men finish the graves and make sure we're left alone.'

'Yes, Sir Philip.'

'You know the power your grandmother has. Have you ever wondered how after a four day siege the fort at Duchies Pass hadn't fallen?'

'I've seen the defences, it's not an easy place to take,' Sir Philip told Roget.

'It took King Edmond four days to get there. The Duchess could have almost destroyed the whole wall in four days. No, she had to lose that battle.'

'Why?' asked Charlotte.

'For the Great Ring of Falconia. Only the rightful ruler of Falconia can wear it and she wanted it for her family.' Roget paused, and even though the others couldn't see his face, they imagined that he smiled. 'Which it is now, but not the way she expected.'

'The way I've been told of the battle of Duchies Pass, her calvary almost got to King Edmond,' Sir Philip said.

'Yes, they did better than she thought they would.

Fortunately, Sir George saved the King. It had to look like she wanted to win. The result of the battle was that King Edmond married the Duchess's daughter, Lady Katerina and within a year King Edmond was dead and the Great Ring of Falconia was in her family.'

'But now the wrong granddaughter has it,' Sir Philip quipped. Queen Charlotte stood saying nothing.

'Your grandmother is the greatest magic user in the entire continent of Strasia. Do not underestimate her. She has not given up her plans.'

Queen Charlotte exclaimed, 'And you want me to give her Scarlett?'

'It is our agreement.'

'I didn't agree to anything.'

'King Philip did, and you will still need my help with your children.'

Queen Charlotte thought for a few seconds. 'I will keep the agreement as soon as Stephen and Julie are fully recovered.'

'That will take a little time. The rose pendants you gave them are keeping them safe.'

'How did you know about them?' Charlotte asked.

'Braidos knows many things,' was the only answer they got.

Charlotte had walked in the castle gardens every day

since the birthday party and had noted that two of the white rose bushes had slightly wilted but were nowhere near dying.

Queen Charlotte asked, 'Why are you telling us this?'

'Braidos does not want your grandmother to become too strong. I am telling you this as a warning.'

'Thank you, Roget,' Queen Charlotte answered. 'But there will still never be another temple to him in Falconia. Now, I must help with the wounded.'

As Queen Charlotte walked back into the camp she saw Burgher Rowles, her godfather. She went and gave him a hug. 'Godfather, what are you doing here?'

'I came to help avenge you.'

'Thank you, but I'm still alive.'

'I'm so glad to see you,' the burgher said, fighting back tears.

Rose returned the Silver wolf ring and the Silver eagle brooch to her mother and then Charlotte did what she could for the wounded, but without magic and the fact she had left her medical bag with the healers at Thomastown, it wasn't as much as she hoped. Edgar reported that there were no enemies in the immediate area, but he was now tired, not being fully recovered from his injuries. The queen thought about sending the Chalice of the Dawn over a mile away but decided that there was still the possibility of enemies being not too far away and could not risk its loss. Fifteen of Captain Watson's men had died and Captain Watson himself and ten more wounded, three seriously. Captain Lipson was the only one wounded from Sir Philip's group and none of Captain Clough's men had taken a wound. After the dead were all buried, they continued their journey with the wounded tied to their horses, where necessary. They travelled slower than they would have liked. There were no more incidents on the journey and in less than three days they were back at Thomastown. The three seriously wounded men died.

CHAPTER THIRTY-EIGHT

On the way to Thomastown, both Queen Charlotte and Sir Philip told each other what had happened to them. Rose told her mother that Roget had saved her life and Queen Charlotte started to feel kinder towards him, although she was still adamant that Braidos would have no more influence in Falconia. Sir Philip told his wife that he had also saved Roget's life to which she replied, 'That's your job.'

Rose also told her mother that Speedy and Slinky had gone to join the Goddess Coralie. Charlotte sadly told her daughter, 'I will really miss them. They were the first of the Silver animals I ever met. Did I ever tell you the story of how they saved me from a pair of harpies and a school of sharks?'

Rose smiled and answered, 'No, please tell me the story.'

Her mother did.

When they got to Thomastown, messages were sent both by crystal and pigeon that the portrait holding Princess Scarlett should be crated up and sent immediately to Passville escorted by the troops that had been sent from the Duchies Pass Fort, after they had returned to Castle Falconia from the Thomastown battle. This was done because they didn't want to take the risk that the Chalice of the Dawn would release Charlotte's twin from the canvas.

Sir George had just about fully recovered, and Queen Charlotte tore up the royal decree. The left-hand side of his face and body showed scars from the burning but otherwise he seemed more than healthy for a man of his age. He gave Lizzy a big hug when he heard they were related, although, he couldn't work out how.

When the crate had left Castle Falconia for Passville, Queen Charlotte, Sir Philip and his party which included Captain Lipson, Captain Clough, Sir George, Colin, Sir Matthew, who had welcomed seeing his brother after several years, and his men, left for Castle Falconia. The wyvern riders stayed.

When they got back, they were met by Sir David

Reading who told them that the lead-lined box had been made and was on a strong wagon. 'We had to take the lead off some of the castle's roofs, so I hope it doesn't rain soon. The dwarfs now have the best lead mines.'

'I'm sure we can come to some sort of trade arrangement with Malgon, but we still have some lead mines. All the lead mined by the Falconian mines will be bought by me,' was Queen Charlotte's reply. 'But first, we must go the laboratory.'

Queen Charlotte, Sir Philip, Colin, Roget and Rose went straight to the Queen's laboratory with Sir Philip carrying the box containing the Chalice of the Dawn. Noah was on duty at the iron door. As the Chalice did not affect crystals Colin told him to send a message to Cooper to remove the crystal barrier. Cooper quite rightly refused. Colin then told Noah to send a message that he was coming down. Twenty minutes later Colin entered the room containing Stephen and Julie. Two spears awaited him, which were lowered as soon as the guards were sure it was him. Cooper had already realised his magic wasn't working. Colin dismantled the yellow crystal screen by taking the large crystal off the staff in the centre of the room. When this was done, one of the guards helped Sir Philip carry the box down the stairs and place it on the table. The lid was taken off and Roget and Rose, taking one handle each, took it out of the box. Colin told Cooper and Noah, 'Bring the ingredients.'

Cooper and Noah went back up the stairs to the laboratory and collected the crushed rubies that the castle magic users had learnt to crush, ten of the red petals of the lace leaf flower, a large bag of the berries of the red mountain ash, a large vial of blue dragon's blood and a granite pestle.

While Rose held the Chalice with her right hand and Roget with his left, Roget used the pestle to grind and mix the crushed rubies, the lace leaf flower petals and the ash berries together. When this was done, he added the blue dragon's blood. The mixture stayed blue. Roget turned to the others, 'The mixture should turn purple. Something is wrong. Let the Chalice go Rose.' Both Roget and Rose let go of the Chalice. 'How old is this dragon's blood?'

Colin answered, 'It should be good, it was Queen Katerina's.'

Roget shook his head. 'Queen Katerina died over fourteen years ago. This blood is too old.'

Queen Charlotte shook her head. 'So, we have to find a dragon.'

A bucket was brought down from the laboratory and the Chalice's contents were poured into it by Roget and Rose who then returned the Chalice to its box. It was then taken to the wagon in the castle's courtyard that held the bigger, heavier, lead-lined box and placed inside. The workers who had made the box had done an excellent job. The lid was topped with steel and was hinged and had a steel ring attached on the top, opposite the hinge. A series of pulleys had been erected in the courtyard with two horses to open and close the lid.

Queen Charlotte sent orders for a bag of rubies to be brought to her and then used her magic to crush them. Sir Philip collected fifty men and then escorted Noah to the Great Forest to get more of the red petals of the lace leaf flower, they still had plenty of red mountain ash berries left.

Colin reset the yellow screen that helped protect Stephen and Julie, then he left the room to see if his main crystal in the laboratory could help find a dragon, the crystal was large, clear and two feet in diameter. Colin had used it many times to find information about various places in Strasia. He knew the only likely place a dragon would be found was in the Infinity Mountains. As the name suggested, the Infinity Mountains covered an extremely large area, larger than Strasia itself, so Colin thought it could take a long time to find a dragon.

Roget, after depositing the Chalice of the Dawn in the protection of the lead box, returned to the laboratory. He waited quietly while Queen Charlotte finished using her magic to crush the rubies. When she had finished, he spoke to her. 'I know how we can find a dragon.'

'How?' asked Colin and the queen together.

'We can ask Braidos.'

'You mean bring Braidos here?' Queen Charlotte asked in amazement.

'He has been to Castle Falconia many times.'

'Yes, and the last time he killed my mother.'

'She was trying to kill you.'

Queen Charlotte looked at Colin. 'How long will it take to find a dragon using your crystal?'

'Maybe five minutes, maybe five months.' Colin shrugged.

'Call Braidos.'

'I will need a large golden chalice containing human blood. Not much, but it must be human.'

Queen Charlotte ordered one of her children's guards, 'Go and get Captain Clough.'

Captain Clough arrived in less than ten minutes. 'Captain Clough, go and talk to the renegade human prisoners and offer a pardon to one of them who will let me use some of his blood. Bring the blood to me in my consulting room, in a large golden chalice.'

Captain Clough looked surprised at the order but said, 'Yes, Your Majesty.' He saluted, turned and left.

The queen turned to Colin. 'Well, would you like to meet Braidos?'

'Will I get to hit him on the head with my staff?'

'I think not,' was the queen's answer.

'Oh well, I will stay here and continue the search, I may be lucky. Send for me when the blood arrives.'

'Roget, please follow me.'

Queen Charlotte and Roget waited for over two hours for the blood to arrive. When it did, the queen asked Captain Clough to go and get Colin. Colin arrived fifteen minutes later. Captain Clough was asked if he would like to meet Braidos and he declined and left the room.

Roget picked up the golden chalice, intoned a few words so quietly no one could hear. He then drank from the chalice and returned it to the table.

The three of them waited silently for over two minutes, then there was a sound like a thunderclap and the room darkened. A black whirlwind started to grow on the far side of the table from where the three were standing. In the centre of the whirlwind a large dark figure started to appear. The dark figure slowly continued to form from the top of the head down. He was bald with scarlet-coloured skin that glowed. The eyes were jet-black, the nose little more than a slit and the lips a deep blood red. He wore a jet-black cloak over his bare back. He looked extremely muscular. His legs were not seen, if they existed, as the whirlwind still swirled below his waist. When he had finished forming, he smiled at Queen Charlotte. 'I never expected to be invited into Castle Falconia again.'

'And you never will again. Unfortunately, I have to ask you a question.'

'You mean you require a favour. What do I get in return?'

'You get Scarlett's portrait as I believe you have already been promised.'

'Correct, but as you say, it has already been promised me.'

'But only when my children have recovered and that could take some time.'

Braidos looked troubled. 'But you have the Chalice of the Dawn. You should have used it by now.' He looked at Roget.

Chapter Thirty-eight

'The dragon's blood they have belonged to Queen Katerina.'

Braidos laughed. 'You should really keep your magical supplies up to date. I can't just magic you some.'

Queen Charlotte spoke, 'I would like to ask you where we can find a dragon?'

Braidos nodded and shut his eyes. 'Roget now knows. I wish you luck. Getting the blood won't be easy.'

'I'll do it. But first I have a question you may be able to answer.'

'I may or may not answer it.'

'Why didn't the Chalice of the Dawn when it arrived here stop the magic that is affecting my children?'

'What is affecting your children is more than ordinary magic. A seed was placed at the top of your children's spines when they were babies. It has grown to take over their brains so now they appear to be in a coma. The Chalice cannot destroy the growth by itself. It needs the potion as well.'

'Thank you for the information. Who planned it?'

'I have answered you one question, the rest you must work out for yourself,' he paused in thought, 'unless you wish to build me another temple.'

'That will never happen.'

Braidos looked around the room. 'It's good being back

in Castle Falconia. What's to stop me from killing you like I did your mother and staying here?'

'I have learnt that some things are more powerful than *The Magic*, such as the Great Ring of Falconia. My mother wasn't wearing it but I am.'

Colin moved to the door. 'If you try to harm any of us, I will knock on this door and the lid of the lead box holding the Chalice of the Dawn will be lifted and then you will lose your magic and be helpless.'

'It will take too long for your message to get to the castle courtyard. I would be gone before then.'

'No, it will be immediate. Outside the door is Lizzy. Lizzy can talk to a raven.'

'I know of this raven.'

'Well, the raven is in the courtyard and if Lizzy tells it to start flapping its wings the lid will be removed and do not think you can harm Lizzy. If Lizzy loses mind-contact with Edgar, Edgar will also start flapping. I wonder how it will go. You here with no magic versus the Great Ring of Falconia.'

'You are a great queen, Charlotte and have loyal helpers. Something your mother didn't have. You will make your grandmother proud. As I said, Roget now has the information to locate a dragon. I wish you luck.'

There was another thunderclap as Braidos clapped

his hands and he shrank back into the whirlwind, which then faded until it disappeared altogether. Queen Charlotte, Colin and Roget went to find a dragon.

421

CHAPTER THIRTY-NINE

Queen Charlotte, Colin and Roget re-entered the laboratory. Colin said, 'Alright Roget, there's a map on that table next to my giant crystal. Where's the dragon?'

Roget walked to the map and studied it. He then pointed. 'It is here, about one hundred miles north-west of here.'

Colin looked at where Roget was pointing and then scryed his crystal. After two minutes he exclaimed, 'I have found it. The dragon's ninety-seven miles almost directly north-west of here.'

Queen Charlotte ordered one of the guards, 'Go and get Prince Rudolf.'

Ten minutes later, Prince Rudolf entered; he was

accompanied by Noah, who had the red petals of the lace leaf flower.

Queen Charlotte spoke to the prince, 'Rudi, could you and your wyverns fly to this place,' she pointed on the map, 'and help me get some dragon's blood?'

'I'd have to take my riders as well,' Rudi joked. 'It doesn't look that far. We fly further than that and back coming here.'

'We will need all of the wyverns, I think.'

'I will have them called here at once. Seven of us should be able to take one dragon.'

'Eight, you forget, I have Great Wing.'

Rudi thought for a second. 'Charlotte, we thought you were dead. Philip was quite distraught, to put it mildly. Falconia needs you. You should not come with us.'

Charlotte asked, 'What weapons do you have to take on a dragon? I am the only person who has a chance to get the blood. I have to go.'

Rudi nodded. 'I will send for the wyverns, and we will leave first thing tomorrow morning.'

The next morning, seven wyverns and their riders gathered in the castle courtyard. Queen Charlotte, wearing armour but without gauntlets, and Sir Philip entered the courtyard to join them. The previous evening, Sir Philip had tried vainly to persuade his wife not to join them, but Queen Charlotte could not be swayed. She touched the eagle brooch, which had been fastened to a scarf around her neck so that she could reach it when her visor was open, and Great Wing, the giant black eagle, appeared. The eagle, more than six feet tall, spread its wings to allow the harness that would carry Queen Charlotte to be attached to its talons, as a person riding on its back would affect its flying. Each of the riders, including Queen Charlotte, had a steel-hinged, lidded container with a clasp for holding the dragon's blood. Queen Charlotte strapped herself in and the wyvern riders mounted up and they all took off flying north-west.

Great Wing had to slow down as he started to outdistance the wyverns. After two and a half hours, they approached the area that had been marked on the map. The group hovered together and organised a search pattern to cover as much territory as possible. 'Any who spot the dragon, fire a signal bolt,' Prince Rudolf told his men. He looked at Charlotte.

'Great Wing will give a loud screech. He can be extremely noisy.'

Less than fifteen minutes later, an exploding arrow

was seen in the sky. Everyone flew towards the signal and regrouped. Less than half a mile away on the ground, a blue dragon was battling a snake. The blue dragon was at least fifty feet long, had a wingspan twice as long, four thick legs and, at its widest, about eight feet in diameter. It had a long snout and a large, well-toothed mouth. It had a long, narrow neck holding its head, which was quite large and its green eyes were the size of fists. It looked as if it was having the better of its battle with the snake.

The snake was seventy feet long and maybe five and a half feet wide, it looked like it had lost the tip of its tail. It had brown, green and grey jagged stripes all the way down its body to its damaged, tapered tail. Its mouth had two long fangs dipping down from the roof of its mouth, both over three feet long, it also had two sets of backward curving teeth, its right eye was yellowy-white with a black vertical slit. Its left eye was milky white as if blind. It had obvious injuries from the fight. Some of its skin was burnt and there was blood showing on various parts of its body.

Prince Rudolf commented to Queen Charlotte, 'From Captain Lipson's description, that looks like his snake.'

'Yes, it does,' the queen replied. 'And he charged it on foot.'

Prince Rudolf called out, 'Sergeant Alexander take

Jack and give the dragon a burst of fire. We'll be ready to follow up.'

Sergeant Alexander and Jack flew up higher so they could gather speed in a dive at the dragon. They dived and as they got closer to the dragon, the wyverns spat their fire. The dragon looked as if it didn't even notice it.

Queen Charlotte told Prince Rudolf, 'My turn.'

She fired a bolt of lightning at the dragon's head. It didn't seem to do any damage, but the dragon flew up twenty feet off the ground and looked around to see where it came from. As it looked around the snake took its chance. It reared up the twenty feet and sank its fangs into the dragon's neck. The dragon gave what sounded like a painful roar and shook the snake away. Blood was pouring from its neck. Sergeant Alexander took a great risk. He flew his wyvern low between the snake and the dragon and, as he did so, had his lidded container open and some of the dragon's blood filled it. He flew back towards his companions covered in dragon's blood. The dragon started to follow.

Queen Charlotte, this time using the Great Ring of Falconia, fired a blast at its head, so strong that would have taken off a salamander's head. The dragon just shook its head, but turned away, flying away from the group and the snake.

The triumphant snake turned its one eye towards the

group and flickered its forked tongue. It then turned and slithered away towards a cave in one of the mountains.

'I have it, Your Majesty, the dragon's blood,' Sergeant Alexander shouted triumphantly.

Queen Charlotte smiled. 'Thank you, you look like you have more blood on you than in the container.'

'It is nothing, Your Majesty.'

Prince Rudolf took over. 'We've succeeded in our mission and saved Captain Lipson's snake. Back to Castle Falconia everybody.'

They flew back to the castle.

When they got back, Queen Charlotte, after greeting her husband, ordered that the small box containing the Chalice of the Dawn be taken to the laboratory and Rose and Roget be sent for. Colin sent a message down to the room the children were in and just over twenty minutes later he removed the main yellow crystal so the room was accessible. The magic user in the room was Sophia, a tall, pale-skinned, seventeen-year-old girl with silver hair and grey eyes. She was allowed to stay, as were the two guards. Prince Rudolf brought the blood and Sir Philip the box and the other ingredients. Also, there was Queen

Chapter Thirty-nine

Charlotte, Colin, Rose and Roget.

Rose and Roget took the Chalice of the Dawn out of the small box. Once again, while Rose held the Chalice with her right hand and Roget with his left, Roget used the pestle to grind and mix the crushed rubies, the lace leaf flower petals and the ash berries together. There was some concern that there may be some of the snake's poison in the dragon's blood. Queen Charlotte used the Great Ring of Falconia to make sure it was pure. Then the dragon's blood was added. This time the mixture turned purple.

Roget and Rose picked up the Chalice and first went to Stephen's bed. Queen Charlotte held his mouth open as half of the mixture was poured into his mouth. Stephen swallowed it. Then they did the same for Julie. 'Now we wait,' Roget told everyone. 'It will take some time for the potion to completely cure them.'

They sat waiting for over three hours before the children began to stir. Half an hour later, Julie tried to sit up and failed. Queen Charlotte gave her a hug then one to Stephen, who had tried to talk. Sir Philip was the next to embrace them, followed by Rose. Colin called up the stairs, 'The children are recovering.' This pronouncement was greeted by a loud cheer from the many people in the laboratory who would normally never go there.

'Feed them with a thin broth for a while,' Roget told Queen Charlotte who immediately ordered that some be brought from the kitchens. 'We must put the Chalice back in its box,' Roget told Rose, and they did so.

Sir Philip ordered the two guards to take the box and put it in the bigger one in the castle courtyard. They left with the box. When the broth arrived, Queen Charlotte and Sir Philip fed their children themselves.

CHAPTER FORTY

The next morning, Queen Charlotte sent a message to the fort at Duchies Pass telling them to arrange a meeting with the Duchess of Mayflor in four days' time. She would have made it three but wanted to spend an extra day with her children. They were recovering well and already sitting up in bed. Both the Queen and Colin thought that the children's rose pendants had helped. Queen Charlotte noted the two slightly wilted roses were now looking healthier. While Queen Charlotte and Sir Philip were sitting with the children shortly before their evening meal of thin broth, which they both complained about, wanting something more substantial, Colin and Prince Rudolf entered the room. Colin hadn't restored the yellow screen, but the number of guards had been tripled and there were always at least two magic users in the room.

Prince Rudolf gave each of the children a hug and then spoke to their parents. 'I will be leaving in the morning. I should go and help my grandfather against the northern tribes.'

Sir Philip and the prince grasped each other's wrists. 'I will never be able to repay you for all the help you have given us.'

Queen Charlotte kissed Prince Rudolf on the cheek. 'If there's ever anything I or Falconia can ever do for you, just ask.'

'I will be stealing one of your magic users. I have asked Lizzy to marry me, and she foolishly said yes.'

Everyone in the room congratulated him. 'I will leave three wyverns here but that includes the wounded one. You'll have more than enough riders. We are going to tie Lizzy to one so she can come and meet my father and grandfather.'

Sir Philip looked at Colin. 'Which reminds me, Colin did you find those documents that show Lizzy is related to Sir George?'

Colin smiled as he took a small sheaf of parchments out of his crystal bag. 'I have them here.'

He gave them to Prince Rudolf who quickly scanned

them. 'The information in these should convince both father and grandpapa.' He then frowned. 'These parchments say the right things, but they look freshly written.'

'Hmm, give them to me.'

Prince Rudolf gave the parchments to Queen Charlotte, who passed her hand over them and then gave the now aged parchments back to him.

'Thank you, Charlotte.'

Sir Philip now spoke, 'Don't forget to send us at least three weeks' notice of the wedding. Charlotte can use Great Wing, but I'll have to ride.'

'I will. Could you bring Jacob with you? I think we have become good friends.'

Earlier that day he had spoken privately with Captain Lipson. 'I saw your snake; it was fighting a dragon and you charged that thing on foot?'

'It seemed a good idea at the time.'

The prince had shaken Captain Lipson's hand. 'You are the bravest man I've ever met. In private call me Rudi.'

'Thank you, Rudi.'

Sir Philip nodded. 'Jacob is a good man to have fighting at your side. I'll bring him but you have to promise I can bring him back.' Sir Philip smiled.

The prince laughed. 'A pity, he would be a great asset to the Concordian army.'

'He is to ours,' was Sir Philip's answer.

The next morning, five wyverns in the castle courtyard were getting ready to fly back to Concordia. Prince Rudolf, Sergeant Alexander and two other riders were preparing them. Prince Rudolf was helping Lizzy. Queen Charlotte, Sir Philip, Colin, Captain Lipson, Rose, Sir George and numerous others were there to see them off. Stephen and Julie, although much recovered, were told they still had to stay in bed, but now they were able to eat more solid food.

Sir George had given his distant *great-niece* a last hug before Prince Rudolf started to tie her to the saddle on the wyvern. Edgar was snuggled in a bag of wool to keep him comfortable for the flight. Prince Rudolf went to stroke him and had his hand pecked as a reward. 'I hope Edgar will come to like me. I like him.'

Lizzy smiled. 'Edgar does like you.'

'Really?'

'Yes, if he didn't like you, he'd peck your eyes.' Lizzy laughed.

Prince Rudolf was taken aback and shook his head as he finished tying Lizzy to the wyvern. He then went round and said goodbye to everyone and mounted his own wyvern and, with a wave, all five wyverns took off and headed north.

Sir Matthew went to talk to Queen Charlotte and Sir Philip. 'My men and I are ready to leave with the prisoners and Roget, whom I believe we are to leave at Passville.'

The Queen answered, 'Yes, Roget is to wait there until we send him a message that he can take the portrait to Mayflor.'

'Well, goodbye. I believe I will be seeing you again soon at the prince's wedding.'

'Yes, it should be a great event.'

Sir Matthew then went and said his goodbyes, finishing with his brother who he gave a hug. Then it was Burgher Rowles's turn to say goodbye. He was going to travel as far as Harbourtown with Sir Matthew and his men. They then mounted their horses and rode out of the castle and town where Sir Matthew's men, Roget and the prisoners were waiting for him.

'My turn to get moving,' Charlotte told her husband. 'I have to go and meet my grandmother.' It had been decided, over Sir Philip's many objections, to leave him behind. Charlotte thought that Sir Philip couldn't be trusted not to try and get information out of her grandmother about Sir Peter.

'But will you be safe?' Sir Philip asked his wife.

'I have Captain Clough, Stuart and fifty men to escort me and the wagon. And I have the Great Ring of Falconia.' Colin was staying to help look after the children.

Rose came up to them. 'I'm going too.'

Queen Charlotte looked down at her daughter. 'It's much too dangerous, you're staying here.'

'More dangerous than getting the Chalice of the Dawn? Besides, Roget will be reasonably close and so should I, in case we have to hold the Chalice.' It had been decided to take the Chalice of the Dawn with them to weaken the Duchess of Mayflor's position.

Her mother made a quick decision. 'You've thought your argument well. You may come.'

Rose gave her mother a hug. 'Thank you.' She ran to get her horse.

The journey to the fort at Duchies Pass went slower than everybody liked. On the way, they stopped to inspect the walls blocking the travelling haze. The work had gone well and there was a strong wall on both sides. They continued the journey, leaving the two magic users and the hundred men guarding the spot. The stonemasons were told they should go back to Castle Falconia where they would get paid.

It was late in the night when they finally got to the fort. Queen Charlotte had used magic to light the way. Sir James Oliver and his wife Margaret welcomed them. After all her men had been billeted, Queen Charlotte asked how fast they could remove the heavy box lid, remove the smaller box and then open that. Sir James told her the best engineers in the whole of Falconia were there, as could be seen from the wall across the pass and the marvel of the fort gate. It would take seconds. They had pulleys, chains, experienced horses, everything that would be needed. Queen Charlotte told them to set everything up the next day inside the fort but in a place that could see the other side of the wall across the pass.

They spent the next day making sure everything was ready. It didn't take long, Sir James was right, the best engineers in Falconia were there. After the pulleys were set up everyone had a quiet day.

CHAPTER FORTY-ONE

Early the next morning, Queen Charlotte floated a large gazebo and five comfortable chairs to a point about fifty yards in front of the pass wall gate. She set up four on the side nearest the gate and one on the opposite side. Queen Charlotte, Captain Clough, Stuart and Rose, wearing their court finery, except for the captain who was wearing his armour, sat on the four chairs nearest the wall and waited. Three hours later, the Duchess of Mayflor with three hundred men and a wagon of her own, rode into the pass. They stopped several hundred yards away from the wall. The Duchess dismounted and several of her men put together a gazebo for her and found her a comfortable chair.

The Duchess, wearing the same black dress and golden

clasp with azure stone she had worn for the last meeting, walked casually towards the other gazebo with her gazebo protecting her from the sun and her chair following. When she was fifty yards away, Queen Charlotte lifted her arm. About ten seconds later her gazebo and chair crashed to the ground. The gazebo collapsed, almost knocking the Duchess over. The Duchess gave herself a shake and continued to walk towards the Queen's gazebo. When she got there, Queen Charlotte indicated that the other chair was for the Duchess.

The Duchess, still standing, said, 'So, you acquired the Chalice of the Dawn. Well done.' She looked at Charlotte. 'Greetings, Granddaughter. I see that the news of your demise was slightly exaggerated.'

'Extremely so, Grandmother.'

'Let's see.' She looked at Captain Clough. 'The inefficient captain of the inefficient troops at Castle Falconia.' She then looked at Stuart. 'A minor magic user who is of no importance.' She then looked at Rose. 'You must be my great granddaughter, Rose. One of the brave few who bought the Chalice of the Dawn to Falconia.'

She walked towards Rose and reached to ruffle her hair. Rose leant back to avoid her hand and fell off her chair. The Duchess smiled as she looked at Rose sprawled on the ground. 'Good girl. Never trust anybody, especially me.'

The Duchess turned and went and sat on the chair that had been left for her, and Rose sat back on her own chair. The Duchess then addressed her granddaughter. 'Well, why did you ask to meet me?'

'To make sure of peace between Falconia and the Seven Duchies. As you have noted, we now have the Chalice of the Dawn. Please watch.' Queen Charlotte used the Great Ring of Falconia to cause a small explosion to destroy a rock about one hundred yards away. 'My ring still works even though *The Magic* doesn't, but I want peace between us.'

'Done,' the Duchess answered. 'I'm not going to attack Falconia. After all, my granddaughter is on the throne, and you have the rest of Strasia as your allies. You also have the Chalice of the Dawn, so Falconia is safe. Has Roget got Scarlett's portrait?'

'Yes, as soon as we finish here a message will be sent to him to bring the portrait to you.'

'Hmm, Scarlett. I must admit, I think Katerina sent the wrong daughter away.'

'Thank you for the compliment, Grandmother, but I don't think I would have liked my mother. The stories about her are not pleasant.'

'Well, it will be good to have Braidos back. Our present main god, er, what's his name?'

'Callica,' prompted Charlotte.

'Yes, Callica. You are right. He is rather incompetent. Is there anything else we need to discuss?'

'Sir Peter, my cousin. He and his men killed sixteen Falconians. We would like him sent to Falconia for trial.'

'I believe the wraith killed most of them.'

'The wraith was acting under Sir Peter's orders.'

'Did you know that Sir Peter killed the man he thought killed you?'

Charlotte looked sceptical but said nothing.

'I do not know where he is and I cannot contact him, so I cannot help you.'

Queen Charlotte decided not to push the issue. 'You may send your ambassador back to Passville if you wish.'

The Duchess smiled. 'I will send a new one. The last one had er ... an accident.'

'That does not surprise me,' Queen Charlotte said under her breath. Louder, she told her grandmother, 'As long as the new one is still subject to the previous conditions, that he's not a relative or magic user.'

'I still have excellent hearing even without *The Magic*. If there is nothing else, I will leave.' She stood. 'Please give my regards to Sir Philip and your children. I am actually glad they have recovered.'

Queen Charlotte glared at her grandmother. 'Really?'

'Yes, believe it or not. Sir Roger Livermore acted without my knowledge. I'm glad Sir George killed him.' The Duchess was quiet for a few seconds. 'Braidos once told me that my granddaughter could become the greatest magic user Strasia has ever seen.' She smiled at Charlotte. 'I think he may be right.'

'Even if it's not Scarlett?'

'Katerina spoiled Scarlett. Scarlett won't be spoiled in Mayflor,' the Duchess said sternly. 'Well, goodbye. We'll meet again sometime.' She turned and started to walk away.

'That wasn't as bad as I expected,' Queen Charlotte told the others. 'But I still don't trust her. Let's go back to the fort. I'll send some men to collect our gazebo and the chairs.'

They had just started to walk back towards the gate in the wall across the pass when the Duchess shouted, 'Charlotte!'

Everyone turned. The Duchess raised her right hand and pointed at Charlotte and a lightning bolt shot towards her. A ray of green light from the Great Ring of Falconia immediately soared towards it, intercepting it with a resultant small explosion. Charlotte and the others were shocked.

The Duchess laughed and held her hands up and open. 'A joke, until next time.' She turned and walked away.

The four Falconians watched her go. Captain Clough spoke first, 'She tried to kill you.'

'No, if she wanted to kill me, she wouldn't have called out so I could see the lightning bolt coming. She knew the Great Ring of Falconia would save me. She's a show-off and is trying to prove something.'

As the Duchess neared her broken gazebo and chair, she clicked her fingers, and both rose up and followed her.

'I will send the idiot who put the Chalice of the Dawn back into its big box to The Field.' Queen Charlotte was angry. Then she was quiet for a few seconds. She then raised her left hand and pointed at a nearby stone to fire a lightning bolt at it. Nothing happened. 'Grandmother is much more powerful than we thought.'

Early the next morning Queen Charlotte and her company set off back to Castle Falconia. As they started early, they reached the castle before dark. When they got back Queen Charlotte first greeted her husband, then checked on Stephen and Julie who were recovering quickly and wanted to get out of bed. Their mother told them, 'Maybe tomorrow.'

She then went to see Mythias at the temple of Craidos.

The temple was a large white building surrounded by carved columns. There were steps leading up to a pair of large, white, wooden doors. Queen Charlotte pushed one open and entered the temple. The temple had an aisle leading to an altar. On either side of the aisle were white chairs facing the altar. The white altar was bare. Everything inside the temple was white even the roof and floor. A dim light emanated from the ceiling with no obvious source. The temple was empty.

Mythias entered from a side door near the altar. 'Charlotte, I'm glad to see you have recovered from your death. What brings you here?'

'I would like to talk to you in private.'

Mythias looked around. 'There is no one else here. But come to my room.' He flicked his hand towards the temple doors. 'The doors are now locked.'

He reopened the door he had just come out of. Charlotte entered a large room panelled with dark wood with a lush brown carpet and a light brown ceiling which emanated a brighter light than the rest of the temple. There was a large bookshelf with many books along one of the walls and on the far side from the door sat a large dark wooden desk with a solid stone chair with bright red cushions. There were also two of the white wooden chairs in the room. Mythias offered Charlotte one of the wooden chairs and went to sit on the stone one.

'I have a stone chair as I keep breaking the wooden ones.' Mythias smiled.

'I've never been in here before.'

'Very few have. Not even the other priests are allowed in here. But I think this talk will have to be very private. Never to be repeated to anyone.'

'I understand. I met with my grandmother, the Duchess of Mayflor yesterday.'

'I know, Craidos was watching to make sure the truce was not broken.'

Charlotte looked surprised. 'Then why didn't he do something when she fired a lightning bolt at me.'

'What could Criados Do? The Chalice of the Dawn nullifies his magic. But even if he could have helped, Craidos, like your grandmother, knows the power of the ring. You were in no danger. If your mother had had it when Braidos killed her, he would have found it a lot more difficult. Why are you here?'

'I want to know why the Chalice of the Dawn didn't work on my grandmother?'

'There are things in this world that are more powerful than *The Magic*. Your ring is one, the chalice is another. Your grandmother has one too. How do you think she managed to banish Braidos?'

Chapter Forty-one

'What is it?'

Mythias pondered for a moment. 'I cannot tell you. It would break Craidos's neutrality.'

'So, it's possible she could attack Falconia?'

'I don't think so. You have the ring and the chalice. Her other magic users, whom I can warn you are at the moment more powerful than yours, would still be useless in battle. Your army is larger and more battle-hardened than hers, even if she calls on the other duchies. You have powerful allies. I think if she starts a war she would lose. She would know this, so I think you are safe from her, at least for the moment. Keep your army strong though.'

'Thank you. I have one other question.'

'You want to know why your daughter Rose was chosen with Roget to procure the Chalice of the Dawn.'

'Yes.' Charlotte leant forward.

Mythias closed his eyes and did not speak for several minutes. Charlotte waited patiently. Mythias opened his eyes. 'When Sir Roger Livermore put the seeds into Stephen and Julie, Craidos put a tiny part of himself into Rose. Not enough to hurt him if she dies but enough to help her get the chalice. He's wanted the chalice off the island for a long time. I've a bit of Craidos inside me. Roget has a bit if Braidos inside him. Roget doesn't really need a golden chalice of human blood to summon Braidos, but it looks more dramatic.'

'So, why didn't you go with Roget?'

'Look at me. Do I look like someone who could go on a dangerous quest? I would squash my horse after only a few miles. He had to choose someone who had a chance to succeed.'

'So, Craidos knew what would happen?' Charlotte asked incredulously.

'Not even the gods know what will happen. They can only try to steer events. Such as having you have Shorman Del Longe paint your children's portraits. But now everything has worked out well. Your children are restored. You have peace with the dwarfs and the duchies. Prince Rudolf should marry your magic user Lizzy. Go and prepare a late birthday party for your children and leave matters that concern the gods to the gods.'

'Thank you for this talk, Mythias. I have learnt much.'

'It must never be repeated.'

'I will never repeat it.'

They both got up and left the room. Mythias unlocked the temple doors with another flick of his hand and Charlotte went to prepare another birthday party.

EPILOGUE

A week later in the throne room tables had been set up in exactly the same way they had been before at the previous birthday party. A long table had been placed parallel to the dais. In the centre were the triplets and the rest of the table was taken by their closest friends, which this time didn't include Prince Rudolf. His spot was taken by Dulgon Steelhammer. Dulgon, even though he was always accompanied by at least two guards and his bedroom always locked and guarded at night, was enjoying exploring Castle Falconia and the town and felt like he was on a great adventure. The rest of the throne room was taken up by tables lengthways to the dais and many children and their parents were seated at them. These were the same ones that had been at the interrupted party almost two months before. The table closest to the balcony once again sat a number of royal advisors and friends, including Shorman Del Longe, the artist.

The still unopened presents had been placed back on the dais. The main difference between this party and the previous one was that, instead of sitting at either end of the table that held the triplets, Queen Charlotte and Sir Philip, wearing his sword, sat on their thrones on the dais.

Queen Charlotte stood. 'King Philip and I wish to thank all of you for coming today. I hope this birthday party doesn't turn out as er ... interesting as the last one.' This caused a small titter amongst some of the gathering. 'I especially want to thank Shorman Del Longe for waiting here in Falconia to paint my children's portraits and not returning to Melita.' Shorman stood up and bowed to applause. 'But before we start the party, there is some official business we have to perform. Everyone by now would know the story of the brave men and women who went to find the Chalice of the Dawn. We are now going to honour three of them.'

Charlotte turned and sat down while the assemblage applauded. King Philip stood. 'Firstly, could Privates John Hand and Tom Mason please come up here?' The two men climbed the stairs that had been placed at the far end of the dais. There was more applause. The two men stood in front of King Philip, who shook both men's hands.

'I thank you both for your bravery and help. You are both promoted to sergeant and you will both be given fifty gold pieces.' Both men saluted by placing their right hand over their hearts and in unison said, 'Thank you, Sir Philip.' They turned and left the dais.

'There is one more. Could Captain Jacob Lipson please come up here?' Captain Lipson did so. 'Captain Lipson, I thank you also for your bravery and help. Kneel.'

Captain Lipson knelt, and Sir Philip took out his sword and tapped the captain on his shoulders with the flat of the blade. 'Rise, Sir Jacob Lipson. The new commander at Fort Philip.'

Sir Jacob stood to rousing applause. King Philip went and stood close to Sir Jacob so no one else could hear him. 'Unfortunately, this will be your last promotion. We can't have a berserker as head of the army.'

Sir Jacob smiled. 'Is that why you resigned and gave the job to Colonel Blayton?'

King Philip laughed. 'You may get there yet.'

Sir Jacob then saluted and left the stage.

King Philip turned back to Queen Charlotte and took her hand as she stood. The queen clapped her hands. 'Well, let the party begin.'

Just as she finished speaking, Gwaine the young magic user rushed into the room holding a letter. 'Your Majesties, you have an invitation to a royal wedding.'

King Philip punched the air. 'Rudi's father and grandfather have agreed to his marriage.'

Queen Charlotte smiled. 'Excellent. We have peace with the dwarfs and Mayflor and now Prince Rudolf and Lizzy are to be married. Future times are going to be magnificent. Read the invitation.'

Gwaine opened the letter. 'To the Majesties, Queen Charlotte and King Philip of Falconia. You are hereby invited to the marriage of the Marquis Sir Peter of Mayflor and Princess Scarlett of Falconia.'